The
by

The series of four historical no ... ...is
youthful alienation from his Eng... ... to
1946 at Nuremberg.

Book 1: The Officer's Code
In 1912, failing at Cambridge in reading Law, Eric Foster rebels against his father's rigid plans for his future as a barrister. While searching to control his own destiny Eric falls in love with the daughter of a minor German baron. To prove his worth to Brigitte's aristocratic family, he exploits the old family connections of his German mother to buy a commission in an elite Prussian cavalry regiment. By joining the most respected, most powerful stratum of Imperial German society, he opens the way to marry his beloved only months before the outbreak of World War One, the war to end all wars.

Book 2: The Versailles Legacy
After the 'War to End All Wars', the German post-war recovery in 1933 still staggers under the crushing terms of the Treaty of Versailles. Erich von Schellendorf, a career cavalry officer, has two desires in life: that his beloved wife, Britt, can break free from the psychological turmoil that prevents her from living life to the full; and that he can ride on the German equestrian team in the 1936 Olympics.

Both dreams seem reasonable, until a British agent named Trudell blackmails Erich into doing a small job for Special Intelligence Services. And a political rabble-rouser named Adolf Hitler seizes absolute control of the German government.

Book 3: The English General
In Berlin, January 1939, Major-General Erich von Schellendorf meets Celia Ashton at the British Ambassador's annual New Year's Levee and steps into a casual affair. By August, on the eve of Hitler's inevitable war, they are dangerously in love. On the brink of war Erich sends Celia home to England. Cornered by the appalling reality of Nazi control over the country, and compelled to pursue his own troubled conscience, he maintains a delicate balance of honour through the most destructive war in history.

Book 4: The Ghosts of War
Hitler's war is over. Lieutenant-General Erich von Schellendorf of the German General Staff is a prisoner of war. Exhausted by the collapse of every aspect of his life, deeply disturbed that he could not moderate the utter destruction of Germany, his only reward is that he survived the most destructive war in history.

But now that the guns have stopped, Erich must ultimately answer his conscience and face his personal ghosts of war.

If you enjoy reading The Officer's Code, I would appreciate your writing a review on any or all of the websites ~

www.amazon.com
www.amazon.ca
www.amazon.co.uk

The Officer's Code

A Novel by

Lyn Alexander

The Officer's Code

Copyright © 2012 by Lyn Alexander

2nd edition, revised

All rights reserved. No part of this book may be reproduced in any form, by any electronic or mechanical means including photocopying, recording, or information storing and retrieval, without permission in writing from the author.

ISBN – 13:978-1500574734
ISBN – 10: 1500574732

Author Website
www.lynalexander.com

Feedback welcome at:
lynraa@xplornet.ca

The Officer's Code is a work of fiction. Apart from well-known, historic personalities, events and locales that figure in the narrative, all names, characters, places and incidents are the product of the Author's imagination, or are used fictitiously. Any resemblance to actual events or locales or living persons is entirely coincidental.

Cover design by R. A. Alexander
Cover elements assembled by Shelley Rogers

A Publisher of Quality Fiction

DEDICATION

To my email friend, reader and guard dog, Professor Emeritus of History, **Karl Larew**, PhD, who made certain I got my historical facts right, and had a few wise words about endings.

ACKNOWLEDGMENT

Heartfelt appreciation once again to **Shelley Rogers** for assembling the cover for yet another of my novels.

PROLOGUE

Easter 1912

His father was raving again. Back and forth he paced behind the desk, clutching that letter like a sword in his hand. Lean pointed face, clipped Edwardian beard, gunmetal-blue eyes like bullets ready to fire. He was dressed for church. The desk clock said eleven minutes after ten. They would be late for Easter services.

Eric stood before the desk, barefoot and in his nightshirt, with the walls closing down about his head. Summoned out of a deep sleep, only half awake even now, he let his father's thunder blast past his ears. There was no point in answering. Or even in listening. He glimpsed a King's College crest on the letter, *"Truth and usefulness"*, the college motto ingrained into every King's student. *Truth and usefulness.*

The room went abruptly quiet. His father sat down in his captain's chair and turned the paper over, as if something extra might be found on its blank side. In the long, frozen silence he did not look up.

Then...

"Where were you last night?"

The question startled Eric rigid. *Where was he last night?* What had last night to do with this letter from King's—?

"Well?"

"We went to the dance over at St. James Pavilion—"

"We? Who are *'we'*?"

"Gordon and Ruth and—"

"And Jenny Henshaw?"

"Yes sir." Eric didn't know why he was drowning in quicksand.

"Jenny Henshaw's mother rang me this morning, said she was up all night, said she was desperate when Jenny didn't come home after the dance. Said she trusted the chaperones. Trusted *you*! So in return, you and this silly girl decided to compromise yourselves and in the same stroke to destroy both your reputations. And mine as well, by the way. Is that it?"

"Nothing like that happened, sir."

"But it's the *appearance* that counts, damn it. Can you not get that through your head?"

"But nothing happened, sir." Now he was mumbling. He took a sharp breath. "I borrowed Gordon's motorcycle and took her for a ride out along—"

"And this ride lasted six or seven hours?"

"No sir, no sir, um... Yes sir, a few hours. But I mean, not the actual ride itself—"

"Ah, so you stopped, did you! Ran out of petrol? In a public place, I do hope?"

Swift image of skidding on gravel in the darkness into a country ditch, landing in a heap together in the dew-drenched grass, giggling in the cool spring night—

"Well?" his father pressed.

"We had a bit of an accident, sir. We had to walk home."

"Can I believe you?"

"You could ask Gordon, sir. The handlebars were bent off line, I couldn't drive it like that, I had to push it all the way from—"

"Oh, no doubt your friend Gordon will back you up on this. That's what friends do, do they not?" He studied the paper, intent and frowning. "What am I to do with you, Eric? I'm a judge. Reputation! Do you understand me? London's a country village when it comes to gossip. And off you go, never a thought for family, gadding about with horses-and-hounds, motors and yachts, and who knows what other bloody falderal? This Henshaw girl, it won't stop there, mark my words. I have enemies enough eager to make use of this sort of rubbish." He crumpled the paper in his fist. His voice crumpled with the paper. "And now this."

Eric's feet were cold on the hardwood. Draughts wafted relentlessly through the house in all seasons, never quite sealed out by closing doors and windows. This was Easter *holiday*. A time for escaping the endless books and papers, every week another paper, another test. Ten days for simple fun. A break in the drudgery.

And now, this.

He knew what was on that paper. It represented tome after tome of common law, of dates and legal decisions and famous jurors' biographies, mindless memorisation that he hadn't caught inside his skull long enough to spew back in the orals.

It was as if his father read his mind. "You came tripping home for the holiday knowing full well you're being sent down, and you did not trouble yourself to tell me." *Those bullet eyes.*

"Sorry sir."

"Answer me then."

"Was it a question, sir?"

"Damn it you young whelp, do not presume to be impudent with me."

"Sorry, sir." He felt his face flush red. He stood immobile and awaited judgment.

"This is quite the end, Eric." His father folded his hands on the desk, a sign that the subject was closed. "I've been up since that woman called, five o'clock this morning, been up with your mother talking it over. This must change. Your mother agrees with me. For once, concerning you, she agrees."

Eric stood mute, staring at his father's Winchester tie.

"Your don told me that you're not likely to go on next term without reviewing the very stuff I sent you up to do. Said you've made no effort. Pity is, you can be so bloody brilliant. *If* you try. *When* it pleases you. So, here's the thing. You'll leave King's and hie yourself over to your mother's *alma mater* at Heidelberg, my God, the thought of it."

"I hardly think—"

"That's right! Please do not presume to *think* at this late hour. We must get you right out of the country, out of reach of this... this... bourgeois woman and her ambitious daughter." He leaned a little forward, his image reflected in the gleaming wood of the tidy desk. "Do you realise the Henshaw woman wants a wedding? To justify your bloody nonsense?"

"Father, it wasn't in the least like that—"

"You're not even nineteen years old! My God! I was thirty, settled in my profession, a partner in The Office before I married your mother. No boy at eighteen knows what in God's name he's fit for, never mind with whom he'll marry and in what circumstances!"

"It isn't that way!"

The room went silent with the shock of Eric shouting.

His father stared at him.

"It was just a ride on a motorcycle." His voice trailed off. *No use, no use...*

"It's all decided. You may thank your mother for this. She's convinced me that Heidelberg may provide the incentive you need to apply yourself. I agree that removing you from your current circle of pals may be half the battle. I'll arrange your admission and reserve your courses, starting at once. There, you'll prepare for The Law once again. I'll give you a year, my boy. If by then you have not pulled up your socks, we shall consider a different path."

Different path?

"I only hope your German is adequate, God help us if it's not."

"I can probably—"

"I'm selling Spats. You'll not need a horse at Heidelberg. Put your nose in your books my boy, and do not look round until next spring. Are we quite clear?"

"Yes sir." He wondered numbly what Spats had to do with it. The punishment, he supposed, for walking Jennie Henshaw safely home.

*

Mid-evening, the house quiet, the sounds of the city distant. His father was in the study poring over a court case. Out of sight, out of trouble.

Eric lay sprawled across his mother's bed while she lounged in her chaise by the window. The gauzy curtains fluttered in a light breeze. This was their special time. Ever since he could remember they had spent the last hour in her bedroom, talking over his day.

"I don't understand," he said again, "why it must be Law. Is there nothing else in life?" They spoke in German, their secret language.

"Ah, you understand well enough, Eric. Don't be stubborn about this."

"But Heidelberg! So far away. I can't come home on the weekends."

"Heidelberg is a wonderful university, *Schätzel*. I was there only a few months, a history course, but I saw enough to love it. I wanted to study at the Sorbonne, you know, where women can study for a baccalaureate..." Her voice drifted off into the memory. She gazed past the billowing curtains.

In the lamplight he studied her face, made smooth with powder. Emphatic chin, long noble nose. Chestnut curls framed the faraway eyes. Always this edge of sadness when she spoke of Heidelberg, as if her dreams were behind her.

"Why don't you go back to it?" He sat upright with this new idea. "Go to Cambridge? King's? Wouldn't that be a joke? Mother and son in the same college?"

"With my terrible English?" She smiled. "You're so young. Life is so hopeful. While you're at Heidelberg be a good boy, na? Do as your father says. Please? Promise me?"

"Why Heidelberg? If your family's in Stettin."

"Stettin is too far, Heidelberg is only two days away."

He mused on it.

"And because," she added, "you know my family wants nothing of... wants nothing of me." She smiled quickly. "We don't need them."

He sank back down on her pillow. He wanted to bury his face in its pervasive scent of rosewater. Vaguely uncomfortable, he shifted back upright against the headboard.

She smiled across at him. "If my family met you they would know you at first sight. You have those Schellendorf eyes, my darling, straight and true. And the curly stiff hair, you know the girls love it, they want to put their fingers through it, they want to tame it." She grew serious. "I want you to be more careful of the girls, Eric. Too easy it is to fall into traps."

He shifted uncomfortably. "I'm a pal, *Mutti*, they don't find me so attractive."

"Yes, but already they do. One day, if you put a little muscle on your skinny bones, you will be such a lady-killer."

He laughed, embarrassed, delighted. He felt his ears go red.

"But let us be serious," she said. "In Heidelberg you must work. Is it so terrible that he wants you in The Office? To carry on the tradition? You know as a judge he can no longer associate with his own office. He needs you, Eric. Do you see that?"

"Why can't he let Colin do it?"

"Ach, Colin!" She threw up her hands as if argument were pointless.

"Father puts all the responsibility on me, and Colin can do anything he pleases... Which," he muttered in English, "is bugger all that I can see."

"You're the elder."

"Why is it important? Colin would die for attention, he'd dig a hole in the moon for half the attention Father puts on me—"

"Colin is not a very bright boy, Eric. He has no capacity. Be realistic."

He subsided.

"This girl, Jenny...?"

He shrugged. "She's a nice girl, Mutti. She's a pal. She makes no claim on me."

"Yes, good."

*

They stood in a knot beside the first class carriage of the Continental Express. Passengers gathered along the platform, steam hissed, baggage carts rattled, carriage doors banged, all in a chorus of noise echoing off high metal girders. The locomotive chuffed quietly on the track ahead.

His mother was crying again. "Hear me, my darling," she said to Eric in German. "Be a good boy and make the best use of your time exactly as your father wishes. And when all is over, you'll have a fine education, and then you're a man, my darling, free to make your own decisions. Only a few more years—"

"Come now!" said his father. "Speak English, you two, you're in public here."

Amidst the press of travellers James and Gordon stood to

one side, waiting to say goodbye. Colin hung behind Mutti, somehow alone. Colin always seemed alone.

Gordon had forgiven the bent handlebars, easily fixed with the proper spanner. But nobody believed Eric had merely walked Jenny home. Among her friends at school she was said to enjoy new distinction as a *femme fatale*, before her family had spirited her off to Switzerland.

"Now do get on," said his father brusquely. "Where's your letter of credit?"

Eric patted his breast pocket.

"Don't trust foreigners, guard your money, keep a sharp eye out for thieves. Work hard, son. Don't let your mother down, this is her idea, you know."

He nodded, unconvinced. He turned to Colin, who hung behind staring down at his shoes. Poor helpless little brother who never seemed to know what time the bell rang, or *if* it had rung at all. Eric went to him and reached out to shake his hand.

"Don't go." Colin wouldn't look up. "I shan't get on without you."

"No choice, old man. You know Father when he's got the wind up."

"Promise you'll come home for the holidays. Promise."

"No promises. I'll be working through." He grasped Colin's hand and shook it, and clapped him roughly on the arm. "But I'll try."

Colin didn't look up. Wordlessly he turned away.

His mother gathered Eric into a tearful embrace. She brushed fingers through his stiff, sandy hair, as if she saw him still a child. "Be cautious," she said in English, "to know vell who are the true friends." After twenty years in England her w's still came out as v's and her r's still rolled in the back of her throat. She released him, and he broke away to his two best chums. Awkwardly he shook hands with them, and they promised to exchange letters and get together over the holidays, conscious of his father's disapproval. Especially Gordon, rolling his eyes and grinning.

The train hooted. On the platform a guard swung his lantern. "Close all doors please!" Eric climbed into the compartment where a porter had tucked his bags. He lowered the window to

lean out. Doors slammed and the guard's whistle shrilled and a blast of steam burst from between the carriage wheels. The train jolted gently forward with a gliding, swaying, accelerating click... click... click... and he waved out the window and they all smiled and waved after him, *Goodbye, goodbye, goodbye...*
One year.
No sailing, no fox hunting, no polo.
No Jenny, no Gordon...
No Father.
A whole year without Father.

* * *

CHAPTER 1

May 1912

He sat alone in the tavern by a little window looking out on the *Haupstrasse*. Students gathered in groups at the other tables, and although he could hear snatches of words and gusts of laughter, no-one paid the slightest attention to him. They wore fraternity scarves and matching leather caps, strange mixes of blues and greens and reds. And gold fraternity rings, they loved gold. They seemed to cherish emblems of membership, of belonging.

Eric did not belong.

He nibbled at salty fat-flecked wurst, and drew in a mouthful of beer, and stared out the dim little window at the road where the sun was shining. He needed something to do, but three weeks in Heidelberg left him vague about what was out there except the castle and the taverns. He'd never gone drinking for the sake of drinking, had never gone into a bar to make new friends. One trip on an excursion boat along the Neckar River had been boredom enough to last forever. Every day he saw horsemen across the river cantering up along the endless pathways of the *Philosophenweg*, but you couldn't meet them unless you had a horse. And Spats, of course, the most willing horse in the world...

"Hey, *Engländer*. What are you doing in this ridiculous place?"

Jolted out of his muse he found a fellow standing above him, hands on hips. Characters like this were everywhere, cocky, superior, aristocratic boors who thought the rest of the world existed merely to serve their comfort. Straw hair, pencil moustache, arrogant blue eyes. Leather breeches, black riding boots to let the world know he was a modern *knight*, for God's sake. Wealthy, brash, rude, and crude.

"Come along with me," said the fellow in casual High German, no sign of a regional accent.

"Why?"

"Why not? But the fact is, you need a friend to set you right."

"Ah, really."

"Ja, really!" Then, to punctuate his point, the fellow took the beer stein from the table and walked away with it out the door to the road.

For just a moment Eric watched in astonishment, then flung down his serviette and followed. He'd paid for that beer.

Outside, the fellow was chugging down the last dregs.

Eric leaned a shoulder against the building. "So that gives you pleasure, my beer?"

He set the stein down on the cobbles and rubbed a suede sleeve across his moustache. "I owe you one, I'll make it up."

"Yes indeed."

"Come along, then. I'll buy you a *Butterbrot*, beer included."

Eric hesitated.

The fellow tugged lightly at Eric's sleeve and walked away across the narrow road toward Karl's Gate and into the tavern, *'Zum Roten Ochsen'*, the Red Ox.

Eric followed.

Until now the noise in this place had kept Eric away, always jammed with students shouting and laughing and slinging bits of food from group to group like children at a party. He followed the fellow into the chaos, tables crowded on several levels, step up, step down, turn a corner, duck under a low beam, dodge the tray on a waiter's shoulder, dodge the students, dodge their missiles, dodge their bodies leaping table to table. The daylight came only dimly through the tiny windows.

The fellow arrived at a massive wooden table, dark and scarred with age, where half a dozen students lounged around it. He stood and waited, hands on hips, until one of them noticed him. Suddenly they almost clambered over each other to move out, carrying food and drink with them, and the table was vacant.

"Take a seat!" shouted the fellow through the wall of noise.

Eric slid onto a massive timber chair. The fellow sat opposite and waved one hand, and a waiter leapt to his side. "Two beers, two wurst sandwiches, and a cheese tray, na? On my account."

The waiter cleared the table to his tray, wiped it, and retreated into the gloom.

"Von Wittingen," said the fellow to Eric. "Gerhardt with a 't'." He held out his hand. "Gerdt."

"Foster. Eric." He leaned over the table to shake hands. It seemed a German obsession.

"But why do you call yourself Foster? When we all know you're a Schellendorf."

"Where did you hear that?"

He shrugged. "Ach, it's a small town. I hear everything. So tell me, what are you doing over in the *Seppl*? Where the Marxists go. The Reds and that shit."

"And so?"

"We're the Whites. The Greens and Blues are artsy-fartsy spring violets. You don't want to bother with them, they study languages, literature, poetry, that shit. We're mainly in military studies. The Greys are law. Now you could be a either a White or a Grey, but the Whites are the best, you should join us."

"This is a fraternity?"

"No, it's a society. You're looking for a fraternity?"

"I just asked. But why would I join military studies?"

Gerdt waved a casual hand. "Well, naturally you could pick up a military course and make yourself a true von Schellendorf."

Eric laughed. Gerdt displayed an unconscious charm that bloomed with every broad, white-toothed smile.

It felt right, to be taken on like this.

*

They walked along the concrete embankment. The Neckar moved silent and black with bits of flotsam carried on a current slower than a walking man. The breeze was brisk in the warm sun. Gerdt slung his jacket on one finger over his shoulder. His riding breeches were hand-tailored, stitched with impeccable arrowheads anchoring the corners of the pockets, and a florid design down the front of each thigh. "If you live in the Seppl," Gerdt said, "you can never meet anybody in anything except politics or poetry, which is so-ho-ho boring. Well! Perhaps you enjoy the ranting of politicians, or to pick apart a lovely poem by Goethe, who knows? What amuses you, Engländer?"

"Horses," he said decisively. "And motorcycles."

"Excellent! Do you fence?"

"I'm good at rapiers."

"There, I knew it. Join our fencing club and earn your scar. You don't belong with those delicate flowers over in the Seppl. You'll move out in the end, you'll see."

"I took what I could find. The pensions were all taken."

"There's an empty bed in our digs."

Ah...

And how much would that cost?

And...

Earn his scar?

*

Gerdt's room was upstairs in a pension-house a block from the Hauptstrasse, only doors away from the Great *Aula*, the main hall where Eric took two of his lectures. The bedroom had a high ceiling and cathedral windows facing west where, Gerdt said, the sun streamed in all afternoon. Two huge beds were stationed at opposite corners, and a captain's desk stood against a wall under a large mirror framed by gilded cherubs with arrows and little wings.

"We have our own private bathroom," said Gerdt, waving toward a closed door, as if he were trying to sell something.

"'We'?" said Eric. "Who are 'we'?"

"Well." Lazy shrug of the shoulders. "You and I, if you like. My former roommate just bombed out and joined the army, he's now living in barracks over at *Schwetzingen*. By the way, it's my father's regiment, in case you need to know."

Eric regarded him in doubtful silence.

"What's the matter, Engländer? You think I'll murder you in your sleep?"

He laughed. "I only wonder why you asked me."

"Well, to help with paying the rent."

"You don't need help with paying the rent."

"Ach, my father gives me only fifty marks a month to spend. If we join forces it means extra cash for each of us."

"So how much is the rent here?"

"Forty a month. Each."

Eric's room at the Seppl was two marks a day. Twenty extra marks at the end of the month? "I suggest this," he said. "I keep my room at the inn this month. I move in with you, and at the end of the month... if it works well... I let the other room go."

Gerdt laughed a lusty, delighted laugh. "But never have I been forced to prove myself."

"Lucky bastard. My life depends on proving myself."

"Lucky, yes. Bastard? No chance."

They both laughed.

Gerdt was an easy roommate, willing to let silences grow, quick to share coffee and books and time. He knew every corner of the town. They went out on the first Friday to a cotillion at the Hotel *zum Ritter* ballroom, where, under the glowering eyes of the chaperones, the unattached young ladies of the best society gathered to look over the competition. Soldiers up from the garrison, Eric noticed, got the prettiest girls.

Within the week he lined up the last of his books into the bookcase by the head of his bed. He'd hung his clothes into half of the huge wardrobe and folded his shirts and underwear into three empty drawers of the dresser. Gerdt pulled the desk away from the wall, and turned it sideways to the window where they sat opposite each other to study.

Eric sat there now, writing a letter home...

> *...met a pleasant fellow taking some of the same classes as I. He is a leader in Heidelberg society, his father being the Baron von Wittingen and a retired colonel in the local cavalry. I have joined his group which concentrates on Military studies ~ there are many such student societies here, and one must be in the vanguard of the class, as well as socially acceptable, to be invited to join, so it is safe to say that I am doing quite well, thus far...*

"You said you ride." Gerdt stamped into high black riding boots. "We're going down to the stables, are you any good?"

"I have no horse. And no riding clothes, no boots."

"So then, it's all right dressed as you are. I'll introduce you to my tailor sometime, he'll fit you up in a few days. We'll find a horse for you, no trouble."

Across the foot bridge at the garrison stables Gerdt ordered the groom to saddle a flighty mare for Eric. "This is my sister's horse," he said. "This one needs a soft hand or she'll jig her nose in the sky and fling herself off balance." Gerdt rode a high-minded stallion. "I'm the only one who rides this one, he needs a strong hand." He aimed the stallion at a gallop away from the stable toward the Philosophenweg that curved for miles along the hillsides above the river. Eric followed more slowly, feeling out the mare, uncomfortable in trousers that wrinkled under the knees, and slick shoes that did not hold the stirrup. When he caught up, three other riders had joined Gerdt on the path. They sat their horses watching Eric approach. By now the mare had softened to his hands and was bending to the snaffle and had lost her anxiety.

"Well!" said one of the boys, "I see that *somebody* can actually make the little fox behave!"

"Which fox?" laughed the second. "The horse fox or the other?"

"Just because you couldn't handle her," said the third, "doesn't mean it can't be done."

"Fellows, I want you to meet the Engländer, Eric Foster von Schellendorf..."

*

Back in their room Eric said to Gerdt, "Why did you introduce me that way? 'Von Schellendorf', my mother's maiden—"

"Well, why not? It breaks the ice, don't you think? Gives you a longer arm, na?"

Well, he mused, why not indeed? *When in Rome.* "And what was it that Franz said about foxes?"

Gerdt snorted. "He was referring to my sister. If ever she hears of it she'll clip his ears, and he knows it. But forget that, he's an idiot. Say, Eric, you have a good hand with a horse. We have a cavalry club, you know—"

"You have a club for everything under the sun."

"We take mounted drills every Thursday afternoon with the regimental master-sergeant. Maybe you'd like to join?"

"I can't afford that kind of time."

"It's the best club, the best people."

"I promised my father—"

"Ach, pass your exams, what else does he care?"

He felt the familiar sideways tug. It had happened last year with the Hunt Club, and the Fencing Club, and the cruises with Gordon on his uncle's yacht out of Southampton. None of that, according to his father, was *useful*.

"Your German is very good," Gerdt said. "For an Engländer."

They had vowed to study for the weekly orals, but Gerdt couldn't settle down. He would sit for five minutes and stare diligently at the page, then leap up and circle the room, or stand, as he stood now, gazing out the window at the darkness.

"My mother is German," Eric said. "Heidelberg's her *alma mater*." He wrote into his notes, *"Clausewitz ~ Attack the best defence ~"*

"Your mother went to university? *Mensch*! What branch of the Schellendorf family?"

"Bronsart—"

"*Bronsart* von Schellendorf? General *Paul Bronsart* von Schellendorf?"

He nodded. "She's his niece." *Attack the best defence...* He couldn't get past that phrase while Gerdt was so restless. "He was my great-uncle." He flung down his pen. "He would leap out of his coffin if he knew how bored I am with Clausewitz."

"You must meet my family. Father will go mad, knowing who you are."

"Who am I?"

"The great-nephew of Bismarck's Minister of War!"

Eric reflected for a moment. "I don't know much about it. My mother came to Heidelberg to live with relatives. Her father was occupied with business affairs. This was where she met my father. It made a scandal of course, they had to leave the country. So I can hardly claim any connection with Bismarck's minister of war."

"What does your father do?"

"He's a judge in London. But at that time he—"

"A judge! *Mensch*! We have no judges *or* generals in our family."

Eric smiled. Ah, Gerdt. Always comparing. "What about you? Where's your family?"

"We have a house here in town, but right now they're in Kleindorf by Baden-Baden."

"Where's that?"

"A village about a hundred kilometres from here. By the Black Forest."

"And your famous sister?"

"Ach, Brigitte. She's one of the reasons they live in the country."

"Why?"

"My father..." He shrugged. "She's so crazy, he keeps her away from Heidelberg, he wants to control her, meet the right people, you know? Not a crowd of crazy students or poor soldiers from the garrison."

"Is that why he retired? To control your sister?"

Gerdt laughed. "No, they tried to give him a staff appointment, but he refused to get out of the saddle. So they gave him the old gold sabre instead."

"And your *Mutti*?"

"She's not well. Tuberculosis. She takes the waters at Baden-Baden."

He nodded. Secluded life in the country, wild daughter, ailing wife, father guarding the cave. It sounded as boring as Clausewitz. "If you have a house here in Heidelberg," he said, "why do you live in a dump like this?"

Gerdt grinned. "The parents come and go, and the house always has servants about the place. You know? Gate-keepers? Spies?"

Eric laughed. He knew.

*

His life settled into routine. German lectures were opposite to the British. German professors were elevated to godhood and did not converse with mere students. They lectured, and were gone. Eric had not realised, leaving Cambridge, how he would miss the exchange of ideas, and the assumption that the student had equal intellect, if not experience, with the teacher. He missed the fellowship of King's, and the subtlety of British humour. German humour seemed based on insult rather than friendship. Often he felt crushed by the weight of German humour.

For the fun side of life he capitulated early. On Thursday afternoons they crossed the river to the garrison stables, and mounted cavalry horses for troop training. The boys sported a self-styled uniform of black boots, white breeches, a semi-military white tunic with brass buttons, and a pith helmet with a white silk scarf wrapped around it. Eric ordered his clothes from Gerdt's tailor and boots from Gerdt's boot-maker. For a few pfennigs he bought a pith helmet in the town's only department store. At the start he felt silly wearing a 'uniform', but after a few rides he got used to it, and fitted in well with the group.

They rode formations on the parade square under the rigid eye of the regimental master-sergeant who addressed his young riders as "sir" in scornful tones and trained them in discipline rather than horsemanship. They rode cavalry formations, two abreast, four abreast, eight abreast... there were only eight riders in the group... each taking turns at the inner and outer wings, in circles and squares and figures-of-eight at different gaits, slow then faster. Eventually when they got it going smoothly at a collected canter, the sergeant put a lance in their hands and they started again at the beginning. After two hours they were allowed to do some individual jumping before turning the horses back to the stable.

On Fridays Gerdt went to the cotillion at the Hotel *zum Ritter*, where he had met a girl. Eric hoped to meet somebody himself, but the girls showed little interest in the Engländer. Gerdt was always dancing, and not good company. Eric only went a few times.

He was invited to join the fencing club where the fencing-master started him into sabres. He liked the heft of a sabre. The light whip of a rapier was replaced by weight and a thicker grip, making the lunge and parry more attack than defence, more deliberate than reflexive, more muscle than speed. "Keep your mask fixed, Schellendorf," the fencing-master insisted. "You don't want a scar in place of a nose, that's not the idea." The fencing-master insisted on using Eric's mother's name. He said it lent dignity. Foster, he said, was not a name.

    Eric let it pass. New friends, new thoughts, new efforts. He loved the sweat that fencing raised. He loved being good at this, and in control. He loved parrying with Gerdt, who was quick and agile and well enough advanced to be carefree at it.

    He loved every moment of it.

    And as Schellendorf he belonged. That counted most of all.

* * *

CHAPTER 2

Summer, 1912

Toward the middle of July, just as they were making their plans for the summer break, the landlady brought letters to their room. "Two from England," she said importantly to Eric. He ripped open the envelope from his father...

> *My dear Son*:
> Dreadful performance. Fourteenth in a class of twenty for Napoleonic Law? Let me be clear. Nothing less than a First will do. Further, why audit mathematics? Yes, you understand me. I am kept informed of your activities.
> I note also membership to no less than three 'clubs'. Returned, I see, to pleasure before duty, untold hours outside classes mucking about with horses and what-not, nothing fundamentally changed except your notion of amusement which grows more liberal in direct ratio to the distance separating us.
> I am currently involved in a significant litigation case. I want no disturbance. Use the holiday to prepare for next term. Pick up the language, if you must. Understand fully the situation, Eric. I am providing you enough rope for you to hang yourself. My boy, if you do not

buckle down in an adult manner before Christmas, I shall reconsider the arrangement between us, perhaps to find you a position in a secretarial capacity with a solicitor. I do not intend to continue eternal support of this dreary performance. If I were you I should ponder this most carefully~
Yours of the 10th inst. ~ Papa

He read it through several times. His father's voice rang through the handwriting, *"If I were you I should ponder this...* Signed *"Papa"*?

Nobody ever called him Papa. Always Father with a capital F. Or *Sir*. Yes, lately it was always *Sir*. He stared at the single sheet of paper, his mind going to numbness. *Enough rope?* A judge provides the *rope?* And *secretarial capacity?* With a *solicitor?*

God God God...

His mother's words rushed into the void, *"...only a few more years a few more years a few more years more years more years..."*

Never.

It would never be.

Because... staring at this letter... he knew that if he gave up all his friends and interests, if he did nothing but study, if he never went anywhere except from this room to the lecture halls to the library to this room... he would never be good enough.

And, *"...kept informed..."*? Spies at Heidelberg? Servants in the house were bad enough, but spies in the university?

He scarcely skimmed the letter from Colin. The usual stuff, *"...promised to come home for the holiday. Life with father is an absolute bugger when you are away. I do wish you would just come home to stay..."*

As if he had the choice.

"Eric!" Gerdt flung his rucksack on his shoulder. "Let's go! I'm starving!"

"Coming."

Nothing in this post from his mother. He refolded the letters and dropped them into the drawer with the others. Easier than keeping a journal, they told the continuing story of his hopeless life.

Perhaps one day he would read them back and smile at all this.

*

"And so, my father doesn't want me home over the holiday."

They were in the Red Ox, competing with the student clamour all around, the shouts and laughter, the pressures building before exams. He was still hungry. He'd eaten a plain 10-pfennig Butterbrot, trying to save his diminishing bank funds.

"You look miserable," Gerdt shouted in the noise.

Eric shrugged. "He wants me to prepare for September." He raised his stein in a toast. "Happy holiday."

A devil twinkled in Gerdt's eye. "How does one prepare for September?"

"I don't know. Take a course and come first. Maybe a course in technical language."

"Take the best thing you do."

"Mathematics."

Gerdt made a face. He stared into his beer stein for a moment, and then a slow smile built on his lips to enhance the devil in his eyes. "I think you need a holiday, my friend."

"Mathematics isn't helpful in preparing for Law. God! I don't want to be a lawyer!" He had to shout over the clamour around them. "I don't want a secretary's job with a solicitor! The last thing in the world I want is to be a lawyer have my father hang over me for the rest of my bloody life, it's like you never escape from home! Damn it, Gerdt, do *you* want to work for *your* father for the rest of your life?"

Gerdt was grinning now. He must think this just a joke.

Disgruntled, Eric clamped his mouth shut.

"Did he say you must take a course?" Gerdt asked through the noise.

"He said I must prepare for—"

"But to take a course?" He leaned closer across the table. "Did he instruct you exactly in so many words to take a course? He said he will be busy with a court case, he said it's time to grow up, that's what he said."

"I know what he said." He took a long draught of beer,

savouring the rich cool froth in his throat. He set down the stein and gazed at Gerdt across the table. Their table. A place of belonging. This was their table in their personal world under their personal control, built upon the magic *Von*.

Two Vons, he thought wryly, do not make a right.

The pun could not translate to German.

"I suggest," said Gerdt, "you take a nice holiday."

Eric rose briefly and turned his empty pockets inside out.

*

The local train chugged at twenty miles an hour from one village to the next, from one grinding stop to the next, following the bank of the Rhine south toward the Alps. People got off and others got on, many carrying bundles or luggage. Students were singing and larking about. Farmers in overalls and mud-caked boots got on at one stop and off at the next, bored businessmen read their newspapers, and soldiers preened in their brilliant finery for the ladies.

On a slotted wooden bench in a crowded third-class coach, his rucksack between his feet, Eric gazed at the scenery gliding past. Every few minutes, filled with an explosive sense of friendship of a kind he'd never known, he would glance at Gerdt sideways. No questions asked, *"Come home with me for the holiday, my parents want to meet you..."* They didn't talk much. After almost a full term spent together, there was little left unsaid between them. He studied the velvet green of the hills and the dark lines of the vineyards and cattle peaceful in their pastures. Gradually the tidy orchards gave way to evergreen forest so dense he could not see between the branches.

"Hansel and Gretel," Eric mused. "Imagine getting lost in that."

"It's the Black Forest. You can't get lost. Pathways everywhere."

At Kleindorf they were the only passengers getting off. Two church steeples dominated each end of a village of a dozen buildings. Beyond the railway platform, a landau waited hitched to a pair of matched chestnuts.

"Let's go!" Gerdt handed over his ticket at the gate and vaulted the barrier.

Eric followed, raising the barrier to walk through.

The driver of the carriage climbed down from the box and touched his hat in salute, opening the side door for them.

"Lower the tonneau, Reinel," said Gerdt. "I'll take the reins."

The driver wore a look of pained fortitude. He folded back the leather tonneau and pushed the rucksacks under the driver's seat. Gerdt sprang up the step and took the reins, and the horses began stamping. "Climb aboard before they go!" cried Gerdt, as if it were out of his control. Eric got in and the driver jumped to the step and Gerdt cracked the whip high in the air. The horses exploded forward. Eric was tossed back into the leather seat. Reinel gripped the carriage frame and stood braced on the outside step for the entire wild ride.

At a dead gallop the open landau clattered and bounced between the village buildings, and out a curving road into the forest of dark evergreens so thick that they shut out the sky. Gerdt sat up on the seat with one boot braced to the footboard and urged the horses by voice and whip. It was hard to know if he drove them or they were bolting for home. A warm wind beat at Eric's face and jacket. He clung to the bucketing right side. Within minutes he saw that Gerdt was a superb driver. He could relax then and appreciate the drama of millions of lance-straight trees, regular as soldiers in their lines, and the dark density of evergreen boughs enclosing both sides of the road.

They drove like that for some miles, the horses slowing to a long trot as they tired. The dust raised from the road caught up with the carriage and enveloped Eric in a brown cloud, adding to the soot from the train. Finally they came around a last curve in the trees. Ahead in a break in the forest stood a massive, three-storey stone mansion with a huge front entrance and turrets on all four corners.

Gerdt whipped up the horses to a gallop right to the steps, then pulled them to a plunging halt in a great billow of dust, and tossed the reins to the unhappy driver. He leaped like a gymnast down from the box. "Halloo the house!" He jerked open the carriage door for Eric and made him a deep mocking bow. "Welcome to Tannenheim!"

*

The great oak door bore a carved coat-of-arms with a stag's head and crossed sabres. The entrance hall reached up two stories. A gallery on the first level ran around the four walls. Racks of antlers and stuffed animal heads hung on every wall, stags and boars and bears, some of them tattered and dusty with age. Closed timber doors ranged along each side of the entrance. A massive staircase at the end led up, then split right and left to gain the gallery. The doors along the gallery stood closed. A sigh of silence.

A man had opened a door on their left. An apparition from the previous century, his long grey hair flew wild in the air. He wore shirtsleeves and rumpled dark breeches with knee-socks, and a white apron, and wooden shoes, like the Dutch. "Welcome home, sir."

"Ho, Hanisch! Where are they?"

"At the Kurhaus, sir. They ask that you make your guest comfortable. The bedroom next to yours is empty. Mistress Brigitte has moved over to the northeast suite."

"And where is she today, then?"

"Riding, sir."

"With whom?"

"Alone, sir."

Gerdt shook his head in a secret smile. To Eric he said, "Come with me. We can wash and change." He led the way up the stairs. "Ask Hanisch for anything you need, don't trouble with the others, they only follow his orders. Military chain of command. Wittingen tradition."

Eric stopped on the stairs, and turned slowly, spreading his arms. "All these trophies. Who's the hunter?"

Gerdt laughed. "Everyone hunts." He clattered on up and turned left along the gallery and opened one of the doors. "Your room, sir. My sister just moved out. I'm directly next door."

The bedroom was enormous, with walls of aged timber, and no stuffed heads. No decorations, no trinkets. Eric dropped his rucksack into a fat eiderdown on the four-poster bed. Heavy carpets lay scattered over the timber floor. The fireplace was banked with fresh logs as thick as his waist, ready to light. He wandered over to the window and looked down on an expanse of grass enclosed by evergreens, a long stable at the edge of the trees, and several horse yards bounded by board fences. Near the carriage house at the far end, the coachman was just unhitching a horse. A stable-boy walked the other horse around an oval track to cool him. Beyond the stable a cluster of small houses and outbuildings pushed under the edge of the forest.

Utopia, he thought. Horses, space, privacy, servants to do the work. The German baronial tradition.

*

It was going toward evening as Gerdt toured him through parts of the manor. Even at the height of summer the rooms were as cool and dank as an old abandoned Scottish castle. They started in the library with a fireplace large enough to spit an ox, and then through a dining room where crossed swords and blunderbusses hung from the walls and suits of armour guarded the four corners. The long table could seat a hundred.

Then into a vast ballroom where twenty crystal chandeliers hung end-to-end from an arched cathedral ceiling. Through the opposite end they came into a maze of connected kitchens where women were working at the stoves and taking down stacks of crystal and china from an immense cabinet. They bowed back to let the young men pass, not a word spoken.

Through a timber door Gerdt led into a narrow room, where the air was as cold as winter. Great blocks of ice lined the walls. Shelves were laden with farm produce and canned and bottled foods. A headless deer carcass, skinned and dressed, hung by the hocks from a hook in the ceiling. The right foreleg and shoulder had been cut away. "Ah," said Gerdt, "venison for dinner." He twirled the carcass on its chain. "Before it rots most of this meat will go to the village."

"The village?"

"To the servants in the village. Come on." He led the way through another corridor into a spiral staircase enclosed by massive wet black stones. Eric counted forty-seven steps to gain a timber door at the top.

"This was once a watchtower." Gerdt climbed to an open turret. From here they looked down on the slate roof of the manor and the other corner turrets. Forest stretched in every direction.

"Our family," Gerdt said, "has owned this land since the Thirty Years' War. You see over there? The red roofs? That's our village for the servants." He swept an arm in the opposite direction. "Baden's over there."

They leaned on the stone parapet, the breeze ruffling their hair. Wealth without limit, Eric mused. Unchallenged power. An ancient, privileged, foreign world...

Out of a long silence Gerdt said in a distant voice, "I know all about fathers."

"Your father too?"

He whipped about. "Do you know how we live? We rent land to farmers for a percentage of their production, we employ villagers to keep up the roads, that sort of thing. We collect taxes for the State and pocket our portion."

"*Scheisse*! I thought that went out with the industrial revolution."

"Well, it's a living, but—"

"Some kind of living!"

"...but not what I want to do. Of course I'll join the regiment, it's expected. The son of the Colonel. You know? Your father wants the same from you. Tradition, ha! So I'll put in five years, why not. But really... just think of this... I really just want to be a farmer."

He thought it was a joke. "What would you do, farming?"

"Ah!" Gerdt came alive. "We have wonderful springs, some of the purest deep water in Europe, and acres of prime land east of Heidelberg. Wine-making would make a good income, we could buy the grapes from growers on the Rhine and use our water to make the wine. Father isn't interested. If it works, I'll grow my own grapes. I'll try it for a few years after I inherit the estates. That's my plan."

After I inherit...?

How many years...?

Both trapped in their own worlds by fixed family tradition.

While they stood in the evening breeze and daylight slipped toward dusk, they heard hooves and carriage wheels grinding on the road below. Soon a closed landau rolled past the trees, then turned out of sight to the front side of the manor.

"There they come," said Gerdt.

*

A fire crackled in the giant fireplace to soften the clammy cool of the evening air. The baron stood with his back to the fire, waving his coat-tails at the flames, a man with narrow hips and massive shoulders, a bullet head with clipped greying hair and magnificent walrus moustache. He resembled a cartoon *Junker* out of *Punch* Magazine. "Ah!" he said to Gerdt in the doorway, "the young Engländer, na?"

"*Vati*, I told you—"

"Come over here, young Engländer."

Eric advanced cautiously, not knowing what to expect from a colonel of the Prussian cavalry.

"Apparently," the baron boomed, "we have much to thank you for. This son of ours has begun to study seriously for the first time in his life. He may even finish his year and thereby be accepted directly for his commission, thanks to your example."

"Thank you sir. If you could explain to my father we would all be happier, I think."

"Why, what's the matter with your father?"

"Sorry sir, nothing." He felt himself blushing. One did not complain about one's father.

"I want you to meet my lovely lady wife, the Baroness Sophie." He extended a hand to a high wing chair turned toward the fire.

Eric stepped around to face the chair. A woman smiled up at him. In spite of the heat from the fireplace, she was bundled in a cocoon of quilts. Her hair was grey, her skin pale, her face lined, her large eyes shadowed; yet in all his life Eric had never seen a more beautiful woman. She held out a thin hand to him. He felt no awkwardness when he bent to kiss it. "Gracious lady." In German it did not sound strange. The hand was cold.

Her smile deepened. "Welcome, my young sir."

The baron rubbed his hands. "Now then, dinner!" As tender as a child's nursemaid, he held out a hand to his wife and drew her to her feet.

Tuberculosis. A tiny sting of sadness shot through Eric.

"Where is that girl!" demanded the baron as they came into the dining room. He held his wife's chair for her, then sat at the head of the table.

Only one end of the long table was set for dinner. Four gold candelabra provided an unsteady light. The Dresden dinnerware was edged in gold, there were gold knives and forks three deep, three kinds of crystal glasses, and a floral centrepiece, all set on white linen. Gerdt waved Eric to sit beside the baroness.

"And what sort of trip," asked the baroness softly, "did you boys have from school?"

They fell easily into table conversation. A maid brought water and filled glasses. Another brought pitchers of fruit juices. Manservants paced regally into the room carrying the joint of venison on a silver platter, followed by covered serving bowls of hot vegetables.

"Where is that girl!" bellowed the baron.

Gerdt winked across the table at Eric.

"She'll be down soon, my dear," said the baroness mildly. "Surely we can begin without her. Everyone is hungry."

The baron went through the ceremony of sharpening the carving knife, swift expert slashes of the blade against stone. "Shot this hind two weeks ago," he said. "Been hanging ever since, should be as tender as a newborn baby's bottom." He began to carve.

Gerdt sat down across from Eric and began to pass the vegetable bowls. The servants withdrew.

The door opened. Everyone paused for an instant, then resumed what they were doing, the way a moving picture show might stutter on the screen in the *Kintopp*. A girl came through the door. Crossing quickly to the table, her boot heels cracked on the bare timber floor. Silhouetted against the bright lamplight from the hall, she was a slight figure dressed in riding breeches and a boy's jacket, hair drawn severely against her skull with a blond halo of wisps in the back-light. The strong scent of horses drifted with her. She stopped to give her father a quick kiss on the top of his head before coming around to a chair beside Gerdt, across from Eric. The baron had just passed Gerdt a plate of sliced venison: the girl calmly took it out of his hand and set it on the table at her own place, and straddled the chair.

"So!" She stared straight at Eric. "This is the Engländer? Does he speak German?"

"I not only speak German," Eric retorted, "but I also speak very well for myself."

"Bravo," murmured Gerdt. "Eric, I present my uncouth *elder* sister, Brigitte."

She laughed, a silvery sound. In the wavering light of the candles her eyes were large and dark as the night, her mouth a delicate rose-pink.

And she was more exquisite than her mother.

Eric could not look at her without staring. He concentrated instead on picking lumps of hot turnip out of a serving bowl.

"Leave some for the rest of us," laughed the girl. Her eyes taunted him. She knew what she could do with those eyes. Eyes of a cat, eyes of a hunter, secretive, searching, watching, laughing... everything at once, as if ordinary life were too slow for her.

Embarrassed, he half rose to pass the bowl across to her.

*

Back in his room late that night, lamps out, even with the breezes sighing through the open window, Eric could not sleep. He leaned on the window sill and stared out at an infinity of stars while Brigitte's eyes flashed inside his head. All through the evening she had teased him. Every move he'd made she had found amusing. She'd laughed at his British accent and mocked the peculiar phrasing of his German. She was rude and sometimes silly, she was in turn haughty or sweet or flirtatious or scornful, and in all her moods she was fascinating. He'd been enthralled by her beauty, by every move she made, by the cunning perfection of her mouth as she spoke, by the lilt of her voice and the choice of her words and the tiniest gestures of sensitive hands. He was fully aware of his own fascination, as he would be fascinated with a perfect horse, a stag bounding in the forest, a classical painting. Everybody else had ignored her, had talked around her.

Now, staring out the window, he could scarcely remember a word she'd said, only the impetuous way she spoke, and this overwhelming image of her beauty.

A tap came at the door, and Gerdt slipped inside. "Are you comfortable?" He leaned his elbows on the sill beside Eric, gazing out the open window.

"Is she always like that?" Eric asked, glad of the darkness.

"Hmmm?"

"Your sister. Your *elder* sister, you said. How old is she?"

"Twenty. Why do you ask?"

Twenty. The number rang in his head. *20. Twenty. 20202020.*

"I only wondered. She acts like a child. Is she... perhaps—"

"*Verrückte*? No, just wild and spoiled. She gets away with it."

"I didn't mean crazy, I meant..." He didn't know what he meant. He meant *taken*. Is she *taken,* he meant. His brain was running in circles with those eyes flashing in his head. She was too old, in any case, she was *twenty* already and he would be nineteen in December...

"Anyway," said Gerdt in the darkness, "she plays for a fool every fellow she meets. That's what she did to you tonight, so don't be bothered by her."

Ah, but it was too late.

* * *

CHAPTER 3

July - August, 1912

They went riding in the morning, Brigitte on a skittish colt, Gerdt on a soft mare, Eric on an edgy bay gelding. "Fastest horse in the stable," Gerdt said, "also the best trained."

"Gerdt usually rides him," added Brigitte, a challenge in her tone.

"But Eric's my guest," said Gerdt.

"Of course, why else?"

"You talk as if it were a mistake to—"

"I merely wanted him to know the honour—"

"Not so much an honour as a gesture of—"

"Ja, but your gestures are always so—"

They talked between them like that, brother and sister, back and forth in constant combat for the final word, with no clear finish to any sentence.

Eventually they ran out of chatter and rode quietly. The forest seemed theirs alone. The path was secluded, fenced in by the marching trees. They came out on a spectacular open hill of grass and bluffs and a small valley, then rode into closed forest again. After another kilometre they trotted through a village and out again before a dog started to bark.

"This is..." Eric searched for the word... "like the... I never thought such... such isolation still exists today."

"Surely you've hiked in the Alps," said Gerdt. "Now, *that* is isolated."

"Well, this is different, it's..." He couldn't admit he'd seen only pictures of the Alps. "You can't live on a mountaintop, all the rocks and snow. But this forest... it makes one imagine so much—"

"Of Hansel and Gretel!" laughed Gerdt. "Fairy tales!"

"Of time before time," said Eric. He stopped his horse. The others eddied on the path until they too came to a stop. Brigitte's colt stamped impatiently. Gerdt's saddle creaked. Eric waited.

"What is it?" Gerdt asked.

Eric shook his head. Brigitte put a finger to her lips.

And finally there was silence among them.

But not a true silence.

There was no wind today, no breeze in the closed forest. The trees were still. Not even the treetops stirred. There was not a sound from animals or people or footsteps or motors or wagon wheels, not the clatter of a distant bucket or the slight scramble of a marten in the branches or even the song of a bird anywhere among the trees.

Just silence.

Yet straining to listen he could hear a constant faint, shifting, *whoosh, whoosh* from millions of sighs overhead surrounding him, as if the trees themselves were breathing. He could almost feel the boughs bending over, looking down at him, breathing, sighing...

Then Eric's horse snorted and pawed the ground and broke the spell.

Gerdt laughed. "There are wolves in this forest, you know."

"Nonsense!" said Brigitte, and rode ahead, her colt's hooves crunching loud on the path.

*

That evening after supper they gathered in the library where a fresh fire had been set in the huge fireplace. Wood smoke clutched at Eric's throat, heat stifled his lungs. They set the wing chairs in a semi-circle before the fire, the baroness buried in quilts which the baron tenderly arranged around her. Then he moved a footstool before her chair and placed her quilted feet upon it. "So, my dearest, so."

A maidservant clattered into the room on wooden shoes. She carried a tray with glasses and a carafe of mulled wine, and deposited it with a thump and a splash upon a small table beside the baroness, and everybody laughed as she retreated out the door. "She's new," said the baroness. "She comes off the streets of Baden, a beggar girl as far as we know. She'll learn the proper ways."

They settled, Eric on the left end of the semi-circle of chairs, Brigitte on the far right, her face half lit by the fire, half in shadow. He was aware of her breathless beauty, aware of energy stretching between them like an invisible elastic band, aware that she studied him under long blond lashes, sly as a fox watching hens through the fence.

Fox...

Out of a stillness, the spitting fire the only sound, Brigitte spoke suddenly. "Her name is Katja. I'll make her my maid. Then you won't be bothered by her."

"Oh my dear," said the baroness, "she's a good girl, nobody is bothered by her."

They talked of small things and sipped at wine so sweet and deep it slid down warm into the stomach and settled in the head like sleep. Gradually the voices faded to reflective silence. They stared into the flames, five bodies slouched in a semi-circle with feet stretched out like spokes toward the hub.

"So you heard it," mused Brigitte.

Her pensive tone startled him. "Who could *not* hear it."

"Some never do. How did you feel?"

"As if I were the first and last creature alive on earth."

She smiled and sipped wine.

"What are you two talking about?" asked Gerdt too loudly.

"The forest," Eric said.

"The *voice* of the forest," said Brigitte in the same breath.

*

Early in the morning she came rapping at Eric's bedroom door. "Aren't you awake yet, *Schlafmütze?*" She advanced on his bed wearing a loose nightdress that floated about her and gave her the look of a mythical sprite. "Are you still asleep, lazy thing? I need an escort to go to Baden today!"

The sun was already bright outside the window. He clutched close the bedclothes as she stood above him and taunted him with those eyes. "I told Gerdt he needn't come." Then she

whirled and danced away to the door where she paused to look back over one tilted shoulder. "I'll beat you getting dressed."
He heard her feet tripping away along the timber gallery.
Like a child...
The drive to Baden with Reinel at the reins took perhaps half an hour at a respectable trot along the *Rotenbachtalweg*. In the core of the town Brigitte got out and walked from one shop to the next while Eric followed along, feeling like an amiable puppy. At each shop she picked up this and that, a book in one shop, slippers in the next, a pair of long white gloves and a ball gown in a tiny boutique, and several pairs of fashionable shoes in a cobbler's shop. As she walked through she dropped the items elsewhere, creating such a clutter that the shop-keepers followed to tidy up behind her. She seemed unaware of the havoc she created. Yet everywhere she went she was treated not as a nuisance but as royalty.

Eric found a strange contentment in watching such glorious unconscious beauty, so animated with delight, as if this were a rare holiday for her, perhaps a day out of jail, he didn't know; just that her eyes danced and she laughed a lot. Everything about Brigitte seemed an exaggeration.

Perhaps a little... *verrückte* after all?

After about an hour of aimless searching she returned along the street to where the landau still waited, the horses sleeping in the sun. She led the way into the bookstore where they had started. She explored several shelves, taking out one book after another and dropping it aside while the clerk hovered closely, *Yes Mam'selle, No Mam'selle*, and he restored the books to their slots and rubbed his hands anxiously and smiled and smiled. At last she chose a small leather volume. Airily she handed it to the clerk. "Deliver this please." And she turned and walked out.

Settled again in the landau she put a hand on Eric's arm. "Wasn't that fun?"

The horses started forward, wheels grinding on cobbles. The spot on his arm tingled. He laughed awkwardly.

"It makes me happy," she said, "to see you laugh. You're entirely too serious."

"I like to see you laugh too." He felt like an idiot.

"Mutti spends most of the day at the Kurhaus. They're too

busy for me. So I don't come very often to town."

He could find nothing to say.

"It's not that I *couldn't*," she said vehemently. "Reinel would take good care of me." She leaned forward and raised her voice over the noise of wheels on cobbles. "Isn't that so, Reinel."

"Absolutely, Miss."

They drove a while.

And then... "Eric, why do you never look at me?"

He had no answer. Was that what she thought? That he never looked at her?

*

She dragged him out riding the next morning. Gerdt said he couldn't bother to go, almost as if he'd set up the situation. Out in the forest Eric heard her laugh, a muffled sound somewhere to the right. She had been riding a few paces ahead, then spurred to a gallop around a bend in the path. When he trotted to the spot she was gone.

"Brigitte?" he called. He stopped the horse to listen.

Another laugh, more distant, and a crash of hooves crackling, fading.

She knew the forest, she'd been raised in the forest.

Did she know that she was a woman? Galloping about on horseback wearing boys' clothes? She was twenty, Gerdt said. Yet she seemed such a child. A reckless, wild child who ignored the rules. A wildling.

She'd be twenty-one next birthday. Almost two years difference. Too wide a chasm. He couldn't even consider the thought. She needed to marry a man, not a boy. A calm, experienced, strong man to take her in hand and gently guide her. A man like the baron, hearty, humorous, rough, tender, wise... Everything that Eric was not. A strong, masterful, mature...

The word struck out of nowhere like a blind-sided blow...

Marry?

Nobody mentioned... *marriage!*

Fifty yards ahead on the path, the colt burst out of the trees, boughs waving in its wake. She rode flattened on the animal's neck. In the clear she raised herself upright in the saddle and pulled to a sudden halt and laughed at him. "What's wrong?

Can't you keep up?"

He rode forward.

Like a frightened hare she whipped the colt away along the path. "Come on!" she called over her shoulder. "Catch me if you can!"

He lifted Gerdt's horse to a hard gallop after her. She flung glances behind as Eric's faster mount gained ground. When he was almost on her heels she leaned to one side in the saddle. The half-trained colt shifted with her weight and dodged in among the trees, whipping under branches, winding among the close trunks, miraculously not crashing. Eric pushed hard to follow. He leaned along the neck to fuse with the horse as it surged through the trees, his cheek buried in mane, his hands close to his own face delicately trying to guide the headlong pursuit. The horse had run in these trees before. It chose its own path on the heels of the colt. In and out between trees they dodged, ducking under branches, scraping arms, hands, faces, knees, thighs. Both horses battered their flanks on the trunks, faster, harder, until Brigitte's braided hair shook loose to fly on the wind. And still she rode dodging and laughing. Finally she burst out on the path again. In a few bounds he overtook her and caught at her horse's bridle and pulled them both up. The horses' lathered flanks heaved for air.

"Do you want to kill these animals?" he asked.

"You could have quit."

"Why would I quit?"

She shrugged, and whipped her horse away along an open wagon road.

He followed at a walk. He would not ride this way. He could not ruin a good animal for the fun of the game.

She soon slowed and stopped to wait for him. "So I win," she said as he came up.

"If you like."

She taunted him with those eyes. "Don't you want to win?"

"I don't like the game."

She laughed, and rode on. Both horses were lathered and breathing heavily. For some time she led at a walk until the lather dried to salt and the horses relaxed without straining to race again.

They came to an opening beside the track where a cottage had once stood, now just an overgrown stone foundation among the trees. She stopped and dismounted, and tied the colt to a low branch. As if to cool herself, she unbuttoned her light jacket, then stood looking up at Eric, waiting for him. He got down. He felt under the girth and found it wet. He turned to check her horse. "We should move on, or they'll blister under the saddle."

She laughed. "What a cautious fellow."

Was he too cautious?

She stood before him in the middle of the little clearing. "So. At least you can ride." She walked a small circle around him, slapping at her boot with her whip, eyeing him haughtily up and down, as if he were up for auction.

"You're an amazing rider," he said, "but very hard on a horse."

"I'm harder on you fellows who try to keep up." She stopped squarely in front of him, the top of her head just level with his nose, the tiniest girl he had ever met. She tilted her face up to him, flaxen hair tumbling loose around her shoulders, hands clasping the whip behind her back, her little breasts thrust up under her light jacket. She gazed at him with lazy tiger eyes that were amethyst by daylight, and she was close enough that he could feel her honey breath. She played those eyes at him and smiled that smile at him, perfect little teeth gleaming tiger white.

It was hard to breathe. He knew what she wanted, yet he didn't know what she wanted, he didn't know what to do, and, like an adolescent fool, he didn't want her to know that he didn't know what to do.

"You may kiss me," she said close to his face.

His confusion surged. He'd never in his life seriously kissed a girl. No more than a peck on the lips in passing He couldn't display his ignorance to her scorn. "Your father," he blurted, "would spank you. I'll spank you myself if you don't behave."

"You wouldn't."

"Yes I would."

And he did not kiss her.

*

On Saturday he went with Gerdt and Brigitte to the dance at the Baden Kurhaus, a splendid weekly affair, held in a huge rococo ballroom, everyone resplendent in formal dress. Gerdt's white-tie-and-tails did not fit Eric well. Gerdt was an inch taller and broader than he, the pants hitched high on braces, the shoulders too wide. When they arrived the ballroom was crowded, and even with every window and door open to the night it was hot enough to melt a candle. The moment they sat down at their table a fellow introduced himself to Gerdt, then away danced Brigitte on his arm, tossing Eric a triumphant glance over her shoulder. He watched with anxious eyes. "Do you know that fellow?" he asked Gerdt.

"Ah, he's a neighbour, he's all right." Gerdt ordered the waiter to bring punch for three, and they settled, watching her whirl in a waltz among a swirling crowd. The music came from far enough distant in the huge ballroom that they could talk in normal tones.

"Do you know why the boys are so idiotic over her?" Gerdt asked.

Eric smiled. "Well it's obvious."

Gerdt gave him a look of lazy amusement. "Ah, she's beautiful, I admit. But she's such an idiot child, how can anyone be serious about her? No, it's because they try to get under her skirts, and rather than giving in to them she despises them for it, which makes her more intriguing to them—"

"She's not an idiot, you know."

Gerdt sighed. "I know what happened in the forest. She said you were an unbendable Engländer without humour. Said you were stodgy. Said you wouldn't kiss her. But in truth I suspect she wanted you to try so she could make you out a fool."

"Why would she want that?"

"I can't say how many times she's done it to other poor fools." Gerdt chuckled. "Look there, she's doing it again to Konrad, right in public on the dance floor. Who can fathom Brigitte?"

Eric watched her out there laughing, whirling with her partner on the crowded floor, gliding, dipping, turning together as if they were attached by an electrical charge. She wore a ball gown of gold stuff, off the shoulder with a fitted bodice that displayed a lovely slim figure, and full flowing skirts that swirled as she moved.

She was simply superb. And how well she knew it.

Inside his head he waltzed with her. The floating made him dizzy. He glanced at Gerdt, on the edge of speaking his mind. Gerdt emptied his punch glass and waved to a waiter for more. "See anyone you like?" he asked lightly, oblivious to Eric's focus.

"Don't worry about me."

After a few moments Eric got up and walked to a table nearby and bowed to the parents of a pretty young lady. "I present myself," he said, playing this new aristocrat game. "I am Eric Foster von Schellendorf, visiting for the holiday with the Baron and Baroness von Wittingen. May I have the honour, Madame, of inviting your daughter for this next dance?"

After that he danced almost every tune with a different girl, long waltzes, animated polkas, tripping foxtrots, in and out to the lilting beat. Now and then he passed near Brigitte as she danced with yet another fellow, and he would catch her eye and smile and circle away, aware that her eyes followed him. Yes, he could play her game.

Late in the evening they all came together at their own table for a sip of punch and a pause for breath before the music ended.

"You're having a fine time with those pretty girls!" Brigitte challenged Eric.

"Would you care to dance this last one with me?"

"I believe I've already promised it to—"

"Whatever you say."

"But if you insist—"

"Fine." *Last word.*

They stepped into the music while Gerdt smiled after them, sipping his punch.

"You're a beast," she said, laughing. She was a feather on his arm.

"Sorry. I don't mean to be."

"You might have asked earlier."

"You were too busy."

"You've wasted most of our evening."

"I'm having a fine time," he lied. "I thought you were also."

"You're a beast, Eric."

*

"I think you're a beast," she said in the afternoon as they rode together in the forest. Before he could reply she galloped ahead, and they were off again, crashing among the trees. Eric followed flattened to his horse, and burst back to the path hard upon her heels. They rode headlong down the slope and into the village and out again with dogs barking behind them, and into the trees. She slowed. He caught up and rode beside her. Suddenly the colt bolted, he saw the white of its eye as it happened. He pulled his own horse down to stop the race. In a few more bounds she gained control and turned and came slowly back.

Eric turned with her and they rode on quietly.

"You didn't ask me to dance," she said, taking it up again. "All night you danced with every girl but me."

He laughed. "You didn't ask *me* to dance."

"Oh! As if I would! Oh, you Engländer! Do English girls ask the boys to dance?"

"Well, but you asked me to kiss you—"

"Oh, worse and worse!" She galloped ahead again. And again he saw her lose control of the colt, and he realised that the chase she'd led him the first day had perhaps been not so much a chase as a runaway. Of course she would never admit it.

She was either very foolish or much too brave.

He rode after her. She brought the colt under control again and waited for him.

"I'll show you something," he said.

"What?"

"I call it a fixed hand. You might like to try it."

"Why would I?"

He smiled. "Try it."

"So, how?"

He showed her how to grip the reins at the exact length to put only the slightest touch on the bit, and then hold the hand rock steady so that when the horse extended his neck, he ran against the bit, and checked his own gait.

For a few minutes they rode like that side by side, and he could see the colt respond by giving at the jaw and bending at the poll.

"You've got it!" he said to her. "You're so quick."

"Don't condescend to me!" And she released the reins and was off again.

He followed at a walk. What did she use for a brain? When he next rode up to her she was sitting straight, and the colt was calm. They continued on, side by side.

"What do you plan for your life?" he asked, to straighten the knot between them.

"Plan!" Outrage in her tone, as if he were stupid. "But what does a girl plan?"

"I meant, will you marry? Go to university?"

"Women don't go to university."

"But of course they do. I know of five women in this year's classes. My mother went to university twenty years ago. I mean, it's old news!"

"All that work!" She snorted. "And after all it's not my fate."

He smiled at that. "What is your fate, then?"

She stopped the colt. He pulled up beside her.

"My fate," she said in disgust, "is to be some rich man's brood mare." She stabbed him with angry eyes. "What must I know for that? How to run a household? How to lie on my back? Like my mother? Do they teach that in university?"

She kicked her colt and galloped away.

Stunned by her fury, he followed at a walk.

*

Every afternoon they rode alone together along miles and miles of pathways under the trees. Hours of challenge and laughter and silliness, and after a while less silliness, a little less laughter, longer silences, fewer hard dashes. Riding quietly, they talked. At first it was little things, "What's your favourite colour?" "I don't know, I never thought about it." "Mine are gold and blue." "That's two colours." "I'm allowed two colours—" "Oh-ho! I see!" Eric could look at her now without staring. He'd got used to her delicate beauty, accustomed to her every graceful move, fluid as a dancer. He rode with her in comfort now.

When she asked about his family, the whole story roared out of him, "He expects perfection, and nobody's perfect, no matter how I try, by God, last term all he could say was that I should have come first even though, damnation, I've never before studied in German..." She didn't ask again. Sometimes they just sat the horses side by side, listening to the forest breathe.

On the last day they stopped and tied the horses and walked a short way on foot to look into a little valley where a green meadow slid down to a brook trickling at the bottom. The air was bright and hot. Midges swarmed in clouds, and in this open place the sounds of birdsongs were everywhere.

He could hardly imagine leaving now. He looked down at her, so elfin fragile, so blindingly beautiful. Her whole character seemed changed since the day they'd met. Her eyes were soft and sad and had lost their challenge. He thought by this time he must be used to her beauty, but each time he looked at her, in quiet moments like this, he was stabbed again in the heart. "Hard to concentrate on my studies," he murmured, "thinking of you."

"You're not like the others."

"The other what?"

"Friends."

"Boyfriends, you mean. Suitors."

She laughed.

"Have you ever..." He left it hanging.

She shrugged. "What do you think?"

"I think not. I think you value yourself too highly to be casual in such things."

"And you?"

"I am completely... Don't ever tell Gerdt. Promise?"

"Completely what?"

"Innocent."

She laughed. "That's why *Vati* lets me ride alone with you. You're so damnably innocent and trustworthy."

Then at last he kissed her. He couldn't imagine going back to Heidelberg without kissing her. It was a soft little kiss, a first little kiss to test her reaction. To discover how. She leaned into him. To look at her she appeared wiry, muscular, energised. To touch her, to hold her like this, he found her soft and yielding. He pressed her hard against him, his hands probing her shape, her substance, all her lovely curves and edges hidden under those rough riding clothes. When he discovered her breasts the breath went out of him, how soft she was, how soft and pliant. He found the buttons and worked them open, and she helped him with her little hands and she watched with wide interested eyes as he probed under her cotton shift into amazing soft warm flesh, and he bent to kiss one breast, to pull on her breast with his lips and tongue and she arched back and with her hands she pressed his head closer against her and she groaned and she whispered yes yes yes...

With a terrible wrenching effort he turned from her. He had to walk away until this scarlet throbbing would settle. He went to his horse and with his back to her braced his hands on the saddle, and stood there until he could catch his breath, until his erection passed, until he stopped trembling.

Then they got on the horses and rode home.

* * *

CHAPTER 4

September 1912

Supper that evening was subdued, with long silences; and when anyone spoke, the intrusive voice seemed too bright. Halfway through the meal the baron boomed, "Well, it's been a fine holiday. So it's back to the books tomorrow, boys."

Brigitte ran from the table out of the room and slammed the door.

"Well I swear!"

"Please don't swear, dear," said the baroness mildly.

"Women's troubles, I suppose."

The baroness glanced sideways at Eric and nodded. "Yes, women's troubles."

Eric laid down his fork and excused himself. As he followed Brigitte out of the room he heard the baron say, "Ah, *those* women's troubles. Well, it's not to be permitted, of course..."

The entrance hall was deserted. Along the walls the lamps flickered in an airy draft. The doors off the gallery were all closed. He stood for a moment scanning the animal heads on the walls. He listened. Not a sound. In the weeks he'd been here he'd never gone to her room. North-eastern suite, the butler had said when they'd first arrived, all that time ago.

He mounted the stairs slowly, listening. At the top he turned along the gallery opposite his own room and walked twenty paces to the nearest closed door. He rapped a knuckle on the timber.

Brigitte's muffled voice came through. "I don't want to talk. I'll come down soon."

He opened the door and stepped inside.

She had curled up in a big wing chair in front of her cold fireplace. Thick carpets lay over the floor and heavy wool hangings covered the walls. The two small windows were thrown wide open to the evening air. Along one wall hung a tapestry with mediaeval armoured knights jousting on horseback. His eye took it all in as he crossed the room; the deep chairs, two sofas, a reading desk, an open door leading to a bedroom beyond with a huge four-poster bed. Without thinking, he swerved to close the bedroom door, and had no idea why he did it. His ears were burning hot, just at sight of her bed.

He reached her side and knelt by her chair. She needed protection, this witch of a girl. From herself, and from the world. Curled up so small in so large a chair she resembled her failing mother. She had been crying.

He took her hand. "What's wrong?"

"I hardly knew you even liked me. Until today. Really."

"It's just that... that you never stand still long enough to—"

"I think I love you," she said in a half whisper.

His heart would crack open and bleed until the world turned red.

"Oh Eric, damn you for being so superior—"

"Superior!"

"You mocked me, you watched me suffer and you just smiled, so superior—"

"When did you suffer?"

"Riding, always just riding, never a word from you, you would rather spank me than kiss me, never a sign until today. And all through that damned dance, you would not condescend to ask me to dance—"

"You danced with everybody else from the moment we arrived. Was I to fight a duel with every man who spoke to you?"

"Why not? Why does a man learn to fence, if not to—"

He laughed.

Tears welled into her eyes and spilled down her face. "I never met anyone like you," she mourned. "From the day you arrived you were impossible, so damned above it all, making saintly judgments on everything I did, sometimes I wanted to slap your face to force you to notice me."

He came to his feet and drew her up into his arms while she went on and on, day after day, about his faults and failures. And he smiled because she knew nothing of his turmoil, and he smiled because she had her arms about him and was leaning into him, her head tucked under his chin, talk talk talk... and all he wanted was to kiss her...

And then she said into his chest, "We can run away."

He drew back. "What?"

"We could go to Paris. I've always wanted to go to Paris."

"How would we live?"

"You could study at the Sorbonne."

"Who would pay for that?"

"Does your father care where you study?"

His father!

He released her. Disentangled her arms. He moved restlessly away from her to circle the room with its priceless mediaeval tapestry. She knew nothing of poverty. He knew nothing of poverty except that poor people existed in the world, some who stood in the dock before his father's bench and often ended in prison or on the gallows.

"My father," he said, pacing, "would disown me."

"Why?"

"What about your father? Would he not disown you?"

"No, he'd come to kill you, and to bring me home."

He stopped and faced her halfway across the room. "Are you crazy?"

She tilted one shoulder in half a shrug. "I suppose then you'd have to kill him first."

She was so forlorn.

"Do you hear yourself?" he asked.

The tears came again, no change of expression, her eyes wide in misery. Abruptly she rushed to him and flung her arms about him. "I think I could do anything, Eric, I could kill with my own hands to be with you. I want you to marry me!"

"You have to be sensible, we've known each other for just a couple of weeks—"

"Forty days, time enough for Noah's flood to cover the earth—"

"Hardly enough to be married, or even—"

"Oh listen, my father has tried for years to find a husband for me, some grey old owl with money and property. Women are born to be married, he says—"

He put a hand over her mouth. He had to wrestle her arms from about his neck. He gripped her by the elbows and lifted her backwards to her wing chair and set her down on it. "This is just a way out for you, Brigitte. For me it..." He didn't know what it was for him.

And again, quicksilver, her eyes filled with tears and tragedy. He drew her up and folded her into his arms and sat with her in the chair. Like a child she laid her head on his shoulder, and like a child she weighed about a feather on his lap.

He'd never met anyone like this. Boy-child one minute, *femme fatale* the next. He didn't think she knew what she was doing. Was she playing him for a fool? Was she truly so naive? Did she even know the meaning of love?

Did he?

He knew this of her. She needed to be cared for. She needed not to be managed, not to be married off, but to be loved. Be *loved*. He wasn't sure, sitting with her like this, so close, so warm... He wasn't sure after today in the forest... he wasn't sure... Nobody had ever told him how to distinguish love from lust.

At this moment he felt such tenderness for her that lust did not exist.

They were still curled together in the chair a few minutes later when Gerdt pounded at the door. "Hallo you two, I know you're in there...!" Such a clatter, it was more warning than greeting. The door burst open and Gerdt charged in like a comedian in a broad stage farce, "Hey you fellows, Vati's been looking for you!"

They left Brigitte there and went downstairs to the library. Outwardly, nothing had changed since supper; but Eric felt at once the slightest chill in the atmosphere. They hesitated in the open doorway. The baroness was lecturing the baron as carefully as a diplomat to a king, "...it is doubtless her fault, not his, my dear, she is so undisciplined, and he may not be aware of correct protocol, I urge you to have patience—"

"Patience is not my best suit—"

"Yes, my dear, I know. Now, I'm certain nothing could have happened or she would have told me, so do not concern yourself, let us be calm, for tomorrow they..." And she looked around from her chair as they came in, and said, "Ah there you are, my boys."

The baron reared back. "Yes, Herr Foster, what took you so long away from dinner!"

"Sorry sir—"

"I want to talk to you, young man."

"Yes sir, gladly—"

"I think," the baron said loudly, "that everyone should leave us alone here!"

Gerdt helped his mother from her chair. She coughed as they crossed the room. Eric had not heard her cough before. The door closed after them and the library fell into a hush, the crackle of the fire the only sound. He turned to face the baron, but the baron was staring into the fire as if Eric were not there.

He waited to one side.

After a long pause, without looking up, the baron said, "So! At least you know when to hold your tongue. A rare quality these days in our free-living offspring!"

He waited.

"What do you think of her, then?"

"Of whom, sir?"

"My daughter. My Brigitte." Now he turned, one hand gripping the arm of the chair. "Before dinner she told her mother she thinks she loves you. What do you say to that?"

He didn't know what to say. This was moving too quickly.

"What happened between you, that she talks such nonsense!"

"Nothing happened, sir. I kissed her, I confess I kissed her, that's all sir." *Echo from the past, his father in his study, Nothing happened sir...*

Dreadful silence.

"But if she said she loves me, sir, it's not from anything I might have done but from what I did not do. I did not treat her as a child, though she acts like one, and I did not take advantage of her loneliness, though she's the loneliest girl I've ever met. She's wild and defenceless and she needs a friend."

The baron half rose. "Did you...? were you...?"

"No sir. We did not."

He subsided again. "Why not?"

Time came to a standstill while he drifted in confusion. *Why not? Why not?* Finally he stuttered, "Because I think I love her also sir—"

The baron burst into laughter. "Bless me, I've never heard that version before. You love her, therefore you made no attempt, etcetera. You're surely one of a kind, young man. Nevertheless, a brash young pup. What have you to offer a girl of her rank and breeding?"

There it was again. The outrage of parents, marriage on their minds, raising hurdles at every turn.

He was not ready for this discussion. "Nothing, sir. I possess nothing."

"Your mother is a Bronsart. The niece of General Paul Bronsart von Schellendorf." The colonel rose out of the chair. "Oh yes, I've looked into it. Otherwise you would not be invited to this house. General Staff? Minister of War in the 'eighties? Author of *'The Duties of the General Staff'*?" A smile blazed on his florid face. "So you're not entirely without background." But he shook his head and sank back into the chair. "Nevertheless I have no interest in any liaison that might take Brigitte away from Germany. What can you offer her, other than the life of an adventurer? In my family a commission with an elite regiment is the only acceptable career. But we would never accept a *Foster* into the regiment. Prussia has a long military history which you English cannot comprehend, you have no concept of the Kaiser's cavalry, or of the Officer Corps' tradition of honour. This is a different world, my boy, one cannot step into it from outside, a man must be born to it, born to the colours. No. Never."

Eric heard this through a fog of numb relief. Twice now he had been pushed to the brink because, for one reason or another, he had found himself alone with a girl.

He did not see her alone again. The next day under a bright morning sun the family lingered on the front step to say farewell and to shake hands all around. Impossible to kiss her goodbye under the baron's formidable scrutiny.

*

In Heidelberg he returned with Gerdt to a room that had been scrubbed spotless top to bottom. Laundered clothes were folded neatly on the beds, and mail lay on the desk. Eric dropped his rucksack inside the door and went at once to open his mail. A letter from Gordon, one from his mother, one from his father. He flung himself on his bed to read the least one first...

> *Dear old sod,* (wrote Gordon)
> *Jenny has returned from Switzerland, non-delectata as it were, and therefore restored to polite society. The important news is, I have decided to go in with my father and he is sending me off to the Singapore office, high adventure in store, new life etc etc. Do drop a note. I shall be embarking on the 17th Oct, and should like to catch up prior, yours till death etc etc usque ad nauseam...*

He smiled and set it aside. What did they expect? That somehow out of a motorcycle accident Jenny would have come up with a child? Bloody foolishness...

He opened his mother's letter, written, as always, in German...

> *My Darling Eric:*
> *"Thank you for your letter. I was sad that you could not come home for the holiday. Colin was very disappointed. It pleases us, however, that you enjoyed your visit to Baden, a lovely part of the country. The Baron and his family can very possibly make a useful contact; but that aside, I wonder if your friend's sister may be more a problem than a friend. She seems somewhat immature and impulsive...*

He ripped open the last letter.

Dear Eric
I expect that you used your time profitably and are now prepared to attack your studies more seriously this term. Remember: only a First will do. I know you are capable if you put your mind to it. Your mother tells me that you absorb the most difficult mathematics precepts with scarcely an effort. From this I know you are capable of similar results in any discipline if you tackle it with sincerity.

Your mother is annoyed with me for keeping you away this holiday. Well my boy, the truth is that you two are as alike as peas in a pod, to the degree that I often suspect that she has conferred upon you her own lack of discipline, which is excusable in a woman but abhorrent in any man worthy of his name. Be a man, Eric. It is my best advice...

Be a man... He sat musing at the last afternoon sunbeam slanting through the window. Be a man. Yes, he could do that. Be a man. At last his father had given him something to grasp.

He took up his rucksack to unpack. Inside lay a parcel wrapped in butcher's brown paper and tied with butcher's waxed string. "Is this yours?" he asked Gerdt across the room.

Gerdt shook his head, reading his mail.

He sat on the bed and untied the string. A book fell out, small, slim, with a familiar hand-tooled leather binding. A single word embossed in gilt, *"Goethe"*.

A book of German poetry. The book she'd bought in Baden that day.

On the first page a note in small spiked handwriting, *"to a Friend."* The ribbon book-mark opened to page 12 printed in illuminated gothic calligraphy, with another handwritten note in the margin, *"my favourite"*...

"*Over all the mountaintops
is peace.
In all the treetops*

> *you detect*
> *hardly a breath.*
> *The little birds rest in the forest..."*

"Ready to go to eat?" Gerdt called from the door.

Eric snapped shut the book, almost embarrassed to be caught reading poetry. "Yes, ready."

Much later that evening, when he returned from boisterous reunions with friends at the Red Ox, he surreptitiously opened the little book to finish reading that poem...

> *"Only wait, soon*
> *you will rest too."*

He slept that night with the book under his pillow and Brigitte's elfin eyes laughing within the darkness of his mind. In that night he made his decision. He must do better. He must not be summoned home. He must make a First. He must not fail because he'd inherited his mother's disordered mind and had no discipline.

*

On his appointment with his academic advisor Eric asked to change his program. "Yes," said Bartók. He scribbled notes on a schedule form. "See what you can make of this."

Eric read it over: *Second level Physics, Boolean Theory, Theory of Numbers, Applied Economics, Forming the German Empire*. Ah good, only one history. The mathematics and physics would give puzzles to challenge his brain. He walked the tour to present his papers to the various professors for approval, in the hope that he would be accepted for at least three. He was accepted into all five. Bartók approved the finalised schedule and smiled and said, "Well, Foster, it's past time that you stretch your mind. You can do this. I have high expectations."

"Oh my God!" he said to Gerdt meeting in The Red Ox for supper. "Look at my schedule! How can I ride with the Dragoons this term? I won't have a free minute all week!"

"But this is too much! Drop the economics and Thursday afternoon will be free. Na?"

"It's my best discipline. If I can't make a First in economics,

I can't—"

"You know, Eric, this will ruin your social life. You're too good a guy to be so damned clever and busy as this."

He shrugged. "Tell my father."

He started into his classes with new heart, but with apprehension. Such a heavy schedule, he wasn't sure he could handle it. But then a strange thing happened. Within the week, after diving into the lectures and the texts and the wonderful physics lab on Tuesdays, he could scarcely wait for what came next. In the evenings he swept through the readings and found time to work a few fascinating problems before Gerdt snapped off his light to sleep. They were both working earnestly these fresh September days.

Another strange thing happened. The White Dragoons missed him, and so they changed their day to Saturday. And because his courses seemed so effortless and he was not kept so long at memorising disconnected facts, he found time on Wednesday evenings for fencing as well. He did not go back to The Historical Society. They took too much of his time.

*

Gerdt had a girl. "It isn't serious," he said. "I met her at the cotillion last spring. Her name's Annette Bressard, she's French. Come to the cotillion this week. She'll be there, you can meet her. Wear your uniform, it will impress the ladies, they all want to dance with military officers—"

"Uniform! That's not a uniform, it's a riding outfit!"

"Ah, but they don't know that. Uniforms impress them. They think we're officer-aspirants."

On Friday when they went down to the dance Gerdt wore his Dragoon 'whites'. Eric put on the usual formal white-tie-and-tails with the high collar, designed, he mused, to keep his head from turning too far out of line. In the magnificent ballroom of the Hotel zum Ritter, marriageable young ladies gathered each week to meet suitable young men under the watchful eyes of parents. It was difficult to talk. The unremitting music of a small Strauss band never stopped, denying any pause for conversation. Along one side wall a refreshment table was guarded by parents to thwart inspired young bucks from adding a splash of something to the fruit punch.

Annette was a lovely girl with languid eyes and glorious chestnut hair. Eric could understand Gerdt's fascination with her. On the ballroom floor they looked the perfect couple.

He didn't want to be here. He danced with a few young ladies, exchanging no more than a few words under the music, and escorted each of them back to her group. A slight bow, a thank-you, and that was all. The ladies were not impressed. It was exactly as Gerdt had warned. Their eyes were for the soldiers from the garrison, magnificent in their sky-blue tunics and gold stripes down their lean trousers and their mirror-black boots.

It didn't matter. Brigitte haunted him all evening, dancing like a puff of air on his arm...

*

"So," he said in mid-morning after Gerdt woke up, "your father isn't bothered about a French girl?"

"My father doesn't know."

"Do you think you'll marry her?"

"My dear Eric, the subject will never arise."

Ah.

Eric went back to his problem in algebra. A very fat, lovely, complex problem.

Gerdt brought two cups of coffee from Frau Hilderman and sat down opposite at the desk. He pushed a cup across to Eric. "So how did you do last night? Meet anyone?"

"I had a fine time. But you were right about the uniforms."

"Ah, it's their loss." He watched as Eric scribbled the last few steps to finish the problem, and set down the result with a satisfied flourish. "How do you do that?"

"What?"

"Those problems. I don't even know what that stuff means, sine, function, and such."

"It's just a puzzle. It needs to be solved."

Gerdt nodded, and sipped the coffee. Then he put down the cup, making another wet ring on the polished wood. "Listen. I want to tell you something important."

Eric looked up at Gerdt's serious tone.

"Listen." He pushed the cup on the desk leaving a trail of wet that would soon set into a soft white stain. "Remember you asked why I wanted you for my roommate?"

"Did I ask that?"

"Yes, the first day. I didn't tell you the real reason."

"No?"

"I said I needed help with the rent."

"An obvious... prevarication."

"A lie. Yes."

"Well?"

"I lie a lot."

"I've noticed."

"Diplomatic lies. I never lie about things that matter."

"No, obviously not."

"Why do you say it like that, 'obviously' not?"

"Because I couldn't be your friend if you lied about things that matter."

"That's it, you see."

"What is '*it*'?"

"I watched you from the day you arrived in my history class. There are things about yourself, Eric, that you don't recognize and I think somebody should tell you, and I don't know anybody better than your best friend."

He set down his pen. Now it would come out, all his little faults. Ah well. The price to pay for a friend's hangover.

"First," said Gerdt, "I wasn't the only fellow to notice you. Everybody did. You walked late into the class and there was an air about you—"

"An air? An air of what?"

"Of... I don't know. Nothing like arrogance or aristocracy, nothing so fashionable. It was... You were saying with your whole being, 'Don't bugger me up, I know who I am'. Very deadly."

"Truly?"

"Like that day I trotted off with your stein of beer and you followed me out and you didn't choose a fight as one might expect. You were amused. You made me look foolish. I then had to make it up to you."

He gazed at Gerdt across the desk, puzzled.

"That's what you do, you see, you force me to do the right thing. I've studied so hard since you moved in with me, my

father's astonished by my performance, my mother's in ecstasy and my sister thinks I've gone quite mad."
"I didn't think you studied at all."
"You mustn't tell anyone. It would destroy my reputation."
Eric laughed. Typical Gerdt, who even lied about studying!

* * *

CHAPTER 5

September to October 1912

My dearest Eric ~
Already I miss you. Already my heart is broken after you left. I ride alone, with only your spirit to keep me company.
~ B.

Her handwriting was small and spiked and as childlike as the way she sometimes spoke. Three short sentences scribbled in purple ink, slanting downhill on pale blue notepaper.

Her heart was broken? He had broken the steely heart of a wood nymph? He read it a dozen times until it lost all meaning. Just words, with her voice laughing behind the words, *heart-is-broken, heart-is-broken.* Teasing? Serious...?

He started a letter, "*My Dear Brigitte, I am studying hard in order to please my father who threatens to call me home if I do not achieve top standing at Christmas...*" He had to keep it calm, keep it friendly. Let her drive the other fellows crazy...

Who were the other fellows?

How many other fellows were there?

He could not stifle the thought. He could not tolerate the idea of other fellows in her life. Men. Boys. Idiots. Competitors? No, no, no...

He could not finish the letter. If he couldn't say "I love you", there was nothing at all to say. He didn't know if this was love or just a distraction, an upheaval in the balance of his brain, which she had now sparked into a fever with three short sentences.

Ridiculous. Magical.

From that time, at odd moments in the day, he found himself interrupted by her note like a banner across his brain, and by those eyes flashing in the dark of his skull. In the middle of a lecture the professor's voice would fade while her laugh echoed in his head. At dinner he would pause, his fork in the air, as he recalled the tilt of her head, the curve of her throat, the silken sheen of her skin. Fencing with Gerdt he simply lost his place and took a slash up the right side of his half jacket. "Wake up, Schellendorf!" thundered the fencing-master. One afternoon he found himself on the train going to Baden. Startled, he got off at the next station and walked perhaps a dozen kilometres back to Heidelberg, and missed his afternoon lectures. Later Gerdt dashed into the room and demanded, "Where were you all day?"

"Walking."

Gerdt tossed his books on the desk and sat over on the edge of his bed. "What's wrong with you?"

"Nothing."

"You live in a dream. Ever since that letter from your father. What did he say?"

Eric thought a moment, then shook himself awake. "Yes, he said if I could do no better I may as well go home and join a solicitor as a secretary."

"So," said Gerdt, "in order to do better you ignore your studies, you dream your days away, you take long walks during lecture time, is that how to do it? And now I find you alone in the dark staring out the window." He reached over and switched on the desk light.

Eric blinked. He hadn't noticed the fall of darkness.

After that he had to concentrate on concentrating. Now when she invaded his mind he would open a book to the toughest problem of the week and work it out on paper step-by-step. In a lecture he would jerk his brain back to the moment, and take his notes in English, and later translate them back to German. In that way he learned it twice over. He must, he *must* do better.

*

They were ten days into October when Gerdt burst into the room where Eric was working some problems at the desk. He waved a letter in the air. "It seems my mother's not receiving any further benefit by taking the waters at Baden-Baden."

Eric half rose in dismay from his chair. "Ah Gerdt, no—"

"So they'll move out of that miserable cold castle back to town for the winter."

He sank back on the chair. "You mean... here?"

Gerdt pulled a crumpled letter from his jacket pocket. "And this came for you."

He couldn't move for a moment. "You mean *here*?" His heart was about to explode out of his chest. "In Heidelberg? For the winter? The whole family?"

Gerdt fell into the chair across the desk and gazed at him with a crooked smile. "Read your damn letter."

Letter from his father...

> *My dear Eric:*
> *I have been in contact with Herr Bartok, and I try to perceive what sort of balderdash is going on in your head. Mathematics? Economics? How will that prepare you for the Law? Your mother and I are equally of the same mind. We want you home now without further delay. Now do be a good fellow and pack it up. You are scheduled in class Monday week. If this appears rather abrupt, it is actually not. We have been contemplating your return for some time, and I have already used my influence to restore you to King's where, if <u>commerce</u> is your bent, you could take up <u>commercial</u> law and still be among people of our own sort...*

The law the law the law... And what was this stuff... this *rubbish*... about "commerce"? Did he see no difference between commerce and economics?

"What's wrong?" Gerdt asked across the desk. "You look like you've been shot."

"My father orders me home."

"When?"

He crushed the letter in his fist. "Now." He tossed the ball of paper over.

Gerdt flattened it on the desk and stared at it, frowning. After a moment he said, "My English is not adequate."

"He's arranged my return to Cambridge. Immediately. My mother agrees."

Gerdt's eyes flicked a silent question.

"I don't care how it looks," Eric burst out, "my mother actually decides, not my father. She always said I must honour my father, and in this letter my father..." He let it slide.

They fell to contemplation.

Then Gerdt said, "Well, one is always obliged to obey one's parents."

"I see no other way."

Gerdt looked miserable. "I've never had so fine a friend. My parents think highly of you also."

"And I you. I love your family. I love..." He did not say it. He had no right to say it.

It occurred to him that he might simply not go home. But his bank account was almost empty. There would be no more money. He couldn't live on friendship, and certainly not on love and air.

He began to organise his things to pack. He'd collected so many books, he had to go out to buy a haversack to pack them all in. All books in German. He paused at that, realising that his whole life was in German, his thoughts and even his dreams at night were in German.

Well, so.

When he gave his notice to Frau Hildermann she promised to pack his trunk for him. "I'm sorry to see you go," she said. "You boys are very quiet and polite, so different from the usual rowdy, drunken types."

The rest of the week Eric made the rounds. He sat his regular lectures, fenced with the club on Wednesday, shook hands with each Dragoon as they encountered each other. He shook hands in the halls, on the Quad, in the streets, shook hands with everyone he knew and many he did not know. Word spread through the university. *The Engländer is going home.*

On Friday he tapped on his advisor's office door. "Yes," said

Herr Bartók, "Your father wrote to me." They went over Eric's records. "There's a unique depth," Herr Bartók said, "in your understanding of mathematics. You must continue to develop such a gift."
    "Thank you sir. I wish someone could convince my father."
    "Shall I write him a letter for you?"
    "He has other plans for my future."
    "A shame." He gave him an envelope. "Well, one does not argue. But it's here in your transcript, he'll be pleased with this excellent performance. I knew you could do it." In the doorway they shook hands. "You've become a good student, Foster. I'll miss having you."
    So different from the casual dismissal of his Cambridge don, *"Brace up, Foster..."*
    Outside the closed office door, alone in the dim corridor, he paused at last. Leaving here would be harder than anything he'd ever had to do. But one had to be tough, control one's feelings, suppress the need to break free, *only a few more years,* she'd said, *a few more years...*
    On Friday evening dozens of students came in streams to surround Eric and Gerdt at their table in the Red Ox. They bought beer and chugged it down in huge hilarity, then, very late, went to mawkish tears when the proprietor tossed them out of the place. Roaring drunk, and singing an endless repertoire of beer songs, bolstered by a phalanx of a hundred noisy others, Eric and Gerdt staggered arm-in-arm back to their pension room. The tumult echoed from the darkened buildings and through the narrow cobbled streets. Lights came on. Heidelbergers shook their fists in the night.

*

Head throbbing, he woke to the smell of coffee. Sunlight battered his eyes. Another letter came yesterday. It still lay on his bedside table. He hadn't bothered to open it before going off to the Red Ox. Now, through the haze of the first hangover of his life, he ripped into it, already knowing what it said...

    ...another week gone by without action or reply.
    It is past time to pack it up. You will return
    forthwith, this very day. No further funds will be

applied to your bank account until we see you home in London. Enclosed is your train ticket...

He sat up cautiously, eyes squeezed shut. A mule kicked inside his skull and set loose an avalanche of rocks. He groaned, and his own voice pounded inside.

Nothing was left to do. His packed trunks were in the hall downstairs, or perhaps already sent over to the station...

"Coffee," said Gerdt. He sat at the desk where a coffee pot steamed on a tray. He bent over like a hunchback, cup between his hands, eyes closed, nose in the steam from his coffee.

Eric edged out of bed, his head swimming, throbbing. Except for shoes and tie he was still dressed from last night. His shoes lay tumbled just inside the door, his tie coiled like a snake on the floor halfway across. "What time is it?"

"Almost noon."

He groaned again and padded across, shedding his jacket as he went. "I've missed the nine o'clock." He fell onto his chair.

"There's another Paris train at six." Gerdt poured coffee and pushed the cup across.

Eric studied the train ticket. First class, dated three days ago. Six-month expiry.

They sat sipping coffee. Rolling rocks filled his head. The weight of the world pressed down his shoulders.

"Frau Hildermann," said Gerdt, "brought up this note with the coffee."

"And?" Perhaps he could die, and not have to catch the train.

"It's from Mutti. They're home today, you know."

"Who?"

"The family."

"Today!" His own voice sent a thunderbolt crashing among the rocks rolling in his head. "Oh my God," he whispered. "I can't move."

Gerdt held a card in the air, his head still bowed, eyes still closed. "Lunch at thirteen hours."

The clock said eleven forty-eight.

*

An hour later they walked up the slope below the Schloss. The cobbled lane curved to a great oak bent over the lane and, fifty yards farther along, a rambling house faced north-eastward to the forests of the Neckar Valley. Gerdt stopped under the oak tree. "So this is home," he said. "Another old fortress. You see why I prefer a room with Frau Hildermann."

The house was of grey stonework, with steep clay roofs and several stone chimneys and a huge window in the front. A stone wall enclosed grass as green and lush as an English lawn. Beds of flowers bloomed against the base of the house.

They crossed a carriage turnabout to the front gate. "Where do you keep the horses?" Eric asked.

"At the garrison stables. We call on the telephone when we want the carriage."

"A telephone! My father has one also."

On the roof above the front entrance an untidy bundle of sticks was jammed against one of the chimneys. "Our storks," said Gerdt proudly. "They fledged, but they'll be back next spring. Mutti calls them our cosmic good fortune." He chuckled. "Vati says it's nonsense."

Just as they reached the step Hanisch opened the door, as if he'd been watching for them. "Welcome home, my young sirs." Today he wore the striped morning suit of a correct butler.

"And welcome home to you also, Hanisch," said Gerdt. "My mother?"

"In the kitchen, sir. Until the rooms are heated."

Gerdt hurried along the hallway, Eric on his heels. He was about to see Brigitte. In that brief interlude along the hall he suddenly understood all the poets of the world and why the heart was the focus of all the odes about love and longing. It pounded through his hangover and made him dizzy. He was about to see her. He had no idea what he would say to her.

They came into the kitchen, a large bright room with a black forged-iron stove and a brick chimney against the far wall. A hot room. Two women worked at a table by the window that looked up the slope toward the Schloss. One of the women moved aside to reveal the baroness sitting at the table in sunlight from the window, hands curled around a large mug. Everything in the room was large except that slight figure.

"Mutti!"

"Ah Gerdt. Ah Eric."

Gerdt ran to her and bent to kiss her on the cheek. She smiled and raised a hand toward Eric. "Come here, come here, let me look at you both. Oh my boys."

Brigitte was not here. Eric smoothed his face, buried his disappointment. He bent to kiss the thin white hand. Skin of cool dry parchment. "Baroness," he murmured.

"Where's Brigitte?" Gerdt asked.

"Reading in the gun room, I think."

Eric straightened abruptly.

"Oh my dear." She smiled, her eyes direct on his face. "Expect nothing. Brigitte's time is not her own."

Gerdt said, "Back along the hall past the stairway, first on your left."

The hall was a long journey. He held his breath the whole way past a staircase to the door on the left that led into a large, masculine room. Books lined one wall. A giant fireplace commanded another wall that was hung with stuffed heads of game animals and rifles and crossed sabres and pistols. In one corner stood a headless manikin wearing a blue cavalry tunic ablaze with magnificent medals over the chest.

A small figure sat reading at the mahogany desk by the far wall.

He stood in the doorway. She did not look up. She was reading in the half light of a table lamp that shone down on the polished desk scattered with writing paraphernalia. Eric stood motionless, gazing at her face in shadow, gathering his senses. He didn't know what to say.

She read. Her total concentration was on the book.

He shuffled in the doorway.

She looked up. "Eric!" She leaped to her feet and darted around the desk and ran at him in a headlong charge. "Oh Eric, oh Eric!" She flew into him. As he staggered back she flung her arms about him and met his lips. He folded her in and sank into the kiss.

*

They sat on the front step. She was bundled up like a Cossack against the October chill in a long black coat, its silver fur collar pulled up around her ears. He wanted to kiss her. The desire was so strong that he had to anchor himself to the step and sink his hands deep in his pockets. He had suffered through a long lunch with the family, he'd sat across from *her* and hardly noticed the food. He'd forgotten his pulsing hangover for the larger pounding in his heart.

When he'd told them that he was packed and ready to go to England, a long silence settled around the table, surprise in every face.

Now this last moment alone together was goodbye. He would not see her again. By this evening he would be on the train to Strasburg and Paris, then on to Calais and the Dover ferry. This was his final time. He could see nothing in the immediate future but England and *Father*. He must control himself, and go forward to face him. Perhaps he could work his way back, perhaps at Christmas...

"I'll die," she said in a small voice. She pulled her coat closer around her.

He smiled

"I can't bear it," she burst out. "Since August I couldn't wait to see you again! I thought in all my life I would never find anyone like you, all those rich, toothless old men looking for a child bride to display at royal functions, I despised them, I turned them away, I laughed in their faces and then I met *you* and now you are gone. I'll kill myself. That's all there is for me."

Eric took her by the shoulders and turned her to face him. Her eyes brimmed over. She clutched at him, and then, sitting side by side on the cold stone step, they held to each other, his face buried in the soft fur of her collar.

He had to collect himself. "Well..." He put her aside with firm purpose. "Certainly it's not worth it to kill yourself just over me."

She jumped to her feet. "Oh yes, make it a joke!" She ran out through the garden gate and slammed it after her. Sleek in that black coat from ears to ankles, black button boots flicking like little target ducks in a shooting gallery, she ran away down the cobbled lane.

He followed more slowly. She ran down to the old oak tree and stopped to lean against its gnarled trunk, its branches bent like an umbrella over her.

He stopped beside her, but didn't dare touch her again. He

didn't know what he might do if he touched her. The warmth of holding her there on the step still burned his chest and drove spikes into a stuttering heart.

"I argued for you," she said. "I made your case, I had Papi convinced." She gazed down the slope at the town spread out below. "And now you're leaving forever."

"Convinced?"

"Well..." She looked up at him. Tragic amethyst eyes. "He said maybe."

His ironic laugh was harsh and dry. He had come only to say goodbye. He had almost not come at all, fearing her witchcraft. He had come out of courtesy, to say goodbye to the family, to do the right thing according to the simple rules of etiquette.

Etiquette! God.

Suddenly nothing was simple. The baron had said...

Maybe...?

"What does he want me to do?" Eric heard himself say.

"He told me a real man will find a way."

They walked. He did not kiss her. They did not hold hands. They walked elbow-to-elbow down to the river and along the busy *Hackteufel* to the footbridge. On the middle of the bridge she stopped and he stopped and they leaned elbow to elbow on the guardrail. Shoulders touching, they stared down at smooth water slipping over the weir. The chill breeze foreshadowed winter.

"When do you go?" she asked the black water.

"I should have left this morning. I missed my train."

"I'm glad."

"I too."

People brushed past them in both directions, unconcerned with tragedy. A busy time, Saturday afternoon. Market day. A man passed carrying a speckled grey hen by the legs upside down, wings half spread, its head craned quietly upward.

She turned to look up at Eric, silver-fox fur framing her delicate face. "Kiss me."

He drew back from her. People walked past, not glancing sideways.

"Why are you so stiff?" she asked.

"I'm not stiff." He turned half away from her, wound tight as a steel spring. "Your father said *maybe* I could find a way. We haven't a millimetre to spare, Britt. We must be careful and not turn your parents against me in any way or..." He broke off at the mischief in her eyes.

Then she laughed outright. "Oh, you are so typical an Engländer, so reserved, so above it all! So precise, such perfect deportment. I could kill you."

He laughed too. "A while ago you wanted to kill yourself. You're quite a killer, you know."

"What did you call me just then?"

"I don't know, what—?"

"Britt. You called me Britt."

"I didn't mean to."

"I like it. Brigitte. Britt!" She laughed again, her sadness of moments ago turned to delight. "And I shall call you Erich..." she drew out the *ch* like the hissing of a cat... "to make you more a German. We meet in the middle of the footbridge."

* * *

CHAPTER 6

October 1912

Late in the night he sat down to write the letter. His packed luggage still waited down in the foyer to be carried wherever it should go. Over in the corner Gerdt was deep asleep. Eric had the night to himself.

He should have done this long ago. He paused a long time, ripped up several sheets of paper putting together the words...

> *Dear Father ~*
> *Sincere apologies for my delay in coming home, but you did promise me a year. I admit to not being the student you expected, but I have done so much better recently, and will certainly work hard at it for the final result. I shall keep the train ticket for Christmas.*
> *Father..."* He paused again... *"Can we agree that although the Law is the foundation of your success, it would be my undoing. This does not mean that I do not value your judgment or advice. I have always appreciated that you are brilliant in your field. For myself, I do not believe that the Law is within my grasp. I have neither capacity for it nor the necessary interest in it. I am sorry if this disappoints you, but I know you would not want a bad lawyer in the*

> *family. My advisor, Herr Bartók, with whom you are in contact, tells me that I am best suited to mathematics and economics. If you do not object, I shall continue in economics, which can lead to any number of useful careers. You promised me a year, and I ask you now to honour that..."*

He wrote a little about the cool autumn weather and finished, *"Much love from your respectful son Eric"*, and blew the ink dry, and read it again. He couldn't predict how his father would see it. As proof of logic and maturity? As rebellion? With nervous fingers he folded it into an envelope.

"*Dearest Mutti...*" he started in German...

This was more difficult. For days he had planned his father's letter. This for his mother came from a deeper place not yet considered. He couldn't think of a diplomatic opening.

> *Dearest Mutti,*
> *I hope this finds you in good health and spirits. I mentioned in an earlier letter this wonderful girl I met in Baden...*

Once started, he filled three pages about Brigitte, about her exquisite beauty, her impulsive personality, her horsemanship, everything that he could think about her that he could put on paper, and how the baron had said *maybe*. But when he'd written everything, he faltered at the end. *"...please do not tell Father about this. He need not know yet about Brigitte, I want him to judge me on my academic performance, which is so greatly improved..."*

He stamped and sealed both envelopes. In the middle of the night he walked all the way over to the post office to drop the letters in the slot. He might lose courage by morning.

*

On Monday morning he sat in his regular history lecture at the Aula, and then went around to Herr Bartók's office. "I want to continue, sir, if it's possible."

"Does your father agree?"

"I don't know yet. I've asked his permission."

Herr Bartók smiled and held out his hand. "Welcome back." That evening, instead of going to the Red Ox, Gerdt marched him up the cobbled lane to the house for supper with the family. "Now that they're home," he said, "maybe we can cadge a few free meals."

At the supper table the baroness led the usual conversation. Brigitte sat in her usual place, casting glances across at Eric at his usual place while he tried not to look at her at all. He was aware of every glance, aware that she talked in tones brighter than natural, aware that she posed and postured and laughed too much and that she watched for his reaction, while he studiously refused to react, not certain of the rules of this game.

After supper they moved into the gun room. Eric loved these evenings sitting with them, chairs in a half circle, feet to a crackling fire, while servants brought fresh logs from time to time. Mulled wine, lazy conversation. Long silences.

Over the next weeks they slipped effortlessly into a new routine. Classes, lunch in the Red Ox with wild debates between tables, fencing Wednesday evening, the Dragoons on Saturday. Almost every evening supper with the family. At the dinner table and afterward in the gun room their conversations ranged from the latest Richard Strauss opera to the Kaiser's ambition for his navy to thirty thousand millionaires dominating the German economy. "Thirty thousand millionaires!" boomed the baron, pounding the table and making the silverware dance, "Not even in America!"

Eric thought ironically, *Easier to be a millionaire in Marks than in dollars...*

Then after nine o'clock he would march with Gerdt down the hill to tackle the books late into the night.

One evening well into October, when he'd begun to feel almost part of the family, when he could sit at supper across from Brigitte without blushing, when he no longer felt that the baron was waiting for him in ambush, he found himself alone in the gun room with the baroness. They'd been sitting in front of the fire, drinking mulled wine, talking, half asleep... and now Gerdt and Britt and the baron had disappeared.

"What are your feelings, Eric?" said the baroness, as if

speaking to the fire.

"Feelings?" He sat upright, alert to danger.

"You understand me."

"I don't... I'm not..." He couldn't say. "The baron..." He gave up.

"Your feelings. Not the baron's or Brigitte's. What do you think of our little girl?"

There it was again. *Our little girl.* A child. "Forgive me, Baroness, she's not a little girl."

The fire crackled. A log fell in a shower of red sparks that whirled up the chimney. After a moment she said, "Brigitte always tells me everything. She thinks she loves you, and in this I feel that she's swimming in very deep water. She hardly knows what love is. Between a man and a woman she knows nothing."

"But if I say I love her also? You know I would—"

"That is not important."

"Love is not important?"

She turned to look at him at last, her eyes mild but direct. A flat voice contradicted the mild eyes. "Life goes on, you see. That's all." She leaned back deep into her high wing chair. "I must tell you, a gentleman has been in communication with me, a Junker in Rastenberg, a gentleman of substance, who plans a visit here after Christmas. We want none of Brigitte's hysterics to disturb his intentions."

He breathed. His head was light. Behind his eyes came a flutter, as if he'd run a race too hard, as if the energy had been drained from his bones. A *gentleman of substance.* Some grey old owl with money and property. He stared into the flames dancing almost smokeless on black logs, grey ash falling below.

"For that reason, Eric..." Wearily she turned to watch him as she spoke. "I count on you to be mature. To be a man. To protect my little girl from herself, from her own impulsive character. Are we understood?"

Again, the demand that he be a man.

"Yes, Baroness. Understood."

*

He walked with Gerdt back down the cobbled lane. The night sky was a deep transparent indigo full of stars so bright that the great oak cast a shadow on the ground. He gazed up with a fury that startled him. Stars were for romance, and there was none. Not even a slight hope. *Junker from Rastenberg.* Bring the lamb intact to the sacrifice. So much for 'finding a way'.

After they came into the *Hauptstrasse* he broke the silence between them. "So what do you know about this *Junker* coming at Christmas,"

Gerdt laughed. "Oh, she'll take care of him soon enough."

"I'll stop seeing her."

"Why?"

"Should I break my own heart? If she's intended for some..." He couldn't finish.

"If you feel so strongly, surely you won't quit."

They came to the Red Ox, still noisy with late evening students. Gerdt started to turn in, but Eric walked on and Gerdt hurried to follow. The crooked rows of houses and shops were shuttered for the night, the streets empty. Only the taverns were open, only the stars and the corner lamps gave light. They passed the Seppl with its quieter crowd.

"She could sign up for a course," Eric said with a new idea. "Then we could see each other more often away from the house, perhaps study together."

Gerdt snorted his scorn. "They wouldn't permit it. Father's precious darling? Anyway, she has no certificate."

"Anyone can audit a history class—"

"I tell you they can't take her, she has no certificate. She's never gone to school."

He stopped short in the street. Gerdt swung to face him in the starlit canyon between the blind buildings and the flickering corner lamps. Gerdt waited him out. Then Eric strode blindly onward, choking with rage, Gerdt at his heels, past the Great Aula, and on to Hildermann's pension house. He had no words. Everything had become too bizarre.

*

Hours after they had got to bed he lay awake staring out the window at the stars, images in his head like little silver fish darting in a deep still pool. Flash of a smile, eyes sparkling mischief, the long slope of her throat. He always wanted to stroke her throat, and slide his hand down, down to the cross of her collarbones and down and down into the valley between her incredible soft warm breasts that once in the sighing great forest...

God!

Some rich man's brood mare? a Junker from Rastenberg? a man of substance...?

"Why?" he asked Gerdt across the darkened room. "Why did she never go to school?"

Gerdt groaned awake. "It's three in the morning. I have a lecture at nine."

"You went to school. Why didn't she?"

"Well that's different." He reared his head off the pillow. "Women don't go to the Cadet College, you know."

"But school? She didn't go to school?"

"Oh God, will you go to sleep? She had tutors. One tutor after another. She got rid of each one as fast as she could, it's what Brigitte does." He turned to face the wall. "Go to sleep."

Eric had made all his friends at school, first at Winchester, then at Cambridge. Some friends came and went, but some stayed. Gordon. Jenny. He'd got a letter from Jenny about her engagement to marry a chap named Bruce she'd met in class, "*...you would get on quite famously, he rides with the Wendover Hunt...*"

Friends made your life, friends understood when nobody else did, friends sat up all night and heard your darkest secrets and kept them safe...

Brigitte had no friends.

He could not imagine such emptiness.

Except... Yes...

Those three weeks when he'd first come to Heidelberg, when nobody had even looked at him. And then Gerdt had stepped in to fill the vacuum. Gerdt snoring across the room.

*

On Saturday at the garrison stables a new member had joined the White Dragoons. When Eric and Gerdt arrived that afternoon, a slight figure in white 'uniform' stood chatting among the boys... then Brigitte turned and smiled at Eric with mischief in those eyes. The boys sported around her swooning and making fools of themselves.

"What are you doing here?" Eric drew her aside. "Are you

permitted—?"

"I'm the Colonel's daughter." Her smile deepened. "I can please myself."

She rode that day on her spirited colt whose prancing and shying disrupted the team. The master-sergeant was gruff but patient. The boys happily adjusted their pace to her. In the next two hours Eric held his position in formation and observed Britt with a warm sense of possession as her colt gave to the bit and settled down under her fixed hand, until they were all back working together as a unit.

After they returned the horses to the stable he walked with her back across the footbridge, two figures in ersatz uniforms and pith helmets, a costume fit for *Fasching*. To stay longer with her he took her in for coffee at *Zum Ritter*, a hotel whose reputation would not allow for gossip. Where coffee for two... one with cream, one without... cost as much as a week of *Butterbrot* at the Red Ox.

From that day on he could hardly wait between Saturdays. Only the mathematics kept him anchored.

*

The letter came, of course. That evening Frau Hildermann stood in the open doorway clutching the mail to her bosom. "I need a word with you boys."

They paused at her tone, Eric just pulling his books from his rucksack.

"I need more money in the next term. Just a warning."

"More money?"

"Two are more trouble than one. Twice the cleaning, twice the laundry, twice the coffee." She waved the letters in the air. "Twice the mail."

Gerdt edged closer. "How much more?"

"Twenty marks." No compromise in her tone.

"Fine, Frau Hildermann, fine." Gerdt held out his hand.

She deposited the letters on his palm and disappeared down the stairs.

Gerdt slapped the letters on Eric's place at the desk and sat down opposite and opened a book.

Eric stirred the envelopes on his blotter: his father's was slim, his mother's stuffed with at least two pages. "I may not even be here next term," he said.

Gerdt raised his eyes, head still bent to his book. "Why don't you find out?"

He turned them over, one by one, and withdrew his hand. "You said you went to Cadet College. When was that?"

"I was a kid. I was eleven going in. Graduated two years ago, it was either university or the War School."

"What is Cadet College? Like public school in England?"

Gerdt closed the book over a finger. "Ah you English. Public school, meaning boarding school? Here we say what we mean. Cadet college, military boarding school, yes."

"How does that work? Cadet College, then university, then... what?"

"I asked my father to come here because with a university certificate it's only months at the War School, not two and a half years. Then five years' service for sure and then I'm free."

Eric leaned his elbows on the desk. "So you don't have to make it a lifelong career."

Gerdt shrugged and opened his book.

"You're serious about farming."

"As serious as anyone can be."

"You're lucky. You have a plan that satisfies everyone."

"Well?"

Eric shifted the letters. "My father's plan has nothing to do with anything I want."

"Open your damn letters and find out."

Another pause between them, long and intense, suspended at the edge of something.

And then, "I love your sister, Gerdt."

"I know."

He opened his father's letter.

> *My dear Eric ~*
> *You have your train ticket, you have your orders. I was serious when I said there would be no funds. I shall cease to recognise you as my son if you continue so wilfully to disobey my specific orders.*
> *Until we see you home...*

No discussion, no alternatives.

He opened his mother's letter, aware that Gerdt watched from the corner of his eye.

> *Dearest Eric* ~ (she wrote in German)
> *Your letter brought fear to my heart. I can only join your father in begging you to come at once home. My suspicions were raised greatly by your last letter about this young woman you met. You wrote so many words about so little, only how beautiful she is. Is beauty the sum of her? Beware of beauty, my darling, and look for the soul within. That was how I met your father. At first sight he was such a handsome man, stalwart and upright, he caught my eye and my heart. So often he seems harsh, concealing a good heart. Everything he says is in concern for your secure future. His harshness is the surface of a wise man deeply worried for his son, who knows no better way to express it.*
>
> *When your father determined to bring me as his bride to England, it was against the wishes of my family, and although they forbade me nothing, nor tried to restrain us from marrying or from leaving the country, they were infuriated when I did so. I was then cut off from my family and homeland. Please, my darling son, do not allow such an outcome in your life. It seems too short a time since you first met this girl to develop such serious intentions as to oppose your father's wishes. Young men fall too easily in love, and just as easily fall out of love. It is the natural way of young men. Please, my dearest son, come home. As a family together we must make a plan...*

No, Mutti, he mused. No more plans.

But she was right. When he'd first met Brigitte her beauty overwhelmed him. Now he could look at her without melting or bursting into fire. There was so much more to her than mere beauty. But *what* was it? That loneliness, that spirit. Whenever he thought of her like this, her eyes pierced into his core and made him weak with the most enormous yearning to touch her. To protect her. To enfold her. To engulf her. To sink deep into her pink and tender flesh...

The image stirred every nerve in his body, and made him want to run out and kill something.

If this was love...

He stared across at Gerdt absorbed in that book, so unaware. Did Gerdt have any idea...?

Maybe, the baron had said.

A real man will find a way, the baron had said.

He stared at Gerdt, and knew the way. It had been there all the time, of course. The baron had known.

"*Dear father...*" He paused to stare out the window at the darkness, at the reflection of the room in the glass, at Gerdt's reflection across the desk from him, pretending to read but just twisting a pen in and out of his fingers.

He bent to his letter. "*Dear Father and Mutti: Things are really going so very well for me, I want to make a suggestion that you will find difficult to argue...*"

He crumpled it. He looked across at Gerdt twisting that pen. The idea had been in his mind for a long time. He didn't know exactly when it had started, but here it was full blown. The time had come. No more pleading, no more letters. He could scarcely breathe with it.

"Gerdt."

Gerdt stretched mightily, arms high over his head, huge yawn. "Hmmm?"

"How do I join the cavalry?"

Gerdt's head snapped about in surprise.

"Your father's regiment, of course."

"Are you crazy?"

"I love her, that's all."

Gerdt stared at him in shock. "You would join the cavalry for her?"

"I would do anything for her."

"You're crazy. You're not a soldier."

"You yourself, you're not a soldier. What's a soldier? A man in uniform. Travel the world and resign in five years. We could go together."

Gerdt smiled out the window.

Eric hunched down, trying to reconcile his father with the Prussian cavalry. "Do you think I'm crazy? My father married the niece of a Prussian general, and he wasn't crazy. How can he forbid what he did himself? I mean, by marriage he did it."

"How do you join the cavalry, you say?" Gerdt braced one boot on the edge of the desk and tilted back his chair. He had the widest grin that Eric had ever seen on him. "You have to buy your commission in the regiment. You must be voted in by your regiment. Most important, you must have a family behind you, an old established family, you need—"

"To change my name."

"To...? To *Bronsart*...?" A light flickered in Gerdt's eyes.

"Von Schellendorf."

Realisation flashed between them with the force of a cannon shot. They stared across the desk at each other, astounded by the simplicity... the enormity... the very *brazenness* of the plan.

* * *

CHAPTER 7

November to December 1912

"...I shall cease to recognise you as my son if you continue so wilfully to disobey my specific orders..."

They sat opposite each other at the desk, shuffling through the stack of blank forms. Proof of citizenship, family sponsor, parental permission, date of birth, proof of education, certificate of health.

Long lists of items for the officer-applicant's kit... Tunic (parade, service, field, drill), Gala dress complete, Pelisse with fur trim, Greatcoat, Officer's cloak, Trousers (dress, drill, field, summer, winter, riding), Boots (dress, riding, field), Cap (dress, walking-out, field), Spiked helmet with Baden shield and white horsehair plume, Sabre, Scabbard, Regimental sword knot... Three hundred and seventy-seven individual items ending with...

One sound young horse.

When the adjutant had thrust the papers across the desk, Eric had accepted them with hardly a downward glance, just stuffing the bundle into his rucksack.

Now he slumped back on the chair. "This is impossible. I have only... how much? Less than twenty pounds in my account, five hundred marks? This...? A hundred thousand at least!"

"Nearly a hundred and fifty thousand, if you count the horse and gear. A junior lieutenant draws about fifteen hundred a year. In case you didn't know."

"My God. My father sold my horse." Ridiculous thought, Spats who shied at shadows...

"Anyway, you signed the application. It's a contract."

Eric was beginning to float in vague panic. It had been so easy to walk into the adjutant's office, sign the papers obviously prepared in advance...

Gerdt shrugged. "Send the bills to your father."

He tried to laugh, but could hardly breathe. He thought of the letter from home, "... *I shall cease to recognise you as my son if you so wilfully continue to disobey my...*" He hadn't yet read it to Gerdt. Perhaps he never would.

Wilfully. Disobey. My. Specific. Orders.

"You could buy your way out," Gerdt said helpfully. "Although God knows I would hate to see you do it. I wanted us to go together, comrades-in-arms, you know?"

"How much to buy my way out?"

"Probably..." He spread his hands. "As much as to buy your way in."

"What's the alternative?"

Gerdt shrugged. "I don't know. Falsify military documents? I don't know. Prison? You still have your rail ticket, you could flee the country. We'll ask Father."

"No! He'll think I'm such a fool!"

"You could enlist as a horse-soldier in the ranks." He was grinning with his own joke. "They have short-term enlistments, eighteen months, two years, three years—"

"Oh, that would be fine. Private Eric Foster reporting for duty, sir, and by the way may I have your daughter's hand in marriage?"

"I'm sorry, Eric, I hadn't realised you were poor, this is my fault for going so fast ahead with—"

"No, no it was my idea."

He had never thought of himself as *poor*!

*

"I tried," he told Brigitte. "The adjutant said I was a good prospect. He said they're building up the army, they need good officers. So I signed the induction paper. But now I have to find a way out of it."

Saturday. They sat at their special table in the *Zum Ritter* dining room. It was the only time they could be alone.

"You can't stop now."

"I can't offer you a good life this way," he muttered. He hitched his chair an inch closer to her and lowered his voice, aware of the steward nearby. "I'll never be out of debt, it's a hundred times an officer's income, and I can't ask my father—"

"Money, money!" She scoffed in her little-girl voice. "Just pay it off one year at a time!"

"Britt..." Then he caught the mischief in her smile. "Why is everything a joke? You and Gerdt, everything's a joke."

She smiled and shrugged, as if money were irrelevant.

He looked away to the stained glass window. He would prefer to be out there riding, but it was cold today. She wanted this warm hushed place, she wanted to commune, to moon, to make little jokes of his anxiety. He didn't know half the time what she wanted. He felt a twinge of impatience with her. She took things too seriously, or not at all. She seemed to recognise no middle ground.

"There's a simple solution," she said.

"Na?"

"Marry me."

He laughed dryly.

"Marry me now. Today. We can run away."

"Oh, Britt, Britt, Britt...!" He laughed again. He wanted to hug her for being the child that she was. He wanted a future with her when she grew a little older, a little wiser, a little less *immediate*. "Britt!" he said again. "My Britt." He sighed. "We can't marry. Cadets aren't permitted to marry. You know that I can't become a cadet until I buy my kit, and I can't buy my kit without—"

"Erich!"

He stopped.

"You men. You think you men know everything. You think women are mere decorations to go along with your greater mission in life."

"Oh shut up, Brigitte. Don't go on as if you were a helpless—"

"Then don't be helpless yourself, Erich! Don't throw away our future for a few thousand marks." Her eyes darkened. The

81

child had disappeared. "There's always an answer." She glanced at the steward still waiting to take their order. She smiled now into Eric's eyes. "Darling, we'll go on with our plans. You will become an officer-candidate and buy your kit." Her smile deepened. "And then you will become an officer of the Regiment and then you will marry me. And then..." She leaned toward him, "...and then my darling, you will pay off your debt with my dowry."

He sat abruptly tall. *"What?"*

Her eyes twinkled in a delighted grin.

"But that's to buy your trousseau, to start your home."

"I have my trousseau," she said. "No, it's for my husband. But then, what if I have no husband? And believe me, I'll marry no other than you."

He thought his heart might stop. There, with a hotel steward near his elbow pretending to be deaf, and with this witch in a boy's white riding 'uniform' across the table laughing at him, the whole stupid game came into sudden focus, as if he had been holding the telescope at the wrong end.

"So! You see?" She laughed. "Everything honourable for you silly men with your ridiculous honour. You would die in honour rather than bend a single step sideways."

"My God," he said. "You're right. If the dowry's enough, everything is possible."

"Oh, it's enough."

They laughed. Eric raised a finger at the immobile steward to make his usual order for two coffees, one with cream, one black. And scarcely enough cash in his pocket to pay for it.

*

Dear Father and Mutti ~
It is difficult to write this letter in fear of
your disapproval. But here it is. I have already
told Mutti about a lovely girl of good family,
actually the sister of my best friend, Gerhardt
von Wittingen. We have become very close. I am
trying to prove to her father that I am worthy,
and when that is all done and accomplished I
intend to marry Brigitte. I hope you will both
find it in your hearts to support me in this.

> *Dear Father, surely you will understand. It is almost as if I am reliving your life, for she is the daughter of the Colonel of the Regiment (Not quite a general!) Like father like son, as they say...*

He mailed it within the hour. Haste driven by fear. He seemed to live in fear from every direction these days.

*

Within that week the letter came from London, a different sort of letter, almost a negotiation, yet still wedged in his father's fixed thinking, as if no other way existed...

> *Eric my boy:* (a hasty scrawl)
> *Your mother has expressed her concern over your latest romantic escapade. I only add this. You <u>shall</u> come home forthwith; and then we <u>may</u> communicate with the girl's family to determine if there is reasonable ground for you to marry, and we <u>must</u> work as two families cooperating, not as one young ass upon a fool's errand. Marriage is not a weekend lark, but a lifelong obligation. If you desire to emulate my unfortunate history, do so at a later stage of life when a modicum of sense and maturity actually set in. DO NOT (as I did) elope with a foreign woman above your station on pain of personal regret and endless social condemnation. I can be no clearer than this. Come home, my boy, and all will be forgiven...*

Forgiven? Was that what he could expect? To be *forgiven?*
Personal regret? Was that how his father looked upon his mother? With *regret...*? He remembered times... he'd been so young... when his father had gone out to big social events, all dressed up in his white tie and tails... without his Mutti. "Don't worry," she would tell him in their special mother/son language. "I don't speak too well. Your father must not be held down by my terrible English..."

He remembered how people used to smile at her English... Made a little joke of it... And how she would become stuck in mid-sentence and blush and look away, and how even as a small boy he would sometimes translate for her.

But he hadn't thought it was a problem. Not a real *problem*. Was that how his father saw it? *'Personal regret and endless condemnation...?*

He would not answer such an insult on his mother.

And then the final threat, *"Until we see you, this is my last communication."*

He crumpled the letter and threw it in the basket.

*

On Tuesday, December third, Eric and Gerdt were summoned to the military hospital for their medical appointment. They missed their morning lectures to suffer through a physical examination, stripped down, thumped, hammered, pummelled, listened to and looked into from every possible angle and orifice. On the way home, still feeling bruised and invaded, they stopped at the *Rathaus* to apply for his legal change of name. The forms were handed over the counter to be filled out on the spot, Gerdt his only witness to his identity. The papers then disappeared into the mysterious machine of officialdom.

Gerdt clapped him on the shoulder. "Erich Bronsart von Schellendorf! The great cosmic wheel is turning!"

All that night he lay awake staring at the ceiling, his father's image inside his head, pointing an accusatory finger and glaring in fearsome condemnation, *Deserter! Ungrateful, irresponsible, love-besotted young pup...! Now you deny your father's name?*

Did he hate his father?

He feared him. He could not hate him. At this distance he felt nothing. He didn't love him, not as a son loves a father.

But he loved his mother. One day he would send for her. Release her from that prison of judgment and censure. God, he missed those evenings in her bedroom, the lamp turned low, the window open to the fog of London, those long talks in their special secret language, as he told of his worries about friends, about school, about the future...

Schellendorf was now his future. These wonderful people. This Heidelberg.

Everything followed upon that day in a sort of dogged dream that unfolded in swift, relentless leaps. Gerdt asked the baron to sponsor Eric's... *Erich's*... application for citizenship. They filled out the form and sent it off. Then they waited a mere week before the baron's attorney, Herr Essen, of *Essen und Mundt*, sent off an enquiring letter to the ministry. Four days later, which gave Erich a hint of the baron's power, they travelled by train to the Baden State office in Karlsruhe, where Erich swore an oath of allegiance to the Prince of Baden and to Kaiser Wilhelm the Second. A shiver went down his spine.

Dual citizen. England-and-Germany. Master of the world.

*

Over the holiday he spent his waking hours with Brigitte. They went to buy little Christmas gifts for the family, using only the smallest part of his remaining bank account. Eric mailed Swiss chocolates home to England.

Every morning they took long rides in the cold, returning in time for hot dinners to melt away the chill. In the afternoons and evenings the family were "at home". Friends and well-wishers dropped by to visit over mulled wine. They sang carols, and listened beside the fire to the baron's old war stories.

On the afternoon of Christmas Eve they gathered in the gun room to decorate the tree, pulling out ornaments and garlands and tiny candle holders from storage boxes and spreading them over the floor. The baroness sat near the fire to supervise while they hung things and drank wine and argued about the arrangement and laughed and laughed. When it was done, they sat in a circle in the deepening dusk to admire their work. The baron settled beside his wife and held her hand in the light of tiny candle flames reflected from the ornaments. Britt leaned her shoulder against Eric's shoulder and stole her hand into his, and they smiled together as if nobody would notice. Then the servants brought in trays of *Butterbrot* and coffee, and they had their supper around the tree.

At midnight they went together to the *Heiliggeistkirche*.

When later they left the church Eric... *Erich*... sensed an anchor with this place. Waiting in the night with Gerdt and Britt, breathing cold air into his lungs, he felt the bond deepen, tighten. Over in the lights of the church step the baron in his ceremonial blues, the baroness in her Russian sable furs, the bishop in his white cassock and purple sash and cope, stood amid a crowd of well-wishers offering handshakes and Christmas greetings.

Then they all walked together back to the house to open little gifts in the German way on this fantasy Christmas Eve.

*

On Friday the twenty-seventh, in the middle of the winter holiday, they were measured for uniforms by the regimental tailor. On Saturday they were summoned down to the garrison where induction papers were set before them on the adjutant's desk. "A good New Year to you both," the adjutant said. "If you sign before the end of this month it means an extra year's seniority." He grinned through magnificent moustaches.

Erich silently questioned Gerdt.

Gerdt winked.

They looked to the adjutant.

"Gentlemen," said the adjutant, "your last day of freedom." He dipped a pen and held it out across the desk.

Gerdt read the paper, then signed at the bottom and passed the pen to Erich.

Erich read his own paper, *"...most gracious Majesty Wilhelm II Emperor by the Grace of God herewith conditionally commissions as an officer applicant his loyal subject <u>Erich Bronsart von Schellendorf</u> hereunder signatory..."* He noted the Imperial stamp and the stabbing scrawl of Kaiser Wilhelm II. The Emperor himself! His scalp prickled. As he signed in the designated space he thought of his mother. She would be proud. His father would explode in frustration. He... *Erich Bronsart von Schellendorf...* had just declared his own emancipation. And signed away five years of service to The Kaiser of Germany.

His father could not challenge the entire German Army.

"Now gentlemen," said the adjutant. "This is a conditional right of entry to the Kaiser's commission, contingent upon your successful completion of officers' training at the war school in Karlsruhe. The passing grade is seventy-five *per centum*. If you fail, you will join a reserve regiment as an enlisted horse soldier for a minimum of three-years. Is that understood?"

They nodded. They could not fail.

"By the first scheduled day at the school you will have

obtained full kits in accordance with lists already provided. You will transport your mounts and equipment to the war school at Karlsruhe, at which time you will be clear of all personal debts and legal encumbrances in accordance with military regulations. Understood?"

Clear of debt...?

"Now then," said the adjutant in the same severe tone, but bursting with a smile, "before you disappear into the rigours of training, let me offer a toast to your success. Na?"

They followed him out of the office into the dark corridor that led past other offices along both sides. Men in uniform were coming and going, heels loud on the boards, eyes focussed hard ahead. A group of four uniforms pressed flat to the wall to allow the adjutant passage, then clattered onward.

"This garrison," said the adjutant, marching them past the officers' dining room, "has a commanding officer, five officers of the line, one adjutant... myself... one quartermaster, and a hundred and fifty under-officers and men. Our regimental headquarters is in Schwetzingen." He reached a door at the far end of the corridor and stepped through.

They came into a lounge. On the wall directly opposite the door hung the Imperial Eagle-and-Crown flanked on the left by the Regimental colour standard and on the right by the gold-red-gold flag of Baden. The windows were draped in regimental gold-and-green. The furnishings were as luxurious as in his father's Law Society. Oak, velvet, crystal, brass and leather. On a late Saturday afternoon the place was deserted.

"Well, gentlemen, last act of freedom." The adjutant leaned one elbow on the bar and snapped his fingers at the bartender. "Future officers, Horst. Line them up."

*

Erich woke Sunday morning with a blinding headache, a dry mouth, and a vague memory of Scotch whisky followed by French cognac, washed down with German schnapps, he didn't know how many times over. He heard Gerdt already splashing in the bathroom basin. He shut his eyes against the sunlight and slumped down at the desk to write the letter that had been spinning in his head for days, perhaps for weeks. He paused, eyes closed, to think a while, but once he started, it came easily through the hangover. Perhaps too much drink erased his final fear.

> *Dear Father and Mutti:*
> *I have been accepted for a commission with the 25th Dragoon Regiment of the German Imperial Cavalry. I was also granted Citizenship as a precondition to joining the army.*
> *I spent many hard days in reaching this decision. Fearing your opinion in advance, I did not discuss it with you. I just wish to add that the King of England himself wears the uniform of the First Prussian Guard, so it is an elite profession in the best tradition. The commitment having been made, I am dedicated to going forward. I have given my written oath. One problem remains. I have entered into debt to buy my kit and commission. If you could find it possible to clear this debt for me, I would go forward without encumbrance.*
> *Father, this is what I must do.*

He read it over. There was no sign of begging or of apology. Not the best petition for financial help, which in any case he did not expect. If he had any courage at all he would have told them his plans long ago, given them a chance to... a chance to... forbid him. Yes, forbid him. That was what it came to. *Enough.* He added a few words about Christmas in Heidelberg and his wish for their good health and good regard. He signed it *"your loving son, Erich"*, blotted it and folded it.

And began to breathe again.

He had broken free.

Erich. His new German name. *Bronsart von Schellendorf.*

The splashing in the bathroom sink ended. Gerdt came out, towelling his freshly shaven face, as bright in the eye as if he had not drunk himself into a staggering daze last night. "Are you ready?" he said. "We're going up to the house for lunch and to celebrate."

"Celebrate!" He groaned and dragged himself to his feet and

went in to shave.

Today was the day. He had gathered his courage last night in the officers' mess, where for the first time in his life he'd been treated as a man. "I mean to do it," he said to Gerdt as they climbed the hill. "I'm going to ask Britt today."

"Better to speak first to Vati."

He should have thought of that. Old family, strict tradition. "Is there a protocol?"

"Not a particular speech, if that's what you mean."

He smiled within himself. He had his speech prepared.

The relaxation in the house struck him the moment they stepped through the door. He imagined that the maid smiled at him more than at Gerdt as they walked along the hall to the kitchen. The baroness stood at the kitchen window leaning on the stone sink, gazing through the scattered trees up the hillside toward the *Schloss*. She turned as the boys came in, and smiled, and sat down at the table. "My young officers."

"How did you hear?" Gerdt bent to kiss her cheek. "We told nobody."

"Word travels quickly in the Regiment. Coffee on the stove."

"Is Vati at home?"

"In the gun room, doing the books. Just go in, he'll welcome a distraction."

Gerdt shot Erich a meaningful look as he crossed to the stove for coffee.

Erich went alone along the hall to the gun room, mouth dry, heart thumping, impressions fleeting in his mind, *father behind his desk lecturing, "Girls and pals, horses-and-hounds..."*

Deep breath. *Go in...*

"Good morning, sir." He closed the door carefully.

The baron sat at his desk, several large ledgers stacked near his elbow, working on the pages of another. He looked up with a wide grin behind the magnificent moustache. "Look at you! As well hung over as a three-week carcass of venison!" He set down the pen.

"Sorry sir." He came to stand before the desk.

"So you've proven me wrong, and here you are."

"Yes sir. Here I am." He didn't know how to start. "In fact here I am, I've been accepted as an officer-candidate for the 25th

Dragoons. Your regiment, sir."

"Yes, we heard some time ago. In fact I sponsored you. And so?"

"It's just that..." It struck him then. "*You* sponsored me?"

"The adjutant sent a query. I recommended you."

Not quite the surprise he'd planned. "Thank you sir. And so, sir..." Now the words came tumbling out of control, "I come today to ask your permission to marry Brigitte von Wittingen, your daughter."

The baron braced his hands on the edge of the desk and pushed himself back in his chair. He met Erich's gaze with quiet humour.

Desperately Erich started, "You said—"

"I know what I said."

"I've answered all your objections, sir. I've met your terms—"

"Yes, you have."

"Sir... for Brigitte I have defied my father, I've turned away from my homeland, I've taken out German citizenship—"

"All this for some romantic notion of winning my little girl."

"Sir..." The challenge at last brought out his memorised speech. "There's nothing left in England for me now. I was sent here as a punishment, but instead I found my heartland in Heidelberg, I found Brigitte whom I love, and in Gerdt I found the best friend a fellow could have. By joining the Regiment I can make an honourable career, and offer Brigitte a good life, and also satisfy you and the baroness."

The baron chuckled. "In joining the regiment, young man, I understand you've put yourself deeply into debt. I would never allow my daughter to marry any foolish young stag eager to start his career deeply in debt. What's your plan for that?"

He drew himself tall and took several deep breaths. "It's true," he said carefully, "that I owe for my kit, and have not yet bought a horse. We've talked about it together—"

"You call her Britt, she tells me."

"Yes, Britt. We concluded that..." *Careful here*... "because her dowry would be more than needed to—"

The baron threw back his head in a huge belly laugh.

"I could borrow against her dowry to—"

"By God, you have the most outrageous impudence!"

There was nothing more to say. He had stated his case.

"Is there no help from your family?"

"I really don't expect it, sir."

Smiling, the baron toyed with the pen on his desk, twirled it on the blotting pad, then put it into the pen stand. "I offered Gerdt the stallion he rides on Saturdays, but he doesn't want him. We're bringing a horse from Baden-Baden for him. Do you want Oberon? The stallion?"

His brain seemed to have seized in panic. "What?"

"I offer you the horse."

His voice collapsed to a whisper. "Thank you, sir."

"Of course you must also take the gear that goes with the horse, it's of no use to me."

"What, you mean the saddle?"

"Saddle, bridle, ceremonial gear, the whole kit for that particular horse."

His mind whispered, *forty, fifty thousand marks...*

The baron leaned forward, the smile gone. "Erich, you're an intelligent young man with great determination and high moral standards. No matter the obstacle we threw in your way, you've never wavered from your purpose. But my real concern is for Brigitte. I've met no man I would rather see her marry, and I am therefore prepared to pay down your debts and accept you as my own son, equal with Gerdt in all things, to ensure that she marries well."

He could not absorb the full weight of this. It rang in his ears, *"...accept you as my own son as my own son as my own..."*

But...

Could he accept it? He did not have to accept it, with her dowry to come. "You mean," he said stupidly, "you want to pay the debt that I have built?"

"Yes, my boy, yes!" The baron's blue eyes danced with anticipation, as if to say, You must now love me, am I not the most wonderful future father-in-law...?

The money involved was almost unimaginable. Three or four years, he'd calculated, of his father's annual income. But... as the baron's second son? A comfortable life, perhaps, bound not to a father, but to a father-in-law? Could he marry Britt, tied in like this?

He drew himself tall. "Sir, you are unreasonably generous. However I find it difficult to accept your offer. I have gone contrary to your warnings, and against my own father's advice. I am prepared to accept the consequences..." His words rambled aimlessly in the fog of nervous shock, something about 'honour' and 'gentlemen' and 'duty' and 'dowry'.

The baron laughed. "Stop." He took up the ebony pen from its gold stand and tapped it on the desk, wood against wood, tap, tap, tap. "So this is the way you want to use Brigitte's dowry. Interest would be added to any loan, you understand. Are you certain?"

"It was her idea, sir, otherwise I'd never have thought—"

"Do you know how much it amounts to, her dowry?"

"No sir."

"A quarter of a million marks. It comes to her on her twenty-first birthday. Is it enough?"

Through the fog of shock he heard himself say, "Yes sir."

Again a belly laugh, and the baron tossed the pen aside. "And you wish to borrow from me using my own money as security!"

"No sir. Using Britt's money."

"God in heaven!" He shook his head with a slow grin of amazement. "How can I reject a loan application so outrageously presented and so impeccably secured?" He took up his pen and waved Erich away. "Let me finish my books now."

The others waited for him sitting around the kitchen table with coffee. He took the empty chair, his back to the window, while the maid named Katja brought coffee for him from the stove. The cup was wet: he saw the ring form on the table, he wanted to wipe it dry; but then he realised the table top was a marble slab that would not stain. Marble. Every room in the house spoke of wealth so long entrenched that it made scarcely a conscious mark upon them.

A quarter of a million marks she brought to a marriage. *Ten thousand pounds sterling.* Twenty years of an average barrister's income... He met her eyes across the table, and she smiled, and her beauty struck him like a fist on the forehead, as it had done the first day he'd met her...

Beside her the baroness smiled into her coffee.
This dream could not be real. And with such money forming a shadow between them, he would jerk awake any moment and she would be gone...
"What did he say?" Brigitte asked.
"I think he said yes."
They laughed, as if his numbness amused them.

*

"My beloved son, my Erich Bronsart von Schellendorf ~" (She wrote in German.)
Her letter arrived on New Year's Eve. He sank down at the desk to read it. A hundred-pound note fluttered from the pages. He caught it before it touched the floor...

> *I am writing to wish you a belated happy nineteenth birthday as well as joy and your heart's desire in the New Year.*
>
> *Your father has forbidden me to write to you further until you have accepted the wisdom of his authority. I enclose a small gift for your birthday, also the address of a trusted friend who will ensure that I receive what letters you send in the future. Please remember that I value your news and wait always to hear from you. Knowing that you are low in funds, I will try to send money to help, although it will not be often, having little of my own. I will ensure continued payment of your university fees.*
>
> *Your father will not write again. He lost himself when you slipped from his control. He will never admit that the fault was his. He rages only to conceal his loss, and fills the emptiness with hard work. If you subscribe to 'The London Times' you probably know he was knighted this month, now "Sir Edward", in recognition of his years of service to the Crown. Erich, do not regret your father's decision. His ways are influenced by a harsh profession and a demanding public life. You must now go forward*

> *to live up to your own capacity and happiness. Tell me more, please, about this beautiful girl and her family. That you join the cavalry is no surprise. The army has been in the Bronsart blood over many generations. Continue to make me proud of my young cavalry officer, and always conduct yourself honourably as a member of your mother's family, and as your father's son. Rather than lose his son forever, I hope he will come to your side in due time...*

He read it again and again. It had come to this, that he must write to her secretly, that he must either capitulate to his father's plan for his life, or never go back. No other road seemed open. He sat at the desk for a long time, staring at the page.

But then something new stirred inside his head. A fleck of thought. A decision.

I'll show them.
I'll make her proud.
I swear.
His first New Year's resolution.

* * *

CHAPTER 8

February 1913

"Gentlemen, good day." Lean and trim in a sky-blue tunic, with a chest of gold braid and medals, the Commandant of the War School stood immobile on the rostrum, face ruddy, grey moustaches bristling with purpose. He scanned the young officer aspirants in their new uniforms, slouched before him on wooden chairs. Under his gaze they sat a little taller.

Day One. This morning two troopers had herded them on horseback three miles from the Karlsruhe railway station to the barrack block, where a master-sergeant introduced them to their future lives. They were assigned bunks and one orderly for each cubicle, two cadets to a cubicle. Then shown the barracks layout, the shower room, the latrines, the boot racks. Handed a book of military regulations and a chart showing the rank structure of His Majesty's Imperial Cavalry. The daily schedule filled two pages of tight handwriting: reveille at 0500, roll-call at 0535, breakfast in the mess at 0545, horse drill at 0615, and on and on. The days were gone, the master-sergeant announced, when they could choose their activities. When they could freely choose anything except their Saturday afternoons.

They were allowed an hour to unpack and, according to rigid regulations, store their belongings into a small wardrobe, two drawers and the footlocker set at the end of each cadet's bunk.

They later gathered in the corridor outside the cubicles to meet and say hello. They were all the same age, all turning nineteen and twenty, with the same casual, arrogant edge that Gerdt presented to the world about him.

Then ordered into field uniform, clean, pressed, buttoned to the neck, boots polished, hands out of pockets, all of an identical stamp, and conscious of a new attitude and expectation.

They marched over to the stables where already their horses had been settled into assigned stalls. As if they were children, the master-sergeant supervised them in the order of their horse kit: saddle on the rack precisely so, with pommel one hand's breadth from the wall, stirrups drawn *up*, leathers pulled *down* through the stirrups, girths unbuckled and laid *over* the seat, bridles on two pegs, utility to the left, ceremonial to the right...

"You are responsible, my little gentlemen," announced the master-sergeant, taking a stand at the head of the stable aisle, "for the supervision of your groom in maintaining your horse, your stall and your kit. If your kit is in any way deficient! If your stall is not sweet and clean! If your mount does not shine like a bloody brass mirror! If his hooves are not cleaned and oiled! You! *not* your groom! will be held to account! You will inspect! And correct! Inspect-and-correct!"

Erich's groom gave him a crooked little smile as he demonstrated spreading the utility saddle blanket folded in four as a dust cover over the saddle. A shy, wiry fellow with the exaggerated bowed legs of a lifelong horseman, his name, he whispered, was Hans. He wore no uniform and bore no rank. As the groom for a mere cadet, he was beneath rank, beneath notice.

From the doorway the master-sergeant bellowed, "Very well, you civilian imposters, regardless of the slovenly habits you may bring with you from your illustrious past, my ugly little parasites, the horse comes first! Lesson number one! Always the horse comes first! Now form up in front of me, two lines, and be quick about it!"

Then they were marched to the lecture hall.

Now the commandant stood on the rostrum, Lieutenant-Colonel Hasso von Wetzlar, Commandant of the Karlsruhe War School.

"Gentlemen, good day. I am your commanding officer. I

have a few comments by which to welcome you. Today you become officer aspirants in the service of Kaiser Wilhelm the Second. This confers upon you many responsibilities. You will be observed at every level, you will be tested every hour, you will be stretched to the limit of your resources. Your lives will change from privilege to arduous duty. Some of you will fail to graduate. Of those who succeed, some will render great service to your country. The weeks ahead will begin an uncompromising life of honour, and you will demonstrate honour or get out." His cool gaze travelled from face to face. "As officer aspirants you will give your whole heart into your training, or quit this school. Any man in this room who does not aspire... who does not *strive*, who does not *intend*... to achieve the rank of general before he retires from service thirty years from today, he does not belong among our sacred society. Be aware that statistically only one of every eleven thousand officers in the German Imperial Army will get so far. But not from lack of striving. Never for lack of heart."

Again he paused to sweep the room with eyes of steel.

He was met by silence. They now sat at stiff attention, not a muscle twitching.

The commandant broke the stillness. "The watchword of every German officer is to lead from the front. Take hold of the reins and lead from the front. Regardless of where duty carries you, each will proudly carry to your grave the honour of your parent regiment, and regardless of your rank you will lead from the front."

They shuffled nervously and exchanged glances. This was ponderous stuff.

Erich met Gerdt's stare. *My God*, he telegraphed, rolling his eyes. *My God...*

What were they in for?

Gerdt spread a broad smile across at him. No surprises there. He'd been born to this. He held up five fingers. Just five years, his fingers said. Not a lifetime.

*

The first week was considerably less confusing than any first week at university. Each minute was run by fixed schedule. The master-sergeant's voice of thunder woke them before dawn,

"*Achtung, achtung,* fifteen minutes to roll-call, my civilian impostors, fifteen minutes, my delicate little gentlemen!" And the cubicle door would slam and a moment later they would hear him shout at the next door, and the next and the next, shouting and slamming doors along the corridor. Then scramble out to the washroom and a fast shave in a row of cold basins, lined up like horses at the water trough, then a quick shower, four or five naked bodies in each stall, all elbows and slippery soap under an ice-cold stream designed to make *men* of them... "*You will be clean, my filthy young aristocrats, and if any of your comrades detect that you have not taken your daily shower, they will toss you into it, uniform and all...*" then back to their cubicles, towelling dry on the run. Then fling into field uniform and stand to attention along the hallway for morning inspection, buttons all buttoned to the neck, boots a mirror-black, stiff as steel rods.

Phew.

By quarter to six they were at breakfast in the cadet mess, food piled high on plates served by soldier-servants, and half an hour to eat. Then clatter double-time out to the stables for two hours of mounted drill. It was the same old drill from the White Dragoons club, and Erich could focus his attention on handling the horse. Oberon was a black Hanoverian with a stubborn brain and an iron mouth, made harder by years of iron hands. Erich clenched his teeth and fixed his hands and did not fight the reins. Gradually he calmed the beast while keeping formation. He said to Gerdt that first morning as they broke off, "I never knew how hard you had to fight this animal. You have my eternal respect as a horseman."

Gerdt laughed. "Now he's your problem."

First lesson in the bare lecture room, wooden chairs, and a knee for a desk to scratch their hasty notes, History of the Baden Cavalry. "Believe me, gentlemen," said the major, "in the heat of battle your chair will be moving on four legs. You will learn to survive, stripped down to basic essentials."

At ten it was Introduction to Military Land Tactics, and Clausewitz, Clausewitz, Clausewitz, with brief mention of Schlieffen, the most modern god of battle, recently retired as Chief of the General Staff.

At eleven it was Introduction to Weapons. Other lectures

through the week introduced them to the army chain of command; to the details of the cavalry uniform and how to wear it in its many variations; to functional differences between the regiments; and to recognition of insignia and colour standards, vital essentials amid the confusion of any land battle.

The instructors all looked alike and spoke alike, lieutenant, captain, or major. It took Erich a few days to distinguish among the uncompromising faces at the lectern.

"Dragoons," intoned the captain, "must be competent on foot and in the saddle, and in battle must be prepared to dismount in support of any formation requiring reinforcement. Lancers will be at the point of every charge and never dismount. Hussars are scouts and messengers. No matter your function, officers will lead from the front. You will demonstrate an example of courage to your men whenever meeting eye to eye with the enemy..."

Erich smiled. *Eye to eye with the enemy...?* He could not imagine it.

"This is amusing, Schellendorf?" barked the captain.

He came out of a half doze and snapped to attention. "Sir."

"Ah yes, you superior English. You English regard military melodrama as your personal source of amusement, true? Boxer Rebellion, Black Hole of Calcutta, Balaclava, Khartoum, quite amusing little shambles. On the contrary, we Badeners, take it most seriously. I would advise you to do the same if you hope to survive the next sixty-three weeks. Understood?"

"Sir."

"Do not delude yourself that being at the top of the class at university confers similar status in this academy. This is a school of command, Schellendorf, with the purpose of training officers to order men to their deaths, to destroy an enemy who may be equally competent. To enter into battle armed with the highest of professional training, moderated by self-discipline, supported by unshakable integrity! Understood?"

"Sir."

"Sit down, Schellendorf. Try to use a degree of self-control to suppress your inappropriate English humour."

Fifteen pairs of eyes smiled upon him. From his days in Winchester he knew that the most dreaded of all things had just happened. He had been picked out from the group.

They were allowed an hour and a half at noon to relax over the main meal of the day, to have a smoke, a drink at the bar, even take a quick nap. In the afternoons they drilled on foot, learning the *Stechschritt*, the 'goose step', which jerked the spine and strained every muscle and quickly exhausted them. The drill sergeant gave them no mercy. "Pick up those feet you lazy fellows, knee high, leg straight... This will make men of you, you will thank me for this after we turn your soft pudding carcass into burnished steel..." *Left right left right left right...*

Or they would mount for field exercises, trot in column of two through the edge of town where people paused to watch them pass, out along the banks of the Rhine, handling weapons on horseback, learning tactical manoeuvres, reading the terrain, and being graded at every stage.

After mess at the end of the day they relaxed together in the cadet lounge for a glass of wine or brandy, stretching out tired muscles and breathing deeply. For the first week or so they exchanged stories of family and friends; but gradually there was little more to say. Then one of them would start to sing and the others would join in. Songs of marching, of farewell, of lost love, of fighting in faraway lands. Songs that Erich had never heard before.

Then back to barracks before lights-out to write letters, Gerdt to his Annette, Erich to Britt and to his Mutti at her secret address. Every evening he added a few lines to the letters, and at the end of the week dropped them in the post.

They drank. It was a necessary part of military life, Gerdt told him. They competed, roaring with laughter, as one after the other tossed back a half measure of schnapps, while the others ringed him round clapping and counting, *"Eins! Zwo! Drei! Vier!..."* When they reached *"Gsuffa!"* you were done. Erich was a weak drinker. Not fast enough to bring the schnapps to his lips or to swallow it whole. Afterward he saw the world through a waterfall of tears, and later he staggered back to barracks and fell fully dressed on his bunk, and slept in a stupor and woke in the morning with a hammering head. The fun of it was unclear.

At the end of the second week he saw his first mess bill. In a daze he wrote out his cheque for the barman to tick *Paid* in the mess ledger, and knew that this was a rich man's game. Excuse enough to stop the drinking. A man had to eat. Twenty pfennigs a day for all meals, it was cheap enough.

Even Sundays were prescribed. Church parade at eight, then confined to camp, obliged to rest for the week ahead. They rode casually, sat in the sun, wrote letters, read books. Some of them practiced fencing, although everybody agreed that fencing would never be required in modern warfare. They did not play cards: cards were forbidden on Sunday, an Evangelistic touch.

Everything was strange and new and exciting, and too demanding to pause for thought.

But at the end of the day after the lights were out and black silence fell, Erich often found hazy reflections wafting in the darkness to keep him awake. A glimpse of his mother's face, Colin's giggle at some silly joke, roaring a motorcycle on a country road, jumping Spats over a hedge in a fox hunt...

Had he been too rash? Too stubborn? Did this vacuum in his chest measure the other world where he had always fit in with no effort or thought? Could he admit to Gerdt, to Britt... to *himself*...? that today he might be in the wrong place?

*

It started in the last week of April. Every Friday before supper, as the final duty of the week, they rode on parade, each cadet in ceremonial regalia wearing the colours and insignia of his parent regiment, inspected by The Colonel Himself. Erich first became aware of the trouble only as he was rushing to dress. Boots stamped on, mirror polish, spurs screwed to heels, pull on the sky-blue tunic, button up the buttons...

Missing a button. The top left frog hung slack.

Two minutes to horse!

He tried to cover the missing button with his dress sash. It kept slipping back to its proper position. Gerdt found a pin and affixed the empty frog in place. They dashed for their horses, seconds ticking off. He was the last to mount. He swung Oberon into his regular position in the double file, still adjusting his helmet, and they started at a quick trot to the parade square. Over the past several weeks the routine had become almost automatic. Today during inspection the colonel drew up his horse before Erich and pierced him with a stony stare, casting a sideways glance to the master-sergeant before riding down the line. The master-sergeant glared at Erich and followed. After inspection the colonel rode back to headquarters, and the master-sergeant held the troop in position, squaring his horse before the line. Every cadet had learned to dread this moment.

"*Fahnenjunker* von Schellendorf!" he bellowed.

"Sir!"

"Improperly dressed! One demerit,! Troop dismissed!"

They turned over their horses to the grooms and went to supper in the mess. Later when they returned to their barrack cubicle, Erich found the missing button on his bunk.

That was the first.

Another afternoon they were on the firing range for live ammunition practice. Erich was beginning to get the feel of the pistol, to steady it and press the trigger gently and to get off eight good rounds into the target. When he reached into his ammunition pouch for the spare magazine... it was not there. He paused in his shooting. Along the row the other cadets stood braced and continued firing, *bam... bambam...*

A crunching boot behind him. "Schellendorf."

The master-sergeant.

"Sir." Sun harsh in his eyes.

"I noted only eight shots from you."

Sweat in the armpits and under the collar. Was the man counting every shot of every shooter?

"Sir!".

"What are you waiting for!" the master-sergeant bellowed.

Erich snapped out the empty magazine and began to load cartridges into it from his belt.

"Where is your spare, man?"

"Sir! Not in my pouch."

"One demerit for undress on the line. Not prepared to fire in combat, five demerits." The boots crunched away.

A chuckle from someone on his left.

Not an accident.

He fired eight more rounds without looking sideways. When he did look up, the others were already exchanging places with the next team of shooters, and he scrambled to catch them up.

Another afternoon the white horsehair plume was gone from his dress helmet. A few days later he could find his left gauntlet but not the right. And each time it happened, directly after evening mess the missing item turned up on his bunk.

And each time he was awarded another dress demerit.

And twice somebody in the troop audibly chuckled.

"Have you any idea who's doing this?" he asked Gerdt. "Or why?"

"Either van Doren or von Ruperthal."

"Or both." He sighed. "If I ever thought of finishing near the top of the class, it's lost now. Stupid buggers. Why do they do it? Ruin a fellow's chances."

"Some people amuse themselves by buggering others."

"*When* do they do it?"

"Maybe an orderly when we're in the shower. And at supper. A little bribery goes a long way."

He hadn't thought of bribery.

On Friday the sword-knot had been cut from his scabbard. Chopped off at the base. On parade the master-sergeant saw it at once. The colonel left the field after inspection without a word about it, but he could not have missed it.

"*Fahnenjunker* von Schellendorf!"

"Sir."

"Remain on parade. Troop dismissed!"

He heard the chuckle to his right. He thought it might be von Ruperthal. He held the stallion in check while the others trotted back to the stables. The master-sergeant waited.

"Schellendorf."

"Sir."

"Your sword-knot.

He glanced down. "Sir."

The master-sergeant nudged his horse closer, two stallions nose to nose. Oberon stamped and snorted restively.

"Schellendorf. Improperly dressed. Automatic demerit."

"Yes sir."

"Because the colonel did not take note, I award one demerit only for this serious deficiency. You cannot support many more demerits for improper dress, Schellendorf. You'll be at the bottom of the class for no good reason. But you understand what happened."

"Sir?"

"You've been hazed. Surely you understand?"

He took a deep breath. Finally nodded. "Yes sir."

"What you do next, Schellendorf, may well decide your future here. You understand me?"

"Yes sir. I'll take care of it."

They rode side-by-side back to the stable, and Erich walked on alone to supper wearing the sword stripped of its regimental knot. He paid attention to his food, looking neither right nor left, leaving Gerdt to observe the others at their tables. He played the game.

When he returned to barracks his beheaded sword-knot lay on the taut grey blanket of his bunk.

Impossible to repair. A hundred and fifty marks to replace...

In the morning he stayed in the cubicle while the others raced to the showers. The days were getting longer, but dawn was still half an hour away. He'd showered last night in preparation. Now he dressed without a shave, and dawdled in the darkness until the others started coming back. Then he left Gerdt on guard while he ran to shave so he would pass inspection. "Nothing yet," he said as they passed.

He lined up in the hall for inspection. After the others had dashed out to breakfast he doused the light and sat on his bunk in the darkness to wait. His ceremonials hung on the usual hangers in his wardrobe.

For several days they followed the same routine, Gerdt and Erich alternating to guard the cubicle, each missing either the morning shower or breakfast. On Friday of the next week Erich sat again in the dark near the door while Gerdt raced out to shower. Within minutes of his vigil, the door opened.

Paul von Ruperthal let himself in, and went in the dark to Erich's wardrobe, and opened it.

Erich stood up, scraping his chair.

Ruperthal whirled to face him.

"So!" Erich lit the paraffin lamp, giving a yellow glow to the tiny room.

Hands in pockets, Ruperthal leaned one casual shoulder to shut the wardrobe door. "So?"

"This requires a public apology. And the replacement of my sword-knot."

Ruperthal laughed. He pushed away from the wardrobe and walked past Erich to the door. "What can you do about it? Guard the place twenty-four hours a day?" He turned in the doorway. "I can dump you down any time I please. You'll have so many demerits, they won't have space to write your dismissal."

"Do you want to tell me why?"

"None of your business, Engländer."

"Bastard." But he spoke to his back as Ruperthal sauntered away along the hall.

Engländer.

That evening in the mess, as they lingered after supper before going into the lounge, Erich stood up to tinkle a knife against his glass. "Gentlemen," he said to fifteen pairs of eyes. "I issue a challenge. This morning I intercepted Paul von Ruperthal in my room. Unauthorised intrusion by any officer into the personal effects of a brother officer is in blatant contravention of the Officer's Code of Honour, and a professional disgrace."

The cadets around their tables had frozen into silence.

"We all know," Erich said, "of my problems at inspection."

Somebody tittered. A few heads turned toward van Doren with von Ruperthal beside him, stiff and frowning.

"And since," Erich persisted, "we can assume the obvious, I hereby challenge Ruperthal to meet me privately on the field of honour."

"Duelling is forbidden!" van Doren shouted across at Erich.

"Lucky for you!" snapped another. "I've seen Schellendorf fence."

"Shut up!" Von Hammersdorf, the class president, stood up. "This is serious."

"I'll tell you what's serious!" shouted von Ruperthal, coming to his feet. "Schellendorf is lying! That's the most serious—"

"I don't think he's lying," another interrupted quietly.

"No, I don't either," said another. "Ruperthal has been too amused by this. I don't think Schellendorf is lying!"

Silence. Ruperthal sat down. "I say Schellendorf is lying."

"I'm all for observing the rules," said Erich. He came to his feet now. "I don't agree to a duel, one of us is bound to be hurt, perhaps forced to resign. I propose a competition of some kind."

All eyes swung upon him.

"What competition?" somebody asked.

Gerdt jumped up, grinning. "On horseback. A jump-off. One man, one horse. The first knock-down is the loser."

"No!" shouted Ruperthal.

Everybody laughed. Ruperthal was not the best horseman.

Then Ruperthal shouted, "The highest clean jump wins!"

"There's no difference between—"

"...big difference—!"

"A jump-off—!"

"The master-sergeant as umpire!" shouted Hammersdorf.

They all began to chatter and shout, heads nodding, satisfied faces.

"One thing more!" shouted Erich over the noise.

Silence.

"This stays among ourselves. We enlist the master-sergeant with no explanation. Just a friendly contest between classmates. And that's the end of it. No matter who wins, that's the end of it." He stared at Ruperthal. "The loser pays for the damned sword-knot."

Ruperthal frowned, then met Erich's eye and laughed. "It won't be me!"

*

Thursday at noon a horse van arrived at the stables. Erich and Gerdt stopped to watch as a lean grey thoroughbred was led down the ramp and into the barn. They went to lunch without thinking much about it. Later during pistol practice a rumour flew through the group that Ruperthal had shipped in his father's international competitive puissance jumper.

"He can't do that!" Gerdt muttered as they left the firing range.

"Why not?"

"It's against the rules."

"What rules?"

"One man, one horse. Our own mounts. He agreed to it."

"I don't think anybody mentioned any particular horses," mused Erich.

"It was understood between gentlemen! We should lodge a complaint."

This thing clicked into place, larger than all of them. Erich stopped in mid-stride. "Gerdt, I refuse to sink that low. In the eyes of the class he has already lost, either way."

Gerdt turned to argue it, then nodded. "I see your point. Bringing in that horse, na?"

They laughed, and walked on.

On Friday after inspection parade as the others were dismissed, the master-sergeant drew Erich aside. "How do you plan to ride the jump-off, Schellendorf?"

"Just ride, sir."

"May I offer you a more tractable animal?"

"I'll go with Oberon, sir."

"Your decision." He lifted the reins, then paused. "And Schellendorf. Sew on that crooked button again, right side up, will you please."

Eye of an eagle.

*

Usually after lunch on Saturday, their only free afternoon, everyone flung off his uniform and disappeared into Karlsruhe. The small city concealed many good revelries, and most of the boys came staggering back late at night full of beer and tales, usually involving '*Les belles Biches*'. But this special Saturday they willingly postponed it for later. After midday they began to gather over at the jumping ring.

When Erich and Gerdt arrived, the fence around the field was lined with cadets and instructors and off-duty soldier-servants and grooms from the stable and soldiers from the regular regiment. Banks of bodies formed a wall of uniforms around the rails.

And just by the gate where the view was best the Regimental Colonel Himself sat relaxed on a canvas picnic chair against the fence, dressed in green Bavarian shorts and a green Bavarian hat with a pheasant feather in the hat-band. Staff officers and ladies surrounded him, taking tea in the sunshine.

The master-sergeant was already mounted in the middle of the ring. Three jumps had been set up, and grooms stood ready at each jump to pick up fallen bars.

They hurried on to the stable. Erich's groom held Oberon saddled in field tack. Ruperthal was inspecting the girth of the grey thoroughbred, cross-tied in the aisle.

"What's going on?" Erich called to him. "All these people! This was for our class only."

"I arranged a few witnesses to keep things honest."

Gerdt snorted. "Only a cheater has to 'keep things *honest*'." He gave Erich a leg up.

Erich and Ruperthal rode out together. Oberon was half a hand taller than the lanky grey and a hundredweight heavier. They drew up before the master-sergeant in mid-arena.

The master-sergeant announced the rules. This was not a race, he bellowed in his parade voice. Each competitor would go over the jumps in turn. After each run the bars would be raised a notch. A knock-down took a penalty of two points. Refusal meant disqualification. When one horse knocked down all the obstacles they would take a ten-minute rest and begin again. Points would be tallied at the end of the second series.

It started on a blast from the master-sergeant's drill whistle. As challenger, Erich would ride second. He sat at the side and watched Ruperthal take his thoroughbred over the jumps, one... two... three... light as air, solid and straight as an engine on a railway track. So simple. So clean. At the far end Ruperthal turned and was signalled to wait there.

Erich started Oberon forward. With jumps in sight the stallion fought the bit and threw up his head to escape the hand, and ran too hard at it. Erich released him one stride before the jump, but as they flew over he heard a hoof rap the bar and down it went. The second jump was higher, but now they had got together and the horse powered over it cleanly. The third jump was perhaps a hand higher than the second. Clear, and a hard landing. Compared with the grey, Oberon was a raging bull in a ballroom. Erich turned him and stopped.

Ruperthal grinned across at him. "Two faults!"

"You haven't the balls to ride your own horse."

"Go to the devil!" He didn't wait for the signal, but spurred his horse forward to take his second run from the wrong direction. If he missed, the bar would jam and could drop the horse. One... two... three... Clean and light and solid.

Oberon was jigging now and wanted to race. Erich lowered his hands to bend him, then rode a long trot around the perimeter to start his second run from the proper end.

It went on a surprising long time. As they warmed up, Oberon settled and gathered his power and flew over leaving more air under him than necessary. The grey conserved his power and slipped over like thistle-down without wasting energy. But each time the bars were raised, Erich was aware that Oberon felt heavier, rose more sluggishly, dropped his hocks, knocked one bar down, then another, dropped his forehand... until at his final run he knocked down the first bar. And the second. And the last.

The master-sergeant blew his drill whistle. "Cool your horses!"

The onlookers around the fences began to shift about and talk and laugh. Gerdt came running into the ring and walked beside his stirrup as Erich cooled the horse. "Listen," he said, "you lost twelve points. I don't know how you'll make it up. I hate to see that bastard win. We must disqualify that horse."

"All I lose is the price of a new sword-knot. My reward..." He leaned over the pommel closer to Gerdt. "My reward is peace. The boys will see to it now." He rode Oberon off to settle him further on a loose rein. Ruperthal had dismounted near the fence and was in friendly conversation with the colonel and the ladies.

A few minutes later six shrill blasts of the whistle pierced the air again. The master-sergeant rode to the middle of the ring. "Gentlemen! Exchange horses!"

Erich rode over to face the master-sergeant. "Sergeant? What is this?"

The master-sergeant almost allowed a smile. "Ah. Did I not say, Schellendorf? I'm levelling this playing field."

Ruperthal galloped the grey across the field. "What the devil are you doing?"

"Switch horses, gentlemen."

"You can't do this!"

"This is not a test of horses, Fahnenjunker von Ruperthal, but of personal honour. Obey the instructions, or forfeit the contest."

Grooms ran out to hold bridles while they exchanged horses and adjusted stirrups.

The master-sergeant signalled Erich to ride first. No whistle yet. Erich took time to move the grey in a wide circle, to feel him out, find his rhythm. It was like riding a cloud. Long easy trot, rocking-chair canter, alert ears and giving mouth. For these few moments Ruperthal sat to one side mounted on Oberon, leaning back, sawing on the reins to keep him checked while the stallion danced in place. The whistle blew. Erich turned into the line of jumps and nudged the grey. Instant response, soft collected gallop, slight shift of gait, the horse did it on his own. This horse knew more about jumping than the rider, gather and rise, such power and control, Erich let him do it alone. Three clean jumps and done. The easiest ride he'd ever had.

Moments later Oberon launched forward at a runaway gallop, shook his hard head to unbalance Ruperthal and in the next stride shied violently at the first jump, flinging his rider over the bar into a heap on the ground. To finish the performance the horse trotted back to the barn under an empty saddle. The bar had not been disturbed from its pegs.

"Refusal!" cracked the master-sergeant. "Disqualified!" He blew a blast on his whistle. "Thank you, gentlemen."

The audience applauded.

*

Ten minutes to lights-out. He was weary and drained and ready to drop. The cadets had gathered in the bar to buy him drinks and Ruperthal had been nowhere in sight and Erich had drunk too much and his head was full of air...

A letter lay on his bunk. *From England.* He leaped upon it, ripped it open. A hundred pound note dropped out on the blanket.

At least now he could order a new sword-knot, should Ruperthal fail to pay up...

He read the letter, his scalp prickling over every scrap of news, "*...a woman may be appointed to the bench... One of the suffragettes has been arrested for exhorting others to blow up the house of Lloyd George... We are nervous over the Balkan events, difficult to untangle the complexities, so I worry about you so close to such political instability... Your father will not discuss it, I think he too is worried...*"

He had a gift for her. Sometime he would write down the silly story and send her his cut-off sword-knot in a pretty little box. She would know what it meant.

His father would not.

And so to hell with him. Life was too good to mourn the end of his former self.

* * *

CHAPTER 9

April - October 1913

Third Sunday in April. Their first visitor's day. They wore their ceremonials after Church Parade, Erich with his new sword-knot. Debt paid by the vanquished.

"Visitor's day," Gerdt joked. "Like prison."

"More like Public School," Erich retorted. "Uniforms and slicked-down hair!"

Gerdt snorted and brushed a hand over the top of his short military clip. His moustache had developed enough to wax the ends into fashionably curled cavalry points. Erich was thinking of a moustache. Everybody was growing one, it was a cavalry tradition, clipped hair and full moustache.

When they came into the mess most of the other cadets were already gathered and stood in a crowd around one table, laughing and preening in their ceremonial finery. Some of the civilian visitors wandered the mess admiring the decor and historic mementos. Some chatted with instructors. The mess orderlies were serving trays of punch and coffee.

Gerdt pulled at Erich's sleeve. "There they are!"

Over by a window in the far corner the baron stood chatting with Colonel von Wetzlar, the baron in full ceremonial regalia taken from that headless manikin. The baroness sat at a table having coffee and cake with the wife of the commandant.

"I don't see Britt," Erich said.

Through clusters of people they crossed in step together to meet Gerdt's parents.

"Damn!" he muttered to Gerdt. "She wrote she was coming." At the ladies' table they crashed to a halt and cracked their heels in unison, then saluted. Startled, they looked at each other and burst out laughing.

"Ah, my boys." The baroness half rose from her chair, and sank back. "How splendid! And oh my! I don't recognise you! The haircuts! Marching like soldiers! I never believed such wild fellows could become so smart in so short a time!"

The two colonels left their corner and strolled to the table, the spare, sunburnt commandant and the bull-chested, ruddy-faced baron. Gerdt and Erich smoothed their smiles and snapped to attention. The commandant dropped a gaze to Erich's sword. "I note you corrected the deficiency, Schellendorf."

"Yes sir."

"Erich," said the baron loudly, "the colonel told me about your jump-off."

"Yes, sir."

"Handled well, I heard!" His booming voice caused a sudden pause throughout the mess. "An officer and a gentleman. Proud of you. Proud of you both!"

Across the room the tight knot of cadets loosened as they turned to stare at the baron. In their midst, like a mythical pixie hiding among blue flowers, Brigitte cocked her head at Erich and waved a little white-gloved hand.

*

They walked away from the others. She wore black buttoned boots and a spring coat of almost the same light blue as his tunic. It made him feel absurdly like one of a pair of Dresden dolls. The feather of her hat brushed his ear. She leaned on his arm, keeping step.

"You're so beautiful," he said.

She laughed. "You look different in uniform! So handsome. They cut off your wavy hair, I hate that." She bent to watch the ground as they walked. "I've been good, you'll be proud of me. I've been trying to be a lady, enough to spew out brown bile."

He laughed at the vision. "I love you as you are, prickles and vinegar."

She smiled. "But I do it for the regimental ladies. To be sure you and Gerdt are voted in. The wife is part of the package, you know."

He was beginning to know. For the next five years the regiment would be the limit of their world.

They walked from the mess around the edge of the square toward the stables. "It's forbidden," he explained, "to cut across. One must be on parade to put a foot on the square."

She laughed. "You'll be a real soldier soon. Just like Papi."

The air was cool, the sunlight warm. From the stable a horse neighed and another answered. Nickering went like echoes around the barn.

"Mother plans it for next May," said Brigitte. "An outdoor ceremony."

"A whole year."

"Papi wants to send us on the Grand Tour. London, Paris, Rome, even Saint Petersburg. He says we should avoid Istanbul and Athens for all the Balkan political strife. A six-month trip, he says. He can arrange for your leave from the regiment. What do you think?"

"Let me just finish here, let me first get into the regiment."

She leaned into him, her head tilted back, inviting a kiss.

They stopped beside the flag pole, in the open for anyone to see. She was reckless, while he was learning prudence. He gave her a light peck on the lips. He walked on, and she put her arm through his and leaned on him as they walked.

"So it's all planned," he said. It seemed that this new life would be mapped out for him. Just his old life turning in a new direction. Do this, go there, obey, obey, obey the regulations, obey *her* father.

"Of course," she said, "it's so long a time from now to next May. I don't know if I want to wait a whole year to... ah.... you know..."

He looked into her face.

She blushed, mischief in her eyes, and looked away.

"We have no choice," he said, deliberately misunderstanding her. "All this yet to do."

At the stables some of the cadets were walking their families in and out and along the aisle to admire the gleaming horses and the gear set out on special display. At the far end Erich saw Oberon's black nose over the loose box, nostrils twitching. He led the way down. The other cadets turned to gaze after Britt, and Erich smiled wickedly at them.

She rubbed Oberon's ear with one white glove. The stallion bent his head to it.

"I'm going to be good at this," Erich said. "I love this military stuff. It suits me."

*

Before the family set off for Heidelberg they sat in the mess again to discuss plans for the wedding and The Grand Tour. Erich said little, but watched Britt's eyes, how bright and happy she seemed when they spoke of the wedding. But about the Grand Tour she became restless, and twisted her gloves, and studied her hands, and did not look up.

The baroness turned to Erich. "You must give us a list of your friends and family. Of course, your family will stay as our guests in Baden. I will love meeting your Mutti. The baron organises hunting parties, I hope your father enjoys shooting. If not, there are many activities..."

Britt rolled her eyes at Erich across the table and gave a shrug of the shoulders as her mother continued planning for the perfect wedding. Erich hardly listened. At this moment he sank his soul into the eyes of this little witch and surrendered to an exquisite sense of... capture.

He walked with them out to their gleaming new automobile, a Benz landau, creamy yellow paint-work with a black leather top and side curtains to keep out the wind. It could travel forever at forty kilometres per hour, the baron said, as long as the road was smooth. He sat in the front beside the driver. Erich helped bundle Britt and the baroness in the back seat under wool blankets, though the day was mild. Forty kilometres an hour would make a strong wind. An orderly cranked the engine and it roared to life with blasts of blue smoke, then settled into a steady rough rumble. Erich stepped back. The monster rolled forward. They all waved through the side-curtains as it trundled away down the hill, sputtering out a cloud of white exhaust.

*

Darling Britt ~
Today was wonderful. How happy I was to see you, surrounded by all those jealous cadets! Two weeks until you come again!
I sensed that The Grand Tour may not be what you desire as a wedding trip. If I am right, express my gratitude to your father, and write to tell me what you want. We can plan it together, and I will make it my small wedding gift to you...

Dearest Mutti: (he wrote in German)
I hope that you and Father and Colin are well. Give them my regards. I write well ahead of time to invite you to two events which will become landmarks in my new life. The first is my graduation at the War School in October. I will advise you of the exact date and place as soon as they are promulgated. The second will be our wedding in May next year.
I can't believe that Father intends never to speak with me again. I would be grateful if all of you could attend both events so that our side of the family will be represented. If only one event is possible, let it be the wedding. You will love Britt, as you will love her family. Please, Mutti, try to inspire Father's sense of justice and family ties. But if he will not yield, please say you will come yourself, and I will certainly make the travel arrangements for both you and Colin. It's still months away. It gives you time to plan...

Dear Father: (he wrote in English)
At some future time soon we will be sending you the formal invitation to our wedding next May. I should be most happy, as would the family of my dear Brigitte, if you were to find it possible...

Dear Colin: (he wrote in English)
  Well old chum, the fat is in the fire and big brother is planning to marry. I haven't heard from you in all this time. Do answer and tell me how school is going and all your news...

Trying to spur Colin into responding, he went on for two pages about Britt and about his military training. He'd had only one letter from Colin since coming to Germany. It was as if his brother no longer existed.

*

From that time onward the family drove from Heidelberg every second weekend, staying in the Kaiserhof Hotel and spending Saturday afternoon and Sunday at the School. So that they could go riding, the wife of the commandant offered Britt her own horse. "Can you see me riding side-saddle!" whispered Britt to Erich. But she accepted the horse rather than not ride; and with Gerdt as chaperone they set out at a sedate walk, followed at a distance by a gaggle of posturing cadets who had suddenly discovered the joys of extra-curricular Saturday riding.

On their next visit Britt brought her boy's riding things and her own saddle. Then there were the usual challenges and dashes and laughter, though the horse of the commandant's wife was a mild and contented creature that did not rise well to competition.

"Let me ride Oberon," she begged Erich.

"Not for a moment. Not even in the jumping ring to show off. I want my bride with no broken bones on our honeymoon."

She didn't argue. They rode on for a while without speaking.

"What is it?" he asked her.

She glanced over her shoulder. Gerdt and two other cadets dawdled twenty metres behind, puffing at cigarettes and blowing smoke in the air, the perfect chaperones.

She nudged her horse closer. "Do *you* want to go to Russia?"

"You don't? But where do you want to go? Paris, maybe? London? We could..." He paused, realizing that he did not expect his family to come for the ceremony. "We could go to London to meet my family. If they don't come for the wedding, that is."

"Do you think they'll come? Do you think they'll like me?"

Deep inside he knew that his father would not like a wild and rebellious Brigitte von Wittingen. "Mutti will love you."

They rode.

After a while she said, "I was thinking of something quite different."

He glanced back. The boys rode on a loose rein back there, admiring the scenery.

"We could take a walking tour."

"A walking tour?"

"Back-packs." The words flooded out of her in a sudden torrent. "You know. In the Alps. Maybe Switzerland. There are hundreds of leagues of hiking trails in the mountains, everybody does it, there are chalets along the way where the hikers stay overnight, hardly any cost at all, we can carry spare clothes and buy provisions as we go and it's very *very* cheap, it would cost nothing at all, don't you think it would be fun? With no worry about what to wear and how to hold my teacup and all such nonsense."

The picture grew in his head...

"Erich?"

"I think it's an amazing idea!"

She laughed and booted the horse of the commandant's wife into a reluctant canter.

Later that evening after supper they sat together in front of the hotel's massive fireplace and stared into the flames and dreamed their getaway, still months ahead.

*

Training intensified through the summer, with strategic exercises at the map table, problems proposed, exposed, expounded, and every word evaluated, balanced, and marked into the record. Reports to write at the end of each day. Written examinations each week, deeper and deeper, more and more detailed, harsher and harsher evaluation, every wayward comma corrected. And now each Friday, regardless of weather, twelve-hour field manoeuvres with the Commandant, no doubt striking black marks into their files.

At the height of summer it was like living in an oven. The Cauldron, they called Karlsruhe, nestled between hills of vineyards and a river running through and the summer breeze wafting up from the south. They trained, no quarter yielded to heat and humidity, hour after hour, day after day, until every horse almost nodded in unison, and every instruction manual committed to memory. For their final manoeuvres several army detachments set up a tent city on the surrounding fields to form opposing armies. The cadets drilled units of men on the parade square to practise their command skills.

The heat broke in September and turned chill in October. The climax to training came with a week of war manoeuvres. Erich commanded a squad of dragoons brought in from Berlin. Gerdt had hussars from Hannover, and they faced each other on opposite sides of the massive conflict. Book studies collapsed. The manoeuvres lasted six frantic, exhilarating days under real combat conditions, with little sleep, and very little time to think beyond their next action.

No more manuals to memorise. Erich felt like a little boy allowed outdoors to play.

*

October graduation. The Chief of the General Staff, General von Moltke himself, had come out from Berlin to take the inspection. Friends and families lined the edges of the parade ground for the march-past, bundled warmly against blustering autumn breezes. The day sparkled in chill white sunshine. The horses danced through the formations. The brass band played stiffly in the cold.

Erich held Oberon at attention in line with the class. He saw Britt on the reviewing dais, on the arm of the baron... *Colonel of the Regiment, ret'd...* in his light blue ceremonials glittering with gold braid, among a crowd of other glittering uniforms. Strong impulse to wave to Britt: then discipline caught him and he snapped his eyes front and turned again to steel.

He'd been assigned the right flank, the marker position of the troop, the place of honour. He'd come first in everything. It was a visceral shock to him. He'd been the *Engländer*, the cadet under closest observation, the cadet with all those dress demerits, the cadet who must marry into privilege just to get his regiment...

First in everything.

The irony was overwhelming. As the inspecting party rode majestically onto the parade square he composed a letter in his mind, *Dear Father, I came first. Are you satisfied...?*

He would never write it.

Von Moltke sagged in the saddle. Under a crisp uniform the mass of his body seemed to settle downward with the pull of gravity. As he rode closer on the inspection, the lines of his face seemed carved in soft butter. A tired old man in uniform.

The command rang out. The cadets snapped through the six-count for the dismount, all in one swift, unified move. Erich gathered the reins near the bit and stood at attention at Oberon's head. The stallion blew steam in his face and nuzzled his shoulder, pushing him almost off balance. *Tsss!* he told him. The horse nibbled his epaulet and settled. From the edge of the square the grooms ran forward to take hold of the horses, backed them out, and waited in a second line behind the troop.

The moment of truth.

"Cadets, prepare to swear the oath!"

God God God... He'd done it. This crazy thing...

"...swear by God this holy oath," he joined his voice in unison with the others, right arm in stiff salute, "that I will render to Wilhelm the Second, Kaiser of the Greater German Empire, Supreme Commander of the Armed Forces, unconditional obedience, and that I am prepared as a brave soldier to risk my life at any time for this oath..."

The band broke into a crisp *"Deutschland über Alles"*.

His new national anthem. Over there on the flagpole, instead of the red-white-blue crosses of the Union Jack, his new black-white-red tricolour fluttered on a stiff breeze...

"And here is our top cadet." Von Moltke stood before him a pace away. He was taller than Erich. On horse he had seemed quite short...

"Congratulations, Lieutenant von Schellendorf. You show great promise. I knew your great-uncle, a fine soldier and a gentleman. You have much to live up to."

"Thank you, sir."

The general held out a scroll.

Erich accepted it. He cracked his heels and saluted.

The general smiled behind his grey moustache and touched a finger to his helmet. He stepped sideways to Hammersdorf, next in line, second in the class. The adjutant followed, carrying scrolls.

The day was organized down to the last centimetre, to the last second, to the last man. When it was over, when the last prizes had been awarded and the last toasts quaffed and the last Important Personage and other guests had dispersed, Erich and Gerdt found themselves in a sudden vacuum of quietude. Much earlier Gerdt's family had left in the Benz for home, the Baroness exhausted by events.

In barracks they gathered their small possessions. Orderlies had already packed their clothes and uniforms and moved their trunks and boxes out to the hall ready for transport. Tomorrow they would travel on the morning train to Schwetzingen.

Night was falling. One more sleep on this tight board of a bunk. They left their little cubicle and walked along the hall and stepped in through the doors along the way and shook hands with any other new officers who hadn't yet departed. He hoped to find von Ruperthal to compare their awards of achievement and to shake his hand at last, the competition over. But the cubicle was empty and Ruperthal's luggage gone.

He wandered with Gerdt to the edge of the parade square. They stopped to contemplate the sky as an early moon climbed over the trees. He breathed in the cold night air, and listened to an owl hooting somewhere. From beyond the square a horse whickered in the barn. The gentle call echoed from horse to horse along the rows of stalls.

He would remember all his life this night when the earth stood still.

* * *

CHAPTER 10

October to Christmas 1913

He wanted to jump out the window and run, so slowly did the train trundle along, swaying and clanking and groaning, and every ten or fifteen minutes stopping at the next little station. He'd waited three long weeks for this journey. He wanted it to fly. Now it was slowing for yet another station. Gerdt read his newspaper, oblivious.

"I wish we could just get there." Erich stared out the window at the trees sliding by. "Do you know how long since I saw Britt?"

"Haven't counted the hours."

"What about you and Annette? Don't you miss her?"

"She stopped writing weeks ago. Months ago."

"Ah. You didn't say."

"Aaagh." He grimaced out the window. "The girls, they come and go. You know?" Then he added, "She doesn't like soldiers. Especially German soldiers." He shook the paper and bent to read. His ears were bright red.

Erich smiled. Gerdt had just admitted that a girl had dropped him.

Another stop, another station. People climbed on and spread out to find seats. A whistle blew and doors slammed, and the train jerked forward at a crawl. A great weariness blunted his impatience. He couldn't wait to see her, yet he needed to sleep for a week. Three long weeks with so much happening, so little sleep...

Last night once again, long after midnight, three drunken officers each carrying a bottle had invaded his room in great hilarity. *"Raus Pupser!* Out of that bed!" Slight stiff bow, click of the heels, in mock formality they introduced themselves by rank and by name, "Your Ordinariness, I present myself, I am Lieutenant von Bräunlingen, my friends call me The Boxer because, you know, I box!" And then Erich in his bedclothes performed the required snapping to attention, bowing, clicking his naked heels, taking a swig from the proffered bottle. "Name the date of the Battle of the Three Sabres!" and several other picayune details of regimental history, a swallow for each. Three officers, three bottles, three swallows, and away they went, singing and crashing along the corridor to search out Gerdt's room.

And days filled with drill, on foot and on horse, drill drill drill, under the uncompromising eye of another master-sergeant, trying to teach by example how to command men, *This is how it's done, you fools.* Trying to instil Tradition. Beating them with regimental history. Perhaps just keeping them out of trouble until assigned their new units.

Drill drill drill. Leading a horse patrol every morning the new officer must determine the objective, ride out in column of two, rest and water the horses, flirt with the local girls, and return in time for the noon break. In the afternoon, two hours of foot drill learning how to command formations of men. Then one hour at the firing range, rifles and pistols. Every other day in field formations, sabres and lances on horse, charging a target, hand-to-hand combat, and finally field manoeuvres against an imaginary enemy, reading terrain, maintaining control, ending with a charge at full gallop. Evaluated each day, no different from the War School.

Evenings in the mess. The butt of every joke. The object of every drinking game. *"Captain Schwann invites you to take a glass with him."* Stand to attention, face the captain across the room, bow, crack the heels, raise the glass, *"Thank you sir, to your good health..."* and swallow it down, *Eins! Zwo! Drei!...* And again and again, from most senior to most junior officer in the mess. Another drink and another drink, until he could no longer see straight enough to raise the glass... when someone would finally bundle him off to bed...

Three weeks like that, day after day.

They were testing him, of course. Burnishing they called it. Either into steel or into a puddle of alcohol. The military had a reason for everything and a man must rise to master it, no matter how bizarre the challenge.

That mess dinner three weeks ago, that had been an amazing event. Full colours unfurled, the regimental band played the officers into the dining room, every regimental officer present, sixty-three officers including those from the Heidelberg garrison, plus the baron... *The Colonel...* They wore ceremonial blues and swords and medals. Until then Erich hadn't realised the exalted position the baron held in the life of the regiment. Even the commandant had bowed to the baron before taking his seat at the long table. Endless food, endless drink, served by a battery of orderlies. By unwritten army law, Erich was obliged to eat and drink everything put before him during endless speeches about the history and glory of the regiment. As a climax the baron stood to introduce Gerdt first. *"You all know my son, a good solid athletic boy, excellent scores at Heidelberg..."* followed by toasts. Then Erich... *"I look upon this young man as my second son..."*

The mess dinner had ended with the vote. Each officer stepped forward to add his name to the formal petition, or to leave it off. Sixty-three out of sixty-three had signed their names.

The rest was waiting. The Kaiser had never gone against a regimental vote.

Three weeks later they were entered into the regimental roll call.

And finally granted a weekend leave.

He still had these moments of astonishment. Two years ago he'd been an average middle-class English student destined to become a lawyer, and desperately failing out of Cambridge to avoid it.

Now this. Travelling on a slow train to Heidelberg in the walking-out uniform of an officer of the Cavalry of His Imperial Majesty, Kaiser Wilhelm II.

Travelling to meet his betrothed.

Daylight was fading when Britt met them at the Station in the November wind. She stood on the platform, a slight figure, fur collar pulled up around her ears, one little glove clutching her coat closed, stamping from foot to foot. She rushed to Erich as they came down the step. He had to catch her to steady her, and she leaned into him under the eyes of all those people getting off the train.

"Kiss me."

He kissed her quickly. Gerdt stood grinning to one side. "Let's go. It's cold here."

They walked up the hill carrying their rucksacks. Britt leaned into Erich at every step.

"How's Mutti?" Gerdt asked her.

"Oh she's a little better."

"Better?"

"She had an episode this week, she's all right now." Then she ran ahead a few steps and turned to face them, skipping backward. "Wait and see what they're building on the house!"

Child phase, Erich thought. Her quick-shifting mood struck sparks in his heart.

"You both look so handsome! I want a uniform for myself! Can you get one for me?"

They laughed, and she came back into the crook of his arm.

At the house they were met in the front hall by three servant girls taking coats and caps and rucksacks, and Hanisch marched them into the dining room where the baron waited for them. "Hello, hello..." They stopped at the table and clicked their heels and bowed to the baron, and slipped into their chairs, as if they had not been gone from this place into another world for nine long months. The baron was already carving the ham.

Britt had taken the empty chair beside Erich. "Mutti's still unwell," she murmured. "She's been taking meals in her room."

The baron passed a plate to Britt and boomed to Gerdt, "Have you seen action yet?"

Erich and Gerdt silently questioned each other across the table.

Gerdt shrugged. "No, Father, not until we—"

"You'll have your chance, I'll see that you have your chance.

The minute they give me my new command."

They turned to the food, puzzled.

"I'll never forget back in 'seventy..." boomed the baron, setting off on another memory of the same old battle.

After dinner Britt drew Erich up the stairs along to the bedroom at the end of the hallway. A soft light shone through the open door. She knocked at the door frame. "Mutti?"

"Come in, darling."

The baroness had been reading in bed. Now she set aside her book, and gave them a weary smile. She was braced upon a bank of pillows and covered with piles of quilts, and she wore a quilted bed-jacket drawn up about her throat. "Hello my darling Erich, I'm glad you're home." She coughed, and covered her mouth with a thin fist.

A fire blazed in the fireplace. The room was unbearably hot.

"How are my boys?" she asked. "Where is Gerdt?" And coughed again.

"He'll come in a minute."

They pulled chairs close to the bedside. Erich kissed the fingers of her cold hand, and held it as if he might warm it. Britt led the conversation, asking Erich about the regiment, and between his answers she gave him bits of news about Heidelberg. Whenever the baroness spoke it caused a dry, weak cough that forced her back to silence. Erich had never seen anyone so ill, had never seen tuberculosis at this extreme degree. Instinctively he felt how close this lovely woman was to dying. He tried to talk cheerfully, told funny stories about the mess and the drinking games, but was almost overwhelmed by a deep ache of sadness. He could not meet her eyes for fear of weeping.

A few minutes later Gerdt came bounding in. At sight of his mother half buried in the piled bedding, his liveliness faded. He pulled a chair over and joined the conversation in subdued tones. After a short while the baroness said that she was ready to sleep. As they eased themselves out of her room, Erich wondered if she would wake again in the morning.

Downstairs, alone in the gun room, Erich and Britt stood facing each other for long moments, his forehead bent to meet her forehead, eyes locked, breath mingling, warming the chill he'd got from that cold hand. At last he accused her, "You didn't write to me how ill she is."

"She's always been ill. Always recovered." Her voice was soft, composed. "But we're prepared now, she more than anyone. She told me this morning not to let her boys be sad."

"Oh... God..." Now the tears came. He felt a fool before her, weeping like a child.

She hugged him and swayed with him as if they were dancing, until he found his balance again.

*

Saturday was warmer. In the morning they gathered in the baroness' bedroom, the servants rustling in and out with food and coffee and cakes, while the family sat about with trays on their knees.

After breakfast the baroness rested. The baron called the boys to him, and they went down to the west end of the house where workmen were building an extension. "This is what she wants," said the baron.

The solarium was half-finished. A cold breeze wafted through open stone buttresses and across the flagstone floor. Two welders worked in a storm of sparks, building a lattice of steel frames that would secure a wall of glass from floor to roof. "You see how bright this will be?" the baron said. "How warm when the sun shines through? And over here..." He pointed to a pipe rising out of the flagstone floor. "That will be a fountain." He swept a hand to encompass the space the size of a tennis court. "We are yet to decide on the fireplace, or perhaps a furnace for better efficiency, and stone benches, and gardens for planting millions of flowers." He nodded reflectively. "Yes, she loves flowers."

Erich and Gerdt exchanged quick glances.

Millions of flowers, Erich mused, in a glass mausoleum.

*

Britt said she wanted him close to her, not on horseback. She wanted to walk together, away from the house, away from the prying eyes of servants, away from Gerdt who acted as if they were all just chums together. She didn't want to talk. They walked arm in arm down to the market square, leaning on each other, not talking.

In the market they drifted from stand to stand, touching this and that, no thought of buying anything, not quite uncomfortable in a chill breeze. Soon he would take her over to the hotel to warm up over coffee.

"Oh!" She stopped at a table of toys. "Oh look! So cunning!" She picked up one after the other, setting each carefully down and picking up the next, "Oh look, it's a pull-toy, it's a little dog, oh Erich, oh look!" Wooden toys painted in reds and greens and blues with moving parts and wheels that turned. "Oh," she cried, "I want to buy them all."

"You want to play with those?"

"For my children!"

"When did you have children?"

She turned on him, laughing. "*Our* children! We have to have children. Yes?"

It struck him hard. He hadn't thought of it. He gazed at her blankly, aware that he was blank.

She punched his arm. "But of course we'll have children."

"Yes, of course..."

She paused another moment, looking into his face; then turned back to the toys. "Oh look at these tin soldiers. I always wanted tin soldiers, I always had to play with Gerdt's." From a box packed with tiny figurines she picked up one after another and set them carefully back again. "I always wanted to grow up to be a soldier. Papi would love me more, don't you think? Look how proud he is of you and Gerdt." She sighed. "Women aren't allowed to do anything."

They walked in the cold along the Hauptstrasse and turned wordlessly into the Hotel zum Ritter. They were reaching that point, he mused, where they didn't have to talk to know which way to go. The rest was discovery. So much to discover. Her notion of children...

God. Children....!

They were still children themselves. He didn't want to be an adult just yet, he wanted to play this game of soldier and parade in his uniform for the admiration of the girls. He wanted to marry this exquisite witch. He wanted to possess her beautiful body. The image turned his ears to fire...

He surrendered his coat and cap to a steward. The maitre d' helped Britt with her fur, and they sat at their regular table by the stained glass window while the steward went to fetch coffee, one with cream and one without.

The weeks passed this way. Five days drilling on horse and afoot, waiting to be assigned a unit of men somewhere in one of the regimental garrisons scattered through the State of Baden, they couldn't predict where.

Two days at home with the family in Heidelberg, deep in plans for the wedding in May.

He loved his weekends with her. He loved his weeks on duty.

*

They allowed him to go on leave at last, and then he would come back to his first posting. He still didn't know where that would be. He took that week to travel alone to London.

As the train pulled into Victoria Station he realised how he missed the city with its endless amusements and fish-and-chips and the high cost of everything and his friends and most especially he missed his mother and Colin and even his father, if the truth could be admitted. He swung down to the platform amid a press of travellers, his bundles buffeted by bodies rushing for the exit. Outside, a row of double-decker horse buses blocked the street, forcing other traffic either to detour or to stop entirely. He pushed through the crowd and swung into the Sloane Street bus. Near the rear door with his army rucksack on one shoulder and his bundles on the floor between his feet, he searched his pockets for the fare. Smallest change was a mark. When the conductor came Erich offered the coin, and the conductor said, "It's foreign dosh, Guv," and Erich said, "It's worth a shilling," and the conductor said in his broadest cockney, "Needs only tuppence, Guv," And Erich pressed the coin into his hand, "It's all I've got, Guv," and turned away.

London.

He'd written to them, *"I'd like to come home at Christmas,"* He'd sent off the letter almost a month ago, when the baroness urged him to make peace with his father. Without the baroness he would have been too proud, too stubborn. He saw it now.

The baroness. The peacemaker. The gentle mover of worlds.

There had been no answer from England. Not even from his mother. At the last moment, when he must either set out or cancel the trip, the baroness had drawn him quietly aside. *"You must go, Erich. It would shatter them to miss your wedding, even if they don't admit it today. Family is more important than anything else."*

He dropped off the bus at Pont Street and walked over. The slight breeze cut through his old civilian coat and made him wish for his cavalry greatcoat that not only blocked the cold but would impress his Mutti greatly.

Winter had stripped the leaves and flowers out of the park, leaving skeleton trees and green turf and mounds of brown flower beds. He cut through the park along the walkway over to the Mews. He looked for someone he knew but saw nobody, not even a carriage. He paused on the pavement before the row of three-storey town houses. Old buildings, old money. Diplomats lived here, he mused, staring up at tall windows behind iron grilles. He opened the wrought-iron gate to his father's door and stepped up three granite steps. He grasped the door-pull and paused like that, holding his breath. Then he jerked it downward and let it go and stepped back a pace.

After a few moments the door opened. In his morning coat Joseph peered down at him before breaking into a wide grin. "Master Eric!" He stepped back to open the door wide. "Ah sir, they've been praying for this. Oh dear, I ought not to have said it." He reached forward. "Let me divest you of your things, sir."

Inside they stood awkwardly for another moment, Joseph holding Erich's parcels and rucksack in his hands and spreading out one burdened arm to take his coat.

"How have you been, Joseph?"

"Excellent health, Master Eric, but oh my goodness you've changed, you look quite the mature young gentleman if you'll pardon my saying so sir."

"Are they at home?"

"Sorry sir, of course, upstairs in the drawing room. Shall I announce you?"

"What do you suggest?"

The strain in the air was palpable. "I'll just set these aside, sir, and announce you." He placed the parcels on the bench and hung Erich's coat on the coat rack. "Oh, I do hope this is a lovely Christmas."

Nothing in the anteroom had changed, yet everything seemed dreamlike as he followed Joseph up the graceful curve of the staircase. Chandelier overhead... Ah! The candles had been replaced by electrical light-bulbs, too bright and brittle. So harsh a light did not define the delicate wall mouldings.

As they approached the drawing room, Erich straightened his spine and tugged at his jacket and took a deep breath. He heard Joseph say to the room, "Madam... Sir... Master Eric is home."

Silence.

He didn't wait for a reaction. He stepped around Joseph's imposing form, taller than he by half a head.

Over by the fireplace his mother rose slowly to her feet, lace tatting limp in one hand, her eyes wide and anxious, looking first to Erich and then to her husband.

His father had been reading the newspaper. He did not move except to rotate his head like a gun on a battleship, and aim his sights at the door.

"Hello Father. Hello Mutti. I've come for Christmas."

"Well I'll be bloody jiggered."

*

They sat at dinner mouthing platitudes about the English weather and their plans for Christmas and the situation between Turkey and Russia, between Serbia and Austria, and the possibility of another Balkan war.

The English struck Erich's ear like a foreign language. From time to time he said some little thing in German to his mother across the table, then caught his father's frown and jumped back to English; but it was a strain. From his wallet he brought out his small print of a photo of Britt on horseback and handed it over for her to see, and his father frowned thunderously and said in his quiet don't-argue-with-me tone, "No pictures at table please."

"Sorry. Where's Colin?" he asked about the empty place-setting.

"On his way, I suppose." He mopped at gravy with a crust of bread, never looking up. "Supper at seven, that's the rule."

End of subject.

His Mutti half whispered, "And my boy is now soldier."

"Ja," he responded automatically in German, "waiting for my first appointment. I should have it by the New Year. And

then we're to marry in May, I told you about..." He caught his father's glare and stopped.

"English only in this house."

Bewildered he glanced at his mother, then took courage. "But Mutti is German, sir, and this house is her home—"

"This house is English. I suggest you not forget it."

They bent in silence to the food.

After supper they returned to the drawing room for port. His father studiously poured two glasses and held one up to catch the light from the new electrical lamp on the reading table. "A good label." He handed it to Erich and sank into the chesterfield.

Erich stood awkwardly, glass in hand. His father had never before taken a drink with him.

"Now," said his father, "you may tell me about the army." He set aside his glass untouched.

"Well to begin, I'm astonished at how much I love the life, and how very well suited to it I—"

"Mindless way of living, stand at attention, salute, march, follow orders, kill people. Utterly mindless."

"Well there's quite a lot to it, tactics, strategy, handling men, handling weapons—"

"And now you need money."

"Well I, um—"

"You've gone quite into debt for this hare-brained scheme."

"Yes, um—"

"How much in debt?"

"Oh, I'm not precisely..." His mind ticked over the figures and transposed German marks into British tender... "About eight hundred guineas, I suppose."

"You *suppose?* You don't know down to the last farthing?"

"It's not that important, sir."

"Not important." He sighed. "Eight hundred guineas, not important. I cannot fathom your logic." He waited, perhaps for an answer.

Erich said nothing.

"Well I've an offer to make you. I've been thinking of this quite a lot and this seems to resolve the entire problem on both sides. I shall fix this for all of us." Immediately he raised a hand like a traffic cop. "Now hear me out, I've looked into it. I shan't buy you *in*, but I can certainly buy you *out*, no matter how much it takes. This will take care of everything. I can buy you *out*, I've made enquiries, and then you'll bring your little girl home and be married here, we'll invite her family over, put them up at the Savoy, I'll pay the whole tab never fear, and when all is done, I'll bring you into Hennessey's office and we'll train you up from there." He gazed up at Erich standing before him. "A bit of a compromise, but our best solution."

Erich had been holding his breath. Now it came explosively out of him. He couldn't find any words. He'd thought this had been settled months ago.

"You'll admit you're in financial trouble," his father pressed.

"No sir, not really."

"Not in trouble! Where would you find eight hundred guineas? Certainly not in the pay of a junior officer."

"No sir." He could not smother his smile. "I've already paid it out."

"Paid it out!" He darted a hard look at his wife, who sat frozen listening to this. "Emilia, have you been sending—"

"No sir!" Erich shouted. "She has not!"

For the second time in his life he'd raised his voice to his father.

A shocked silence folded down over them.

"My Brigitte," Erich broke the pause, "has offered her dowry as security for—"

"You took money from a *woman*?"

"In fact there was no need, her father already had me in his sights, as it happened, he paid out my commission, I didn't touch the—"

"I've heard enough. I'm appalled. Utterly appalled. You accepted money to marry this girl! Joined the German army for money!" He took up his glass and in two gulps swallowed the port like water and slammed down the empty glass. "Don't you realise Austria is drumming up to war? Do you not see where that puts you, wearing the Kaiser's uniform? Backing up the Hapsburg war monger?"

Weakly he said, "It's only in the Balkans, sir."

"Great God! Did I beget this? Do I deserve it? *Two* bloody fools for sons?"

The evening stretched too long. After almost two years apart they felt they must keep talking, yet there was nothing more to say. They waited for Colin, but he did not appear. "He knew you were coming home," his father kept grumbling. "I hardly know what's happening to young people these days, defy their parents, no respect for tradition, no thought of family. Colin now, there's a case in point, he *knew* you were coming..."

Finally toward ten his father stirred out of his chair. "I have a court case in the morning. Will you come to observe? Perhaps it might stir up a modicum of interest...?" Without waiting for an answer he turned away as if too weary to go on. "Excuse me, I've a brief to read."

The door closed after him.

And silence remained.

His mother's face reflected her pain. She took up the port decanter and poured a glass. For a moment she studied the dark translucent red. Without looking up, she drank it slowly down.

In the past two years she had gained weight and now stood tall in a black gown, square and somehow regal in her sturdiness. She radiated that same tough inner resilience as the baroness. Erich had never noticed that before.

"Come inside," she said.

He set down his glass and followed her around the hall to her bedroom. Here was her domain, her personal haven from the world. Here nothing had changed in two years except for a new electrical lamp by her bedside and new curtains at the window.

She sat in the chaise near the window, the electrical light shining half her face into hard shadow. "You have defeated him," she said in German. "I never thought it possible."

Erich sat on the bed and let the silence descend. Silence between them had never been a strain. He'd thought he would have a lot to tell her, yet nothing came now. She knew his mind from his letters, sent in secret as if hiding from the enemy.

An enemy defeated.

"I have," she said, "several times communicated with the baroness."

"Really? You know them?"

"Yes my darling, we have planned your future together."

"*What?*"

"Oh, I've been with you all along. You should know we're all connected in some way, by family or by tradition. It's so different from the society your father knows, you can't expect an Engländer to understand."

"Then you'll come to our wedding."

"No darling, we will not be there. The baroness understands. She's a brilliant woman. If your Brigitte is half so wonderful, you marry a treasure."

"But forget father, come yourself, bring Colin—"

"Do you love this girl? Truthfully? Or is she your way to escape your father? Don't answer me without careful thought."

Erich took in several long deep breaths. This was not a new question in his own mind, but he had buried it beneath the rush of events. The answer was either too simple or too complex. He could consider in pieces the elements of this new life with Britt, her family, the cavalry, his friendship with Gerdt... or he could fit together all the parts of the jigsaw puzzle into the final, the amazing grand picture...

"I love everything about her and the army and the life we'll have together."

"I think you do. From your letters I think you do."

"Then please, you must come to the wedding."

"I can't go against your father."

"Oh let him go to the devil—"

"Darling." *Warning tone.*

He stopped.

"Never make the mistake to believe I don't love your father. I live my life for him in his world, as you go to live with these people, your new family, in theirs. Can you understand?"

He shook his head. "I don't understand. Such a stubborn monster—"

"No! This is the man I married. If you love Brigitte, you will understand. If you cannot understand, you know nothing of genuine, enduring love."

He thought of Britt's pixie eyes and her little-girl mischief and her rare bursts of wisdom and the glorious adventure of her soul. He thought back in little spikes, back to the day he'd first met her, back to their rides in the forest, to his powerful desire for her and the subtle battle day by day to suppress his drive to touch her, kiss her, enfold her, to bury himself into her flesh...

He blushed.

Watching his face, his mother laughed. "You've become something of a devil."

He felt the blush inflame his ears and raise the hair on the back of his neck.

"My handsome, placid, wise, very young, elder son has become a cavalier." She pointed to her bedside table. "I have something special for you. Get me the small box in the drawer. I planned to present it on Christmas day, but I wish you instead to spend Christmas with your German family. Na?"

"Wait a minute." He ran out to his own bedroom. Nothing here had changed, even to the same blue silk spread on the bed and the two fox tails pinned on the wall. He didn't pause for sentiment: this was his baby room, it had nothing to say to him now. He opened his rucksack where Joseph had set it on the chair, and found the little gift he'd brought for her, and carried it back to her room. Along the hall he paused by the open door to look through to his father in his study reading from a stack of papers. He couldn't remember the last time he'd seen his father laugh.

Enough. He would not live that way.

He'd brought her his sword-knot. He'd written about it when it happened, the challenge, and the ride-off. Now he gave the cut knot to her in a small walnut box he'd bought in the Heidelberg market. "Baden Dragoons," he said proudly. "Happy Christmas, Mutti."

"Ah." She fondled it and turned it every way in her hands. "Your father will not understand. I shall keep it forever. This is your true heritage."

"I know. I feel it."

"And this for you." She handed him a small velvet ring box. "This too is your heritage."

The ring was of warmly glowing gold, the stone was wine red, held by claws on four corners in a square setting. Heavy in his palm. Solid. He slipped it on his finger, and it fit as if made for him.

"That," she said softly, "is hand-beaten gold. The ruby is our family gemstone. In a financial sense it is very valuable. As a keepsake it is priceless. It was handed down from generation to generation since the Thirty Years War. I have never worn it. I didn't earn my way to wear it. You have earned it. I give it to you now, and when the time comes you will pass it on to your eldest child. And more than I was ever able, you will honour the family maxim."

"Which is?"

"Look inside."

He held the ring to the light. A tiny inscription, *"Dienst ~ Mut ~ Treue"*

Duty. Courage. Fidelity.

The moment pressed down hard upon him. *Duty ~ Courage ~ Fidelity.*

"On the left hand, Erich. To show that you're engaged. When you marry you'll wear it on the right hand in the German tradition."

He put it back on his finger. "Mutti, I swear I'll make you proud—"

"Now, my son, go home to Germany and give your life to that high purpose."

* * *

CHAPTER 11

May 1914

Erich floated in a daze through the day. When he'd fumbled with his buttons, Gerdt helped him to dress, first in his walking-out uniform for the trip to Baden, and later in his ceremonials for the afternoon's main event. In a state of mild shock he met Britt at the altar under a bower of flowers and vines. Amethyst eyes drew him forward. A veil of patterned lace covered her flaxen hair, the white satin gown clung to her delicate form, high in the neck, studded with pearls, and sweeping a regal train over the grass. Her eyes held Erich's eyes in a smiling promise, *Soon.* The guests spread out on the open lawns in the magical May sunshine. He scarcely heard the bishop's words. Scarcely knew when he responded as they'd rehearsed it. He slipped the ring on her finger, and, foreheads meeting in the moment, she put his ring on him. A quick, awkward kiss, and then it was done.

The six-man cavalry band played the official march of the Twenty-Fifth Dragoons. As Erich turned with Britt away from the bower, twelve fellow officers in regimental ceremonials crashed to attention to form a guard of honour on either side of the path. Gerdt snapped out commands. Twelve sabres flashed an arch of steel blades glinting in the sun.

He glanced down at Britt. She gave a little laugh and drew on his arm to move him forward. Applause burst from the guests gathered over the lawn, parting now to open a path from the bower to the manor. He gripped the hilt of his sabre to steady it, and moved with her under the arch, his brain detached to a little distance as though observing from other eyes, yet at the same time aware of the weight of gold on his right ring finger, her hand light on his arm, and of his heart hammering inside his chest and pulsing in his throat.

They'd first been married this morning in the Baden *Rathaus*. A few words, a five-minute signing of the record, a mere legality that didn't count. Afterward Britt was whisked away from him to prepare for her wedding. And now this ceremony, too, was done...

They were married.

The past week had been an enormous social brawl. Erich had spent much of the time hiding in Gerdt's rooms, or out together riding in the forest. No convention allowed the bridegroom to participate in his own wedding arrangements. "You're not even supposed to be here," Gerdt told him. "The groom only arrives in time for the rehearsal."

Erich saw Britt at dinner, but they had hardly a moment to talk. She was involved in mysterious preparations of her own, guided and guarded by her mother and a flock of spirited bridesmaids.

Every room in the manor was filled with guests and their servants; maids and footmen, and chambermaids brought in from the villages to help with the endless cleaning. The stables and yards overflowed with horses. Cars and carriages were parked over the lawns and along the roadway. Guests with steamer trunks arrived from every part of Germany and Prussia and Austria to stay the week. Wedding guests filled all the rooms of all the inns in Baden-Baden and all the surrounding villages.

At the manor they held outdoor tea parties, and tennis and lawn-bowling matches. Children raced wild in the woods and by the pond, over in the stables, and up and down the manor stairs, their sharp little voices echoing in the tower and along every hallway. Each dawn the male guests met beyond the stables for the daily hunt. Villagers spread out in the forest to beat the bush, wild animals flying out of every copse, shots blasting like a battleground, the carcasses collected and laid out in rows, rabbits, pheasants, grouse and pigeons, a few boar, a few deer.

Erich went shooting with them on the first morning. After that he could not face the slaughter. "Slaughter!" laughed Gerdt. "Where else do we get enough meat to feed so many guests?"

Each morning servants decorated the great hall with fresh flowers. Ancestral trappings of war had been brought out to decorate every wall, swords and halberds and daggers and rifles and cavalry spears and baldrics, each bearing the family coat-of-arms, each with a history of some old campaign. The best silverware and china were laid out on tables. Platters were filled hourly with fresh fruits and breads and cheeses and cold meats for guests to help themselves in passing. Roving stewards served beer and wine and spirits, until some of the guests sank into an intoxicated fog, scarcely aware of what went on around them. Full meals were served to order at any hour. The games room had become a gambling hall, with card tables and dicing tables and a roulette wheel where the play never stopped. That was the most popular room of all.

The day before the wedding, the regiment invaded the estate. They arrived in a military convoy by wagon and on horse in column of two. The troopers erected a small tent city on the high ground under the trees to take up housekeeping for the weekend. It was, the colonel announced, an excellent field exercise.

Erich wandered unrecognised among strangers, pausing here and there to watch. He was almost glad that his family had not come. Their Edwardian sensibilities would be scandalised by such an orgy of opulence and waste.

"No, you don't understand," said Gerdt. "Nothing is wasted, and cost is of no concern. The Wittingen tradition requires us to demonstrate a suitable generosity to our guests."

Now Erich was married into the Wittingen tradition.

*

A full orchestra accompanied the dinner in the ballroom. Strings, brass, drums and a harp. A conductor in black cutaway played muted classics while the vast company dined on pheasant or venison or river trout and six kinds of exotic vegetables from Spain. One course followed upon the next. Erich and Britt sat at last side by side, flanked by her parents. His head was reeling from too much food, too much drink, too many people. His stomach felt tense. The gold-crusted collar of his ceremonial tunic choked him. Dessert, and wine, and the toasts drifted above his floating head, followed by liqueurs and coffee, and the orchestra played, almost drowned by a chorus of voices and the clinking of silver on china.

"*We must dance.*" Britt's voice in his ear.

Numb, smiling, he rose from his chair and unbuckled his scabbard. Several hundred guests applauded. The orchestra fell abruptly silent. Britt rose, and waited for him. "*Take me out on the floor,*" she mouthed the words in a suddenly silent room.

He offered his arm, and she set her little glove on his sleeve and smiled into his eyes as he led her out to the floor. In the vast silence he could hear his own heart pounding. They paused, quite alone on the open floor. She turned to face him and lifted her chin like a ballet dancer. She took up her train in her right hand and touched her left fingertips to his gold epaulet. On that signal the orchestra swept into a Strauss waltz. Alone on the floor they began the dance.

It went on for hours. He wondered how these people, stuffed with food and staggering with drink, could continue on and on. Now, done in, he sat beside Gerdt and sipped wine, scanning the crowd in vain for a flash of white satin. Her parents, too, had disappeared.

"I've lost Britt," he said.

Gerdt chuckled. "She's in the library with Mutti. No doubt getting her bridal instructions."

Erich pushed his way through the crowd into a rear corridor to avoid people, and slipped the long way around to the library. He closed the library door behind him and leaned against it. The room was hushed and dark except for a weak glow in the giant fireplace. The noise of the festivities echoed from a distance.

"Erich?"

Britt peeked at him over the high back of a wing chair before the fire.

He went across to join her.

The baroness sat half hidden in another chair. The firelight intensified the shadows of her deep-set eyes and deepened the lines on her face as she smiled. "Come kiss your mother-in-law before I go to bed. We'll talk about the Grand Tour Tomorrow. Tonight the master suite has been prepared for my newly-weds."

He bent to kiss her cheek.

With surprising intensity her hands gripped his arms, then released him. "My dear son," she murmured. "You've made me very happy today."

He pulled over a third chair. Britt leaned back in a crumple of white satin and lace. They stared reflectively into the dying fire. At last he put together the words he'd been hoarding for the past crazy week. "Frau Freiherr von—"

"I am Mother now," she interrupted. "Mutti, if you prefer."

He took a deep breath. "Frau Mutti..."

They released a chorus of laughter.

"Mutti," he began again, "I hope I am not impudent, but..." He swept Britt into it with a sideways glance. "Neither Britt nor I have any desire to go on the Grand Tour."

"No?" She turned to Britt.

Britt stared at him with widened eyes. Then little white teeth flashed in a smile.

"With your good wishes," Erich said more bravely, "we want to take a private trip. My wedding gift to my wife..."

Wife!

"What trip?" The baroness rose higher in her chair.

"Just... a walking tour. If we have your approval, we catch the overnight train to Zurich at eleven. We should hurry."

Her eyes wavered in doubt.

"We cannot go," Erich added, "without your approval."

She seemed to gather herself inward. "Then go. With my love and good wishes. And take extraordinary care of my little girl. Of your wife."

They all paused one more instant. Then Erich leaped impulsively to her and kissed her again on the cheek. "God bless you, Baroness." Then, red-faced, he added, "Mutti."

Again, teetering almost at the edge of hysteria, they laughed.

"One moment."

They turned, poised to fly.

"Erich." Her voice had a hard edge to it. "I regret the rupture with your family. Perhaps the fault was ours, for opening our home to you, but it was not your fault for joining us."

"Thank you—"

"At risk of insult, my darling Erich, your father is a fool."

*

In Gerdt's bedroom Erich tore off his ceremonials. Acting as his valet, Gerdt tucked away all the bits and pieces of braid and sash and lanyard and white kid gloves into bureau drawers. Erich pulled on his rough pants, thick socks, cotton shirt, wool sweater, hiking boots, heavy loden jacket.

"I packed extra money in your rucksack," said Gerdt. "should you run into problems. Your *Soldbuch* is in the money belt, the first compartment, along with your army orders." He grinned. "In case you're arrested or something."

Erich snugged the belt about his waist and pulled the sweater down to cover it. On the bureau he found his wool gloves and the train tickets and stuffed them into his jacket pocket. After a week of languishing in the background of his own wedding, his blood was raging for freedom.

Gerdt leaned against the tall bedpost as if it were a street lamp. His eyes thoughtful, he stood gazing across at Erich.

Erich, too, stopped. A wonderful calm settled between them.

"Now truly," said Gerdt, "my brother."

"We are brothers."

Another silence. A stillness between two minds. Then Gerdt thrust away from the bedpost. "I must go and whip up Britt."

"She has her maid."

"Ja, ja, but we need forty minutes to get to the train station, and women are women." Again he paused, his eyes meeting Erich's eyes. Gerdt held out his hand and they shook warmly, strongly, briefly; and then, embarrassed, continued onward, the pact complete.

*

When Erich and Britt stepped off the train the next morning, he had no idea where in the mountains they were. Earlier at the Swiss frontier they'd spoken to a customs officer, who suggested this was the place to begin their trek. The land fell away from the tracks down to a village clinging to the shadowed side of the mountain a few hundred metres below. The early sun hung silver over snow peaks.

A few other passengers who had also got off walked away to their own purposes. The train, a mere three carriages behind the engine, chugged away toward Zurich, leaving Erich and Britt finally alone in a vast quietude.

He felt strangely fresh after the slow ride from Baden-Baden, after stop-and-starting at many stations through the night, lurching ever higher into the mountains. "I thought," he said to her, "we'd hike to the Bodensee and then cross by ferry back to Germany."

She swept her gaze over the magnificent scenery, grassy meadows down long sweeping slopes strewn with boulders, stands of dark evergreens, steep walls of rock and crag and, far below, the twisting thread of a stream. "How far," she asked, "to the Bodensee?"

"I don't know. I didn't bring a map."

Her eyes darted to his face. "You're crazy!"

They stood staring at each other. Then both began to laugh.

The sun rose clear of the mountaintop as they shrugged on their rucksacks and gave their tickets to the agent and walked off the platform. They adjusted the loads on their backs. At the road they paused again, looking left and right. "We go east," he said, pointing left.

They set off with the morning sun in their eyes.

*

Around noon the road took them into a small village where they turned into the marketplace for food. "I haven't eaten since the banquet," she said, "and I didn't eat very much even then."

"Are you tired?"

"Not a bit." But her voice was too sprightly and her back too stiff. In the past half hour he'd noticed how her steps had slowed and her heels occasionally scuffed the road.

In the market the village women wore ankle-length dirndls, voluminous embroidered blouses and bonnets. In her rough boys' clothes Britt walked among them, obviously not a boy. The villagers gave her sidelong frowning glances. With Erich at her heels she moved slowly past tables of vegetables and cheeses, wood carvings and leather goods, painted cuckoo clocks and wooden toys. She fingered the toys, and gave Erich a lingering gaze. He smiled, and turned away to buy a leather bag to carry food. Last autumn's apples, a loaf of heavy black bread, a wedge of hard grey cheese. He wrapped the foods in proffered waxed paper and stuffed them into the bag.

Four other hikers strode into the market from the opposite direction, stout walking sticks in hand and laden with rucksacks. One of them hallooed Britt and Erich, and they came together to shake hands all around. "Where are you heading?" and, "How is the road?" and, "How far have you come today?"

Erich said, "My wife and I are on the way to the Bodensee." He felt his ears prickle red. *Wife*... "Which is the road?"

"That way," said one of the boys, waving a hand eastward. "You take the first fork left." He spoke in a heavy Austrian accent. "The right fork leads over toward Zurich."

Another said, "If you need a map, just pick one up at the next hostel, it's only half a day along."

They shook hands all around again. *"Tschüss!"*

"Wiederseh'n!"

At the edge of the village they stopped under a bridge and set down their rucksacks. Erich refilled the water canteens from the icy stream. They sat on its bank in the grass to rest. Erich took the food out of the leather bag, and with his pocket-knife he cut a wedge of bread, then cut the wedge in half and offered it to her. "We could rest here for the night at the chalet over there." He tilted his head toward a steep-roofed inn across the stream.

"It's only midday."

"And you're not tired."

"Not a bit." She plucked bread out of his hand and wrestled it with her teeth.

The stream bubbled and rippled under the stone bridge. From a branch above a kingfisher streaked blue and white into an eddy, a tiny *plunk*, gone! A few moments later it flashed out downstream and flew up with a fish in its bill.

"It might be a good idea to stop here," Erich ventured.

"I see no reason to stop here."

"We were just married, Britt!"

She hugged her knees. "Oh... I don't know—"

"Why not?"

"It just seems... in the middle of the day...? And this is such a small village, everyone would notice. Those... farm wives."

She'd teased him for months, and now... reluctant? He'd expected her to be feeling hot and urgent. He wasn't certain now what he was supposed to do. "Well... tonight we'll find a larger

village and a larger inn."
She blushed.
They ate, and rested awhile, and then walked on.

*

Endless sky, endless wilderness, distant snow peaks, sweeping valleys that smelled of ice and green growing things, and air so clear he could almost count the feathers of an eagle soaring half a mile above the valley. The space and isolation overwhelmed him. The wind sighed, the eagle keened a long cry, and the rest was silence. They did not talk very much. Nothing seemed important in these vast spaces. They walked forever, a little bowed by their rucksacks. Along the way he cut a walking stick for her because she stumbled. Later he cut one for himself. Along the way they met other hikers, stopped a moment to chat, and then walked on. The only sounds were the crunch of boots and their breathing, deep and regular. The high altitude began to tell on him. His legs felt heavy, he who had just come out of hard military training. How much keener she must feel it. But not a word from her. She matched him hour by hour, stride for stride.

By nightfall they were nowhere.

"I thought," said Britt, "the hostels were half a day apart."

They stopped in the middle of the path and stared at each other.

They had walked the whole day.

They had not seen a human being for hours, or a village for the past few miles. He looked forward and back. The path lay low in the valley along the side of undulating slopes. Here and there under the trees other footpaths branched downward toward the inevitable stream at the bottom. But no villages. No hostels.

"We have to stop," he said.

"Here?"

"It's coming night. We might take a wrong path in the dark. I don't want us falling down a cliff." He shrugged the rucksack from his aching shoulders and felt suddenly light as he set it on the ground. Twenty kilos lifted from his back. Hers was twelve, he'd weighed them both on the kitchen spring scales yesterday.

"I refuse to sleep here."

He laughed.

"Erich I'm serious! I will not sleep here." She dropped her

rucksack to the ground and arched backwards, hands on hips. "I want my bath, I want my supper!"

"Well..." He turned in a slow circle. "I don't believe we'll find a hostel tonight, my darling. In the meantime, it seems this paradise belongs to us alone."

For a moment she stood still, only her eyes turning. Then she let out her breath and laughed. "Father would throw a fit! Are there bears, do you think?"

He laughed.

In the fading light they found a level space under a spreading fir tree. He snapped many small branches from the tree and showed her how to interlock them on the ground. "This is the most comfortable mattress in the world," he said. "They taught us this at the War School."

He was weary as he worked. She would be weary too. Too weary perhaps... He was nervous now. This moment had dwelt in his mind on and off for weeks. He had no idea... no real idea... Just a crazy image from years of adolescent wet dreams and wild imaginings...

He released the cords of the rucksacks, unrolling the half-tents and shaking them out, and laid them side by side over the boughs. He snapped them together. "When it rains," he told her, "this makes a tent for two. You see the over-flap? It's perfectly waterproof." Babbling to calm his nerves...

"Where did you find these?"

"Part of our field kit. One is mine, the other's Gerdt's."

"Ah."

"So," he teased her, "you might say that Gerdt is with us tonight."

"Oh God." She laughed a nervous laugh.

He pulled the blankets out of the rucksacks and folded each lengthwise and laid them side by side on the ground sheet. "You see? Then we fold the rest of the half-tent over the blanket and it keeps in the heat even if it freezes. though it won't get that cold of course." His heart was pattering. Thumping. *Thudding.*

"Where's my pillow?"

He laughed.

She crumpled down to sit on one side of the makeshift bed. "I'll sleep anyway. I've never..." she met his eyes, "...been so tired." Then, without removing her boots, she got into her blanket and pulled the groundsheet over herself and turned on her side away from him, and settled. It was almost too dark now to see if she had closed her eyes.

He jerked off his boots and got inside the folded blanket. Drew the groundsheet over himself.

Settled.

Tried to settle...

Turned to face her. She didn't move. He couldn't hear her breathing. Didn't dare to touch her, to disturb her. Waited, hardly breathing.

"Erich?" Her voice was muffled. She turned toward him in a great upheaval of boughs and blanket. She settled again, facing him. Her breath was warm on his face. "You're right, this is most comfortable."

He held his breath.

"Erich?" She touched his chest.

"Mmm?" His heart under her fingertips would explode...

"I was teasing you."

"Do you think...?"

And now that it was allowed, now that it was *expected*, they hardly knew what to do with each other. Fumbling in the dark, nerves turned to action, buttons and cloth, layers of *stuff*, coats and sweaters and boots and more buttons, and the awkwardness of breeches, fumbling, hurrying, and underwear ripped away and tossed aside. Naked together they burrowed into the blankets, warm now from the struggle, the night air cold on his back and her damp heat down the belly into his loins, his hands worked down her body and her hands helped to guide him to the place where she parted for him and he thrust deep into her and she groaned and then she screamed and bit him and it all came together in hot stabbing spasms of red energy...

And...

Gone.

Withered to nothing in warm wet radiating exhaustion.

"My God!" he said.

"My God," she echoed softly. "That was awful."

*

Within the week they put it all together, a map to find the trails, the distance between hostels, the casual fellowship of passing hikers, meeting with others in the hostels to share bread and a kettle of soup and a dormitory with double bunks lined up in quasi-military precision, lights out at eleven. As the lamps were doused to sudden darkness they would hear "good-night" in half a dozen languages before there fell a gradual silence.

They found no privacy in the hostels, so by day at the first impulse they would slip off the path to find secluded places in the warming spring sun, until they knew the map of every perfect hill and vale of the other's body, and how to waken and how to please each other.

On the thirteenth day near noon, a narrow strip of water glinted into view through the trees below the north-facing slope. They strode strongly now, hardened by the miles of tramping, browned by the sun, breathing easily in the high altitude. From time to time their eyes would meet in deep smiles and wordless astonishment.

The paths here were crowded with hikers as if approaching civilization. A last fork led them up a long rise to a lookout point where other hikers stood in gawking groups, and they joined them at the guardrail to stare across a spectacular panorama. The strip of water had broadened to a lake as far as the eye could see, the opposite shore a grey smudge of ragged mountains. Cerulean water reflected a clear cerulean sky. A distant steamship inched toward this shore among many small pleasure boats cluttering the water.

"The Bodensee," she said. "We found it."

"So by evening we should be back in Germany."

"Are we in a race?" She let her rucksack slide to the ground and leaned against him. "Do you think we could... perhaps... hike back to Eisendorf? And go home from there?"

He laughed. "Why not?" And unabashed in front of those other hikers he pulled her to him and kissed her roundly.

*

In mid-morning they got off the train at the Karlstor Station and lugged their rucksacks up one last hill to the house. Britt was bounding with energy. Erich had begun to worry. At home he would get a tongue-lashing from his father for dodging the Grand Tour and wasting an expensive investment. He expected nothing less from the baron.

At the oak tree out of habit they stopped to look out upon the town and the river. Britt was even more beautiful today than yesterday. Her face was suntanned darker than her pale hair, and had a rosy glow from marching those many miles. Her eyes flashed energy. "Come on!" She pulled at his sleeve. "I can't wait to see them!"

At the house they were greeted as returning heroes. The baron himself came booming in great humour to meet them at the front door, and dragged them to the new solarium where the baroness waited, surrounded by an indoor garden of flowers and flagstones and green rolling lawns. "How are my darlings?" She did not try to rise.

Britt bent to kiss the pallid forehead, her suntan like earth against snow. "Mutti, you were right, it was such an adventure! I'm so happy! I love him, oh Mutti, I do love him, you said I would!"

The baroness patted Britt's arm and smiled up at Erich. "My children. Now go up and change from these dusty clothes." Her smile widened. "Don't be too long, I want to hear it all." She laughed. "Almost all."

Katja led the way upstairs to a bedroom with a low ceiling and a fireplace against the long wall and a window of many panes under sloping eaves. The bed was the size of a hay wagon with high carved corner posts and cushions piled halfway to the ceiling and quilts thick enough to hide in.

On a bedside table a letter caught his eye. *London postmark.*

"Oh look!" Britt cried at an inside doorway. "They put in a bathroom while we were away!"

A small room opened to the side, with an iron tub on curled claw feet, and a washing bowl on a vanity stand. And their own commode hidden behind a discrete ground-glass panel with ornamental flower motif. Britt turned on a tap in the tub. Water spurted out in a fast stream. After a moment she said in wonder, "The water's hot."

"You first," he said.

While she bathed he sat on the edge of the plush, springy bed to read his letter.

My Darling Erich, (she wrote in German)
I apologise that we could not come to your wedding. Although your Father still seems angry I ask you to forgive us. and beg you to bring your bride here to meet...

He was still on leave until the end of June. Time enough for a trip to London.

Later that evening he showed Britt the letter.

She read it quickly. "Of course we must go."

He laughed nervously. "Mutti loves you already. For a long time she's been writing to your mother, did you know? When my father meets you he has to love you also."

She smiled. She thought it was true.

* * *

CHAPTER 12

Into June 1914

In London the motor vehicles glutted the streets more than ever, but horse traffic still took the right-of-way. Huge drays crushed over the cobbles, and hansom cabs dodged in and out among trolleys on their tracks and among coaches and omnibuses and the double-decker horse-trolleys. Coming out of Victoria Station Erich took Britt's arm. People bumped and thrust about them. Out on the pavement the porter with their luggage caught up. Erich hailed a cab. A man pushed him aside and jumped into it ahead of him, and the porter dashed out into the street for the next hansom and caught the bridle of the horse. "Oy!" he shouted, "Hold up there Guv!" Erich pressed a shilling into his hand, a royal tip. Then he got Britt out of the crowd while the porter shouldered their trunk and valises into the boot. A crack of the whip and the cab moved gently into traffic.

They checked in at the Savoy on the Strand. A week would swallow most of his remaining bank funds. He was now almost stone-broke. A strange sensation. Never before had he wondered where it came from, it had always been there. He still had a few pounds left from the hundred pound note his Mutti had sent, but when that was gone he'd be on a soldier's pay. Britt had no idea of living at that level. *He* had no real idea of living at that level...

He stood now in the window, staring out at the Victoria Embankment and a spectacular view of London Bridge and the Blackfriar's Bridge and all the boats and barges between, plying the water that he'd never before stopped to study. He felt a flood of affection for this old town, largest city in the world, that once was home.

In the bathroom Britt was splashing happily in a huge gilded tub, while the hotel maid unpacked their luggage. Erich sat down at the Queen Ann desk, and braced his hands on its ornate curved edges. Gold pen, gold inkwell, embossed hotel stationery. The opulence of kings. From his pocket he took out his new calling cards with gothic text...

Erich Bronsart von Schellendorf, Leutnant
25te Dragoner Reg., Baden.

On hotel stationery he wrote in a careful hand, *"Sir: I wish to inform you that my wife, Brigitte, and I arrived today in London and beg to call upon you at your earliest convenience. Please convey loving greetings to Mutti. With sincere respect, your son Eric."* He slipped his card with the note into a hotel envelope, and sent it off by messenger.

*

In the next two days he took Britt to view some of the tourist places, Buckingham Palace, the Tower of London with the Crown Jewels, St. James' Palace and the Coldstream Guards in their tall black bearskins, the Houses of Parliament, Westminster Abbey with kings and bishops in their stone tombs, the flower market in Covent Garden where they bought trinkets to send home to Heidelberg. They took long strolls, admired buildings that went back to Roman times, paused to sniff the flowers in public gardens, and dodged under her umbrella in the occasional rain showers. Thirstily he drank in the voices of strangers around him speaking every accent of English and Scottish and Welsh and even a little bit of Irish here and there. But they seemed to him drab and dispirited. He kept overhearing rumours about partitioning Ireland, he read the government debates over the Irish question, and strikes in the coal mines and the shipyards. They saw men lining up in the labour exchange and waiting on the docks and in the streets for odd jobs.

Newspaper headlines speculated about the troubled Balkan settlement, and would the Habsburgs take it to war? Why, he wondered uneasily, would England stick their noses into the Balkans?

He hadn't really thought of war.

Last Christmas his father was already thinking of war. Erich had dismissed it at the time. Now the possibility mounted.

What would he do if it came to war?

He'd be stuck with it. An officer obeyed orders and passed them on. Simple as that. In any case, the Balkans had nothing to do with England, so England would have no part in any new flare-up. Russia had been sabre-rattling in defence of Serbia, but England had nothing directly to do with either Russia or Serbia. An easy fix; the King and the Kaiser and the Tsar of Russia, all blood related, would surely keep their connections calm...

The Times headline caught his eye in the tea shop...

"DEEPER AND BROADER KIEL CANAL PRESENTS INCREASING GERMAN THREAT!"

He bought the newspaper and glanced over the front page story while they waited for their tea. *"...permits passage of the largest German battleships directly between the Baltic and North Seas..."* The story of a parliamentary debate made it appear that deepening the canal was Kaiser Wilhelm's personal declaration of war against Russia and the entire British Empire.

"You know," he said to her, tossing the newspaper aside, "the British seized the Suez Canal to get to India, and now they resent us widening our Kiel Canal. They accuse us of aggression, but they talk more every day about war than we do in a year. Who's guilty of aggression now?"

She shrugged.

The waitress brought their tea.

Was he trying to convince Britt?

Or himself...?

Tea shops, restaurants, theatre tickets, gifts for home were more expensive here than in Heidelberg. "We must conserve," he said to her on Thursday as they dressed for the day.

"Conserve what?"

"Money, my darling. Money."

"Oh pah! Charge it to Papi."

"I can't do that."

"Why not? I always do."

He laughed. "Because I'm responsible for you now, not your father."

"And *your* father, what of him?" She was smiling.

"I can't charge anything to—"

"Why has he not answered your note?"

"I don't know."

"We both know. He won't face you. He's too stubborn."

"Well I can't change him."

"You also are too stubborn."

"I'm not too stubborn to come all this way to see him."

Her smile widened. "You're both too stubborn."

She was teasing again, but he recognised the truth of it. He could not change his father's resolve. He would never change his own. It was not a question of winning or losing, but of different desires. They were two stubborn men of identical minds heading in opposite directions. And now after all these months of military training and a honeymoon, he had grown from pup to dog. His father would not see it. Would never admit it. Erich saw no way to close the breech unless they could face each other equally and talk like men,.

"We will go!" he announced. "Damn him, whether he invites us or not, we will go!"

"I don't want to meet your father. What kind of man will not answer his son? Go if you like. I don't like this city, it's too big and dirty. Visit them alone. I can wait for you here."

"They will meet you." Then, smiling, "And they will love you." His smile was false. His heart was beating too hard.

He took up the gold telephone and asked the operator for a connection to the home of Sir Edward Foster, and gave the address. Then stood listening to the clicks and buzzes and faint voices on the wire of unseen people. A distant *bzz-bzz... bzz-bzz... bzz-bzz...*

Then another click and another distant voice, "Foster residence."

"Who is this, please?" Erich spoke loudly.

"Who is calling?"

"It's Eric. I'm calling for my father."

"Ah Master Eric! How extraordinary! Joseph speaking."

"Aha, Joseph!" He winked across at Britt. "Please inform my father that we're coming to the house sometime before luncheon. I and my wife."

"Absolutely, sir. Absolutely. Oh how fortuitous, they'll be at home until the weekend."

By eleven o'clock they were riding in a fine clean hansom cab across the inner city. Britt had changed from tourist clothes into a fashionable blue outfit designed to impress, with heirloom pearls at her throat. She sat beside him staring out of the cab, her rolled umbrella firmly anchored between her toes.

At the house they got down, and the hansom rolled away along the street, hoof-beats lazy in the sunshine. He didn't know if his pounding heart was fear of his father, or impatience to see his mother again. End the letters. Introduce Britt. Talk and talk and talk.

An upper-floor curtain swayed. As it went still, he imagined eyes looking out at him...

He stepped up to the door, and grasped the door-pull and jerked it downward and let it go and stepped back. Britt stood one step below. Her eyes were calm.

The door opened inward. Joseph stood just inside looking down a long nose at them, his eyes impersonal. "Yes, sir?"

"Hello Joseph."

"Sorry, sir." He did not step aside. "I am instructed to say that neither the judge nor Madame is at home."

"But of course they're at home!" He stepped forward half a pace.

Joseph did not move aside. "Sir, I am instructed to say that if the gentleman would care to return alone at some later hour, that is without the young lady, he would be most welcome to enter."

Erich turned to look at Britt.

She was still smiling. She did not understand English.

Through a failing spirit he turned again to the butler, so impeccable in his morning suit. "Thank you, Joseph." He dug into his inner breast pocket and brought out his key ring with three keys attached. Carefully, deliberately, he worked one key from the ring and held it out. "Convey to my father my profound disappointment. I shall not return unless invited."

A slight bow as Joseph accepted the key. "Thank you sir."
He turned to go.
"Master Eric? May I...?"
He paused on the step.
"May I say, sir, this is most dreadfully regrettable."
Helpless, furious, he waved off the apology. He took Britt by the elbow and propelled her down the step to the pavement.
"What happened?" She stared up at the gently closing door. "They're not at home?"
"No. My father will never be at home."

* * *

CHAPTER 13

June to July 28, 1914

He trotted out at the head of his squad, twenty-two troopers two abreast, and one lance-corporal who carried the red-and-yellow regimental streamer fluttering from his lance. Hooves blended in grinding rasps over the road. From the drill field all the way out past the gate the men had laughed and chatted among themselves as if on a holiday picnic.

He'd born this for three days. He'd thought they would settle down, but during the drills with the other squads they moved like a herd of cows wading in a swamp.

Past the gate he turned the squad into the throughway, and just before they came under the trees, Erich raised high his hand, and behind him the lance-corporal called the halt.

He swung Oberon about and watched the squad stop like kids in a school yard jostling into line, high-spirited, unfocused. Horses lunged and bumped each other. Lances swayed, as if the men had never before held a lance. Pedestrians along the verge had to step into the grass to dodge stirrups and restless rumps and switching tails. Traffic in the roadway swerved around them.

Erich cringed that civilians saw this.

His squad.

He nudged Oberon across the middle of the road. "Lance-Corporal Merckel!"

"Sir!"

A wagon veered on the road to avoid crowding him. He held Oberon steady. "Form up the squad line-abreast."

The lance-corporal roared out the command.

Raggedly they turned into line to face him, horses backed against the verge.

For the love of God, he thought, *straighten up, straighten up...!* "Right dress, Lance-Corporal!"

"Squad...!" the lance-corporal roared... "Right...! *DRESS!*"

They shuffled. One horse shied and broke the line. Then every horse shuffled out of line. Holding himself tight, keeping a wooden face, a hand on Oberon's withers to steady the stallion, he studied each rider, one face to the next.

This was *his* squad. His responsibility. His embarrassment.

They settled into the line, properly spaced, not precise, but straight enough for the moment.

"Eyes front!" the lance-corporal bellowed, his face red.

Two wagons came from one direction, a motor lorry from the other, engine sputtering. All stopped and waited. Pedestrians turned to watch.

"You men," he announced loud enough to be heard by every trooper and by the civilians on all sides, "you gossip and giggle like old ladies at tea. You ride like schoolgirls. You can't form a straight line on the road. You can't keep your horses in hand."

He saw them along the line stiffen in the saddle, eyes front.

"You ride like infantry!" It was the ultimate insult. He let it sink in. He did not glance at the pedestrians gathered to watch. Witnesses to the squad's shame. Part of his plan.

"You're cavalry, not infantry! You're regular, not reservists! We will ride as usual to the river, and when we return, Lance-Corporal Merckel will drill you until you show me perfection. There will be no weekend passes until I see perfection. Is that clear, Lance-Corporal?"

The lance-corporal looked startled, and melted to dismay. "Yes sir."

"Form into column of two."

They turned into marching order, moving smarter now.

He rode forward and raised his hand. They trotted on.

He'd been assigned the squad on Monday, his first day back from leave, his first day with the Second Squadron, Twenty-Fifth

Dragoons. *His* regiment. Initiation into the mess was apparently over, nobody challenged him now to buy the drinks, and he'd been allowed to sleep undisturbed through the night.

As he trotted Oberon into the Schwetzingen Landstrasse, civilian traffic yielded to the squad. Pedestrians paused to turn and smile and wave as if it were a parade. Erich was aware of his own deep-stirring pride that this was *his* squad and he was in command. On his second day of duty, the captain had told him, "They're all yours. Take them out every morning exactly ten kilometres, post-to-post. Toughen them up for the route march." Erich had called in the master-sergeant and worked out a route, five kilometres out, five back - not four, not six - then trotted them out, ragged and happily unruly, down along the river and back, exactly ten kilometres post-to-post. "Now," the captain said afterward, "whip these devils into shape."

He loved it. Trotting the squad, riding his precious, steady, responsive Oberon, he loved it. His mind swarmed with ideas for taming these men as he had tamed the stallion; a fixed hand, solid routine, hard exercise, and no damned foolishness.

The squad trotted on, a little straighter than before, and quiet. He'd caught their attention.

*

The pace of the sortie was faster than yesterday, bringing him back to the mess too early for lunch. Half a dozen junior officers had gathered in the bar. Among them Erich was the newest and youngest, still months short of his twentieth birthday. He'd not yet found his place among them. Like the new boy at school, he had to watch every step, every word, and yield to every man here. Today as he came in they parted at the bar to make place for him. *Oberleutnant* Jurgen Kästner gave him a rough, comradely slap on the back. "What's yours? I'm buying this round." He held a Pilsener glass in his hand. Erich ordered one for himself. The barman slid it along the bar to him. "Thanks." He raised it in silent salute.

Gerdt came through the door and signalled the barman, and stood quietly at the end of the bar to take up his glass.

"So how did it go with Zed Squad?" Kästner asked Erich.

The others chuckled, sharing a private joke.

"Zed Squad?"

"That's what we call them. Zed. End of the alphabet, end of the line. The regular squads are A, B, C, D and then there's Zed. The ultimate knuckleheads. So how is it so far?"

He shrugged. Every eye was on him, and he knew he was the butt of yet another mysterious joke. It seemed a pattern in this mess, target the new officers. Gerdt was wise to stay out of it. "I think they'll shape up," he said. "We'll see what weekend drill does for them."

They laughed. Some of them raised a glass to him, and they turned again to the serious business of drinking. "Did you hear?" he heard one say. "Two new hussar squadrons being formed—"

"Yes, but not for us, it's for the Bavarians, bring them up to regimental standard—"

"Well I heard it's a general call-up, not just the Bavarians..."

Gerdt came to stand beside Erich now. "Well I heard it's national mobilisation."

Abrupt silence.

Then, "Where did you hear that?"

"My father, he has friends in Berlin. The Kaiser's all for wiping out Serbia, never mind just putting her in her place."

"So we may have a chance for combat?"

"Who knows. Remember the Moroccan crisis, nothing but talk. And the Balkan wars, they didn't even invite us in."

"We'd have put them in their proper place—"

"But war! Really?"

"My God, do you think...?"

The air turned electric. One of them raised his glass. "Here's to a fast fight, and a chance for quick promotion!"

"Are we ready?"

"Oh God, are we ready! Champing at the bit!"

The bell announced the dining room open for lunch. They filed in, carrying their drinks.

He'd gotten used to the opulence of the officers' mess, with white linen table cloths and porcelain tableware and silverware stamped with the regimental crest. A regimental colour standard hung behind the head table, so firmly imprinted in his brain that it fluttered in his dreams...

"Sit with us, Wittingen?" Kästner offered chairs to them. "Schellendorf?"

An invitation, not an order.

As orderlies rushed to serve the food, the talk among the tables was all of war. Erich could put a name to each officer now, had decided which might be friend and which to ignore...

"...But!" announced Captain von Hardenberg to the room. "Nothing was resolved in the Balkans. Austria needs a major victory to regain status, but they can't do it without German support. And Russia supports Serbia, gentlemen, and France has an alliance with Russia, you understand the fine balance? As always, we're surrounded by powerful opponents. One careless word, and Boom!"

"Let me at them!" Lieutenant von Belov rose from his chair and held his glass aloft. "I'll lead the first charge!"

They raised their glasses. Belov sat down.

Erich could not imagine charging through an enemy line, swinging a sabre, enemies collapsing in every direction, *what did a Serb actually look like?* while survivors flung down weapons and cowered in abject surrender...

Or... fired modern repeating rifles point blank at charging horses...

"...must polish our manoeuvres," the captain said to the room, which fell into a respectful silence for their superior. "To that end we drill the men pitilessly. Especially the charge."

"Especially," somebody murmured in the quiet room, "Zed Squad."

Uproarious laughter.

It was time to stand his ground.

"Well, I don't know," Erich said loudly through the laughter.

As if insulted, every man in the room turned to stare at him.

"What's the point," Erich asked, "of drilling the charge?"

"You understand," the captain quoted the cavalry manual, "'In action, a vigorous cavalry attack...'"

"'...is the surest way to victory,'" Erich finished the quote.

"Exactly!" exploded the captain. "And your Squad Zed is the least prepared, Schellendorf. Look to it sharply. Shape them up!"

The other officers nodded and murmured agreement.

"I must just wonder..." ventured Erich...

"Yes?"

He did not really mean it as a challenge, he only wanted to

be seen as thinking, rather than blindly following. "I mean, sir..." He spoke across three tables directly to the captain. "I mean, is it possible for mounted troops to charge against an entrenched enemy armed with repeating rifles and machine guns?"

A dreadful silence descended on the room. The orderlies paused in serving the tables.

"What did you say?" The captain's voice was a whisper.

"I mean, sir, in previous wars the army used breech-loading, single-shot, smooth-bore carbines with a limited range and poor precision. Today the infantry has long-range repeating rifles. And machine guns that fire off five hundred rounds per minute. Can we charge close enough to unsheathe our steel?"

"Why... Why..." The captain paused, then bellowed, "One uses terrain, you idiot! Terrain! You study the terrain! That's your job!"

He felt his face go red with embarrassment, not for himself but for an aging captain who had no worthy answer, who had perhaps waited long years for a war to fight, and for promotions that had never come.

"And make certain," the captain said to the room, "that every man here drills the charge! It *will* decide battles!"

The orderlies resumed serving. The men bent to their food.

"You know," muttered Kästner, leaning close to Erich in the silence, "you're right."

"Of course I'm right." He glanced over to Gerdt, who raised his eyebrows. *Keep your mouth shut, stupid...*

After lunch Erich was about to go back to review his squad's progress when Kästner drew him aside. "Just a little piece of... what shall we say? Advice?"

"I know. Keep my mouth—"

"No, no, not that. About your squad."

"Yes?"

"Zed Squad. It's a joke—"

"I know. I'm the butt of jokes."

"But it's a test, you see. Every new shave-tail gets a Zed Squad. Wittingen had his while you went on your honeymoon. They're the troublemakers from every unit in the squadron. Shows the C.O. what you're made of."

Ah. Not a joke. "Thanks, Kästner."

They shook hands. Everything in the army was a test.

*

Britt met them at the train. He was proud, how smart they looked together, she in exquisite style, he and Gerdt in walking-out uniforms, sharp, clean, perfect. People smiled to watch them go.

She leaned against him as they walked. "How was it, your first week?"

"I command twenty-two very rough men. I have to whip them into shape."

"You and Gerdt, you're both real soldiers now." She hooked her arm in his as they started up the hill in the darkness, the lamps from the Schloss above casting long shadows through the trees. They stopped together at the old oak to look at the town below. Yellow street lamps outlined crooked lines of buildings, and the river glittered obsidian between its banks. A magic time, together in the night walking up the ancient cobbled lane.

At the house they quietly let themselves in. "Mutti went to bed," she whispered. "Papi is down in the mess. The servants have retired."

"What of Gerdt?" he whispered to her, watching Gerdt walk forward to the gun room.

"Let Gerdt take care of himself."

"Do you know," he whispered on the stairs, "how much I missed you this past week?" He followed one step behind her, every nerve and muscle in his body reaching for her, as if she were magnetised.

In the lamplight of her extravagant bedroom, she turned to him like a tiger.

*

June 28. Sunday. No special day.

On this bright warm summer Sunday, a day that would hang forever in history, the Archduke Franz Ferdinand of Austria was shot to death by a Serbian student in Sarajevo. In Heidelberg the news came in mid-afternoon by telegraph and was made public by the garrison cannon firing into the opposite mountainside. A resounding boom, a dead shell, a puff of flying dirt.

Riding the Philosophenweg, Erich and Britt had stopped to sit on the ground opposite the Schloss. They sat braced against the straight trunk of a tree, shoulder-to-shoulder, half turned away from each other, not quite touching, not needing even to look at each other. The horses dozed, tethered nearby in the shade. The sun melted the sky.

They hadn't spoken since they'd dismounted some time ago. Nothing broke the timeless peace of the hillside until the cannon boomed, shattering the quietude. It echoed down the open valley, and was gone. The air settled back to tranquillity.

"Erich," she said softly.

"Hmmm."

"Do you feel it?" She was not speaking of the cannon.

"Yes."

"The forest that day."

"Yes. The same."

Something was there, he wasn't sure. This was not the same as the Black Forest breathing, but something deeper, as if they sat enclosed together in a small shimmering pocket of infinity. As if an invisible glass wall kept them safe from the outrages of the outside world.

"We've become the same," she said softly. "We think the same."

He nodded. She couldn't see him nod, but he knew that she knew he nodded. It was like that within this tiny pocket. They didn't need to see each other. They hardly had to talk.

"How is it possible," she broke his muse, "to be so happy, and not explode?"

*

Monday morning he was back before his squad on the drill field. He turned Oberon into line for the little talk he'd composed over the weekend.

"Squad Zed!" he announced to the men. "Squad Zed! That is the reputation you enjoy in this squadron. End of the alphabet. Bottom of the heap. Squad Zed. Is this how you want it?"

Silence. The horses along the line shifted restively.

"Squad Zed! Is that how you want to be known?"

"No *SIR!*" they bellowed in unison.

At least, he mused, they had got their answer together.

"The colonel expects you to fail. Do you expect to fail?"

"No *SIR!*"

"Are you ready to prove the colonel wrong?"

"Yes *SIR!*"

He glanced across at the lance corporal and gave him the slightest nod of approval.

He reprised his own training from the War School. Over the next weeks he drilled them on horse and on foot, in formations and overland manoeuvres and weapons handling and hand-to-hand combat. Lances, carbines, pistols. Firing the carbine prone, then kneeling, then on foot, and while charging forward on foot, six blind shots, pause, kneel, reload. Firing at the gallop, then dismounting to lean over the saddle using the horse as a brace and a shield, using blank ammunition, training the horse to stand firm. Charging with lances at full gallop, in line one at a time, stabbing into straw dummy forms. Charging in column of two, column of four, then twenty riders charging line abreast, and bringing up in good order...

At the end of the third week he issued weekend passes for all the troopers.

*

"Where will they send you?" she asked, as they rode on the Philosophenweg.

"God knows. Serbia? Albania? Turkey? What does your father think?"

"He says there'll probably be no war at all."

"I'm just as happy."

He didn't often see the baron. Who seemed to spend his mornings sleeping and his afternoons down at the garrison with his old regiment whooping up fervour for a war that might never come. Then to return home late at night, red of face, and too groggy for conversation.

"He's drinking too much," he said to Britt.

"He's old," Britt shot back. "He's sixty-six, Erich. He can't bear this excitement. Everyone wants to go to war and he can't go. So he drinks."

"He's drunk, mostly."

"Not truly drunk, just..." She never could see a flaw in the perfection of her father.

They rode on, enjoying the summer day.

*

On July 28, all diplomatic efforts having failed, Austria-Hungary opened an artillery barrage on Belgrade, the only strategic target in immediate range.

On July 29 news came that St. Petersburg had mobilised two Russian military districts along the German frontier. Berlin sent diplomats to demand Russia stand down, and to Paris warning French circumspection along Alsace and Lorraine. The First and Second German Imperial Armies mustered on the French and Belgian frontiers. Crown Prince Rupprecht of Bavaria ordered his Fifth Army up to war readiness, and in the same week the First Squadron of the Twenty-Fifth Dragoons in Karlsruhe was attached to the newly formed Seventh Army under General von Heeringen.

On July 30, Russia announced national mobilisation. France and England remained silent.

On August 1, at 16:30 in the hushed summer afternoon, the Heidelberg cannon fired twenty times into the mountainside directly above the grey stone house, cutting down a swath of trees and opening a fine new ski run for some future snowfall.

Erich was home in Heidelberg that weekend. Before the last echo faded down the valley the whole town came alive. Jubilant crowds came thronging out of the houses, greeting each other in the streets, exchanging rumours and recalling the last war with France and the victory of 1870. This one too, they said, would be finished in no time. The Kaiser had promised it. God would see to it. Crowds flowed to the newspaper office to read the news posted hourly in the front window. This time a single headline:

WAR!

*

Britt sat on the edge of the bed watching as he pulled on his tunic and buttoned every button to the throat.

"Do you think it's actually war?" she whispered.

He refused to think of it. He shot his cuffs, part of the ritual of the uniform, and tugged at his tunic skirts.

"We could take one more ride," she said in a small voice.

"My train is in an hour."

Too many things suddenly pushed at him from every side: parting from Britt, reporting for duty, war declared between Austria and Serbia, Russian intervention in Serbia, the French army on red alert in the west, England still standing silent. All the combinations of international reaction were spinning in his head as he stood wearing this uniform on the edge of a tottering precipice. He had joined the cavalry to prove something. He had joined to win Britt. To escape his father. He had joined for adventure, for comradeship, for a respected career and early retirement, for the uniform and the esteem it brought him and the security it promised. He had become a soldier...

For every reason except war.

And here he was. On the precipice. Stomach choking up in his throat.

They went downstairs. He put an arm about her shoulders, felt the soft, wiry strength of her, and knew her fearlessness. She would go on with what she knew. For himself, he thought he knew what he was going to. Adventure, battle, glory. That was what they all said, those who knew.

"I'll miss you," he said on the stairs.

"I'll miss you," she echoed.

"Write to me."

"Yes, write to me also. Every day. Promise."

Gerdt met them at the foot of the stairs. "Erich, Mutti wants you in her room."

*

She seemed weaker. This hot weather seemed to press her down. Hottest summer in memory, they said. Excellent crops this year, they said. A wonderful year, Erich mused ironically, for a good war. The late sun slanted through the window to light the corners of the room.

She patted the edge of her bed, and he sat there, and she reached for his hand and held it. From her bank of pillows she smiled into his eyes. "My handsome boy. My second son."

He felt a flush rise red in his ears.

"You are my hope," she said.

Involuntarily his hand drew back.

She gripped him with a surprising surge of strength and did not release his hand. "Gerdt is..." She shook her head. "I have something to tell you before you go."

Gerdt? What of Gerdt?

"I have," she said haltingly, "a terrible confession to make to you. You may hate me when I say it, but if you must go to war..." she coughed, "...I must be honest."

He reached for the camphor on her bedside table, and she took a moment to breathe it in.

"My dear Erich," she said, "I confess a family conspiracy."

"What?" He almost laughed in relief. This was not serious.

"From the first day. Gerdt never admits to being impressed, so when he wrote to us about this Engländer of Schellendorf heritage—"

"I know less than nothing of my heritage."

She waved an impatient hand. "It was the first thing about you we investigated."

He remembered suddenly his mother at Christmas, *"...with the baroness... we planned your future together."*

"When Gerdt first brought you home," the baroness said, "you impressed us greatly. You never put a foot wrong or said a wrong thing since we've known you. But most important was Britt." She smiled. "You see? We all call her Britt now. We saw in her an immediate change. You yourself saw how she changed. To us it was a small miracle. Brigitte... the old Brigitte... we were always terrified that she would beat off every prospective suitor, and never marry. That she would run away. That in her wildness she would do herself harm. But then you came, Erich, and she changed. You were so sweet with her. So careful, may I say. And we saw in you, with your Prussian family background... even though you didn't see it yourself... we saw in you the perfect prospect for Brigitte. And so like a fish we reeled you in. From the very first day. Gerdt with his friendship, the baron with his challenges, I with my indulgence. And you, my darling, fell so cheerfully into the net."

He struggled with the thought.

"Will you forgive us?" she asked, still holding his hand.

He nodded mutely.

"Because..." she whispered, her voice spent now, "I had to see my daughter settled in life. You understand? You were the only one who ever turned her head. Whom she respects. Whom she compares with her father. I saw in you the perfect prospect, everything looked perfect, your family roots, your fine character, everything."

"I'm grateful for—"

"I had to see her marry, you understand. Nobody is certain... not even the doctor... how long I may have yet to live—"

"Ah Mutti—"

"Let us not be emotional. I'm greatly relieved that you know everything now. Don't hate us for our deceit."

"Hate you? I love you. You've become my family."

"And your own family? In England?"

He half rose. She tightened her grip on his hand. He sank down again.

"No, you needn't answer that." She smiled, and the sunlight seemed to brighten in the room. "You make me happy, Erich. Especially how things are turning. You see it yourself, the baron is slipping into his dotage. His health is excellent, no trouble there, but his mind wanders more and more to the past."

"Yes, we understand."

"And Gerdt, of course, he has his own life to live and the estates to handle without the burden of a wild, disorderly sister." She smiled with mischief in her eyes. "She's your burden now."

He laughed.

"So, my darling Erich, I want you to make to me one solemn promise."

"Yes?"

"That no matter what happens to me or to the baron, or in this war, or in life itself, you will keep my daughter safe."

"But there's no question. It's the vow we took—"

"Forever. As long as you live. Promise me now."

"I so swear."

She smiled, and her head sank back on the pillows. "Now go along to your war."

Erich kissed her cold fingers, and reluctantly left her.

* * *

CHAPTER 14

August - October 1914

They were given a ceremonial send-off with the regimental band leading off and the whole squadron turning out to parade them to the train. Full regimental colours flew at the vanguard. Red-and-yellow streamers fluttered from every trooper's lance. The whole city seemed to have come out to cheer them on. Erich was going, Gerdt was not. He didn't know where they were going, just that his troop and two others were being detached to support an infantry battalion somewhere.

He rode at the head of Troop Zed, with a newly-assigned sergeant at his side. Gerdt's troop was just ahead. They brought up the rear of the parade, last ones in, last ones out. They rode in column of four, too far back from the band to hear more than the drumbeat over the cheering crowds. He was proud of his men now. After these weeks of intense drill they rode as a unit, eyes front, heads high. Their nickname 'Troop Zed' had become a source of wicked pride to the men. They couldn't wait for a good fight to prove the squadron all wrong.

The townsfolk along the route, dressed in their Sunday best, waved little Kaiser flags and cheered and pressed forward,. The horses began to dance with crowds closing around their heels. "Steady!" Erich ordered the sergeant half a horse to his rear. "Steady!" the sergeant barked to the troop. Erich silently prayed that no horse would lash out with nervous hooves. The battalion ranks filled the road ahead. Field-grey tunics, pennants fluttering on lances, white plumes on metal helmets flashing in sunlight. The grandeur of the parade flanked by cheering crowds filled his heart. It was the perfect August day to go to war.

At the rail yards a train was already loading. Crowds crushed against the outer fence to wave and cheer them on. Gerdt's unit turned aside and marched to the perimeter to join the mounted honour guard forming there. Erich halted Troop Zed and ordered the sergeant to dismount the troopers and loosen girths for the journey.

"Hurry up and wait," the men laughed. "Hurry up and wait!" Erich dismounted with them. Kropp, his new batman, took hold of Oberon.

Sergeant Moos watched all this through alert, hooded eyes. According to his personnel file he came from East Prussia where the Russian army was now approaching his family's home a few kilometres inside the Prussian-Polish frontier.

The horses were led up the ramp into the stock car and hitched four deep, with troopers standing close to keep them calm. Infantrymen climbed into third-class coaches, slamming doors and leaning out through open windows to cheer and wave back at the crowds. Several wagons drew forward, carrying a hospital and supplies and ordnance and fodder for almost two hundred horses. One by one the wagons were rolled up onto flatcars and anchored there with chains.

At the War School there had been a few quick lectures about logistics, but Erich could hardly imagine the organisation needed to bring together all these essentials of the smallest part of an army. At the beginning of the month over a million men and horses had travelled a similar road to Belgium. The complexity boggled the mind...

"Schellendorf." The adjutant had come to stand beside him. "Your orders."

He accepted the envelope.

"When you reach Königsberg—"

"Königsberg, Captain?"

He nodded to the envelope. "It's all in there. The Russians have forced a German retreat in East Prussia, and General von Moltke has posted elements from a number of regiments to build the Königsberg defences." His smile widened to a wolfish grin. "So you brown-nosed with Moltke and got the best job fighting the Russians? While the rest of us sit here on our royal arses?"

"What?"

"Good ride and good luck." With the flip of a finger he returned Erich's salute and walked away.

At his elbow Sergeant Moos said, "Officers got a coach of their own, Lieutenant. I'll git this bunch loaded."

And he too turned away.

In that mass of horses and men and cheering crowds, Erich stood suddenly alone.

Brown-nosed with General von Moltke?

*

As the train pulled out north-eastward the officers opened their orders and obeyed the first step, putting away the white horsehair plumes and fitting their helmets with the green canvas covers they'd been issued to block the flash of metal.

This would be the real thing.

It was a long two days to Königsberg. The men broke out the decks of playing cards for endless games of Skat. Erich spent his time staring from the window at a land he did not really know. Over the hours it unfolded from hills and small farms to broad tracts of ripening crops and grazing livestock, and streams and villages among scattered stands of forest. His country now. This was all his country.

He dozed, forehead pressed to the glass. In his dream a letter appeared, floating in the dark, he could see his father's personal letterhead, but when he tried to rip open the envelope it burst into flames, it burned his fingers, and although he could not read the message he knew his father had sent him precise instructions for going home to England...

He jerked awake, and stared forward at the morning sky paling in the east.

*

On the first day at Fortress Königsberg the commandant briefed the officers. Cavalry would form the vanguard of a forced march of a hundred and fifty kilometres to reach First Reserve Corps. Each officer was issued the map marked with the route from Königsberg to HQ near Angerburg on the Angerapp River. The cavalry reconnaissance troop would lead exactly five kilometres in advance of the main body, scout the country, and report back to Captain Sonderheim. Time was critical. A major battle had been joined near Gumbinnen, so fluid that nobody was certain hour-to-hour where the enemy stood.

Erich studied his map and led Troop Zed out as the sun reached noon. An infantry company marched behind the troop, followed by a hospital wagon, two quartermaster wagons, and four artillery limbers in the rear. Sergeant Moos riding at Erich's side was still unknown. Erich tried to conceal the thrill, and the terror, of being in the lead. He had been trained for this, he told himself. He repeated it again and again to himself, *you've been trained for this, you've been trained...*

They rode at a trot. After an hour they stopped and Erich sent the scout back, and the troops loosened girths and checked hooves for stones and loose shoes until the infantry caught up. Then they mounted and followed the map along roads and tracks, through small villages and large farms, through scrub forest running with little brooks, then into hills of heavy forest where they rode nervously with weapons at the ready.

The summer sun fell heavily on Erich's shoulders. Dust rose to choke his throat. Horses lathered in the heat, and dust stuck grey on the lather. They marched south-westward, scanning the country. Erich sent scouts fanning out. They rested when they found another stream, watering the horses and waiting for the infantry. Then on again and on, hour after hour, to the rhythmic, hypnotic scrape of steel hooves on stony roads. Behind them the foot-soldiers strode along loose-limbed, complaining and joking, even singing from time to time, and swigging their water bottles. In the middle of the afternoon the company halted by a riverside to break out rations and to give the foot-soldiers a rest. Then onward again, hour after hour, pushing to cover twelve kilometres every hour. They did not know how close to the advancing Russians they might be. Villagers and peasants in the fields grinned and waved, and some of the young girls ran alongside the horses, offering bunches of wildflowers gathered at the roadside, then fell back as the troop trotted on.

The long evening sun touched the horizon as they came into a village along the road, a collection of wooden houses with thatched roofs, a couple of larger brick buildings, a water-well in the middle, a shop, a baker, and the usual blacksmith shop. The captain called a halt. Staff officers rode out to check the area, and posted guards around the perimeter. The infantry moved in and added to the mass. The sun fell below the horizon.

Erich's shoulders felt heavy with weariness, his hips ached, his spine was stiff as steel. He told the sergeant to order the men not to off-saddle, but to loosen girths and stand for inspection. The sergeant darted him irritable glances and obeyed. The men stood bent with weariness at the heads of their mounts. Erich braced back his shoulders and walked the line. One by one he checked the gear, checked their weapons, checked their saddlebags, and ran a hand under each saddle. Four times he paused at a slight swelling under a saddle, and ordered those troopers to walk their horses thirty minutes before unsaddling. The rest were in good condition. At one point the sergeant whispered at his elbow, "This is my duty, sir."

"Thank you sergeant." He continued relentlessly down the line. He was weary. They were all weary, but he was intent on pushing beyond mere weariness and forcing these men to follow. *Lead from the front...* When he finished inspection he gave the sergeant orders... he knew it was unnecessary... to water the horses sparingly, to bed them down, to break out grain rations from the supply train, all of it before dismissing the men to the mess wagon for a hot meal. Erich knew the sergeant knew all of this, and when he finally turned away, he caught the sergeant rolling his eyes at the sky.

It was hard to sleep that night. He thought he was tough enough for this, he'd gone through this at the War School, had been under pressure from five in the morning until eleven at night, had been challenged in brain and body to his ultimate stretch, but never... *never!* had he been this sore, this weary, or this wide awake. The midges gathered, whining about his ears. He pulled the half-tent over his head, suffering heat better than insects. Curled up on the ground under a wagon, he didn't know when he fell asleep until he woke to reveille.

The next day they marched closer to the fighting. Sometimes Erich could hear the boom of artillery in the distance.

Quite early his forward riders came at the gallop to report

Russian infantry ahead. "About a hundred foot soldiers, sir, no wagons, no horses."

"Resting? Marching?"

"Double-marching, sir. Away from us. Southeast."

"Did they see you?"

"Not as I know."

"Report back to the captain."

He called a rest halt and posted perimeter guards. He told himself he was following orders not to engage, but inside he felt his fear rise like green bile in his throat. To control it he made a quick inspection, hooves, saddles, saddlebags, weapons. "Load carbines," he ordered the sergeant. The word passed quietly. Clicks and scrapes along the line as men charged their weapons, then shouldered arms and gripped their lances closer.

The sergeant darted him a sideways, sardonic, knowing grin. *He* knew the signs of fear, the avoidance, the delaying tactics. And Erich knew that he knew.

The infantry caught up. The officers held a quick conference. Captain Sonderheim decided to continue forward unless the enemy was encountered. "Don't seek them out," he told Erich. "Our orders are for Angerburg."

They trotted on. Trees spotted the rugged farmlands on their right, scrub and wetlands on their left, and Russians somewhere near. "Don't wander off the track," the sergeant warned him. "Horses get mired in them swamps."

"I understand you're from Gumbinnen," Erich said.

The sergeant nodded. "I know this country. They gave you to me so's to keep you safe." Sardonically he added, "Sir."

*

Erich dismounted the troop in dense woods that screened them from the Russian enemy fire. They stood with hands over the muzzles of the horses to prevent them whinnying. From here they could see nothing of the enemy. The lookouts on the points reported perhaps fifty rifles and one machine gun in the village below the long slope. Erich stared down at the clump of thatched roofs. His frozen mind kept saying, *Russians Russians Russians Russians...!*

For two hours the infantry had tried to push the Russians from this village, firing at every sign of movement down there.

Rifles raked blindly in both directions. The entire march had ground to a halt, and now they waited for the artillery to move up and open a barrage. The infantry company lay above the open slope, pinned there by the Russian fire.

A runner reported to Erich that the limbers had mired trying to cut across swampy ground, and had to be levered out to regain the road. It would take a while.

A scout returned. "There's a way, sir."

"Which way?"

"Below the woods, sir." The scout unfolded a paper to show Erich the rough map he'd drawn. "See, a cedar hedgerow goes around to a roadway the far side of the village. A windbreak, sir. Tall as a horse."

"Guarded, of course?"

"No outposts I could see, sir. They's formed up down there in the square, the hedgerow lies on their right flank with houses between. On the far side an open field goes down to a marsh. No enemy seen in the marsh, sir."

"What do you think, Sergeant?"

"They bin careless, Lieutenant. Not to guard the hedgerow." He tightened his saddle girth, an unspoken signal for action.

In training it had been repeated again and again. *Lead from the front...*

"Mount the troop, Sergeant Moos." His mouth was dry with terror. "Load carbines. Leave the lances, free the hands." He turned again to the scout. "You're sure? No outposts? We have to take outposts if—"

"Certain, sir, no outposts."

"Mount the troop," he said again to the sergeant. "We move fast. Follow on my lead, two columns in line." To the scout he said, "Report back to the Captain that we're going forward. Tell him, when we start the charge I want his rifles to divert Russian fire from the hedges, and when we outflank them, tell him to advance the company." He tightened Oberon's girth, then checked his pistol. His stomach was churning. *He might die today.* They had trained him for this *they had trained him for this they had...*

The troop thundered along the screen of thick cedars. Erich rode flattened to Oberon's neck below the level of the hedge.

Fear had vanished with action, his brain was focussed. His eye caught every branch that swayed on the breeze, every stone and clump of grass under Oberon's hooves. His ear was tuned to the hoof-beats behind him and to the faint shouts of the Russians shifting position, he heard the *crack* of many rifles, heard bullets rip through the hedge, saw a spent bullet tumble out from the hedge ahead of the horse. In moments the troop thundered around behind the village, Erich with pistol in hand, the troopers firing and reloading at the gallop. From the hill the German infantry laid down a punishing small-arms fire to keep the Russians pinned.

At a dead gallop they crashed into the village from the rear, seeking brown uniforms, firing point-plank into frightened faces, the horses breasting over any man dodging in their path. Erich emptied his pistol and drew his sabre, and coldly chose his human targets, swinging, chopping at forms too slow to dodge, bones crunching, blood spurting in the air, his brain in a cold rage to kill...

Russians dropped their weapons and flung up their hands.

The troopers milled in the square, rounding up prisoners.

It was suddenly done.

His blood was up. His first charge, his first real engagement. His first enemy prisoners. He was aware that the sergeant looked upon him with surprise and new respect in those hooded eyes. Flushed with exhilaration, they rode around the square as the Russians began to pick up their dead. Three of them stood silently in a circle gazing down, and Erich rode over to boot them onward. A Russian officer lay in a disjointed heap in the mud, his neck almost separated from the shoulders by a great gaping wound where the sabre had hacked at an angle down into his chest. Erich tasted bitter bile in his mouth. His first kill. *Face-to-face with the enemy*. And this, the bloody garbage left.

"My God," he whispered.

"Yes sir," said the sergeant beside him. "The lieutenant sure done him in."

Erich found his voice. "The poor *Arschloch* only wanted to surrender."

"That's the enemy sir."

"But if—"

"That's the enemy sir." Respectful tone, all condescension gone. "If the lieutenant never cut him down, maybe the bastards wouldn't of quit so easy."

He turned the stallion away as the prisoners bent to pick up their officer.

The sergeant turned beside him. "Two men hit, Johannsen and Bertsch. Flesh wounds. One horse down, the rider bust his ankle. No other casualties." He held out Erich's empty pistol. "The lieutenant dropped this, sir."

Momentary blank.

The sergeant grinned. "When he took out his sword, sir. Threw down his pistol. Empty."

"Thank you sergeant."

"Wouldn't want to lose it, sir." The reproach was gentle, proprietary. "Might cost a pile o' pocket money."

"Report ammunition expended, Sergeant."

"Yes sir." The salute was snappy.

He smiled inwardly. So he was now 'the lieutenant', not merely the contemptible 'sir'.

From the high ground the German infantry was advancing to spread out through the village. The medics drove down to take charge of the wounded. Precise, textbook. Had it been too easy? He hadn't seen any Russians escape from the village. Were they over there in the woods, regrouping for a counter attack? Where was their main force?

Another runner rode up to him in the square. "The captain orders the lieutenant to report, sir."

He followed the runner back to Company. The captain was bound to tear into him for an unauthorised charge. He tried to gather his argument.

The Russian officer dead in the dust burned inside his head.

* * *

CHAPTER 15

October - December 1914

Company HQ occupied a farmhouse a kilometre back from the village. A wagon stood hitched beside the barn, and as they rode across the yard Erich heard shrill squealing from the open barn door. Two soldiers came out carrying the bloody skinned carcass of a butchered pig and slung it into the wagon bed, then went back inside. Squealing still ripped the air.

Beside the large farmhouse Erich dismounted and tossed his reins to the runner.

"Fresh pork for dinner," the runner said.

Erich escaped into a huge kitchen. Warm aromas arrested him at the doorway; seared meat... *pork*... and soup bubbling on a wood range, and bread baking in the oven. Three cooks worked in the heat, barking like sergeants back and forth at each other. As Erich came in, they sprang to attention facing three directions, like mechanical toys run down.

"Officers through there, sir," said one, pointing to a door. "Hospital upstairs."

In the main room a clerk sat at a large table smashing at the keys of his typewriter. Several officers scribbled reports to be typed, and Captain Sonderheim was flipping files. "Excellent action," he said, waving Erich to the table. "Fill out your report."

Erich took up a blank report form.

Runners came in to report to the captain, who took their bits of paper and wrote his responses and sent them out again. "It looks quiet for now," he said to Erich. "You covered almost a hundred kilometres today. Excellent pace."

Erich paused over his paper. "Can we comb out the woods?"

"We take our orders from Battalion."

"But... the Russkis... They almost lined up to surrender."

"So you want to take prisoners."

"I want to win this war."

The captain threw back his head in a huge laugh. "*Herrgott*. These cavalry...!" Then he sobered. "Schellendorf, two Russian armies, one from the east, one from the south, are encircling the Eighth Army, the only German force defending all East Prussia. Now. Von Hindenburg has shifted the main elements of the Eighth to meet the Russians in the south. This morning Insterburg and Angerburg fell and we're in general retreat there. You have the picture?"

He felt the breath leave him. "Yes sir."

"You and I." He paused, holding Erich's eye. "You and I are part of a small force with the task to trick the Russians into believing that the First Reserve Regiment... *Us*... is the entire Eighth Army. Us alone. We cover the Insterburg Gap. We're short of cavalry. You boys will be strung fine. Understood?"

"Yes sir," he whispered. He didn't know if this heart-thumping was fear or excitement.

"Then rest your men tonight and we'll start in the morning. Report here, 0500 hours. We'll have our orders then."

*

When he got back to his troop, the infantry had dug in around the village. Ordnance and fresh supplies had come up, and the field guns had finally taken up the high ground. Dusk was falling. The breeze dropped, leaving the air close and hot and whining with clouds of midges.

A wagon shed had been commandeered for the horses. He rode inside, and Private Kramer ran to take the stallion's bridle. He slapped Oberon's neck. "I'll bed him down, sir."

"Where's Kropp? He can do that."

"That's fine, sir. He went back for the lieutenant's kit." He led the stallion to the picket line strung along the walls and tethered him at the end and began to strip off the gear. Erich made a quick inspection. The other horses had been rubbed dry and now stood in straw, ears slack, eyes half closed, noses deep in their grain bags.

"Where are the men, Kramer?"

"Down by the well in the village square, sir. The kitchen's caught up." He rubbed the stallion with fists of straw. "I'm on horse detail."

Erich found the rest of his troop lined up at the kitchen wagon, mess tins and mugs in hand. Erich joined at the rear of the line, seventeen men ahead of him, he could put a name to each face now. At the wagon a cook was ladling potatoes and cabbage and chunks of boiled pork out of a large stew pot into mess tins. A helper handed a half loaf of black bread to each man. Another helper poured hot coffee into tin mugs, and laced the coffee with schnapps.

One of the troopers snapped, "Officer present, turn out!"

The men shuffled, eyed Erich sideways, and stepped aside for him to move ahead.

"Does anyone have a spare mess tin?"

Silence among them. Then suddenly with childlike eagerness every trooper reached out toward Erich a forest of mess tins. Something caught in his throat as he turned them down.

The cook found a mess tin among the kitchen provisions.

They carried their rations to the shed among the munching horses. The men spread out between horses to sit with backs braced along the walls. Erich tossed a bale of straw to the shed doorway and sat in a freshening breeze to watch the last light fall below the western horizon. The air was cooler now. Looking south he could see flashes of lightning along the dark forest horizon.

Sergeant Moos came to join him. He set his mess tin and coffee mug on the ground and pulled over a bale. He sat down and took up his mess tin. "All set, sir?"

He nodded, vaguely numb. The Russian officer, bloody in the dust, pervaded his mind.

"Mail caught up, sir. Letter for the lieutenant." He pulled papers out of a tunic pocket.

From Heidelberg.

The sergeant began to attack his rations.

A letter from Britt. He ripped it open...

> *My dearest darling Erich, Gerdt now has his turn to go to war, I know not where. Papi tells us Lorraine, but does he really know? I suppose he does, he is in a position of great trust if no responsibility. He fights on the garrison map in the mess, and his ammunition is Drink. You were right, he is drinking every day too much. I think because Mutti is quite ill. I think he is quite worried, my poor dear Papi, though it is nothing new and has certainly been with us for many years. Mutti's illness, I mean. The news is that while the war in France is going well (so they say) the casualties are heavy and Dr. Kirschner tells me that they are in great need of volunteers at the hospital. My darling my darling husband husband <u>HUSBAND</u>, I have a request to make of you, but I will wait until a better moment, Papi is just home, wanting his supper at this late hour...*

Husband husband HUSBAND... He smiled and turned the page.

> *It is much later in the middle of the night, and I cannot sleep. Here is what I wanted to ask. Please write to Dr. Kirschner with permission to work as a volunteer at the hospital. It is only to roll bandages. Dr. Kirschner says that any kind of help is needed, and he will ensure that I am not to be a qualified nurse or doctor, but I will not be permitted to work without my husband's permission, please, please... Think how I would worry if my husband, a fighting soldier, were wounded and they had no bandages...*

Sergeant Moos, devouring his pork, was watching him. Erich tucked it away to finish later. "Letter from home."
"Your mama?" Friendly. Inquisitive. Barriers lowered.

"My wife."

"Ach. The lieutenant looks too young for having a wife." He broke a piece of bread and dabbed it in his tin, and chewed.

"Are you married, Sergeant?"

"The lieutenant seen it in my Soldbuch."

"Yes, so I did." He swallowed the last of his overcooked cabbage, cold now, and soggy. "Do you miss her? Your wife?"

"Nah. I get the urge, I just go find a milkmaid some'eres and stack her up in a hayloft."

He hoped he didn't blush. He hadn't meant it quite that way. He finished his supper in this new comradeship and, mimicking the sergeant, wiped the mess tin clean with bread. He did not think about tomorrow. "That was good work today," he said. "Tell the men for me."

"That was easy work today, sir." He gulped down a last crust of bread. "It'll come harder when we hit the real war. I seen it in the Crimea." He pulled out his pipe and lit it on a long match, and puffed smoke into the quiet air.

In the tranquillity of the horses and men resting around him Erich tried to think of Britt. Her letter crackled in his tunic pocket, bringing her spirit so near to his heart that he could usually conjure up the warm, damp, horse-sweat scent of her. But today he'd killed a man. Swung full force down with his sabre and cleaved deep into the chest, instant death, collapsed to the ground like a wet string. The image filled his head, the startled eyes, the twisted mouth, the fling of blood, the troop galloping on a few more paces before hauling up.

On his knee by the light of a guttering candle he opened his field notebook to start a letter to Britt. *All is going well, I am getting to know the men better. I led a successful charge on the Russians today. My sergeant expresses a hint of respect. The stars in the evening sky would make you weep with the beauty. I shall write a letter for your doctor...*

He did not mention killing a man today.

He did not think about tomorrow.

*

The land echoed with explosions somewhere eastward. Erich was not concerned with battle positions, his job was to hunt out Russian scouts slipping through the thin German defence lines.

Hunt them. Stop them. Wound them when he could, and send them back alive to give false reports on German positions. He lost men, one killed here, another wounded there. Carried out his casualties, dead and alive alike. He had no fear of death as long as there were no faces. As men fell they were replaced. As officers fell, their troopers were shifted to other squads. As other officers fell his own troop grew. He did not ask the names of the new men joining him. He did not inspect dead bodies. He told his men to remove them, told his sergeant to list the names.

None of it was difficult for him if his own men had no names and the enemy had no faces. He had not checked a Soldbuch since he'd got off the train in August.

Day by day the Germans gave ground to the Russians. The squad rode as long as the daylight lasted, reporting by night to Battalion's next mobile bivouac a few kilometres to the rear. Supper with the men at the wagon. Briefing with the officers. Sleeping the sleep of the dead in a half-tent under the stars. Bathed in sweat in the heat of the summer night, swathed by clouds of midges, face and hands pockmarked with midge bites, worse than war, inescapable. Oberon lost condition. His gleaming coat grew dull and dry. All his ribs showed through. Erich sent him to Division at Feste Boyen for a rest, assigning Kropp to care for him, and rode out on a remount mare that was fat, sound and responsive. Erich too lost condition. He lived in weariness and had to shake out his brain while on patrol, to watch, to react... To survive.

Hunt the enemy, hit the enemy, dodge the enemy. Stay alive.

Then at the end of the month came reports of a great German victory at a battle near Tannenberg.

*

On the sixth day of September the heat broke. Erich had breakfast at the wagon with the men, veterans now. Not much chatter among them. Eeyes stared away to the distance. The cool morning air seemed to have grounded the midges. For the first time in a month the men drank their coffee in comfort.

A runner came out from Battalion. "All officers to report to Regiment, sir."

At Regiment they gathered around a kitchen table with the strategy map spread open. It showed all of East Prussia, and the manoeuvres marked in different coloured pencils where in four days the German Eighth Army had surrounded and destroyed the Russian Second Army. "We've had twelve-thousand casualties," said the colonel. "Dreadful cost. But we took a hundred thousand prisoners and drove the remnants back into Poland. The Russian Second Army is wiped out. Their general has shot himself."

The officers crowded around the table to study the coloured arrows on the map.

"And now," the colonel said, "we turn to face the Russian First Army." He stabbed the map with a forefinger and traced a northwest arc cutting East Prussia almost in half. "There's the front line. Today I received word that we've been given two new corps from the Belgian Front, which will hold the ground in this sector. Hindenberg will launch a full-scale two-pronged attack from south of the Masurian Lakes, roll up the enemy's left flank, cut them off from their lines of communication, and destroy the First Army as he did the Second." His gaze travelled around the circle of officers. "Our objective now is to hold. We are a fulcrum, gentlemen. Kill them, take prisoners, capture guns, and hold this damn position."

Erich's troop rode now as part of the squadron, across a vast terrain dotted with large farms and small villages, of meadows and brush and woodlands and running brooks and standing marshes. No longer dodging, when they encountered a Russian formation they would bear down at the gallop with the whine of bullets from every direction, crash into the enemy line, shoot into Russian faces, and scatter them for infantry to mop up prisoners. Then in the early darkness they regrouped to tend the horses, rubbing them down, cleaning hooves amid contented munching in nose-bags of grain. When the field kitchen finally caught up, the men gathered, eating out of mess-tins. In the deep quietude, being still alive, Erich called roll, and counted the casualties...

That was always the miracle, being still alive...

Every hour more infantry formations marched from the railhead to fill the gaps. More casualties fell every hour as they pressed the Russians back. Shells exploded among them in great eruptions of earth and rock and broken trees. Smoke rose before them as the Russians burned everything. They called it scorched-earth, a strategy from the days of Napoleon at Moscow, *if you cannot hold it, burn it.* The roads became cluttered with wrecked equipment, dead horses, broken wagons, abandoned guns, bodies in brown uniforms and others in grey, left together to bloat in the sun until the guns had moved on. The victor had to bury them.

They were only supposed to hold the position, not drive the enemy back, but when the Russians began to collapse, Division sent down the order to push the buggers right back into Poland.

*

The war had come through this village twice in the past month. It was the same village. From the same stand of woods on the long downslope, Erich saw smoke spewing out from the blacksmith shed in flames. Russians were somewhere down there.

In the woods he turned to Sergeant Moos. "We'll take the village, Sergeant. Send a runner back to bring up the infantry."

A scout came in. "There's a squad of Cossacks in the village, sir. They're burning everything. They look drunk, sir, they're shooting at the villagers."

"Where are their outposts?"

"No outposts sir."

"Order the charge, Sergeant Moos."

As if in a recurring dream they thundered down behind the cedars. Erich rode with a coldness that had settled into his brain over the months at war. Men had died next to him, yet he had driven through. Never touched. Never would be touched. He could hear rifles firing over there, and he thought, yes you bloody drunken bastards, empty your weapons. He'd never met a Cossack but God, he hated Cossacks. Wild beasts on horseback...

The troop thundered around and burst into the village, firing weapons, reloading at the gallop. In the square the Cossacks in black blouses turned to meet them. Small horses seemed suddenly riderless, but the riders had slipped sideways out of the saddle to the far side, firing under the animal's neck point-blank at the troop. The forces met midway in the square. A pistol was useless, Erich could find no target. Then as a Russian pony dodged past him his mare jolted as if she'd hit a wall, and Erich struck the ground, dazed by an impact he hadn't felt. In the same moment he heard rifle fire rattle down from the top of the hill where the German infantry was coming up. He tried to scramble to his feet, but fell back.

The square went abruptly quiet. He found himself lying on the ground. Half of his men had been hit, most of the horses were down. His mare had fallen and now struggled to rise on three legs, her right foreleg dangling from the knee by a ribbon of tendon. Blood pumped out of the stump...

Oh God oh God...

In charging past, a Cossack sabre had slashed through the joint of her knee.

He aimed the Luger for that spot below the mare' ear and he pressed the trigger, and she hobbled a few steps before sinking to the ground. She rolled on her side and lay slowly kicking one hind leg in the air.

An old man bent over him. "May I help your honour? Praise God you saved us." He pulled Erich by the arm to help him up.

Pain exploded in his arm and down his side, and the day went dark.

He woke in waves of pain. Somebody was lifting him into a hammock of some sort. A man at his head and another at his feet heaved him off the ground, and he said, "Ah no, whoa!" but they carried him gently and set him down somewhere else. He became aware of flames crackling around the square, and the smell of smoke. He was lying under a tree among a row of wounded men. He sat up. The pain struck, became focussed, manageable. His left sleeve was torn and bloody at the shoulder.

"You caught a bullet, sir." An orderly bent over him. "Wait for the doctor."

The square was littered with dead horses and dead soldiers in field-grey and dead civilians. Even a bloody baby over there by the well... *neatly cleaved in half... God...!* Survivors stumbled about searching in the carnage. But nowhere did he see the black blouse of a Cossack, living or dead.

Later in the *Lazarett* he heard that the Cossacks had ridden into the village that morning only minutes before Erich's troop. They'd fired off their guns and swung curved blades at villagers wherever they found them. Everything that moved, men, women, children, dogs, pigs. Started tossing torches into buildings. Fired their weapons in the air, danced their ponies around the square...

Not one Cossack body had been left behind.

*

"A flesh wound," said the doctor. He ripped the left sleeve from Erich's tunic and beckoned to a medical orderly. "Clean and dress this." He laid a hand on Erich's right shoulder. "We'll take out the bullet when I have time." He patted encouragement and turned to a trooper with a gut wound. Erich had seen gut wounds before, intestines oozing out through ripped cloth. He thought the man would die.

In the next hour they tore off his tunic and scrubbed his bloody shoulder and laid him on a table. He looked up through the roar of pain. The doctor said, smiling, "Sorry, this is minor, we have to save on the chloroform for serious cases." He poured alcohol into the wound. Pain engulfed him. He felt nothing else when the doctor tugged at the shoulder. A moment later the doctor straightened, smiling, and held up an instrument clasping a bit of ragged lead. "Saved your arm," he said. "A ricochet. It was spent before it hit you."

Well, Erich mused through the fog of torture, if that bullet had been spent... he would hate to take a full blast.

He slept.

*

He was shipped to Feste Boyen, pivot for German forces at the mid-point of the Masurian Lakes. Flanked by the lakes and dense forest, during the August invasion the immense fortress had been surrounded and assailed by everything the Russians could throw at it, but never was breached. Feste Boyen was headquarters for the Eighth Cavalry Division, and the central supply depot for the German armed forces all along the eastern front.

Erich reported to the garrison colonel. His arm was in a sling applied merely to remind him not to use it.

"What's the matter with you?" the colonel asked.

"Just a flesh wound, sir. Not allowed to ride."

"Report to the Intendant. They can use a pencil-pusher over there."

In the next eight weeks he caught a glimpse into the world of logistics and supply, stacks of this and tons of that, loaded on wagons and shipped up the road to the fighting sectors. Assigned to keep ledgers, he saw battles on the planning map before they ever happened, and the waste they left behind.

Then, as winter rolled over the land, the divisional medical officer shipped him back to his troop, a blooded veteran worthy at last, Erich mused, of leading men.

*

He woke cold that morning. December thirtieth. His birthday. *Happy birthday, Erich...*

A sentry's boot crunched near his head. He opened his eyes to the half-light of a late dawn and listened to the silence while the cold penetrated slowly into his bones. At eye level the world was white under a fresh fall of snow.

Six months ago the Kaiser had promised the war would be over by Christmas. The Russians had apparently not heard about that.

Good morning, Britt...

He crawled out from under the supply wagon and shook snow from his half-tent. Around him the trees stood black against a white sparkle of first sun. The winter forest, he mused, made his troopers a clear target in a flat white shooting gallery.

Almost fifty horses dozed along the picket line, heads down, snow dusting their manes and their canvas-blanketed backs. The sentry paced along the line, slapping a neck here, checking a halter there. Erich appreciated his sensitivity. Not many troopers kept up their love for horses. After the first serious battle you discarded all feelings for the horse in favour of survival.

First battle... second battle... tenth battle... They all blurred together now. Another month of constant movement, seek out the enemy, blasts of fire, return fire, send a runner back to report to the line, engage the enemy until the infantry came up. Then out again to scout the river, use the terrain, search out the enemy, report back. Two men down last week, careless chitchat when they should have paid attention. *Bam-bam,* fell to the ground before they knew the Russkies were there.

The sentry paced to the end where Oberon stood. He reached a hand to the stallion. The black head jerked sideways flinging off snow. Teeth flashed, and the trooper leaped nimbly out of the way. In the deep silence of the forest Erich heard him mutter, "You fuckin' old shit, if it weren't for the lieutenant I'd put a bullet in your brain."

Around the bivouac, bodies rose like ghosts in their half-tents, stretching and shrugging off snow in all directions. None of them had shaved for days. Erich's face was sand-paper. They would not even wash today, never mind shave, unless it was by using snow for water. They all smelled like pigs.

The men grumbled to each other and gathered up their mess tins for breakfast.

They rode out within the hour, the troop heading southward, the two wagons turning west to Battalion to restock. At sunset they would meet at their regular every-other-day rendezvous in a copse of trees five kilometres east of Goldap. It had become routine: northeast corner one night, southwest the next. This way they had a hot meal at least once a day. In their saddle bags they carried black bread and cold sausage. Their drinking water lay white on the ground. The horses had grain this morning, would get an hour grazing at noon wherever they could find grass, and grain again tonight. At the end of the week the troop would take a day's rest. A hard, simple life. The sector between Stallupönen and Goldap was Erich's to scout. Standing order, "Search and destroy." He never knew where pockets of enemy might be found, it was still fluid. Back and forth, back and forth. The latest he'd heard, the Germans were retreating out of Bzura again. Any day now the front might crash back into Prussian land.

He rode at the head of the column upon fresh snow, winding silently among black skeleton trees and solid evergreens. The two point riders paced them ahead, keeping just in sight, left and right. The only sounds were the creak of saddle leathers and the chink of bits. The troop rode in single file a horse-length apart, rifles slung ready on their shoulders. To the northeast the first rifle fire of the day started up, a crackling in the winter air, north to south, like strings of firecrackers. Artillery boomed a long way off, perhaps twenty kilometres north. The usual morning chorus.

Deliberately he kept among the trees. The men followed silently. In single file it was hard for them to chat; and that was Erich's purpose. Forty-six riders in his troop stretched out in silent single file. Their only objective was to seek out the last tags of the retreated enemy, attack and destroy, or take prisoners. Battalion preferred no prisoners.

Up ahead the left point rider, Braun, had halted, dark against the white expanse. Erich raised his arm, and Sergeant Moos raised his arm, and back along the single file each man raised his arm; and within a few seconds the last rider had halted, a half kilometre behind. Perfect coordination.

Braun backed his horse. Erich analysed it as it happened: he backed the horse to mask the movement, or not to expose his broad side... *something ahead*... Then turned and came down at a gallop, flinging up white clods from the knee-deep snow. He pulled to a sliding halt. "Riders ahead, sir."

"Russians?"

"Cossacks, sir. Down on the far bank watering the horses."

Cossacks.

God, he hated Cossacks.

Ponies the size of a large dog, nimble as a rabbit. At a gallop a Cossack swung sideways on his saddle using his horse as a shield and fired from under the horse' neck and, coming to grips, aimed at the enemy horse's legs with that curved cutlass. It was like fighting a swarm of hornets, nothing to hit, no target to shoot at, bloodthirsty as vampires, totally without fear.

But he couldn't let enemy scouts gather even a suspicion of how the Germans were building up and reforming in the rear.

"How many?"

"Seventeen, one officer."

The image flicked through Erich's head, a depression on the far riverbank below a wall of rock, a stretch of forest beyond. This was his terrain, he knew every rock and tree and hillock by now. "What was the range from your position?"

"Maybe seventy metres."

"Sergeant, bring up the troop."

The sergeant waved a hand. The men galloped in and slotted into a circle around Erich. He felt the flush of pride in them, discipline from drill, knowing exactly what to do, how to do it.

"Cossacks," he announced.

They bunched in closer and fingered their rifle slings.

"We leave the horses here," he said in the quiet air. "We advance on foot, rifles and ammunition pouches only, ambush them from the crest of the slope. Not one is to get out."

The distant artillery had started rumbling again. It would cover their noise, if they made any noise in the snow.

"Remember," he told them. "Cossacks don't dismount. Drop the horses and we have them. The first thing a horse moves is the head, so aim for the heart. Sergeant, assign your horse holders."

They dismounted into the snow and shrugged out of their packs and set them on the ground. He kept his sword, didn't know if he might need it, didn't trust the devils not to charge into the barrage. He ran forward on foot with the men hard behind him, snow slippery under his boots. He drew his Luger, although at seventy metres he had no thought of using it. Toward the brow of the slope they bent to a crouch, and finally dropped prone to crawl up the last few metres. The wet snow penetrated almost at once through knees and elbows and then to his belly and chest.

Cossacks. Down there, chatting in their strange language. And laughing. Dark beards. Sun-slitted eyes under fleece hats. The long-skirted *cherkessa* coats and the cartridge clips on their chests branded them instantly as the wild men of the Ukrainian steppe. They sat their saddles in a half-moon on the river bank while the horses bent their heads to the water.

Their guns remained sheathed on the saddles. Careless black targets in a white shooting gallery. *Unforgivable arrogance.*

Erich searched the river bank and trees beyond, and the quiet dark river within view. Nothing else moved. They were at least a mile inside the German line. Damned Cossacks. Laughing and chatting deep in enemy territory as if they owned the world.

Erich had never ordered the deliberate slaughter of horses. He waited for a last click as his troopers cocked their rifles. He held his breath.

A Cossack laughed, sharp in the clear air.

Then... in a low voice... Erich said...

"Fire."

The air exploded in a massed barrage along the crest of the slope. The horses below reared and leaped and fell back in the water. Through the mêlée riders kicked free of falling horses and scrambled for their weapons. He heard his own nerve-raw voice shouting, "Fire fire fire!"

They fired until nothing moved. He signalled to wait. The cold seeped into his belly. Nothing moved. He waited long minutes. In the distant north and south the guns stuttered their morning chorus. Finally when nothing had moved he stood up and beckoned to the holders to bring up the horses. They mounted and rode down to the riverbank.

Bodies lay in clumps and piles in the snow and in black water, bizarre tangles of arms and legs splashed in blood, horses twisted with humans, the men's faces swarthy after a lifetime of sun, abruptly immobile, the half-open eyes fixed on eternity.

"Sergeant, put ropes on the carcasses, pull them out of the water so the river isn't poisoned, search pockets and saddles for papers. Find the officer and strip his insignia."

"Does the lieutenant want them buried?"

"With what, Sergeant? Bayonets?"

An hour later the troopers finished the terrible task. Leaving bodies where they piled them on the bank, they handed up insignia and papers to the sergeant, who stuffed them into his ammunition pouch. Then they rode away to pick up their packs left in the snow. Nobody looked back.

Reprisal complete, honour served. The wolves in the forest would eat well this winter.

Happy birthday.

* * *

CHAPTER 16

January to Easter 1915

Britt wrote every Sunday, her only free day, she said. The letters came on Thursdays. She never had news. Her letter of the next week almost echoed her letter of the last...

> *My darling darling darling, I miss you so. I long for you mostly at night, for we are very busy during the day when I have no time to dream. Mutti is as well as can be. Papi is seldom at home. I am kept busy at the hospital and at night I am always much too tired, but I lie every night awake dreaming of you. The menservants were called to their reserve units, although some of them are able to work for us until they are actually called for the fighting. The farmers are exempt. We are lucky having the farms, for food grows short in the market as winter goes on. They say most of the harvest this year went to the army...*

He yearned to go home. At night he dreamed he lay beside the damp velvet heat of her in their opulent bed, her eyes laughing, her lips kissing him, her tongue caressing him, her hands bold along his body... *God!* She kept him awake half the night in this cold land, wrapped in his half-tent in yet another Prussian farmer's barn.

They lived like animals these days. Attack. Retreat. Back and forth across the Angerapp River, one week holding the west bank, the next week taking back the east bank. Horses fell horribly, men rode out doubled up on animals scarcely strong enough to bear one rider. They carried out the wounded, but he sometimes had to leave the dead behind. Then the following week, back over the same ground, the Russians once again in retreat. Now he could pick up his dead in wagons bouncing over frozen ground, only to retreat again under a new curtain of enemy artillery. They could not break through. Poland was only a ride away, and they could not break through...

> M*y dear brother*, (Gerdt wrote) *I send Greetings from the Real War* ~
> *Thank you for your letters. How pleasant it must be to sit at peace with your comrades after a day galloping in the field. Here we lie night after day in these glorious underground chalk 'apartments' in the Second Line, surrounded by all ranks, entertained by the unceasing music of artillery drum rolls, and occasionally visited without invitation by our neighbours from the opposite side who seem excessively interested in procuring our valuable real estate of broken trees, artillery holes and mud. Yesterday we had two such visits, one before dawn following an artillery bombardment which announced the impending social call, and another visit totally unannounced in early afternoon in the middle of a heavy sleet storm. Our defences are such that we expelled the visitors immediately, but what excitement and havoc, and with what casualties! You cannot picture it until you see it in the flesh, how the enemy run straight into our machine gun fire. If we seek relief from living inside this kettle-drum, we need only volunteer for a tour as Duty Officer. In any case we are assigned such*

duty at least once a week, which means that for 24 hours we supervise discipline in the rear ~ twenty-four blessed hours out of range of enemy artillery. The French have an establishment in the local village called an 'Estaminet', usually known in German as 'Brothel', but cleverly disguised as a bistro, serving bad food for astonishing prices, and two or three labels of wine ~ red, white, and muddy (hm!). Here we may also indulge in delousing, a warm bath and, for a few Pfennig more, a pretty (hm-hm!) young French maid to pour the rinse water, etcetera.

Erich, for Easter I plan to take leave. What a fine plan if you could do the same...

*

The trains had never been so slow. He stared out the window at the passing land, white giving way to new green, as if in a few hours the train had carried him from winter into spring. Between Danzig and Berlin the third-class carriage was jammed with soldiers going on leave, civilians with their bundles, and babies crying, children whining, their mothers staring into space...

At Berlin he had to change trains. Between Berlin and Karlsruhe he stood the whole way, eyes closed in a semi-stupor, twelve hours jostled into a cramped corner by bodies coming in and others going out. At Karlsruhe he had to change trains again, but it was the middle of the night and the next train to Mannheim didn't come through until 0622. He had no money for a hotel or even for a cup of coffee at the kiosk. He found a bench where he collapsed and slept hard, his rucksack for a pillow. The stationmaster shook him awake in time for his next train.

On the last short leg from Mannheim he grabbed a vacated spot and sat with forehead braced to the window as the familiar open valley slipped past, cattle in the fields, cherry trees in first bloom on the easy hills, teams of giant Belgian horses ploughing up the black earth. Yet he hardly saw any of it for the stronger image of Britt mirrored in the window, waiting for him, eyes full of sparkle and mischief, perhaps dressed in boy's riding gear to shock the locals...

She was not there.

He walked alone from the Karlstor station across the grass and up the cobbled lane. The air was crisp, the sun pallid behind a thin veil of cloud. He stopped at the old oak to look down at the ragged rooftops and windows of the town, and the river curving black below. He stood, weary to the bone, basking in the chill spring air.

"Erich!"

He turned to see her burst through the gate above, one arm high in the air shrugging into a coat, its long skirts flapping about her riding boots as she ran toward him. He set down his rucksack. Still pulling the coat about her she ran at him, and he opened his arms. She struck him in full stride driving him half a step back, and he closed his arms about her. "You didn't meet me at the train."

"You didn't tell me which train!"

"I didn't know which train!"

They laughed.

He kissed her at last, deep and hot and urgent. He took up his rucksack, and she leaned into him under his arm and gripped him about his waist as they walked melded up the lane.

"How long are you home?"

"Two days."

"Is that all?" Tone of outrage.

"This is the army, my darling."

Her arm tightened about him.

They slipped into the house. One of the maids met them in the hall, but Britt put a finger to her lips, *Shhh*, and the girl smiled and turned back to the kitchen. Britt dragged him by the elbow up the stairs. "Papi's not at home, Mutti's in the solarium, we have time..."

In their bridal bedroom they ripped off their clothes and burrowed into the huge four poster bed and disappeared into the moment.

*

The baroness lay on a chaise bundled up to her chin in quilts, although the solarium temperature was tropical. Water tinkled in the fountain beside her
, and little brown sparrows chirped and hopped around the pond.

"Ah, my handsome son." She held her arms open to him.

He bent to embrace her, and lowered her gently back.

"You look thin," she said. "Have you eaten?"

"Not yet today."

"Ah, you must take better care of yourself. I'll call Katja to bring sandwiches." She rang a little hand bell on the table beside her. Her open book lay there, face down. A coffee carafe sat on a metal stand over a guttering candle that kept it warm.

This was where she lived, this spacious corner of the house, flowers growing all around, sparrows in restless little flocks drinking from the fountain, pecking at seeds scattered for them, darting back and forth in spurts of joy.

Dying, she surrounded herself with life.

"Has Gerdt come too?" Erich asked.

"He was here last week," Britt said. "He had to go back, to allow the married officers home for Easter."

"Ah. I'm sorry."

"I hate the army," she murmured. "War. So much killing. The absurdity of men."

The baron came to the doorway, dressed in his ceremonial blues, brisk and impatient. "Hello hello," he said to Erich, "are you coming? You said you'd come with me to the mess."

He couldn't remember saying that. He glanced at Britt.

She shrugged submission.

They drove down in the Benz, the baron at the wheel. "My driver was called up last month. I've learned to handle this thing myself." He happily clashed the gears with each shift. "Quicker than a brace of horses, I must say, but when you're blind drunk it doesn't carry you home again."

Erich chuckled. "How do we get home, then?"

The baron roared with laughter.

The officers' bar was empty when they came in. Nothing had changed since that day the adjutant had raised a toast to Erich and Gerdt, *"Well, gentlemen, last act of freedom..."* The same banners hung on the wall, the same warm mahogany, the same crystal and brass fixtures, the same barman. Nothing ever changed in the army.

"Fill us up, Horst," thundered the baron. "My tab!"

Horst drew two steins of lager and placed them into their hands.

"You know my best son here?" the baron challenged Horst.

"Yes sir, Lieutenant von Schellendorf. Still a member in the mess."

"Led a cavalry charge, saved a village in East Prussia, did you know?"

"Yes sir, you gave us the news earlier, just after Christmas I believe." He winked at Erich.

The baron raised his stein. "Led a charge, Horst! Saved a village! Was wounded! Probably get a medal for it, if I have anything to say!" He drank deeply, froth edging his grey moustache. "My other son sits on his arse in a trench looking at the enemy across a bloody cow pasture!" He shook his head and emptied the stein in a series of long gulps, then held it out for a refill. "Drink up!" he commanded Erich.

*

Easter Sunday morning he woke with a throbbing hangover, and he lay very still to keep it quiet. Couldn't open his eyes to the light. Couldn't remember coming to bed last night. He'd never in his life drunk that much, glass for glass keeping up with the baron. Started with lager, went to schnapps... and he vaguely remembered going on to cognac. How did the old man do it? Day after day after day...?

"Ummm..." Britt stirred beside him, then heaved upright to sit looking down at him. Usually she woke gradually, as if she had to think about it.

"Good morning." His own voice bounced pain inside his head.

"Good morning."

"Sorry about last night."

She bent down to kiss his nose. "You talk in your sleep."

"What did I say?"

"Talked about horses and Cossacks. And you said, 'No! No! No!' In English. Many times over, No...! No...! No...! Like that."

"In English!"

She snuggled down beside him. "You often speak English in your sleep."

Three years in Germany, and still he spoke English in his sleep? Three years while the world had turned upside down from where it should be, when every king was a cousin of every other king and used to attend each other's weddings and coronations and funerals... now fighting a war to the death against each other in a world gone mad...

"Kiss me," she said. "Love me again. Before we have to go down to breakfast."

*

They went with the baron to church and came out toward twelve, anticipating the Easter feast of roast lamb from their own farm, quartered and hung for three weeks, the baron said.

The servants had set up a dining table out in the solarium. Sparrows fluttered about them and sunshine slanted through the glass roof as they sat down to the meal, the baroness in her chair to the baron's right side with Erich next to her and Britt opposite him where he could smile into her eyes. Gerdt's chair stood ceremoniously empty.

The baroness said grace in a small firm voice, "God bless this food, this house, this family and our precious sons away at war. God bless our fighting soldiers and bring them swift victory, in Jesus' name..."

Afterward as they stood up from the table the baron collared Erich. "Need your help."

"The children want to go riding," the baroness protested. "They have so little time."

"Only take a minute!"

In the gun room the baron pointed the way to his desk where several great ledger books were piled one upon the other. "Have a look. Gerdt tells me you're a genius with numbers." He placed a ledger on the large ink blotter, then waved Erich to the chair, and opened the book.

Standing, Erich ran his eye across ten columns of figures. "What am I looking for?"

"We have deficits. Never in two hundred years have we had deficits."

"These figures are correct."

"Sit down, sit down! How can you say the figures are correct if you don't look at them?"

"I looked at them." He sat down, uncomfortable in the baron's sacred chair. He turned back two pages to February and scanned each column. Correct... correct... "Perhaps it's just the war."

From behind the chair the baron pressed his hands down on Erich's shoulders. "A year ago we had three hundred thousand marks in this account alone. Today..." He flipped forward again to March, "You see we're in arrears four thousand eight hundred fifty-two marks and change. We keep an account for each farm. The other farms have similar arrears, this one is the worst."

"Who keeps these books?"

"Why, I do myself."

"Perhaps if your accountant examines—"

"I pay my accountant when I see the need. Show me where it started to go wrong. Then I'll call in the accountant."

Erich turned back pages, glancing at each bottom line. Each page showed a loss. September last year he came upon the first monthly deficit. He scanned the figures, correct... correct... *Damn!* He was losing his time to ride with Britt. She'd called the garrison earlier, they would have brought up the horses by now.

He began to check the remarks column... *17 September... turnips, 5016 kilos... Baden Intendant... debit column... M 1153.68...* no cheque number recorded, was it by cash?

"Why," he asked the baron who leaned over his shoulder breathing warm stale cognac on him, "would you buy from the government five thousand kilos of turnips at 23 pfennig a kilo?"

"No no, we don't *buy* turnips, we sell..." He straightened abruptly.

Erich looked up at a face gone bright red. Realisation struck them both in the same moment. He laughed and came to his feet and clapped the baron on both shoulders. "Call the accountant, sir. I'm taking my wife out to ride."

*

They rode in a perfect spring afternoon, the sun warm, the air cool, the pathways crowded. People dressed in their Easter finery stepped aside as the horses passed, and touched fingers to their foreheads as if in salute. Erich thought the salute was for Britt the baron's daughter, but Britt said it was for her officer husband in his walking-out cavalry blues. They smiled and saluted back, and rode upward. This was his world, he thought in wonder. Common people looked up to him as uncommon. He carried the Kaiser's commission, he wore the insignia of a fashionable regiment, he was married to the most beautiful princess in the world...

"It's been almost nine months since you were home," Britt said. "I counted every day."

"It's the army, darling."

"Don't blame the army. Gerdt's been home three times."

"It's a different sort of war in Poland. We never stop. We sleep under the trees, we—"

"Yes, yes, you told me."

He glanced at her riding beside him, a prim little frown crowding her brow. He couldn't admit to her that he hadn't thought to apply for leave. Had watched men come and go on leave, had yearned to see her, yet hadn't thought about leave. "Well," he said, "They gave me a week, most of it spent on the train."

"Then ask for more. You could go to the garrison adjutant and request an extension. Gerdt did that after Christmas, he was home until New Year."

"He doesn't have so far to travel, darling."

"Oh, I don't want to talk about it." She spurred her horse into a sudden gallop away across the open hillside. He followed, keeping pace.

After a while they dropped to a walk once more side by side, the horses relaxed. Again the adjutant had sent up his grey Hungarian gelding, the most comfortable horse Erich had ever ridden, soft, responsive, yet eager to move. Britt would not like this peaceful horse.

"Maybe," he said to her, "I could rent a little house in Königsberg."

"Why?"

"I could get there from Angerap in hours."

"Oh!" She laughed harshly. "So that two or three times a year *I* could ride three days on the trains to meet you on your leave?"

He laughed too, gently. "No," he ventured, "so you could make your own home and live with your husband the way any regular army wife lives with her husband."

She turned astonished eyes upon him. "*I* should live in Königsberg?"

"Why yes, why not?"

"I... I... What in the world would I do in Königsberg? I don't know anybody in Königsberg! And then you'd be transferred and we would have to start again in the new posting, and on and on to the end of time! No thank you."

Her reaction was so absolute, so *instant*.

"I thought..." He didn't know how to say it. "I thought you wanted us to be together."

"Well of course I do. Oh Erich, I die every night without you. But *Königsberg*...!" As if that were explanation enough. "You could request a closer posting. Perhaps right here in the garrison—"

"No darling. I go where they send me—"

"You don't understand anything."

They were approaching their special tree in its little pocket of infinity. She turned off the pathway and got down from her horse. He followed and tied the horses to the nearby tree that had grown a low branch just especially for them to tie their horses. A childish notion, he mused. As if providence were on their side.

The town lay below, red roofs bright in the sun.

"What don't I understand?" he asked.

She folded down to sit braced against the trunk and patted the ground beside her.

The ground was still damp. It chilled his seat. Probably chilled hers too. He could match her stoicism any time.

She leaned shoulder to shoulder against him. "I'm needed here. It's the first time I've been needed in my life anywhere. Mutti is worse and worse, she can't even get out of bed without my help—"

"The maidservants could—"

"But Erich, she's dying. Should she die alone?"

"She has her husband." A vague, newly growing despair drifted in.

"Papi is never there. He runs away to the mess, he's terrified of her dying. I'm much calmer about it, I see people at the hospital every day dying—"

"You said you only roll bandages—"

"Oh Erich, I do everything, I hold hands with men after a leg is amputated, for God's sake, I do everything! I carry bedpans, I cut off bloody bandages, I clean pus from wounds, I bring their dinner trays and help them to eat, I change their beds, I wash their filthy sheets. I do it all, Erich! The baron's daughter, who never raised a finger to help anyone, can you believe it? For the first time useful!"

He put an arm about her and drew her to his chest.

She curled in, her hair fragrant under his chin. "I love you above all, Erich," she whispered. "I miss you so. This stupid war. When it's over the regiment will come home again and we'll be back to normal. It can't last much longer."

But it could, he reflected, staring down at the peaceful town.

*

They returned early to the house. It seemed selfish to spend too much time away, leaving the baroness alone. But when they came out to the solarium she was not alone, they found a visitor sitting with her, a tall young man of their own generation with wavy blond hair and generous side-whiskers and a cotton jacket loose over a large, square frame. He rose to meet them when they came through the door. Britt ran forward, and he opened his arms and folded her into a giant hug. "Hallo my darling, this is the husband?"

"This is my Erich."

They made introductions, Lieutenant Erich Bronsart von Schellendorf, Herr Doctor Peter Kirschner. Shook hands. Erich was surprised by the humour shining from the doctor's eyes. A doctor ought to be remote, serious. And older. This fellow didn't look old enough to be a doctor.

They pulled chairs into a circle around the baroness and settled down. The maid came to set a fresh pot of coffee over the everlasting candle.

"My patient is in fine condition this afternoon," said the doctor to the unspoken question. "It was a good day for her."

"How did you spend your Easter morning?" the baroness asked him.

He laughed. "At the hospital, how else?"

"Well at Christmas you must join us for dinner. You and your wife."

He smiled. "I'm sure she'll be pleased."

They gazed at the sparrows playing about the fountain.

"This is a lovely place," the doctor said to the baroness. "I never come to examine you, you know, I come only to watch the sparrows." He leaned back in his garden chair, gazing upward. "Where do they fly in?"

"Oh, there's an opening somewhere. They build nests up in the rafters, you can see little brown bundles of sticks, like a hornet's nest, with a door."

They all sat searching the metal rafters for brown bundles of sticks.

Then Doctor Kirschner said to Erich, "This lovely woman, your wife, is a marvel at the hospital."

"Truly?"

"She came to us a little girl seeking praise and some useful little thing to fill her time, and now, only a few months later? Praise is unnecessary, get out of my way she says, out of my way!"

Erich smiled. He felt strangely light, floating in a peaceful space.

"She's grown from *enfante terrible* into an amazing young woman."

"You can thank Erich for that," said the baroness. "They're so in love."

"Well honestly," the doctor retorted, "they married some considerable time before she came to us, she had her chance with him. It was surely the hospital."

"They talk about us," Britt laughed to Erich, "as if we're not here."

Erich nodded, eyes closed, smiling, floating. The quietude and the heat in the solarium were putting him to sleep. His vague notion of protecting her from the horrors of the hospital faded. She was an adult, a woman.

Tomorrow morning he had to start back.

* * *

CHAPTER 17

May to September 1915

In May the Germans opened advances all along the Russian front from Memel on the Baltic to the Carpathian Mountains. The Eighth Army was spread thin in the north, while the Eleventh Army in the south massed alongside the Austrians. In field briefings Erich saw on the situation maps where the great forces lay, but for himself he felt like an ant in an anthill, carried along with an ant's view of the world. He had his orders, he pursued his objectives. The horses were on point. They were supposed to break the enemy lines for the infantry, that was the goal, it was what they had been trained to do, but the ride was rough and casualties were high.

As they pushed eastward the land grew wilder with greater distances to cover, more forests, more streams and marshes, with villages widely separated. Step by step they drove the Russians back. Half a kilometre was a good advance. A few days pushing, then a sudden stop when the Russians turned to push back. Once into Poland the Russians no longer burned everything, but the clutter accumulated. Abandoned supplies, Russian weapons, dead horses.

When put on the defensive the horse troopers were sent to the rear for a day of rest in a Polish barn. Erich wanted nothing more than to lie in dry straw with Oberon bending over him munching Polish grain in warm contentment. But he was the officer, he could not rest. He moved among the men, kicked them to their feet. "Curry the horses," he ordered. "Check every inch of hide for infection or blister, check hooves, have them re-shod if needed." The men groaned and dragged themselves to obey.

He had a leisurely shave in hot water, lined up for a bath in the horse trough, and got one of the troopers to cut his hair. Kropp caught up with him, bringing fresh clothes and socks and underwear. Then the next day, back into the line to move forward. He sent Oberon to the rear with Kropp. He did not want to lose Oberon.

All spring they thrashed at the Russians. Here in his own small sector it was back and forth. The Niemen River was the obstacle, the Russians dug in this side of Grodno. In a Polish farmhouse kitchen on the situation map they saw where the two German armies would try again for a wide encirclement around Brest-Litovsk. But here on the north they were not part of it, they formed a holding action only to divert Russian forces from the real fighting.

For a mere holding action, he thought numbly, his men were dying.

In the last week of August his troop was ordered to support a break-through at Grodno to keep pace with the rest of the German front. An hour before dawn a mounted force of almost two hundred horses grouped to go in with lances and force a breach on the weak eastern edge of the village. Two infantry battalions were massed to follow.

They started in full darkness, overcast sky, no moon. In the black night they rode forward stirrup to stirrup over rough ground, through a row of evergreens and across a roadway, down a sudden dip into trees again. Horses stumbled in the dip and a branch rasped across Erich's eyes, excruciating pain, he swayed in the saddle almost off the horse with the shock to his eyes. Then suddenly from the left came the rattle of a machine gun and shouts in a Slavic language. He drew his pistol as they struck the enemy in the dark, troopers stabbing with their lances. Flashes of gunfire lit the night. Black forms rose up from the ground. He shot at them and saw forms crumple to formlessness. Something clawed at his knee and he aimed his pistol down at it, blindly firing, and it was gone. A grenade exploded a fiery blast to his left and the machine gun went silent. His cheek brushed down on the mane as if the horse could be a shield from the flying shrapnel. Somewhere ahead a horse screamed and other horses behind it crashed into a pile-up and men fell cursing. And then a cannon thundered almost in his face and instantly he was on the ground under the crash of bodies. From behind him a German foot-soldier clambered over him, then a whole mass of foot-soldiers charged in, trying to fire their Mausers without hitting their own, and horses continued thrashing ahead.

Erich's leg was pinned under his dead horse. He couldn't get up. Foot-soldiers clambered over him as if he were just another lump of soft ground. Another machine gun stuttered on the left, and a man screamed directly above him and fell on him like a sack of wet sand almost crushing him, then rolling off, dead. From ahead came a wall of rifle fire, staccato bursts suddenly firing together, he knew the sound, the organised wall of bullets directed by a single officer, and he knew the horse charge was finished with those useless damned lances, and all he had to do now was to get his men back alive.

In the darkness eastward he saw the grey haze of dawn along a black ragged horizon of trees. He struggled to lever his leg from under the dead horse. In that early light he saw vague violent black forms of infantrymen pushing forward into the rain of bullets. Somewhere a whistle blew four short sharp blasts.

They had broken through.

The infantry would finish it. In the light of day against the Russian machine guns, horses made too broad a target.

The troop mustered around him. One offered his horse, but Erich shook his head, and in a group of perhaps half the horses that started out this morning, they staggered to the rear, some riding, some on foot. He limped along, his leg still hurting from the crush under the dead horse, his hand holding the stirrup of a trooper. Eastward, northward, the fighting thundered, crackled, boomed.

That afternoon, after almost three months of constant front-line action, his troop was pulled out and sent to Feste Boyen for a scheduled rest.

*

"New orders," said the adjutant. "Report to the Intendant at 0900 hours tomorrow."

"Not again."

The adjutant grinned at him.

"I'm not wounded."

The grin widened. "No, but the rest of your troop has been attached to other commands and you've been taken out of the line. Did you write to the parents of the casualties?"

"Yes, last night." *Taken out of the line...?*

"How many?"

"Sixteen."

"God. Sixteen in one action."

He nodded. "Half my troop."

"Was it bad?"

"Quite bad. I lost my horse yesterday."

"Not the—?"

"No, not the stallion. I don't take him into the line anymore."

"Smart."

His *sang froid* was fake. He could pretend cold-bloodedness at any time. No harm in impressing people. Nobody had to know how confounded he'd been in the dark. How he'd lost sight of the target. How in the thick of it he hadn't known whether that hand on his knee had been friend or enemy...

He was glad to be out of it, if only for a while.

*

"Hey! Engländer!"

The voice cracked across the room like a rifle shot, and the whole mess, perhaps thirty officers, went to silence.

Erich turned slowly, one elbow anchored to the bar, his wine glass partway raised.

Engländer.

An officer walked toward him, and the group opened as he passed, swivelling to watch.

Ruperthal of the slashed sword-knot.

Grinning, his head tilted at a cocky angle, he sauntered to the bar next to Erich and turned to raise his glass to the room, "Here is my old buddy from training days, going to work for the Intendant, I hear. I didn't even speak his name, but he knew who the Engländer is. Prosit, Engländer!"

Erich stood like a fool, speechless.

"Did you hear?" Ruperthal said loudly to the room, his glass raised high, eyes now hard on Erich's face. "In January our Zeppelins dropped bombs on England. Did you hear?"

The glove had been flung down, demanding a response.

"Yes, I heard. Over Norfolk. What is your point?"

"Also London. Perhaps you have friends in London, Engländer!"

He found his balance and laughed. "No Paul, I have no friends in London."

Ruperthal swept his gaze across the room. "Gentlemen! Did you know this fellow is English? Well, how could you not know! What do you think? Is he a spy, do you think?"

Erich couldn't stop himself. His wine glass jerked forward, splattering Ruperthal's left ear and face. "Sorry!" He took out his handkerchief to pat Ruperthal's face. "Reflexes."

Ruperthal ripped the handkerchief from his hand and rubbed at his ear, his neck, his face.

There had to be a fight. Point of honour, unavoidable after that splash of wine. "Swords or pistols?" he heard himself say. "Or would you prefer another jump-off?"

"Enough!" Another voice penetrated over the murmur of the crowd. The divisional general, red collar tabs blazing, stepped forward into the open floor. "We will have no duelling here, gentlemen. Settle this after the war."

"Yes sir."

"Sorry sir."

"I'm serious, gentlemen. One wrong step and you'll be in the stockade. Locked together in the same cell. Understood?"

Relieved, Erich turned away and ordered a fresh glass from the barman. Nothing he wanted less than a duel.

From the far side of the room came an outburst of laughter. Ruperthal stepped into a small, tight circle of smirking friends.

Ah, Ruperthal...

*

My darling Britt (he wrote that night) *you cannot guess who is here at Division and looking for trouble. Remember my slashed sword-knot...?*

*

The Intendant's office silently opened ranks around him, and he took up his old desk as if it belonged to him. He enjoyed the quiet. He enjoyed the numbers and how they stacked up into a picture of how the war was being fought. A wise general, he mused, would watch the numbers. As a lieutenant he merely wrote them down.

Nothing happened with Ruperthal that he could tell. His uniforms in his quarters were left alone, his gear went untouched. Perhaps Ruperthal had learned a lesson. Probably not. People didn't change, they just got wiser. Craftier.

Ruperthal and his crowd avoided Erich. Sometimes when they met in the mess somebody would mention *Engländer*, or *Supply*, the worst insult for any cavalryman, off horse and into support services. He ignored it all.

Then one morning when he rode out for his regular exercise, Oberon went lame. He didn't think much of it. He took him back to the barn and ran a hand down the left foreleg but found no sensitivity. He checked the shoe, but it was solid. No stones. The hoof was clean. Ah well.

The next day Oberon could scarcely hobble. Erich called for the veterinarian. Joints were sound, no muscle tenderness, no swellings. They spent an hour together and found nothing.

On the third day when he checked, he found blood in the straw. He ran his hand down the foreleg and came away from the fetlock with a smear of blood. Probing with his fingers he felt the slightest depression all around the fetlock, and had to dig deep to find the wire. For a few minutes, digging to get under the wire, he thought only that Oberon had run into something in the yard and it had somehow wrapped around the fetlock. He called the stableman to help. Together, fighting the horse for half an hour and finally throwing him off his feet, they worked with pliers to cut under the wire.

It had been twisted on.

By hand.

A fine black wire invisible in the black hair, twisted tight.

He straightened and stared at the stableman.

"Who woulda done such a thing?" the man asked.

"Can you put a guard on this animal?"

"No sir, I just don't got the manpower."

Fury so deep he could scarcely think. "Why," he whispered to Oberon, "didn't you kick him in the head?"

Then came the helpless dismay.

He found Kropp and set him to guard Oberon twenty-four hours a day. He would have to leave his kit unattended.

And he thought, All right you bastard, you win.

He wrote out a request for transfer back to the line where he could face his enemy.

*

Within a week he was called into the chief administrator's office. The colonel came to his feet to return Erich's salute. "A little gift from the Kaiser, Schellendorf." He held out a small black velvet box.

Erich opened it gingerly. The Iron Cross lay inside with its black-and-white ribbon neatly folded. At the top stamped with a crown, at the bottom, '1914'. He turned the medal and found his name etched on the reverse, *'Schellendorf'*.

"For those wounded," the colonel announced, "in active service for the Kaiser." He sat down again. "You have the right to wear the ribbon at the second button of your field uniform, and the medal itself on all dress tunics."

"Thank you sir."

"And now this." He held up a paper. "You were expecting this?"

"What is it sir?"

The colonel gave him a long, penetrating stare.

Consciously he held his ground.

"This is your transfer to the Twenty-Fifth Dragoons. In Lorraine France." His stiff bearing shouted censure.

"France, sir? I only requested—"

"The signature is that of von Moltke himself."

He struggled to absorb it. *Von Moltke*.

"You knew about this, of course."

"No sir."

The major smiled coldly. "You go on the morning hospital train to Königsberg."

"Tomorrow?"

"Leave your horse with us. We need every officer's remount we can find."

"I'll take him with me sir. He belongs to the Baron von Wittingen."

"Ah yes, ah yes. So! I see. The baron would be the architect of this little transfer, nu?"

"What?"

"You're very fortunate having friends in such high places."

"Sir, I didn't—"

"Of course not. No honourable officer would go over the head of his commander. Dismissed, Schellendorf."

*

A week later, with no leave permitted on the journey, he arrived in Essey, a French village as small as its name. In the chill rain of a September morning the lorry stopped in the square among crowds of horses and foot-soldiers and a supply convoy being loaded out of a large storage shed.

The driver jumped down and came around to the rear. He dumped Erich's rucksack out on the ground and beckoned him to climb down. "Here we go, Lieutenant."

Erich dropped into mud. His polished boots were instantly smeared. A cold breeze whistled through his greatcoat. Rain tapped lightly on his new steel helmet. He stretched, stiff from the long, rough lorry ride, and picked up his rucksack, coated now with a mess of mud.

The driver grinned cheekily. "Welcome to the war, sir." He swung into the driver's seat and the lorry rattled away, gears grinding, wheels slewing mud clots into the air.

Most of the village buildings had been damaged. The church stood open to the sky, the houses on two sides of the square had burned to the ground, leaving only vacant stone foundations. On the south side he saw a row of scarred buildings where civilians and German soldiers were going about their morning errands, shoulders hunched against the weather.

"Acht geben!"

Heavy draft horses bore down upon him. He leaped out of the way as the double box of an ammunition wagon trundled through. Tucked beneath the steel fore-carriage, the driver was scarcely visible behind the horses' great haunches.

Erich turned a slow turn. A hand-painted sign *"BAON 42"* hung over a blacksmith shop on the east side of the square. He went under the sign into a cobbled courtyard. Horses were tied along the walls of the smithy, their saddles and harnesses loosened. A soldier wearing the metal gorget of the military police demanded his papers, and with a vague salute waved Erich to a sign over the shop door that repeated the outer sign, *"Baon 42 HQ".*

A tool room had been converted into an orderly room, with two battered desks back-to-back in the middle of the timber floor and a bank of filing cabinets against a wall. Blacksmith tools had been tossed into hedgehog piles in one corner. Two soldiers hammering on typewriters at the desks did not look up. A sergeant yelled over a telephone and slammed it into its box. "New officer? Come with me." No salute, no clicking heels, no protocol.

He followed the sergeant along a dark hall to a room lit by oil lanterns. No electricity here.

"Erich!" Gerdt leaped up from writing at a desk.

Erich froze speechless in the doorway.

"I heard you were coming!" Gerdt dashed around the desk, arms wide, and met Erich and embraced him roughly, then shook him by the shoulders. "God, I missed you!"

They stood gaping at each other. Among two million German soldiers on the western front, here was Gerdt, as if, in a lottery of two million tickets, they had won the right to stand in the same place and breathe the same air.

A slow grin split Erich's face. "My God. Gerdt."

"Come on, meet the major." Gerdt laughed. "You'll hate your appointment."

The major sat in an office at a table covered with stacks of paper and maps. He rose now to meet them. "Altmann," he said.

Erich snapped a salute. The major grinned and stuck a cold pipe between his teeth, then shook hands across the desk as if they were old friends meeting on a street corner. "Welcome to the Forty-Second," he said around his pipe. "So you're the Engländer?"

Erich glanced at Gerdt.

Gerdt shrugged, and grinned.

"No shame in the English," the major said. "They give us hell up north, second best fighters in the world. Here we only face French pigs." His eyes flicked irony. "I'll put you in charge of Battalion transport, you'll see the hellish mess we're in, our baggage-master was killed a week ago, jumped when he should've ducked. I hope you'll keep your damn head down. Average lifespan at the front for you green-noses is a few days. After that there's hope."

"Sir." He clicked his heels. "Not exactly a green-nose."

The major smiled bleakly. "Your predecessor had no talent for figures. Take charge of these records. I hear you're a genius with figures."

He glanced again at Gerdt who gave a little shrug. The major stepped away from the desk and waved Erich into his hard-backed kitchen chair.

He sat down gingerly and took up the first paper from the untidy pile. He tossed the major's maps aside and began to sort papers into categories, a pile here, another there, until every sheet of a thousand papers had found a place among two dozen piles. He began then to sort them by date, earliest at the bottom. The earliest dates were at least four months old.

When he looked up next, he was alone. The duty sergeant reported that Gerdt had gone back down to the trench and would meet him again at supper.

* * *

CHAPTER 18

November 1915

This was a different war. Not much moved, except replacement soldiers in and out of the line. Occasional errant shells flew over to keep them all awake. "Our responsibility," Gerdt told him, "is to hold the line. The French over there, they'll send us an hour of artillery, which gives us the warning, and then they attack and we beat them back, and so it goes. We don't attack. Stupid way to win a war."

The infantry sat in trenches a few kilometres beyond the village, Germans on this side, the French over there across no-man's-land guarded by barbed wire on both sides strung in great unbroken rolls across the open farmlands. By day sharp-shooters fired off sporadic rounds at each other. By night both sides sent out patrols across no-man's-land to scout the enemy and to bring back prisoners for interrogation. By night Erich could stand outside the headquarters to watch distant artillery flashes along the north-western horizon at Verdun. In this sector occasional artillery barrages from both sides blazed the darkness, leaving behind more casualties, more shattered trees, and a few more dead cows in their shell-pitted pastures.

He settled into his work. Every morning he supervised assembling the supply convoy according to requisitions telephoned in from the front line. Every couple of days he went down to check their work. Today he swung up beside the driver of the lead wagon. The November dawn had a feel of winter in the air. "Smells like snow," he said to the driver. He pulled his half-tent around his shoulders against a cold drizzle.

The fellow whistled, and the four-horse team strained into harness, jolting the wagon over the pocked and rutted road out of the village down toward the marshes. In the pastures cattle grazed on autumn stubble among shell holes filled with polluted water and trees stripped of branches by the fighting that had twice passed through this sloping plain. They drove in silence, four wagons in line. They drove past farmhouses and barns, past farmers who waved at them as they tilled the autumn ground to prepare for spring planting.

Company headquarters were separated half a mile apart along the Third Position, with fewer than three hundred soldiers to cover the line between. A desperately thin line, if the enemy only knew. Erich hopped down from the wagon at the field infirmary, a camp of tents on high ground with red crosses painted on the canvas roofs in hopes of being bypassed by enemy artillery fire. In the north at Verdun the *crump-crrrrump* of German artillery had already started the usual morning exchange. Erich scarcely noticed. Hardly a war zone. yesterday one man had been killed by a low-flying French biplane on reconnaissance. The full day's activity in a waiting war.

He stepped to the senior medical officer's tent. "Are you getting your proper rations, sir?"

"Oh, find us green vegetables, would you, Schellendorf?"

He laughed and tossed a cheerful salute as he left.

The ground here was soft from constant foot traffic. He followed a boardwalk down the slope to the trench of the Third Position. The wagons had separated along the line to their own company depots. Second Company had already sent men up to unload. They grunted under the weight of sacks and crates as they slid in mud down into the underground depot. Each man carried his rifle with him every step of every day, a double load to curse. And a lot of rough humour when a man slid off his feet or stumbled into water. Their uniforms had turned mud-brown over the regulation field-grey.

"Ho, Lieutenant!" called one soldier, resting a moment on his way back up to the wagon. "Where's our water wagon?"

"Coming."

"Today?"

"Get on about your business, soldier."

The man laughed and went by. Erich noted that his rifle was clean. A good soldier kept his rifle clean, no matter how filthy was the rest of him.

He stopped at Second Company Headquarters in a Third Position bunker. A huge complex, its walls were dense grey chalk dug deep underground. Stone steps led down to a dry floor of wooden planks. Every corner was filled this morning with off-duty soldiers resting out of the weather, leaving scarcely any space to step inside the opening. Erich poked his head through and shouted, "Lieutenant von Wittingen?"

"Wittingen? He's up on the line this morning."

He waved thanks. The bakery squad had slung rods through the side handles of the portable wood-stove, and shouldered the supplies to bring hot rations to the line. Erich fell in behind. They walked out into a traverse, a trench only shoulder deep this far back in rolling farmland, fields broken by stone walls and hedges and shell-shattered barns and patches of woods. No cattle here. No life in these fields. Far ahead a flash was followed by the boom of a French gun. It was answered by a barrage of German artillery, shells whistling over their heads from the rear, *wheeeee... whoosh, whoooosh...*

The traverse suddenly deepened, and turned in zigzags built to block enemy bullets coming straight in. For ten minutes they walked down the modest slope in single file, brushing past men going back. Forgotten was even the thought of parade dress and polished boots. The men's clothes were rumpled, and smeared with grey crusts of mud. Erich wore what every rifleman wore, rubber galoshes over jackboots and loose trousers that he had stolen out of his own stores. No pips on his epaulets. In these days of the long-range sharp-shooter, officers were under orders to cover all badges of rank and to wear the infantryman's steel helmet against stray bullets or shrapnel. A man couldn't tell an officer from a *Landser*, except by knowing the face.

They reached the Second Position guarded at regular intervals by machine-gun posts like concrete hat boxes. Men shouted back and forth, heads popped up out of holes dug into the trench walls. From along the trench men rose out of nowhere and began to gather near the bunker, mess tins in hand. They'd already built a fire. Now two soldiers shovelled the burning wood into the cook-stove, and there was instant heat. The drizzle had let up. The sky had begun to lighten a little. One man joked about a possible day without rain; another retorted that rain was better than snow. Ragged boys with day-old beards lined up for hot food, a ration of rum, and the water wagon. It was nearing noon.

"Wittingen?" he asked a soldier passing.

"On the line." A jerk of the thumb over his shoulder.

He could walk upright in this traverse that rose a good metre above his head. It was uphill from here, up to the brow of the slope to the First Position. This was The Trench, the last jump off before the tangled rolls of barbed wire, before no-man's-land, and the enemy beyond.

He dodged guards peeping over the top with box periscopes, and past cubby-holes where men slept curled around their carbines. Digging out a rock-fall, a crew flattened against the wall to let him pass, then went back to shovelling debris to fill puddles along the floor. He found Gerdt with a sergeant in a small storage bunker counting out flares and cans of fuel and small-arms ammunition. "Hallo, good morning."

Gerdt told the sergeant to finish the count.

"How does it look?" Erich asked.

"Something may be coming." Gerdt walked with him back along the trench past the turn of the traverse to a machine-gun post that stood just high enough to see over the crest of the slope. It was made of thick steel armour plate with several firing slits along the four sides, and camouflaged in front by a hedge of cut evergreens. One of the guards stepped down to let them squeeze up the timber step. "Look there," said Gerdt. He handed Erich his binoculars. "Tell me what you see."

Through a firing slit Erich scanned the slope down to the river depression on the right and the farmland sweeping upward left. Scanned the tight rolls of wire between posts, the expanse of shell-pitted, water-soaked pastureland and shattered trees, and, five hundred metres across the devastation, the distant lines of French barbed wire and a pale line of sandbags that marked the forward rim of the enemy trench... and the brief sharp reflection of a rifle-sight looking back at him.

He snapped away from the firing slit. A strange glow warmed him, as if the ghost of a French bullet had brushed his forehead.

"You saw him, did you." Gerdt laughed. "Don't stick your head up."

They went out to the trench again, and hunched down, backs to the parapet wall, their feet in mud. Erich was still wearing his half-tent. Now he folded it into a rubber cushion on the rifle step. Drizzle had changed to pale sunshine. White clumps of cloud were breaking up in a new blue sky.

"Did you see all that movement over there?" Gerdt asked. "The French are building up, at least two regiments by the latest intelligence reports."

Erich's scalp prickled. "Regiments?"

"How is it at Battalion?" Gerdt asked him. "Are we bringing up fresh cannon meat?"

"I don't know."

"You organise supplies and you don't know?"

"I just count what's there and order more."

Gerdt laughed. "Me too. We just count what's over there and bring back the intelligence. Two fresh regiments."

They trekked back to the company bunker. It had been expanded since Erich's last visit a week ago, deeper, wider, longer, with brick steps down and a kind of dam at the top of the steps to prevent run-off water from the trench. Concrete over the entrance protected against shrapnel fragments. Heavy timbers shored up the walls against concussion, electric wires were strung over the ceiling. A big wood stove stood by a side wall, planks on the floor covered the chalky mud beneath, electric lights shone overhead, and tiers of bunks were lined up along the walls. Men hunkered on their heels hip to hip, or sat on the steel bunks, eating their only hot ration of the day. The bakery crew had fried slices of ham on the hot stove surface, and reheated a tub of white beans. An open vat of coffee steamed on the stove. Gerdt and Erich took up tin mugs to dip in. Then they went back outside to sit in the open trench under the fresh sky.

"So how do you like the Army Service Corps?"

Erich felt his face and ears go red. Lowest of the low. "Do you know why we're here?" he asked. "I mean here, you and I with the Infantry, instead of our own Dragoons?"

Gerdt laughed drily. "To fight for God and the Kaiser?"

"Because your father pulled a lot of strings to keep us out of the fighting sectors."

There was a silence.

Gerdt said quietly, "I know."

Again a long silence between them. An uncomfortable, restless silence.

Then Gerdt said, "I don't object, if truth be known. I do my weekly reconnaissance and get back alive. I can't wait for this to be over! Truth be known, I just want to be a farmer."

"We all want to survive, Gerdt. But this... as if we're hiding from it. This is not... This is not honourable."

"God damn honour. All my life I've had honour booted up my arse."

Erich paused to put the thought together. It had been forming since the first day, but he'd buried it, concentrating on the daily effort of staying alive. "You're going to be a farmer," he said at last. "But I *must* be a soldier, I have no choice."

"You think I have a choice?"

"When this is over you'll have a choice."

"And you don't?"

He shook his head. "It all started so... harmlessly. Just a... an adventure." He looked into Gerdt's eyes. "But this is all I have, you see. I can't be buried like this in the Army Service Corps. I should have stayed in East Prussia. I can't ask for a transfer, a soldier does the job he's given. Ask no questions, seize the day, do the job."

A smile spread over Gerdt's face. "You didn't take all those lectures seriously!"

He nodded. "This is my profession. I have to be good at this, Gerdt, don't you see? Because of this war I'll never be able to go home to England again."

"Home..." Gerdt stared blindly down at the mud under his crumpled boots.

*

Twenty-third November 1915. A cold autumn morning. Dry

leaves tumbled across the road and spooked horses that did not twitch an ear at gunfire. Erich checked the papers one more time and waved the drivers on. Artillery had started up again. Erich stood in the doorway, staring northeast at the morning thunder. Something was happening. They were pulling units out from this sector, sending them north to Flanders. To the heavy fighting.

"Altmann wants you sir," said a corporal passing.

When he stepped inside the major's office, he found Gerdt ahead of him, slumped in a chair staring out the window.

Erich saluted Altmann and removed his cap.

"Bad news, Schellendorf." Altmann held out a paper. "This is your leave pass. You have six days, two each way and two at home. Try to be back on time, we can't afford you away."

They rode remounts on farm roads about ten miles across country to catch a train at the railway line at Vigneulles.

"Overnight," Gerdt said. "Just gone."

"I hope she was... you know... at least... not uncomfortable."

"How is it comfortable when you can't breathe?"

He'd never seen anyone die of tuberculosis. He'd never seen anyone die of any disease. "It must have been quick. Britt never wrote a thing about it to me."

"She's too full of her horses and her hospital work, she was gone night and day. Mutti had no-one. Vati spends his time in the garrison mess, you know how it is..."

Within two hours they were on the hospital train to Metz. Strange, he thought, watching trees slip past the train window, how easy it was, even in wartime, for a regimental colonel *ret'd* to get them home for a funeral.

Such an empty black feeling. Had she died alone?

The trees slipped by.

*

Mourners overflowed the Heiliggeist Church out to the road. Erich listened numbly to the eulogy. He could not recognise the baroness in the pastor's distant words, and so he turned inward to see her shadowed eyes in his mind, her gentle smile. To hear her voice, *"Oh my dear..."* and when the tears came at last he groped for Britt's hand. As if his own mother had died.

They followed the casket out of the church in a cold hard wind from the north, just as it began to rain. By her graveside the pastor briefly spoke of ashes-to-ashes, the German words strange in Erich's ears. They took turns to drop a handful of wet earth into the open grave while the wind battered at their clothes and faces and blew the clumps of fresh earth sideways. The rain flooded down to camouflage his tears. The crowds broke now and hurried away to shelter. An officer from the garrison urged the baron to go down to the mess for hot rum to warm his bones.

Gerdt and Britt and Erich remained, buffeted by the wind, chilled by the rain, but too benumbed in spirit to abandon her yet. Perhaps an hour later, arms linked, they walked back up to the house.

The house had died too. Servants whispered and disappeared out of the way behind doors. The dining table had been set lavishly for a cold lunch, but nobody had come. Erich and Gerdt and Britt changed out of their wet clothes, then met around the table to pick at the food. "We go back tomorrow," said Erich to Britt. "At eighteen hundred."

"I know," said Britt.

Later in the afternoon the baron returned, flushed and happy, still in the wet ceremonials that he'd worn to the funeral. He came to join them in the dining room where they still sat in numb reflection, nibbling at bits of food. He unhooked his sabre and tossed it clattering on the sideboard.

"Papi," said Britt, "you must change or you'll catch a cold."

He glanced over the table. "What's all this food? Don't you know there's a war on?"

"It was just... I forgot to send out invitations."

"Where's Mutti? Has she eaten yet? I'll get her!" And he darted out the door again.

Britt hurried after him. Their footsteps echoed away along the parquet hall floor and faded up the stairs.

Erich stared at Gerdt.

Gerdt stared at Erich. "It's been coming. You know it's been coming. The whole garrison knew it was coming."

Erich shrugged. "He's harmless enough."

"I don't know, harmless." He paused, then said, "I was looking at the ledgers."

Erich smiled. "I know about that. Hasn't he called in the accountant?"

"No idea. He tells me it's not my business."

"But it is. You'll inherit all this."

"You also."

"No, no—"

"Yes. Don't forget, as we sit here, we're equal in Father's will."

"No...!" He sat back in the chair, his brain turning in loops. "No, no I don't... Will you be serious for a moment?"

"You have to persuade him to bring in the accountant. He doesn't listen to me. Not since..." He pressed his hands to his forehead and sat in glum silence amid all that wasted food.

Erich waited.

"You remember Annette Bressard?"

He shook his head, puzzled.

"The cotillions at the Ritter Hotel. You remember?"

He shrugged. Flash of chestnut hair dancing by...

"Her family lives in Metz. I've been... I mean, since I was posted to the Salient..." He flushed red about the ears. "I've been visiting every chance I get."

Erich smiled a slow smile. "You sly dog."

"No no, it's not like that! No, just... I love her, Erich. I want to marry her, and I love her family too, and they think I'm a fine fellow for her and..." He stared at Erich in misery. "And Father threatens to dispossess me if I persist."

Ah. Sons and fathers, fathers and sons. The endless conflict.

*

He lay awake long after Britt had relaxed into sleep. They had made love, a guilty love with the funeral only a few hours past. A deep, unhurried, satisfying love. She'd beguiled him with hands that knew his sensitive places, nails that scraped at his nerves over chest and ribs and down the midline of his belly, "Come on, come on..." She'd put a wet tongue in his ear, "The doctor said when I feel this way we could start a baby, Erich, don't you want a baby? Oh come on..."

A baby?

He'd never thought of babies. The idea of a baby put him into a panic. There was a war on, they were in the front line. Her father was stumbling into senility and her mother was gone, and Britt was the only one left who could take care of the house...

And now she wanted a baby?
Had they just started a baby?
God.
She slept so peacefully, so totally. She had no perception of the problems.

And her father...

How could she manage that bombastic, senile old man and a household full of servants and thirteen farms on seven estates with seven feudal villages? And her deadly work at the hospital, she must give that up. She would be plagued with problems. Nobody could help her. The army wouldn't help her. The army would not allow her husband or her brother to take a furlough any time she might need help. Didn't she realise? And now she wanted a *baby*?

She could not manage this. She could not bully her father or charm him into taking better care over the books, her father would tell her it was not a woman's business. It didn't matter that he adored her, or that she easily twisted him around her finger for those little luxuries she desired in life. She could not control him. The baroness had been able to control him, and the baroness was gone.

*

It was harder to leave her this time. Although Oberon was down in the garrison stable, they had neither time nor desire to ride. "You'll ride him while I'm away, will you?" he'd said to Britt, and she had promised. The baron had gone out early to the mess to supervise his personal war. Then Erich and Gerdt and Britt spent the morning with the accountant, tracing back the beginnings of the errant entries in the books. The accountant packed up the ledgers to take to his office and complete the revision. "You realise," he said, going out the door, "that this puts a new picture on your tax structure. Instead of deficits you have taxable profits. Therefore outstanding taxes."

"Report to me," said Gerdt, and gave him his military postal address. "Speak with my sister. Avoid discussion with the baron, in peril of your life, you understand?"

The accountant chuckled. He thought it was a joke.

They helped him carry the heavy books out to his carriage waiting in the roundabout.

And now the train was due in fifteen minutes, and still Erich could not go out the door. He could not even voice his fears.

She was so small, so young and innocent. She was older than he, yet such a child still, such a child.

"Gerdt is waiting," she said.

Gerdt leaned patiently on the gate, rucksack at his feet. Under a fresh sun the garden glistened with yesterday's rain. The breeze was cold. Hanisch waited in the Benz to drive them down to the station.

"Write to me every day," Erich said. "Tell me everything."

"I always do."

"You didn't tell me how ill she was."

"Oh Erich, go! She was always ill, how could we tell the difference?"

"Let us know how the baron goes."

"Papi's a bull! Nothing will happen. I'll keep an eye on the books, I'll help him keep up the records, I'll learn how to do it, I promise. Now go, or you'll miss the train, and then what? Up on court martial."

"I want you to quit that job—"

"Go." She pushed him toward the step. She reminded him suddenly of the baroness.

He turned away and slung the rucksack over his shoulder.

"Erich?"

He paused.

"Don't you dare to leave without kissing me."

He came back and dropped the rucksack to take her into his arms.

"If I'm possibly with child," she whispered into his ear, "I'll stop working. Does that suit you?" She kissed him to stop his argument. She bent to pick up his bundle and pushed it against his chest. "Don't miss your train."

*

They rode in a train so overcrowded with soldiers that it was impossible to carry on a conversation. There was no longer any distinction between officers and men: you grabbed a spot and clung to it and hoped that not too many others would step on you when pushing through. They were all on the way back to the war. With each stop the carriage gained more travellers and lost none. Trains going the opposite direction were packed with men on leave and walking wounded, with a couple of cars reserved for medical crews and their stretcher casualties. Trains like this carried soldiers west to the front. These days not many civilians travelled west.

They had to change trains at Metz and wait for a troop train to Vigneulles. Two, three hours, the Metz stationmaster said. The city swarmed with soldiers going to and from several different battlefields. The restaurants and cafes were full. Men lined up for a cup of coffee and were told there was no coffee, there was a war on, didn't they know? There was bread if they wanted it, "But no wurst, no meat at all, no beer, some potato soup, and that's all!" It was as if they blamed the soldiers for the shortages.

Erich and Gerdt walked into a nearby park with a spring fountain, and lined up for water with other soldiers. Gerdt had brought his mess tin. He had trench experience, he knew the value of a mess tin. They filled it with water and walked over to a bench where three privates sat laughing and joking: privates who, laughing like that, had obviously not yet seen front-line service. Erich swung his rank to send them packing, and took over the bench. They sat now at last in relative solitude under a cold blue sky. Gerdt offered him first water. He drank, and handed it back.

"So this Annette," Erich ventured. "You want to marry... *but*?"

"Now that Mutti's gone I can go ahead without breaking her heart. It's terrible, though, to see her death as... as opening a door."

"But we can look at her death as a release for her. So hard, for so many years."

Gerdt nodded and sipped water. Then after a moment he said, "Will you stand up with me?"

"Sure. Absolutely."

"Father may not like it."

"Ah well."

"So then I expect you and Britt will be the heirs. Mainly you, in fact."

"He's that serious?"

"One can't talk sense with him. He's ready to dispossess me. His mind is set."

"Ah, fathers! Maybe next week he'll forget it."

Gerdt nodded glumly. "Our positions are now reversed, you and I. Ironic, isn't it?"

"So you'll marry Annette, and then?"

Unexpectedly Gerdt's face split into a wide grin. "And then I become a farmer! They have a nice farm, you know. Quite small. But they'll be glad of the help. Once the war is over."

*

Late that night, back in his bunk behind Battalion, Erich opened the little poetry book that had travelled with him all this way. By candlelight he found a favourite poem, *'Welcome and Farewell'*, which always made him think of Britt. He scanned down to the last stanza...

"I went; you stood and looked to the ground
and watched me go with moistened eyes.
And yet, what bliss to be loved,
and to love, my God, what bliss..."

That was it exactly. The reason he was here.

Now Gerdt was following his pattern. It had to be worth it. So much to give up. Much more than Erich had ever given up. Wealth, title, lands, position...

When the old baron was gone, as the heir Erich could always turn things more to Gerdt's advantage. He could not imagine himself living the Wittingen baronial style of life. The ledgers were quite enough, he could do that. But to handle all those people would be nothing so easy as commanding a formation of cavalry.

No. For him the army would be enough. After the baron was gone, Gerdt would manage the estates and distribute the profits.

He put Goethe away. He swung his feet over the side of the bunk and took up his notebook to write a letter on his knee.

* * *

CHAPTER 19

February to May 1916

February, and bitterly cold. Yet the ground did not quite freeze. Under a thin blanket of fresh snow the horses laboured to move loads while wagon wheels sank into six inches of stiff mud. Last evening two of his horses on different teams had dropped dead of exhaustion. Now he must find replacements. Since midnight he'd been on the telephone to the Intendant, and to the remount station in Vigneulles, and to Detachment C headquarters, trying to obtain a priority for horses. And he was failing on all fronts because the entire St. Mihiel Salient was the lowest priority in the grand scheme of things.

He was still on the telephone at 0400 hours when he heard new artillery. A single *boom*! Heavy stuff, far away. Then another. German guns, he could tell by the dull echo along the ground. Somewhere north. A single distant boom, then every few seconds another distant *boom*.

"There they go," said Major Altmann.

Erich jumped. He hadn't heard Altmann come in. "Who goes where?"

"We've opened an offensive at Verdun."

"Do we have new orders?"

"Stand on alert in case of a French breakthrough here to outflank the Meuse. This will be a big one, perhaps change the course of the war."

Erich slung the phone in its box. "Two draft horses dead last night, I can't find remounts."

The major smiled in his dry way. "Make do."

To reduce the numbers of teams he began to calculate new numbers for twenty percent lighter wagon loads. It meant more trips for each team, longer hours at work, longer exposure to the wayward artillery shells.

His head swam with numbers. He was now supplying not only the Battalion, but every artillery battery along the whole sector between the Meuse and Moselle rivers.

"If we had a medal for organisation," said the major, "I would put you up for it."

"Just give me more horses," he said.

The organisation weighed him down. He felt smothered with attaching numbers to objects and guiding the objects to their destinations. The war itself raged in the north, but this sector was reasonably quiet. The war had become an abstract exercise for him, without attachment to the men who died in violent ways out there, or were carried back with legs and arms blown off, or simply disappeared into a shell hole in shattered bursts of bone, blood, cloth and mud. Every morning the enemy sent over barrages all along the line. Every morning the German guns, rationing shells, aimed a few lobs back at enemy cannon flashes. Every night the patrols sneaked out in deep darkness, like foxes into a chicken coop, returning with scraps of intelligence, and carrying their wounded or dead.

That February morning just before dawn the artillery up north opened a drumfire barrage that filled the air with distant, unremitting rumbles that would last the next three hundred days. They soon got used to it. Just another phase in a pointless war. Over the weeks he read the communiqués as the German Fifth Army battered at the French First Army over Verdun. In his little office piled with papers he followed the war on the map and felt nothing.

*

Spring sneaked in on him. One afternoon he looked out to see birds fluttering in the hedge. The normalcy of it startled him. He paused in the doorway to watch them. The guns never stopped. North at Verdun men were dying. Thousands of men every day.

Yet here the little birds twittered happily in their own innocent world, unaware.

The mail was in. Somebody had stopped a few minutes ago in his open office doorway, "Letter for you, Lieutenant."

Still he couldn't take his eyes from the birds. Suddenly they swooped, a little cloud of black-and-white birds in a shrieking tangle of wings, and flew away. At Verdun the guns rumbled their background music, but here the sky was blue.

Mail. He went through the dark hall to the orderly room. A letter from Britt. She hadn't written in almost three weeks. He carried it back to his desk...

> *My dearest Erich* ~ (in schoolgirl handwriting)
> *Nothing new here to report. I am well. Father is well. He spends his days at the garrison, and I at the hospital. I ride when possible, usually on the weekend, although my time is dictated by the numbers of wounded rather than by the day of the week. We experience difficult penalties of the war which Father has not noticed. Hanisch has been called up to be a soldier-servant for General Behrendt. This year the government has imposed severe price restrictions on farm produce, and the major percentage of our crops must be sold to the government for the war effort at prices that barely cover production costs.*
> *Father sends his regards...*

'*Father*'? When had she ever called her Papi '*Father*'? Reports about *farm production*...?

Something had happened. He read the letter again and again. When the desk telephone rang he answered some questions from down the line, and flung it back in the box and looked again at her letter. Three weeks without a word from her, and now this letter from a stranger.

The war, this dreadful war. Something had hurt her in some dreadful way that he would only know when he saw her again. She hadn't explained anything in her letter. It distracted him from his work all day, it took too much space in his head.

That night he lay long awake, then lit the lamp and read the letter again. Not once did she write *I love you*, and not once did she call him *darling*, or *husband,* and nowhere did she fling her words into her usual beguiling silliness. He wanted to show the letter to Gerdt, but Gerdt had not read any of her previous letters, and would not understand.

In the morning he put in a request for leave. He was not due yet. They'd had six days for the funeral in November.

The major threw back his application. "You're quite insane, Schellendorf. You know the extent of the French build-up over there, and you ask for leave?"

"Sorry, sir."

"And we have nothing to answer them with. Every available unit has shipped north to Verdun or Flanders. We'll get nothing more in this sector except men on rest duty."

"Yes, sir."

"Trouble at home?"

"No sir!" He was too emphatic. He added lamely, "Wife's birthday."

The major gave him a sharp glare, then returned to his map.

Bread 700 grams, egg biscuit 250 grams, field biscuit 300 grams, meat 325 grams...

He sighed. Every item of food had been reduced once again, changing all the ratios. Every field issue must be repacked. More men to feed, less food per man. Even less for those like himself in support positions, or resting behind the lines. Lucky they could send the orderlies out to fish at the river. Rumour had it that the soldiers had been stealing pigs and chickens and eggs from local farms. Against regulations, but who was watching? The military police accepted their share of the plunder in smiling good grace.

As he worked at his new numbers, suddenly French artillery opened up, crashes instead of rumbles. A shell whistled overhead and an instant later the building rocked. Erich leaped to his feet. He reached across the desk for the pistol holster that he was supposed to wear at all times, did not quite get his hand on it, another explosion hit somewhere close throwing him off his feet, dust and debris filled the air, *damn me* his mind registered in

English, *they found our range*, and a *BOOM...!*

He picked himself off the floor and came nose to nose with the major, who had jumped across the room to help him.

His head was spinning, his ears seemed filled with syrup.

"All in order?" the major shouted.

He nodded. Shells screamed in both directions. "They're shelling the village!" he shouted to the major.

"Stupid bastards!"

He found his holster and pistol under the desk that was crushed by a shattered roof beam. One corner of the room had been grazed by a shell, debris all over the floor, papers scattered, dust everywhere choking him. He strapped on the pistol.

Somewhere a horse screamed.

They ran to jerk open the door. The hallway was exposed to the sky. Flames crackled up one wall. The kitchen beyond had been blown out, the stove shattered. A fire was climbing out of the warped fire bed. The table leaned in splinters on two legs. A huge hole in the floor was filled with rubble. Half buried in dust lay the bloody shreds of a body who only moments ago had been preparing lunch for the officers.

The orderly room beyond was smoking rubble. In the smithy courtyard several horses lunged frantically in half circles on their tethers. One horse lay stiff on the ground, its head twisted up, still attached by its halter to the wall. Another had broken loose and staggered on three legs in a circle, one foreleg dragging in bloody pulp from its shoulder. The head drooped low, eyes half closed in blazing pain, silent in the way of horses. Without another thought Erich aimed his pistol and shot it in the eye. It dropped like a back of rocks. *Good shot.*

The major had gone back. Erich paused in the orderly room amid smashed walls, rubble in heaps, a typewriter among bricks, scattered shards of window glass, the splintered desk, and paper, paper everywhere. Bodies must be somewhere. Erich saw none. He brushed through rising flames back along the hall to find the major. The thunder of explosions filled his head.

In the destroyed headquarters room the major cranked the field telephone to raise Division. "It's dead," he shouted to Erich through the thunder.

The German artillery now opened up along the line, air

pressure blasting overhead, he could feel the pressure pass. A squad of soldiers came crashing in from the burning hallway.

Erich shouted at the corporal at their head, "Get the records out!"

They grabbed indiscriminately at papers, the filing cabinet, the dead telephone, the drawers out of the major's splintered desk. They battered out the window glass with their rifle butts. In the hall the fire rose to an inferno, cutting off that path of escape. Smoke billowed into the room. One of the men slammed shut the door against it. The only way out now was the window, too small to fit more than one man through at a time.

He could die here. They could all die here. He felt his mind turn on its own, slow and clear and cold as ice, *Do not push, do not fumble, take something in your hands, throw it out the window, do not block the window, take the situation maps off the floor, watch that man...* He moved like a machine, fine-tuned, precise, fitting his body into the actions of the soldiers, eight soldiers, the major, the corporal, all moving together to pitch things out one window while the flames crackled through the door and the room filled again with smoke.

"Now!" The major's voice cut under the thunder of artillery, "One man at a time, everybody carry something and get out! One at a time, one at a time!" He stood by the smashed window like a policeman at an intersection and bodily thrust one man after another out the cramped hole. Erich pushed himself out, his arms laden with crushed maps, the major propelling his hind end.

The artillery went to drumfire, a solid wall of concussion that beat the brain and obliterated all thought. Outside they gathered up papers from the ground just as the fire inside filled the window. Nowhere now to hide from the shells, no trench, no wall to protect them. The shells whistled over and crashed in the village. Across the road a small house jumped from its foundation flinging stones through the air, and collapsed, leaving a cloud of dust and half a wall standing. A runaway bay horse galloped past. Its harness slipped off sideways and hung from the collar and became entangled in its legs, and it fell and struggled. In that sharpened moment, Erich saw the whites of its eyes, and through the wall of artillery thunder he heard the *snap*, saw a hind leg turn into an unnatural angle, and his brain whispered *fracture...'*

And he jerked out his pistol, and he shot the horse.

Killed two horses in the same day.

Fresh meat for the troops.

Nothing wasted.

In the hush that followed his mind went into a blank place. He sat down to rest, and did not know what time had passed when he found himself with his back braced to the hot stone ruin of the smithy. The syrupy feel of the air lingered, as if a bright liquid curtain protected his eyes and cushioned his ears.

"Wounded, are you?" The major stood over him in the sunshine.

"No sir." He scrambled to his feet, and swayed. His head throbbed. His pistol weighed heavy in his hand. He stared at it in vague surprise.

"Then get busy. Send for the butchering squad to clear up the horse carcasses. Then set up a new headquarters over at the Cormier farm. Take Sergeant Horn and a squad with you to evict them, they're French, send them packing. Are those the maps?"

He still gripped a bundle of crushed maps under his left arm. "Yes sir."

The major clapped him on the shoulder. "Good work, Schellendorf. Carry on."

*

Once they'd moved to the Cormier farm the officers of Battalion met daily at 1600 hours to write out reports in the huge kitchen. They sat around the timber table and drank a little wine until the kitchen crew dumped mounds of food before them. They ate well. The Cormier farm raised beef cattle, reserved by higher command for Detachment C Headquarters and Division staffs. The Cormier barn was still half full of stored fodder.

He saw Gerdt every day at supper. Gerdt had lost weight in the trenches and gained the faraway gaze of a soldier who'd seen too much. One night they sat outside after supper before Gerdt went back down to the line. Gerdt was in a reflective mood. He hadn't spoken through supper.

"So," Erich said, "what's happening with you?"

"I'm going to ask her. Maybe she'll say yes. Maybe not. Her heart is with the French."

"Who, Annette?"
Gerdt nodded.
"You need regimental permission."
"Where did you find the courage?"
"What courage? You fill out the proper forms—"
"To defy your father." He turned to Erich. "Do you think I can do it? Defy him?"
Erich grinned. "Sure you can." Then he added, half joking, "He might not even notice."

*

At the end of May it rained for days. The farmers had put in the April crops, and the unseasonal rain came down and washed out newly sprouted crops, and the overflow drained down into the lowest trenches. It was a continuing joke that the French lines lay lower than the German. "We'll flush our piss and shit down on them!" And, "If we can't kill them with bullets, we can just let them drown!"

Over the past two years the artillery barrages had splintered most trees in the region, and now men went out in the rain to cut up the wood to shore up the trench walls and to lay down new boardwalks against the rising water.

Another letter came from Britt this morning. *"My dearest Erich..."* Somebody had died, a manservant had been called up, farm prices were down again, while the civilian rationing had almost doubled since last autumn...

Erich thrust the letter into his pocket and threw his half-tent over his head and went out to ride with the daily supply convoy. The rain came down. At the Third Position he supervised dividing the loads, then went down to the Second Position bunker to have coffee with Gerdt. The men out in the trench were lining up for a hot meal, their half-tents a grey forest of canvas peaks in the driving rain.

"I asked Annette, you know," Gerdt said over his coffee. "Last night."

"It took you all this time? And?"

"But she said yes, what do you think! Of course she said yes! To hell with the war, she said!"

"What about the regiment? What will the colonel say?"

"To hell with—"

Down in the First Position rifles and machine guns roared suddenly into life. A distant gong clanged, and whistles shrilled. The men lining up at the stove threw down their mess tins and seized their rifles. Gerdt leapt to his feet, spilling his coffee over the timber floor. Erich followed more cautiously. He did not belong to this lot.

"Stay there!" shouted Gerdt at him, pistol suddenly in his hand. He darted away at the head of a squad of riflemen.

Erich pulled his pistol and followed, buffeted among soldiers charging down the zigzag traverse. As they ran forward, the crack and rattle of small arms intensified, like an avalanche of stones crashing over concrete. Soldiers thrust him out of the way to race past him. Men's voices ahead called out orders in French, in German. A man cried out in the rattle of gunfire. Running, Erich was blinded by rain washing into his eyes and buffeted by unwashed pungent wet bodies pushing past him...

"Fire! fire! fire...!" Gerdt's voice came back to him from far ahead. Gunfire swelled to a roar. Men screamed. The air exploded with blasts and the cries of men, and the rain came down...

Then came a stutter in the noise.

Gradually the shots and movement tailed off as Erich finally reached the forward trench. The men ahead of him were stopping now. He'd never fired his pistol, he'd seen no French targets, just this mass of wet grey German uniforms, now slowing, gathering, regrouping...

"*Ach nein!*"

He heard that little grunt ahead, and felt a chill go through him, he didn't know why.

A hand touched his shoulder. "It's fine now, Lieutenant, we sent the buggers packing. We never follow, we let them go."

Rifles still fired sporadically. From the pillbox a machine gun hammered a long chattering burst. Somebody said, "They never so much as sent over one artillery shell this time—"

"Never gave even a warning—"

"Only madmen attack in such rain!"

"Crazy French...!"

The rain came down. Erich moved forward among the men. He felt he was drowning in rain. The soldiers bent over bodies in the mud, checking identity tags, searching pockets for papers. Blood, mud, crumpled bodies. The rain came down.

"Wounded here." A voice ahead.

"Any prisoners?"

"Give a hand here. The lieutenant caught one."

No, Erich thought, *I'm not hit, I'm fine...*

Except...

He pushed his way forward. The men parted to let him through. Stood back, watched him. Nervous. Eyes shifting. Rain dripped from helmets...

He stepped over the strewn lumps of uniforms and scattered guns, the bodies with blind eyes staring out, the rain hammering down, blood mingling with mud, a wounded French soldier still moving, groaning, cried out, "Au secours! Kamerad...! "

A landser fired point blank into his face. One jerk, and silence.

And beyond...

Gerdt.

In the mud.

Erich stumbled forward over bodies.

"He's wounded, sir," one of the men said to him. "I'll get a stretcher."

"Don't wait for a stretcher!" Another pushed in. "Use a half-tent."

Gerdt lay on the trench floor, half covered in mud, streaming with rain. His left arm was jammed awkwardly under his chest exactly as he had fallen.

Erich reached him and knelt beside him. Didn't dare to touch him. He couldn't see a wound. Lying prone, Gerdt's head was twisted sideways in mud mixing thick with blood, his face in the mud white as chalk, his eyes clenched shut.

"Gerdt...?"

His head turned an inch out of the mud, he opened his eyes. "Tell Annette..."

And, smiling, he died.

* * *

CHAPTER 20

May 1916

Erich sat alone in the baggage car among the trunks and crates and mail packages and twenty-three coffins going to Mannheim and Heidelberg. Neatly stacked in six rows, each coffin had a metal name tag nailed to the top right corner to identify the burden within. The scent of raw wood blended with smoke and grit from the locomotive.

He sat beside Gerdt's box. The train master had brought him a folding chair, suitably uncomfortable. It let him guard the box, and the discomfort kept him awake. The whole journey home he fingered the French bayonet he'd picked up in the trench, a token of Gerdt's moment of death...

Perhaps he would bury it with Gerdt.

But no. It was an enemy bayonet...

The colonel had ordered Gerdt buried in the regimental cemetery at Schwetzingen, but Erich had gone to the top, to General von Fuchs himself at Detachment C, the first time he had ever gone against a superior officer's decision. Fuchs was a lean dry man with direct eyes and a stillness about him that gave Erich his full attention. "You represent the family," he said after hearing him out. "I'll provide a written order. The family plot in Heidelberg, you say?"

"Thank you sir."

During the long ride from Metz through Saarbrücken and

Kaiserslautern and Mannheim he had all that time to think. The wrong people died. Gerdt the farmer, Gerdt the lover longing to marry. Gerdt would not want a French bayonet buried with him.

The wrong people died and the wrong people lived. Erich hadn't thought much about it until now.

For two years this war had bogged-down on one decision of one man, when the First Army forming the right wing had turned east of Paris instead of circling west and south. Just over a month into the war when they still could have pulled it off... a commander-in-chief had blinked...

Von Moltke. Erich's own sponsor, benefactor, whatever they called it...

Had blinked.

And now this. Trench warfare. Nobody ever dreamed of trenches when they'd started out. Trenches changed the tradition of warfare. There were no rules today. No motion, no strategy. Just fire blind and hope. A war of mud and explosions and millions of bodies. Germans used gas, the British used gas, everybody cried foul and perfected more deadly kinds of gas, and across all of France from Flanders to Switzerland an open strip lay between opposing armies called no-man's-land, where corpses rotted without burial, without dignity. He'd been trained to fight in honour, but there was no honour in this. You just killed whatever you could kill.

At least he could bury Gerdt.

And when that was done he would go back and apply for Gerdt's command and go out with a Frenchman's bayonet and kill a few Frenchmen...

*

The train slid to a gentle stop. A whistle blew. The baggage-car door opened with a crash. The afternoon sun flooded in. A squad of infantrymen lined up on the platform to begin loading coffins onto the truck beds to go to the hospital.

He stepped down from the metal footplate into sunshine. He searched for Britt but didn't see her along the platform in the crowd that now began to break into little groups, "Hello, hello, so good to see you home...!" Embraces. Kisses. The laughter seemed incongruous, with Gerdt lying there in a box. Behind him the corporal in charge of coffins muttered his commands to his squad of bearers. Erich hitched his rucksack over one shoulder and walked off the platform.

"Erich!"

He swung about. She came from the street through the breaking crowd, pale hair, pale skin, eyes of amethyst fixed upon his face. She met him and stopped. For a magic moment he stood a pace from her, absorbing the *realness* of her, close enough to touch, tidy little figure in a black mourning frock and black button shoes.

"It's so terrible," she whispered. She opened wide her arms and gripped him around his chest, her face pressed under his throat. "Hold me," she whispered. "Just hold me."

They walked together up the cobbled lane, rucksack over his shoulder, Britt hanging on his arm. He could not pin down the feeling that something dreadful had happened. Not just her brother's death out there in the war, but something more. Something *here*. This girl who clung to him was not Britt. *Where is my tiger*, he wanted to ask. Aloud to her he said, "How's the colt?"

"How did it happen?"

"It happens, that's all. Tell me about the colt."

"Well he's fine, he's fine." Impatient. "He's coming well. But why were you with Gerdt when it happened? Are you not far from the fighting? We're doing everything we can to bring you home, you know."

"I know. I heard."

A few steps farther on she asked, "Well?"

He stopped under the great oak tree, its new leaves still a bright green before darkening into summer. "Are you trying to manage my war? You and your father?"

"Of course!" And suddenly she was crying. "Of course I am, I want you here, I want you out of the fighting, I don't want you to die like Gerdt, you're my husband, I need you here to take care of things, oh my God..."

He dropped the rucksack and held her, and they stood wrapped together under the great oak, sunlight dappling through the boughs. His body awakened to her body, heating now, pulsing. He pulled apart from her. He took up his rucksack and they walked faster now.

"Darling," he said, "I'm a soldier. Your father's a soldier. You know all about it, a soldier does his duty, no favours asked."

She didn't speak.

He glanced sideways at her. She trudged on, her eyes on the cobbles.

The house seemed empty when they went in. He dropped his rucksack to the floor and took her into his arms again. And now at last, here in the gloom of the hallway, he pressed her to him and forced her mouth open with his kiss and searched down deep and hot. With his fingers he kneaded her breasts through the stiff stays of her bodice, and probed down over her corset to the solid pad of hips and buttocks, seeking a break in the armour, while his pulsing started to rise again... "Come on." He broke free and took her hand and started toward the stairs.

"But wait." Her eyes darted along the hall to the kitchen, then back toward the gun room, searching.

"Wait? Who cares! The servants know I'm home." He pulled her hand up the stairs. She came, dragging back on his hand.

In the bedroom he stripped out of his tunic and tossed it over the chair and slipped his braces over his shoulders...

She stood watching him, her eyes without expression.

"Are you all right?"

She shrugged. "I'm sorry."

"Not on Gerdt's account. He would sit up and cheer."

Again she shrugged, and turned away to the window. "I'm sorry, Erich, it's... It's the... It's the wrong time of the month."

Ice water over the head. He took several deep breaths, and sat on the edge of the plush marriage bed, and stared over at her.

"I can't," she whispered. "I'm sorry. I only started today."

He sank on his back across the bed and flung his arms wide like a crucifix, and rested there gazing at the ceiling. *It had been months...*

And now this... and now this... According to her calendar, eight days of *this*. According to his calendar, only two days at home...

God.

*

They sat alone for supper in the large dining room, with only the housemaid, Katja, to serve, and a nameless cook in the kitchen.

Potatoes and turnip and a bit of fresh carp caught in the river by an enterprising fellow who hawked his catch door-to-door. "But we produce pork on the farms," Erich said to Britt across the table. "And lamb in the spring and fall, na? We're not short of meat are we?"

"The government takes most of it." She seemed on the verge of tears. "For the army."

He'd never seen before such a sadness in her eyes, as if her spark had flickered out. He dropped his fork and knife and went around and put his hands softly on her shoulders and bent over and kissed the top of her hair, scent of lavender, feel of silk. "I'm sorry, darling. I'm sorry. It's war."

She gripped his hand and quietly wept.

He stroked her hair. He felt the same way. He went back to his chair and pretended enthusiasm for the food. The fish was flabby, tasteless, dry. "What we need," he tried to make a joke, "is perhaps a better cook."

In the quiet evening they waited for the baron to come home from the garrison mess. Restless after supper, Erich searched the books in the gun room and picked out a title, "*Reconnaissance on Foot, on Horse, and by Motor*" and sat in a wing chair by the cold fireplace blindly turning pages. Britt took a chair beside him. Something separated them that he couldn't define, almost the same invisible barrier that once had enclosed them to keep out the rest of the world. But now it separated them instead.

"Tell me more about your work," he said to her.

She spoke. He hardly heard the words. Her voice was measured, without expression. So many bedpans carried and emptied, so many patients sponged and dried, bandages rolled, letters home written for men who'd lost arms or hands or eyes, or simply hadn't the strength to hold a pen. Long days surrounded by unspeakable horror. She mourned the blood and pain, the men dying.

"I think," he said after she'd gone silent for a time, "you must stop working at the hospital."

"Are you crazy?" Flash of energy in her voice. "They need me! The poor wounded men. The doctors and nurses."

"It's exhausting you."

"It keeps me alive! It's all that holds me together while

you're away. You have your war, Erich. I have mine."

He looked across through the barrier between them. "I can forbid you. If it makes you ill, I will forbid you."

She hunched deeper in the large wing chair. "You may forbid me. You cannot stop me."

He let it lie there. They talked then, sporadically, of little things that didn't matter. They avoided talk of Gerdt. At ten they had a glass of wine to relax. After eleven when the baron did not appear, Erich rose and held out his hand, and they went together up to bed. She disappeared into the bathroom to undress. He understood. She never wanted him to see her naked in that condition. When she came out wearing her flannel gown, he went in, and looked about for the evidence.

The hand-washed, rust-tinged rags that she always hung to dry on her special towel rack were... already dry.

She would never leave them there for him to see. Once they were dry, she always folded them away out of sight.

He got into bed, half buried in the eiderdown mattress beside her, and turned out the bedside lamp, and lay there, holding his breath in the darkness, his head gently drifting with the wine and vague confusion of unanswered thoughts...

She turned to him with a little whimper. "I love you my darling. I love you I love you."

He held himself steady, he refused his body's silent scream of desire for this lovely creature pressed against him. He enfolded her and held her quietly. In this time and place it came together again, the reason he loved Germany, the reason he stayed to fight, the reason for his very existence. His destiny. So simple. This woman. All.

But in the close warmth of their bed he did not detect the faint, pungent, musty odour of clotted blood that she always gave off at her woman's time-of-the-month.

She lied.

*

The baron was already at breakfast, dressed for the day in his 1870 blues. He boomed a welcome when Erich came into the kitchen, and immediately poured three cups of coffee out of the pot. "Where's that girl this morning? Did you wear her out last night?"

The question stuck in the air. Erich stared at him sitting there raising a cup to his blameless lips, as if he had not just uttered, soldier to soldier, a lewd and outrageous thing.

Erich swallowed some coffee. He sat down at his place at the table. A breadboard had been set out, with hot biscuits and fruit preserves and cutlery in a tray.

"How was the fighting in Russia?" the baron boomed. "I heard you led a cavalry charge!"

A year ago... "How did you hear of that, sir?"

"Oh I hear everything that goes." He set down his cup. "Proud of you."

It was as if a year were missing from his time.

He had grown quickly old since the death of the baroness. Heartiness gone to heaviness, hairline receding, turkey-wattle neck spilling over the high tight collar, ruddy skin gone to a pallid paste.

"Recommended you for General Staff training."

"Time enough for that when the war's over."

"When the war is won, you mean."

"When the war is won, yes sir. Absolutely."

Britt came in. She wore her riding breeches and boots this morning, and one of Erich's own white shirts tucked into a tiny waist, the sleeves rolled in large loops back to the elbows, the starched collar engulfing her slender neck. She circled behind Erich to give him a quick kiss on the top of his head in passing, and sat in the chair next to him and lifted his coffee cup out of his hand. He slid the third full cup over for himself.

"Why do you dress like a man?" boomed her father.

She sipped the coffee. She picked a biscuit from the tray and began to nibble at it, and did not look at him.

It was proof of the lie. She would never go riding during her time of the month, she'd always believed a woman riding astride would bleed out...

"After breakfast," the baron said to Erich, "I want you to examine the ledgers. Gerdt tells me you're good at such things. He has no interest in bookkeeping."

"After breakfast, sir, we have a funeral."

He looked blankly at Erich. "Another funeral?"

*

The funeral was quiet. Only seven officers wearing ceremonial blues had come from the garrison at Schwetzingen. Erich knew none of them. Beside the open grave they saluted with sabres as the coffin was lowered. A few words by the garrison chaplain. That was all.

Later Erich drove with the baron down to the garrison. "I want to see where his mind is," he told Britt. "I'll be home in an hour." He'd never lied to her before. Then, instead of going into the mess, he left the baron there and walked alone around to the hospital, where he searched out the office of Dr Kirschner. He waited in the office for a long time. Occasionally the nurse-secretary looked in the door to apologise. "So very busy, sir. So many demands." And rushed off again.

Almost two hours wasted out of his time with Britt.

Two hours invested, he answered himself.

"Hello, hello!" The doctor burst through the door, white coattails sailing behind. "How are you managing? Terrible about Gerdt! Sorry I missed the funeral. Wounded coming through every day."

"No, I understand."

Kirschner flung into the chair behind his desk and laid down his stethoscope and folded his hands on the desk. "Something I can help you with?" Lines grew deep about the tired eyes. He seemed to have aged by ten years.

"It's my wife," Erich said.

"Ah Brigitte, yes."

"Something is wrong."

"Just tell me, I'm a busy man, don't make me guess."

"I don't know. Something happened." He tried to describe what he felt, but could not find the proper words. "The way she writes her letters, all her love and enthusiasm gone. She seems exhausted. She doesn't smile. And her excuses..." He couldn't say it.

"Excuses about?"

"She... claimed to have... uh... Well, she denied me... uh—"

"Trouble in the bedroom?"

"Yes sir." He straightened stiffly. He had to be honest here. "She claimed to be at her time of the month, but she lied."

"Why would she lie?

"I ask you. You're her doctor. Why would she lie? She's a... she's a tiger in bed. Except now suddenly..." He shrugged and gave a little shake of the head. "I blame it on the hospital work. I think it exhausts her. I think it shocks her, so many men dying."

"So you think she should stop working here?"

"She won't stop. Even if I forbid her. She says it keeps her engaged."

"So you don't forbid her?"

"I don't know what to do. I can't be here for her. She seems exhausted."

Kirschner gazed at him for another moment, then jumped to his feet. "I'll keep a watch out, how does that suit you? If I feel she goes beyond her limits? Maybe cut back her hours. Will that suit you?" He came around the desk and held out his hand.

Erich shook hands with him. "Thank you sir."

The doctor disappeared out the door in a flap of flying white coat tails.

*

When he got off the train at Metz he stood for a while feeling the faint rumbling through the ground, like a distant earthquake shaking the platform under his feet. Artillery from Verdun, only sixty kilometres away, artillery by day, artillery by night. Millions of shells in both directions. *Millions.*

After the week away he'd somehow thought the world would have changed. Gerdt had died. The war should stop now. But nothing had changed. The abortive Verdun offensive continued, and people didn't even talk about it these days. Last February Falkenhayn had given Germany a moment of hope for real victory. By now it had turned into just another massive meat factory. German boys were dying under guns they could not even see. Death by astonishment. Squashed, cut through the middle, divided from top to bottom, blown into shreds, guts turned inside out, bits of bloody raw meat, shattered arms and legs mixed in with boots and grey wool cloth and grinning skulls hammered into muddy shell holes and left to rot...

In his mind's eye Gerdt smiled up at him. *"Tell Annette..."*

Lucky Gerdt. Buried in one piece...

Annette's family... Bressard... lived here in Metz.

He could not face Annette. In the railway station he sought

out a public desk and took from it a yellow telegram form, and stood leaning his elbows on the desk for a time wondering what he could say.

"My dear Annette ~ I hope this finds you in good health, and that you remember me for being Gerdt's brother-in-law as well as his best friend..."

It took a long time to find the words. When he was done, he tossed away the half-dozen sheets he'd spoiled, and took up an envelope from the desk supply and wrote her name on it, "Mlle. Annette Bressard", and he went to the station master's cubicle to ask for the Bressard address from the town records there, and he wrote down her address.

So it was done.

He had not written down his military address. Live and let live.

*

Back at Battalion it was coming into sunset on the Cormier farm. Major Altmann looked up from his desk with mild surprise. "What are you doing here?"

"Back on duty, sir. Sorry if I'm late—"

"You're supposed to be at Detachment C."

"I received no orders, sir."

"*Scheisse!*" He turned the telephone crank in a spasm of fury. "*Gottverdammt*, didn't you hear? They took you away from me?" When nothing happened on the telephone he flung it back in its box and bellowed for the corporal to call in a pioneer squad to repair the line. Then he sat back down and glared at Erich. "You're to report to Colonel Steiff. Your orderly has moved your kit over to Hattonville." His face split in a wide grin. "You organised Battalion Supply so prettily they want you up the line. You now have Fuchs himself to answer to." His grin widened. "Not an easy man to work for."

Erich stood stock still. *Not again, not again...* "Excuse me sir, did somebody...? Did this come down from von Moltke?"

Altmann peered at him more keenly. "Why do you think that?"

"My father-in-law has connections, sir, he sometimes interferes... He's, uh—"

"This came down from von Fuchs, Schellendorf, because

you went over the colonel's head about the funeral." He grinned again, wolfishly. "You're promoted to *first* lieutenant temporary grade. Colonel Steiff doesn't want a junior lieutenant in *his* office."

"*What?*"

"Get a runner to guide you over."

He turned to go. Along the Meuse all the way from Verdun the regular drumfire from the French stuttered into the evening rumble. *Welcome back to the war...*

"How did the funeral go?"

He paused, a hand on the door latch. "Very quiet, thank you sir. Only a few of the regiment could come to see him off."

"But you were there. That's what counts."

* * *

CHAPTER 21

May to September 1916

Near the heart of the St. Mihiel Salient, surrounded by farms and forests that had been chopped and splintered by almost two years of fighting, the Detachment C headquarters occupied a French chateau on the crest of a hill. Horses filled every stall, wagons and automobiles and lorries were parked in every yard. Every outbuilding was used for storage. Soldiers kipped down in the main barn and took their ease on the football pitch. The officers were quartered in the chateau attics and in a row of guest chalets according to seniority, lowest rank farthest out. Erich had been assigned a chalet by the railway track which shuddered on its foundation every time a locomotive rolled past in the night. Kropp had found a bunk somewhere else.

Early that first morning Erich walked alone up the hill to report to Colonel Steiff for duty.

*

"You'll be my adjutant in Logistics."

Colonel Steiff was dapper in walking-out uniform and highly polished boots and his sleek hair touched up, Erich thought, with a hint of henna. The ruddy moustache was neatly clipped in the latest drawing room style, not the waxed handlebars so popular among cavalry officers.

"That means," the colonel said, "you will collate the daily supply requirements for the detachment and have the figures on my desk by 1200 hours each day."

"Where do I obtain these figures?"

"Your sergeant will deliver daily reports to your desk in the war room."

The sergeant spoke in grunts as he showed Erich to his desk. The war room in the rear of the chateau had once been a drawing room, spacious and gracious, with old master paintings on the walls and a crystal chandelier overhead. The original furniture had been cleared out, replaced by utilitarian filing cabinets, nine army desks, a dozen chairs, and a large situation map on one wall.

His desk was a bare kitchen table, with a kitchen chair to sit on. Behind the desk a French door opened to a grove of chestnut trees. For a few minutes Erich stood outside gazing at a town named Hattonville, a quarter mile down a long hill.

"Hello there, so you're the new fellow!"

An officer in shirtsleeves leaned out the open door. Behind him the sergeant was already piling papers on Erich's table.

Erich returned inside.

"I'm Remer," the fellow said. "Captain Hans Remer. You must be Schellendorf. We don't salute around here. Well, except for Steiff, watch out for Steiff. And the general."

They shook hands.

"I work for Steiff," Erich said.

"Yes, well too bad for you." He glanced at the table, now piled with papers. "You'll be busy. We've all had a hand at this, so good luck. Come and meet the fellows."

The fellows were having coffee in the officers' mess. Any time of the day or night, Remer told Erich, they could ring the bell for service. Service was quick, the food excellent, cooked by French chefs on duty twenty-four hours of every day. No black bread or white beans here, a general occupied the second floor. *Coq au Vin*, rack of lamb, venison with truffles, fully stocked wine cellar.

Within the first week he heard it again: *Engländer*. He said nothing. The *Engländer* worked in the Army Service Corps, the lowest of the low, never mind his parent regiment. He smiled and attended to his papers. Everything, including the distant rumble of artillery, became background for the endless records.

He soon got to know the other officers, got to know who drank too much, who talked too much, who brooded. He too was a brooder, he knew that. Yet when he sat down to lunch in the mess, somebody was bound to sit with him at his table. It was as if they were seeking new blood, new eyes, new stories. They all seemed in low spirits. Their jokes were forced and too jolly, their silences long. An air of oppression hung over them.

With the colonel, Erich learned to work in silence. Had to be there, had to be one jump ahead, but be silent. Colonel Steiff did not like his job, said it was demeaning for a fighting officer to count things; and when Erich stepped in Steiff's way, he was fired upon with sarcastic harangues for the rest of that day.

"God," said Remer, "I've been stuck here two years now. Once you're in the Salient, your career comes to an end. None of us has been promoted since joining the Detachment."

"You could put in for a transfer."

"Oh sure, and be sent into the trenches. That's how to get killed for sure."

"I know, I just lost my brother there, my best friend."

"Ah..."

The distant artillery rarely paused. The chateau was out of range, at least fifteen kilometres from French guns in any direction, and nobody paid attention to it. "That's from Verdun," Remer told him. "In this place, you know, from time to time we see a French reconnaissance airplane. We take pot shots at them, it's our best entertainment."

"Is there no fighting here at all?"

"Well, the French opposite, they're undermanned. We're just ninety kilometres from Paris, we only need to mount up and attack, if somebody would give the order. The High Command in their wisdom, however, has made this a rest area."

"But the records... we don't have the manpower to attack."

Remer grinned. "Ah, you and your records. Can't fight a war with records."

Erich smiled. Couldn't fight without them.

Once he got into the rhythm of the work he often found time heavy on his hands.

The chateau seemed a busy place, always somebody driving up or driving away. At each entrance a foot-guard marched a regular beat, and slapped rifle stocks for every visitor coming and going. A horse was usually tied at the front post, a lorry parked by the steps. The general's staff auto always stood ready and occasionally drove off in a cloud of dust.

"Come along," said Remer one summer afternoon. "We're going fishing."

They went out in a group, five of the officers with their orderlies who carried the fishing poles as well as a magnum of champagne in a portable ice chest. Out by a little stream they took off their shirts in the sun and sat along the bank and dangled fish-lines into the water for a couple of hours and drank champagne until it was gone. Then they put on their shirts over painful new sunburns and walked back to the chateau.

Another afternoon they rode out ten kilometres to Lac de Madine, where they shed their clothes and unsaddled the horses and rode out in the water to swim in joyful splashings of naked freedom. It was well after dark before they got back.

And of course there was the village.

Only once did Erich go down with the boys to the village. It was crowded with soldiers on rest leave from the trenches, some posted here until assigned to new units. They answered daily roll-call and took drill in the mornings, but by afternoon they had nothing to do. Erich heard many dialects among them. Units were all mixed up, Austrians, Prussians, Badeners, Swabians, and Hungarians and Turks who spoke their own language. Many got into trouble one way or another. Too much to drink, too many ladies of the night. Too much battle-weariness, too many arguments and fist-fights. Too many soldiers having nothing to do. The evening that Erich went down with the boys, they were assailed on every side by the ladies from the local *estaminet*, and he had to battle his way back to the little chalet.

*

Britt did not often write. Days went by between her letters. At supper he read the latest with the same stranger's tone ...*We are both well, we are lucky to have eggs from the farms, but the crops this year were very poorly started due to the unusual rains. Father was distressed to hear of the death in June of General von Moltke, his old friend of many years and comrade-at-arms...*

Von Moltke was dead? He'd missed it in the newspapers?

But she wrote nothing of herself, she did not call him darling or write that she loved him or missed him or...

She'd lied to him. That was what he could not sort out.

She had lied to him.

A gust of laughter at the next table turned his head. Remer caught his eye and half rose from his ornate Louis XIV chair. "Join us, Engländer." He waved a hand at an empty place between the others at his table, von Hase, junior liaison to the Fifth Army at Verdun, and Zintner, captain of the Detachment guardroom.

Immediately a steward drew Erich's chair back from under him. Another carried his plate and glass to the next table, so that he was left without a decision in the matter.

"So how is it going with Steiff?" Hase asked.

"No trouble."

Remer grinned. "We all had a nose full of Steiff. So you're in good company here."

"I just do my work, it's all he wants."

Even as he said it, Colonel Steiff walked into the mess. He ran a sharp glance over the table as he passed to the bar to order a drink. Then he stood, one elbow braced on the bar, studying the group of officers.

"Watch," muttered Hase. "He'll come this way. He'll soon spoil our dessert."

"Schellendorf!" barked the colonel across the room.

Erich came to his feet and clicked his heels.

"Over here."

Erich laid down his serviette and walked across, reviewing everything he'd done this morning. His supper was effectively over.

"Have a drink with me," ordered the colonel.

"Thank you sir. Lager for me."

The colonel rapped his knuckles twice on the bar, and the barman rushed to fill a stein from the keg. It seemed to Erich a strange repetition of that other evening with the baron, while the baroness had been slowly dying in her opulent solarium.

"I've noticed," the colonel nudged the stein into Erich's hand, "that your work does not keep you fully occupied."

"It's less detailed than anything I've done before, sir."

"We lost a man this morning." The distant artillery barrage vibrated the window panes.

"Only one, sir?"

The colonel snorted. "Schellendorf, You display a wicked humour."

He wondered if humour made a difference.

"I understand you commanded a cavalry troop in Prussia,

"Yes sir." His heart lifted. Then slumped when he thought about dying horses.

"Can you do my paper work in the mornings and be free for evening patrol duty?"

"Yes, sir."

"Fine." He took another sip, then seemed to recall... "By the way. Major Altmann?"

"Yes sir?"

"He caught shrapnel yesterday. On the way to supper. Side of the head. Instant."

Aaaagh.

"Could have been you," the colonel added almost wistfully, and drank down his cognac.

*

The guardhouse was in the middle of the village at the base of the long hill. Erich reported at 1600 to Zintner, captain of the guard, who spoke in barks. "You're cavalry!"

"Yes Captain." He would not call this fellow 'sir'.

"Then you'll wear your cavalry uniform!"

He couldn't help smiling. "Gladly, Captain."

"Report back when you've changed."

*

"Fill me in," Erich told the sergeant as the troop rode through the village in column-of-two. "I haven't pulled this duty before." He wore his cavalry field-greys with the insignia of his parent regiment. He'd drawn a quiet bay gelding from the officers' stable, and felt more lively than in months. The late afternoon air was fresh on his face.

The sergeant was an older man, perhaps in his forties, with deep lines on his ruddy face from years in the weather, a light hand on the rein, and an easy way with the men.

The ten troopers behind them were a little slack and untidy.

"Fill me in," Erich prodded the sergeant.

"We watch for deserters, that's all. And we keep the peace."

"Sir!" said Erich.

The sergeant shot him a sharp look.

"You address me as 'sir'. I call you 'sergeant'." He used the familiar *'Du'*.

"If that's what the lieutenant wants."

"That's what the lieutenant wants."

"Yes SIR."

They rode. The French villagers went about their business, eyes on the ground. Infantrymen on 48-hour passes from the front had ridden in on the little train today and were sitting in the late sun, or wandering through the marketplace, flirting with girls on the street, lining up outside the public bath. Scruffy, filthy uniforms, long hair, unshaven jaws. They needed a bath and delousing; and they needed to be checked for their papers and their passes.

"How," Erich asked the sergeant, "do you tell a deserter from a soldier on legitimate pass?"

"Ah, we can usually tell." Then laconically he added, "Sir."

It was going to be like that.

"There!" The sergeant raised a sudden hand. "Take them!" The entire troop charged forward and left Erich gaping. They galloped down upon two soldiers who dodged desperately through the market crowd. The horses quickly surrounded them, battering civilians out of the way and overturning a table of vegetables.

Erich pressed forward to regain control.

"Papers!" the sergeant barked. The troop eddied around the two soldiers.

Erich rode up beside him. "Show me their papers, Sergeant."

"They got no papers, Lieutenant, that's the thing." Then he turned in the saddle and waved forward a trooper. "Fritsch, take three men with you, escort 'em back and lock 'em up. Then follow us on." He muttered sideways to Erich, "Probably put the cowards up against the wall. Sir."

He watched while the two were marched away at the point of four mounted lances.

"Sergeant."

"Sir?"

"We can do it this way, or we can do it the army way. You want to bring me into the picture."

"Sir, I got no time to horse around."

"Oh yes we do have time, Sergeant. Plenty of time. Just fill me in as we ride."

Then, before the sergeant could call for column-of-two, Erich gave the hand signal to form up the troop again and they continued on the patrol. It would carry them into the night along the road to Vigneulles, and by another road back to the chateau by midnight, watching, watching for any suspicious movements. Foot patrols were doing similar duty in every camp and village behind the front. As the war dragged on, there were more and more deserters.

A shock to Erich, he hadn't heard about desertion. It was not advertised.

The next morning he was at his desk when he heard the volley of rifle fire down in the village. He didn't think about it; but later when he joined the troop for the evening patrol, he heard.

"They shot them two deserters," the sergeant told him. "*Sir.*"

"Ah." It seemed too sudden.

"Cap'n wants to see you. *Sir.*"

"Form up the troop then, Sergeant. I won't be long. And try not to be impudent."

In the guardhouse he saluted Zintner and stood at ease before the desk. The captain pushed papers across the desk at him. "Names of the two deserters."

"Yes sir?"

"Need letters to the parents. Explain how they died."

"Why not their own officer, Captain?"

"You were the officer who caught them. Their own officer will lie about it, make them out to be heroes."

"Didn't they even have a court martial, Captain?"

"We don't court-martial cowards."

Summary justice. *His father would have a fit.* In the doorway, in the middle of this French village, with artillery thundering all along the distant line, he paused with a sudden, eerie sense of dislocation.

His father would have a fit?
What did his father think of all this? Of this war. Of Erich in this war. What would his father think of such summary injustice? He forced himself onward to start the evening patrol.

*

My Dear Frau Kesel...
He mulled over it a long time, trying to find the words to tell a mother that her son had been shot as a coward. His father still haunted him, even after eight hours on patrol. Nothing much had happened this evening. A long ride, with his father's spirit drifting in the dark shadows beside him.

Outside the open window of his little chalet a strange silence hung over the night. The train had not moved all evening. The artillery was silent, the whole night was silent. Not even a nightingale. He listened a while, appreciating the peace. Even if only a temporary peace...

He bent to tackle the letter.

He could not tell a mother the terrible truth. *My dear Frau Kesel, it is my duty to inform you of the unfortunate death of your son Paul Wilhelm Kesel while on active duty. Another comrade stood by his side as they came under a heavy volley of rifle fire. Both soldiers died bravely and without suffering...*

Such were the facts. He folded and sealed the letter and wrote the mother's address on it. When the censors checked it, what would they know? If the captain opened it, Erich was in trouble.

Ah well.

He started on the second letter. *My dear Frau Steglitz...*

* * *

CHAPTER 22

September to November 1916

My darling Britt ~
How are you these days? I hear almost nothing from you. My life continues divided between endless paper work and police duties.
I have not had a note from you in almost two weeks. The last you wrote you were tired, having worked all night at the hospital. My darling Britt, you have not answered my question: when did you begin working at night? And no word from you at all for these past two...

The world was coming to an end. The guns never stopped. All along the trench lines from Flanders to Switzerland they seldom paused. In the heat of the passing summer the smell of death rose in sweet thick clouds from thousands of unburied bodies in no-man's land twenty kilometres away. The stench hung on the air, it moved with every breeze, it curdled Erich's stomach and clung to his skin. He could not wash it off. He went to bed at night with death in his nostrils, and woke in the morning with death in his throat. How much more horrifying it must be for the soldiers at the front.

And flies everywhere, and fleas in his blankets and lice in his hair that had to be cleared out with petrol. Rats scurried in the barns fouling the grain and making the horses sick with colic.

Much worse at the front, with rats and two kinds of lice in the trenches.

Many crops had failed this year, first from the heavy rains and then from the heat wave that stretched into a summer-long drought. Poor crops had already led to scarce animal feeds. And now the Intendant was confiscating livestock to feed the army, and farmers were hiding their animals to conserve their breeding stock; and this left no meat for the markets. There were few potatoes, few cereals, a poor wheat crop from Prussia. Butter was *ersatz,* a disgusting mix of curdled milk and sugar and food colouring. Bread had picked up a new name... *War Bread...* made of oats and rice, dried bean meal, corn meal and even pea meal, all ground together, mixed with water, and baked into small hard grey loaves too tough to cut. Erich knew all this firsthand as part of the Supply complex, though none of it ever reached the general's table.

Every afternoon when he rode with the troop on patrol, he saw the funeral processions, not for fallen soldiers, but funerals for old people and new babies. Starvation was in the air along with the stench of the unburied dead.

And lately he was hearing how the British Blockade in the Atlantic had successfully cut off Germany from world trade while the Kaiser's fleet huddled safely in the Baltic. There would be no outside relief from famine this year unless somehow the Kaiser's submarine squadron could break the blockade. The war now seemed to depend on the navy.

Britt had to live with this too. Somewhere in the middle of her personal war at the hospital she would be running the estates and keeping the ledgers, and trying to manage a father whose mind constantly drifted back to a better time...

*

> *In your latest letter* (he wrote) *you made no mention of the baron. How is he now? Does he continue drinking his days away in the mess? Are you able to make sense of the ledgers? Are you helping to run the estates? Oh my darling Britt, it is so difficult even to ask such questions, but your silence causes me to think in such terms. Please I beg you to keep me informed...*

At least once a month since he had transferred here, he'd applied for a few days' leave, and had been denied. "No," said the colonel, "this may seem a minor job to you, Schellendorf, but nobody else has managed it so well. If you find an efficient replacement for yourself..."

But none of the other officers would volunteer to work for the colonel, even for a few days.

> ...*but being a policeman* (he wrote) *is not in my nature. My men know it. I have seen young men broken through this work, and it does not make me proud. We sent three more men before the firing squad in the past week, which makes sixteen condemned to death since I began commanding these patrols back in July, most of them very young. This is not the war I started out to fight.*
>
> *The rest is merely numbers. I have become a pencil-pusher...*

He looked over his letter, two pages of complaints. He would not send it to her. It only aired his dissatisfaction, and would do nothing to cheer her. It might even make her feel guilty for putting him in this position.

Yes. She had done this. She had not intended it, but she had worked at the baron until he had worked at his friend, von Moltke, and this was the result. Out of a successful junior cavalry commander came a successful policeman. It looked to be permanent. Von Moltke had died.

*

"The general wants to see you." A corporal leaned in through the hall door, his hands braced on the door frames.

No 'sir'? No salute?

"What is your name, Corporal?"

"Braun, sir." The man straightened to attention. "Corporal Helmut Braun."

"Put yourself on report. Insubordination. Improper address, no salute."

"Sorry sir."

"Take me first to the general."

Damn. One should expect discipline in a headquarters... Everyone suffered the same depressed spirit.

He followed the corporal up the curving Louis XV staircase. The day was dull, the weather cold, with winter definitely on the way. Even inside the manor the air carried a bite of frost. Artillery rumbled faintly through closed windows.

The corporal opened the office door for Erich, and dodged away.

"Schellendorf." General von Fuchs stood up with his hand outstretched across the desk. "We meet again."

Erich cracked his heels as they shook hands.

He waved Erich to a chair, and sat down behind the desk covered with maps. "Not the work you trained for."

"Not really, sir."

"You've requested leave a few times."

He felt a stirring of hope.

"Well, you're going to get your leave, Schellendorf. I don't know for exactly how long, I leave that to your discretion. Unfortunately it is not as you hoped. It comes on compassionate grounds."

"Compassionate, sir?"

"I received this telegram a few minutes ago. Your wife is apparently quite ill in hospital. The situation may be serious." He handed the yellow paper across the desk.

"*...UNDERWENT EMERGENCY SURGERY AT 04:00 TUESDAY...*"

"Ride directly to Vigneulles," the general said. "A hospital train will wait there for you only fifteen minutes, it's the last train to Metz before tomorrow." He handed Erich a leave pass. "Don't worry about anything here, cable us when you arrive."

Erich stopped at his own desk only for his coat and cap. He carried a little money in his pocket, he could get more in Heidelberg. He ran around the corridors to the front entrance where somebody's horse would be tethered. Two were there; he chose the bay and rode away at a gallop without a word even to the guard at the step. Nobody stopped him.

*

Almost eighteen hours later he came into Heidelberg by the same train, simple blind luck that its destination was one of the largest hospitals in the country. Along the length of the platform a squadron of ambulances lined up to carry casualties to *her* hospital. Where she worked. Where she now lay after surgery.

Wearily he walked the half mile to the hospital. Ambulances passed him one by one, a slow procession. People turned in the street to watch them go.

At the hospital there were still no answers. The doctor was not yet in, and the night staff would not tell him where Britt was lying after surgery. At the desk all the sister would say was, yes, Frau *Oberleutnant* von Schellendorf was a patient here.

"But," he protested, "I'm her husband. I must see her."

"Sir, it is not yet seven in the morning. You must wait for doctor's permission."

"Is she alive?"

"Yes sir, she is resting." She smiled a gentle smile. "Why don't you go home and get a little sleep? And perhaps have a shave before she sees you? Around noon, perhaps?"

He walked slowly up to the grey stone house.

Katja met him at the front door. She took his cap and coat and hung them away. "Will you have breakfast, sir?"

She looked as if she had not slept either. Her hair was awry, her clothing rumpled.

"What happened, Katja?" He led the way out to the kitchen.

She followed silently. She was a strange girl, always silent, often clumsy. In the kitchen she moved the coffee pot from the warming plate over to the hot element, as if she could not bother to brew a fresh pot. Her eyes were dull.

He sat at the table. "What happened?" he asked again.

She sat down. It fleetingly astonished him that a servant would sit at the table with the master. But Katja had always been odd. She did not speak at once.

He waited.

Finally she gave a great sigh. "She had an accident, sir."

"What kind of accident?"

She shrugged, and would not look at him. "The doctor will have to explain it, sir."

"What, did she fall from a horse? Did she break bones?"

"Oh, nothing like that sir."

"Then what? You were with her, were you not?"

Another deep breath. Finally she looked at him. "A woman's accident, sir."

"A woman's...? *What?*"

Another pause. Then in careful words, "She had a haemorrhage, sir. She might of died, but we got her there in time. The doctor will have to tell you."

"Oh! My! God!"

It had burst out of him in English...

She got up from the table and went to the stove to draw him a cup of reheated coffee, black and strong as cast-iron. After the filth of army coffee, it tasted fine. He wondered vaguely where real coffee came from in these lean days. From Turkey, across the Bosporus? No farm in Germany could grow coffee beans, and South America was cut off by the British fleet...

*

She was not really awake. She saw him there and smiled, and closed her eyes. In the darkness of Erich's own fatigue *Gerdt smiled... and closed his eyes... and died...*

He caught his breath...

Her skin was a strange mix of pallor and faded summer tan, dry and hot to touch. He sat a long time beside her bed, watching her face, stroking her cheek, closing his mind to Gerdt's last smile. Occasionally her eyelids fluttered, but did not open again after that first look.

"Is she all right?" he whispered to the sister who stopped to check the chart.

She nodded.

"Why won't she wake?"

"She's had morphia, sir. For the pain."

He half rose from the chair. "The pain? Is she in pain? What happ—?"

"Wait for the doctor." And she prepared a needle to inject morphia into Britt's limp shoulder.

*

"So sorry!" said Dr Kirschner. "I've been in surgery since eight this morning. A new shipment of fresh hamburger from Verdun." He pulled a chair beside Britt's bed and collapsed on it like an empty sack. His white coat was smeared with blood. He pulled off his surgery mask and let it fall to the floor. "Well!"

It was almost five in the evening.

"How could this happen?" Erich asked. "I entrusted her to you."

"Oh my dear fellow..." He flipped open his pocket watch. "Come, let's have something to eat together, I'll tell you what I can." Then before they left he put a stethoscope to her chest for another moment, and was satisfied.

They went along corridors and up a flight of stairs past nuns rustling busily in their silence, yet bombarded by the moans and groans of men in pain. Kirschner's small office was filled with books jammed into bookshelves and piled over his desk. The window looked out toward the Schloss. Somebody had set sandwiches on the cluttered desk, and a jug of milk. "Goat's milk," he announced. "Better than cow's milk, and it's not rationed." He sat behind the desk.

Erich took the other chair.

"Have you seen the baron?" the doctor asked. "He hasn't come to visit her yet."

"I didn't see him."

"Something's going on there."

"What do you mean?"

"I don't know." He concentrated on choosing a sandwich, and pushed the plate toward Erich. "I thought you might know."

Erich pushed it back. "What happened Monday night?"

The doctor chewed. He watched Erich's face while he ate half a sandwich. Then finally he said, "In the middle of the night she had a haemorrhage of the uterus. We could not stop the bleeding by medical means, we have limited resources in that way. We had to—"

"*We?*"

"Me! I had to make a decision. I couldn't find the baron, and you were away at the front."

Erich held his breath.

"To save her life," the doctor said. "I had to open her up and perform a hysterectomy."

"*What?*" He didn't know that word. "What's that?"

"Extensive damage causing a massive haemorrhage in the uterus. Massive. Hysterectomy. Removed the uterus."

They contemplated each other across the desk.

The doctor took up another sandwich. "Sorry. I won't have another chance to eat. Rounds in ten minutes. Please, help yourself. I'm sure you haven't eaten since you arrived."

Reluctantly surrendering to his own hunger, Erich took up a sandwich. "Haemorrhage? How did she come to haemorrhage?"

"Something we have yet to determine. Extensive damage inside. But..." He poured milk into a glass. "The most important thing, perhaps..." He set aside the sandwich and milk, and leaned his elbows on the desk. "I have to tell you..." A long pause...

Would she be crippled? Would she die?

"I'm sorry... I'm sorry..." Another pause.

"Please. Say it."

He leaned forward, watching Erich's face. "There was a foetus. Probably four months along." His eyes never wavered. "We lost it of course."

He sat staring at the doctor. His mind rejected the thought. The world would stop. *God... Please God...*

A foetus?

Aaagh... God... God... God...

Whose foetus?

*

He sat with her all night. She woke and slept. While she slept she cried in pain and when she woke she spoke to him in slurred and rambling words. A sister came by every few hours to give her a drink of water, applied a bedpan and gave another little needle in the arm. From along the corridor came sounds of groaning and moaning and the cries of men. In the half light shining from the open doorway he sat through the hours and watched her face. She had not changed. In sleep, even in pain, she was still the most beautiful creature he had ever seen.

Face of an angel. This was his Britt, this pixie, this laughing devil, his darling, his beloved...

A foetus, *foetus foetus... some other man's filthy foetus... a monstrosity...*

Four months.

Not his. Not possibly his...

This was his beloved Britt. She could not have done this awful thing to him...

All through the night the orderlies and sisters on silent shoes hurried from time to time along the lighted corridor past the open door. In the deepest night a man in another part of the wing began to scream and for two hours he screamed with every breath, and then suddenly he stopped. Erich had heard enough of that to know the man had died.

In the morning as the sun came through the window Britt opened her eyes and smiled at him. "I dreamed you were here." Her voice was a hoarse murmur.

"I'm here. I've been here all night."

"I'm sorry."

"How do you feel now? Are you in pain?"

"I'm sorry, Erich, I'm so sorry..." She was weeping. Again and again, over and over, "I'm sorry I'm sorry..." until she faded back to sleep.

Only she knew all there was to know.

She would not tell him. It didn't matter whether she told him or not. He couldn't believe her. She had lied before.

*

Back in the house he took a shower. Today was Thursday. Somewhere he had lost a day, and still had not slept or eaten. He changed out of his filthy clothes at last, putting on his walking-out cavalry blues, the only uniform in the wardrobe. It was regulation in wartime that he wear the uniform even on leave, and so be always on call to bear arms where needed.

In the kitchen he found the baron, Colonel of the Regiment, in his 1870 field blues, poised to ride off to war.

"Ah, Erich! Where is that daughter of mine? Have you seen the baroness? Where is everybody?"

* * *

CHAPTER 23

November 1916

They drove in the Benz down to the garrison. "I never know where anybody is," the baron complained. "The house is always empty! Where do they go?" He drove at full throttle, while pedestrians dodged in the narrow lane. "Idiots!" he shouted. "Out of the way!" His right hand steered the car, his left hand pumped the horn, *OOgah-OOgah!*

Erich held to the side door. They thundered across the Karl Theodore Bridge, scattering pedestrians. He turned left into the Neuenheimer Strasse, and Erich thought, Ah good, he's going to the hospital... But partway along the baron drew the car to the verge and looked about in confusion. "Where the hell did it go?"

"What are we looking for, sir?"

"The mess, of course!"

Erich cocked a thumb over his shoulder. "Back there."

"Ach!" And he turned the car around in the road, bouncing the wheels over the verge on both sides, barely missing a team of horses on the towpath hauling a river barge.

It was as wild a ride as any cavalry charge.

At the mess they went into the dining room. "I eat here most of the time," said the baron. "Can't find the cook at home!" He didn't seem to question it. He led the way to a table by a window and sat down and waved Erich into the opposite chair. Early yet, the dining room was deserted.

"Tell me how it is out there, are you still killing Russians? What do you hear from Gerdt?"

Erich sat down carefully. "Um..." He had no idea what to say. "Sir, we buried Gerdt last—"

"Of course we did!" He banged his fist on the table, and the silverware jumped. "Where's the steward?"

The steward leaped forward, and they ordered.

"I'm confused," said the baron when the steward had left.

"In what way, sir?"

"I don't know. Just..." His bluster had melted to uncertainty. He looked at Erich with tragic eyes. "Everybody is gone, Erich."

"I know, sir."

He brightened. "You know?"

"Yes, sir. The menservants are gone to the war, and—"

"Oh so I don't imagine it! I thought I was going mad! I couldn't find anybody!" Then he seemed to shrink into himself. "Don't tell anybody about this. This confusion."

He smiled. "Of course not, sir."

"You were always a sensible boy. Much more sensible than my own." He leaned forward brightly. "What do you hear from Gerdt?"

*

They stood at the bar after lunch. The few officers in residence stopped as they came in to greet the baron in the mess tradition, clicking their heels and raising their glasses. With each new toast the baron raised his glass and took another sip. When he ordered a second cognac, Erich silently shook his head to the barman and gave a little wave of the hand. Leaving the baron to drink his daily measure with his officers, Erich put on his cap and coat and walked out of the garrison mess.

He walked slowly on the tow-path along the riverbank. Here the Neckar ran slow and deep and black. Out in the channel an empty lumber barge inched east toward the mountains, steel chains rattling over its deck sprockets, propelling it against the current. The rattle echoed from the hills on both sides, a lonely, cold, chattering sound.

The first time he'd ever walked this embankment, Gerdt had sauntered along with him, suede jacket slung from two fingers over his shoulder, *"What amuses you, Engländer...?"*

His first German friend. His brother.

But Gerdt was gone. The baroness was gone. The baron was almost gone inside a mind that bumped into its own memories, and confused today with yesterday.

Britt.

It whirled around in his head, Britt was gone too, *Britt was gone.*

He had not seen her since April. Seven months. Not since she had lied about her time-of-the-month and turned away from him. Fundamental fact. No matter how he might try, he could not equate himself with a foetus only four months developed.

She'd carried another man's baby.

Who was the man?

In his mind he saw her pale and weak on a hard hospital bed tucked away in a closet-sized room in a huge hospital bursting with war wounded. Small and delicate, numb with pain and narcotics, scarcely able to open her eyes...

Sweet... Beautiful... Helpless...

Guilty.

Who was the man?

He couldn't confront her with it yet. He could not even think of it. He must first recover his own composure, prepare himself, and... and give her time to... to devise another lie if that was what she needed, and let her build up the lie to a truth, so that... so that...

So that she would not tear them apart...

So that he would not lose her...

Because...

...if he lost her...

What was he doing here? In this place? In this war...?

Sometime later he found himself in Dr Kirschner's office. He hadn't come intentionally. He bumped into the secretary in the corridor outside the office door, who assumed he was here on an appointment.

He sat down obediently to wait.

After a while the doctor dashed in with coattails flying, saw Erich sitting on that chair, and stopped abruptly. "I just came from her," he said. "She's much improved." He moved behind his desk. "Excellent progress. Out of danger. She might go home in another week, ten days."

Erich didn't know what to ask. That was the whole answer. She was out of danger.

"What am I to do?" he finally asked. "What am I to do? I have to go back to the war. I have to leave her like this. How can I leave her like this?"

Kirschner nodded thoughtfully. "How much time do you have?"

He shrugged. "General von Fuchs left it open. No more than a few days."

"I could contact the general directly and obtain an extension, perhaps another month. She'll need somebody. Does she have any other family? An uncle? Cousin? Someone to give support? Someone to come and help for a while?"

"Not locally. I don't know who to ask."

"But we ask her of course."

He wasn't thinking clearly.

"Do you wonder," the doctor said carefully, toying with his pen on the desk, "who might be responsible for this?"

"I can't... I can't think about it."

"Do not blame your wife for it."

Erich sat abruptly straight on the chair.

"No no, you're too tired for this. I'm going to send a cable to the general to extend your leave, and we can talk later. I want you to find out who might help. Na?" He too sat up straight. "Now go home and get some sleep, and don't come back until morning." He came to his feet. "General von Fuchs, you say?"

"I want to see her," he whispered. His brain was exploding now with questions and hope.

*

He stood for a while looking down on her as she slept. Her face was at peace. He absorbed the beauty of her, swallowed her beauty like nourishment into his being.

The question was... If she was not to blame...

Rape?

A word never spoken aloud. A word too foul to contemplate.

A word that condemned the victim more surely than the perpetrator. *She asked for it*, that was what they always said...

Don't blame the man. When a woman asks for it, men will do

what men will do...
How?
Who?
When...?
He knew when. Sometime before last April, when her letters had changed. Before she'd lied.
But it couldn't be that long ago.
Four months ago. Only four months ago...
He'd seen no difference in her letters four months ago, nothing seemed to have changed in her life *four months ago*.
She stirred. Smiled. Then winced as the pain struck into her wakening.
Unclean his mind whispered.
No!
Do not blame your wife the doctor said...
She looked up at him. "Hello my darling."
He bent to touch her lips in a light kiss. "Hello my darling. How do you feel?"
"Oh Erich, oh Erich, I love you so much! Oh God, oh God, I thank God you came back...!" She opened her arms to him. He bent again, and she clutched at his arms with weak fingers.
He sank down to sit on the hard bed beside her, and bent sideways over her so that he would not hurt her to hold her, and she clutched close to him and cried.

*

Over the next days he came to see her during regular visiting hours in the early afternoons. In the mornings he went through the ledgers with the accountant. They were in chaos. He asked the accountant to take them to his office, to bring them properly up to date and keep them current. "But the baron, sir!" the accountant protested. "What if he objects, what will I do then?"
"The baron will not miss the work."
"Ah yes, I understand. But—"
"My wife has power-of-attorney to sign all papers..."
He went to the office of *Essen und Mundt*. Essen, the family attorney, could not see him, but turned him over to Mundt, the junior partner. Protocol was at work here, Erich realised. The Wittingen family had been relegated to a lesser status.
"Herr Mundt," he told the young man across the desk, "if

you check into the Baron's will, you'll note that I'm the sole remaining heir to the Wittingen estates." He was not certain of the German terms, but he remembered the English legal terms well enough. "I ask therefore that I, and also my wife, be given full signatory power in order to carry out the business of the estates."

The attorney shifted uncomfortably. He was a squat figure, hard in his body and eyes, with square powerful hands. "As the baron is still living I have to obtain his approval for that, Herr Oberleutnant. It may require a court action."

So correct, so forbidding.

"Very well. But before it comes to that perhaps you could come up to the house." He would not allow this fellow to control the situation. "It has to be tomorrow morning while I'm here on leave and while the baron is still at home. He goes out for the rest of the day. It's the only hour to find us together." He'd explained too much. No doubt a weakness in the judgment of the attorney. "We'll have him sign approval. You will prepare such a paper."

"As you wish, sir. Shall we—"

"Shall we say, nine o'clock?"

"As you wish, sir."

"Now I want you to look up the family records and find any Wittingen family members who might assist in family matters."

"As you wish, sir."

Better. "And I want Essen-und-Mundt prepared to handle the family estates in case I should be killed in action."

"Oh my good sir!" He half rose from his chair.

"The possibility is always there."

He sank back. "Yes sir, I understand."

"And I want this put in place before I go back to duty within the week."

Another thought had occurred to him sometime in a sleepless night. In case, when this was over... in case he should go home again to England.

*

That afternoon he found Britt sitting up in her bed. Her skin looked less pasty. Her eyes were bright. She opened her arms to invite an embrace as he came in. "I had a good lunch today," she said.

He bent to fold her in. "How does it feel? The surgery. Still painful?"

"I can bear it."

"No doubt." He released her and sat in the chair. "You were always a tough one. But how does it feel? Did you want to go home soon? Katja is..."

Her face stopped him. Her eyes had clouded over, and she looked away from him.

"I don't mean today." *What was it about Katja?*

"Not yet," she said in a small voice.

"No no, not today, I didn't mean today. When the doctor allows it. But soon, I meant to say."

Still she would not look at him.

"Darling, I'm sorry." Then he stopped, because a baby had not been mentioned, and he could not start that subject, it must come from her... "Darling, you'll stay until you're ready. I promise. Na?"

She stared down at her hands on the blanket.

"I'll be here a while yet," he said, to see her reaction.

She smiled.

"Shall I dismiss Katja?" he asked.

Instant anxiety in her eyes. "No no, Katja is a jewel!" She fell back into the piled pillows, exhausted again. In that moment he saw her mother there, ashen, weak, drained.

Then what should I do? he wanted to shout. Aloud he said, "Who can come? To help you through this time?"

She rolled her head wearily on the pillows. "Oh, could you come home to stay? Take a local posting? Ask Father? He would make it possible."

She surprised him every time. *Father?* She called him *Father?*

"Could we bring in a relative, perhaps? A friend of the family? Who can I call?"

She shrugged without interest. "Look in the safe. Everything about the family is there."

"The safe? Where's the safe?"

She shook her head. "Ask Father."

He had never seen a safe in the house. Would the baron even

remember where it was kept, never mind the combination for the lock?

*

At nine in the morning the attorney arrived, catching the baron at breakfast in the kitchen. They carried coffee around to the gun room and sat at the desk to look over the papers. "This is power of attorney for the lieutenant," said Mundt to the baron, placing a paper on the blotting pad. "It allows him to handle your business for you."

"Ah good!" The baron signed with a flourish.

"This..." Another paper... "is power of attorney for Frau Oberleutnant von Schellendorf, your daughter—"

"I know who my daughter is!"

"...while the lieutenant is away on duty. This allows you freedom from concerns, day to day."

"My daughter?"

"In each instance she will obviously seek your permission, or obtain the lieutenant's counsel. Here, you see, in the fourth paragraph—"

"Ah well, in that case..." He signed the paper. "Women, you know. Not made for business."

"This document..." He placed it on the blotting pad. "This transfers the full responsibility for the management of the estates to your sole heir, Erich Bronsart von Schellendorf, quite apart from power of attorney and apart from your last will and testament. It removes signatory power out of your hands."

"Ah yes! He's a good boy, you know." And he signed the paper. "He's a genius with numbers, you know. My best son. You don't know the trouble we had getting him safely married into the family. Ask my wife, the baroness..." And he paused, confused. "No, naturally not."

"And finally, sir, this states that you are legally aware of the significance of this action and are in full agreement."

"Of course I'm in agreement! And this is the last of it!" And he signed with a flourishing stab. He looked up at Erich. "Thank you, my boy. It eases this old man, that you'll be here to handle matters."

*

They stood in the hall at the top of the stairs. Erich had asked to open the safe, and this was where they'd come. "Right there!" said the baron, pointing into the open door of an empty storage nook in the hall. "The cord man! The cord!"

A short fine cord hung where the wall met the low ceiling.

"Pull the damn cord!"

The cord resisted Erich's hand. He had to put his strength into it, and he thought it might break. Then it shifted slightly, and he pulled harder, and the ceiling panel swung down to reveal an opening above.

"The ladder." The baron waved upward. "Pull it down."

A ladder was just visible at the edge of the opening. Erich grasped the lowest rung and worked it outward. As soon as it moved it swung easily down to meet the floor.

"Why," he asked, "couldn't we just go up the attic stairs?"

The baron laughed, and waved him up.

At the top he looked into a black hole.

"Take this," the baron said. He'd brought a lantern and lit a match to it and passed it up.

It seemed somewhat melodramatic. Through a veil of clinging cobwebs Erich lifted the lantern into the dark space and set it on the floor. It revealed a compartment about a metre from side to side, running the width of the house. It smelled of dry must and dust. The heavy beams and angled roof overhead made the space even more cramped. At the far end the lamplight shone only dimly upon a safe that was too massive to be moved through this hatch.

"They built the safe right into the house?"

"No, no, we moved it in through the inside wall." The baron pushed up behind Erich. "They built this partition during the Napoleonic wars. For hiding political fugitives. The safe was put in later."

They squeezed up into the compartment. Erich brought the lantern with him. A blanket of dust covered everything.

"Twenty-one left," said the baron. "Fifteen right, all the way back around left to eighteen, then right to forty-seven."

Doubtfully Erich twirled the lock. *The old man couldn't remember breakfast this morning...* He felt a click on the last number. Turned the handle. A bit of a shock when the door swung open.

The first thing he saw was the gleam of gold bars.

*

"Nothing here helps." In the gun room he sat at the baron's desk with the baron leaning over his shoulder. Stock certificates, bonds long matured, expired contracts, certificates of land ownership. Everything about business, nothing of family. He was not surprised by the vast fortune the papers represented. But it would not help in Britt's recovery.

"What do you mean, nothing there?" the baron asked.

"We might have these papers evaluated. I was looking for family records." He shuffled the papers into a neat pile to return them upstairs. "I need somebody." He looked up to the baron. "A woman, a friend, to help Britt recover from surgery. Who could I call on?"

"Why... why... I uh—"

"Do any family members live close by?"

"Close by! No, my dear boy, they are all in Königsberg or Berlin. We don't even know them. Our branch of the family... *my* branch came here after the King of Prussia granted the lands, long before Waterloo, I remember all the stories when I was a boy..." He began to recount the family history over the past two hundred years, not a detail left unsaid...

*

Britt guided his hand under her hospital gown to touch the incision line bumping across the velvet plain of her belly. He could not imagine her body cut open and surgeon's hands reaching inside to pull out a mass of bleeding womb. He jerked away, shocked. She could have died. *She could have died...*

"I never thought you were squeamish," she laughed, and winced with laughing.

"But I must go back," he said. "The cable came this morning from General von Fuchs. I go back tomorrow."

"Tell them no. Tell them you won't go."

He laughed grimly. Men stood before a firing squad for less. He couldn't tell her that. He took up her hand again and held it. "So darling, please, think of someone you would want with you in the house when you're out of here."

"I have Katja."

"She's a servant. She's no company for you. She wouldn't

know what to do if—"

"She knew well enough what to do when it happened."

"You want somebody of reasonable authority. Somebody to rely on. A friend, not a servant. What about the wives of the Regiment?"

"I don't know them, Erich. I don't like them."

He held her hand. Despair was rising in a huge wave that threatened to drown his reason. He must think. He could not think. He was too damned weary to think. In the past five days he'd had one full night of sleep, and the rest had been a constant overwhelming worry for her, and for the baron. She couldn't do this alone.

The doctor came in. He stopped at the end of the bed to read her chart. "So it's tomorrow."

"Yes. My train's at noon."

"I thought everyone in the army was expendable."

Erich laughed. "Disposable yes, replaceable no."

"I have a thought," said the doctor.

"Na?"

"This little lady will come to stay with us until she's well. My wife will take good care of her. They'll enjoy each other's company."

"Oh Erich..." Protest was in Britt's eyes.

"You'll do as you're told." He leaned over to kiss her cool forehead. "Let me go back with a free mind."

* * *

CHAPTER 24

Into 1917

The winter was warm this year. Not *warm*, of course, but it did not freeze or even snow this year in the St. Mihiel Salient, where on the overloaded roads the mud came up to the wagon hubs and horses dropped in their traces. Every afternoon through the winter he changed uniforms from infantry to cavalry greys and pulled on his polished black boots and his cavalry greatcoat with the ankle-length divided skirts and the metal gorget around his neck that identified him as a policeman. Then he rode out with his little troop to patrol the back rest areas and pick up dodgers. That was where he saw the horses dying. He connected horse deaths with his own work. His numbers determined the loads that they dragged along those mud roads. Everybody thought it was the colonel who gave the orders. Nobody knew that a mere first lieutenant (temporary grade) gave the colonel the numbers upon which to base his orders. So the lieutenant was, by logical extension, the killer of horses. He had to harden, or he would lose his soul.

As he rode with the troop, whenever he encountered a horse dying, he would stop and order the driver to shoot it. Or shoot it himself. At least he could do that. He understood why a driver would hesitate. This was *his* horse, his responsibility. He had signed a piece of paper for it, after all. And also perhaps this was his... his friend. But time and resources could not be wasted on animals that had been worked until their hearts and legs gave out.

> *My Darling Erich ~*
> *I am home from the hospital at last in time for Christmas, which I shall spend at the home of our dear doctor. Father will also join us here for the holiday meal. Please try to come as well. I am being very good and following orders. Of course it is difficult to disobey the doctor while he watches me so closely. I have not yet gone riding, for the weather is terrible, wet and windy, and I must confess my surgery is not yet comfortable and feels that it will tear apart at the first little bump...*

On the twentieth he put in a request for Christmas leave. He thought it would go through. This sector was so quiet that they had a running joke that many of the boys took up housekeeping with village ladies and were raising blond, bilingual babies.

But on the twenty-first his request form was back on his desk stamped *"DENIED"*. He went then up the stairs to the colonel's office overlooking the distant Woëvre Plain where the French army quietly lay at the far end of the colonel's telescope.

"You took leave only last month," the colonel reminded him.

"That was my first leave in—"

"Eight months, yes, I understand. And it will be another eight months, Schellendorf before the next. I need you here. You went over my head last time. You will never do that again."

"Sir, I didn't go over your head, the general himself called me in—"

"Don't argue. Dismissed."

The following morning Erich heard that the colonel had left by motorcar on Christmas leave. He thought, *May his wheels get stuck in the mud.* It gave him the only smile he could muster that morning...

*

> *My Darling Britt,* (he wrote) *how good to know you are on the road to recovery. When you ride*

> *again, I suggest you borrow the adjutant's grey gelding, a responsive mount, and as soft as any cushion. Tell me about how you get along with Frau Doktor Kirschner. I am very glad that she is there for you and will keep you company as you recover...*

His letters had begun to sound as cool as hers...

> *...I'm sorry to report that I am unable to come home at Christmas. They tell me that I had leave in November, no matter the reason, and it may be another several months before my next leave. It seems I have become indispensable to the colonel, who, incidentally, has himself just departed on Christmas leave...*

The other question still hung there. *Who was the man?* He'd planned to ask her this time on leave. He couldn't ask her in a letter.

Who was the man? How did it happen? *Where* did it happen? How did such a foul thing happen to his fearless Britt who tolerated no nonsense from any man? Was it her work at the hospital, where so many lonely men saw her every day? Was it because she'd started working at night?

He couldn't put together the time factor. From his collected cigar boxes he gathered her letters, and put them in order of dates, and began to read...

Her letters had first changed a few weeks after they'd buried the baroness. Long before she had started into night work. Long long *long* before this terrible thing had happened.

He couldn't put it together.

All he knew was an approximate date of the... the *Incident*. Four months before her surgery.

Five or six months after she had turned away from him. *After she had lied.*

He took up a new sheet of memo paper. He stared at it a moment, blank on the desk, then put the pen to it. "Oberleutnant Erich Bronsart von Schellendorf, temporary grade, respectfully requests..."

He crushed the sheet and started again. "Oberleutnant Erich Bronsart von Schellendorf..." No need to remind them the rank was temporary... "respectfully requests a transfer to his parent regiment; and in the meantime permission to join his family on leave for the Christmas holiday."

He addressed the request to General von Fuchs. Over the colonel's head.

Bloody bastard.

*

"You misunderstand the situation," the general said.

"Nobody explains the situation to me, sir. I do numbers."

"Precisely. You do all the numbers."

Puzzled, he waited.

This morning a cold drizzle fell through a fog as thick as a London pea-souper. He'd got wet just walking up from his chalet to present the application by hand to the general. In this fog the guns had gone silent even over Verdun.

"Are you actually this thick?" the general said. "A fellow as bright as you? Do you really believe that everybody can integrate sheets of solid numbers and understand them?"

Erich frowned. Then he caught the glint of humour in the general's eye, and he laughed. "But what has that got to do with Christmas leave?"

"I'm sure you noticed that while you were away for those few days last month, our logistics became fouled."

"But..." He did not understand. "What did you do before I transferred in?"

"Schellendorf... We have eight divisions in this sector, a brigade in the line, plus several separate units in reserve, all of them brought in from every part of the western front from other army groups. This is a designated rest area. In this sector my soldiers are weary, their regiments are decimated. Their morale is the lowest in the entire Imperial armed forces. You, on the contrary, are fresh and healthy. You've had your leave. Allow the colonel his." Then he added, "I'll check about returning you to your regiment. In the meantime, consider this temporary until we find the right man."

Temporary.

Numbly he watched the general slash his pen across the page, *"DENIED".*

"You see..." He tossed the paper into his basket, "If both you and Colonel Steiff go on leave at the same time, the logistics of the entire St. Mihiel Salient would collapse. Speaking frankly..." He grinned through his moustache. "The colonel has seniority."

*

On New Year's Eve he brought the men to his chalet where he'd ordered in a festive supper for them from the officers' mess. For a while they sat crowded elbow to elbow around the table that Kropp had set up, eating politely, speaking politely, using their best manners. Then after supper Erich broke open bottles of Sekt and they toasted *Sylvesternacht* amid gusts of laughter loosened by the wine. Later they all closed inward to sadness.

The year turned. The winter hardened.

There was little war news. Nothing much shifted along the trenches. Some bitter fighting in the north, a few local engagements, more casualties on both sides, a few metres lost eastward, a few gained westward, nothing of strategic value. It became the standard news of the day: *Im Westen nichts Neues.*

All quiet on the western front.

Then into February they began hearing reports from Ypres and Serre and Neuve Chapelle and Warlencourt... the giving of ground, evacuating villages, tightening the German line. A feeling of pressure. Short withdrawals, usually regained with heavy casualties.

Not always regained.

*

> *My dearest Erich* ~ (she wrote) *We think of you often, and wish you could be with us. Even though I am well recovered, I have moved back with the doctor and his wife who is presently in confinement, their baby being due sometime in May. She is glad of my help. We are lucky in so many ways to have such good friends as this. Peter is very thoughtful and attentive, bringing flowers every day and taking us out to dinner at least once a week at the Ritter Hotel. He has bought an automobile to take us out for rides in*

the countryside on Sunday.
Father is hopeless. He thinks everything is as it always was and nobody can waken him to the truth. Will you please write a letter to him and urge him to instruct the farmers what to do? I must say he is happy that I conduct much of the business for him now, but the farmers do not listen to a woman. I have been around to all of the estates ~ Oh my dear, I should not trouble you with this, but you are the only one who knows anything. Please tell me what shall we do to plant the crops in the spring...

Buy seed, he thought irritably. *Buy seed.* Sell a gold ingot from the safe in the attic.

He sat down to write instructions to her, *My darling Britt...*

*

The night was cold and clear with a million stars in an indigo sky. As he rode with the troop he could look up and feel himself weightless, drifting upward into that endless expanse of black empty space. No, they said, outer space was not empty, but was filled with strange dead worlds floating in circles around distant suns, every star a sun with its own cluster of spinning planets.

And suddenly, out of that innocent, aimless muse...

The doctor.

It came from nowhere. It had been hiding deep behind his brain, like a spider under a rock, ever since he'd last sat with the doctor at Britt's hospital bedside...

Oh, it had been so easy. "*I'll take care of everything,*" said Kirschner. Oh yes. He'd already taken care of it. With surgery in the middle of the night he'd eradicated their guilt. Then with cold singular purpose, had brought the most beautiful woman in Europe to live in his home under the very eyes of his trusting wife. How otherwise explain the distant tone of Britt's letters...?

"Halt!"

The sergeant's bellow jolted him out of his musing.

Ahead in the road two forms ran in the starlight, ducking aside into a field. "Forward!" the sergeant shouted, and he led the troop after the dodging men. Erich sat staring after them. One man flung himself down on the uneven ground and disappeared in the darkness. The other had darted the opposite way around shell craters where the footing was too dangerous to run a horse. The troop closed about the man on the ground. "Two men take him back," the sergeant ordered.

A shot rang out. A second shot. Some of the troopers had followed the other man and were now firing down on him.

"Hold fire!" shouted Erich.

Too late. Dimly in the starlight he watched as the form crumpled, heard the splash as he collapsed into a shell hole. They arrested the man on the ground and put him under guard. Erich led the rest of the troop around the craters to search for the second. Through the doctor's face swimming in his brain, he took command back from the sergeant. They found the other fugitive where he had dropped, limp, inert, head and shoulders submerged in filthy cold sludge.

"Get him out," Erich ordered.

Two men dismounted and wrestled the body from the crater.

"Dead?"

"Yes sir."

"Leave him by the road for pick-up."

He rode on in silent fury. Shot a man, for what?

Later at the end of the tour he called them into his chalet. Since New Year it had become a place for the troop to gather, to chat and play cards and write letters home. It was a tight fit for all twelve men together in a group. They stood nervously about the room, not knowing why they'd been called together so late. Everyone was tired after a long patrol.

It was for his own benefit, he knew. Get rid of the doctor in his brain...

"Gentlemen," he began.

All eyes turned to him.

"Tonight we killed one of our own."

They shuffled restively.

"There's no reason under the sun that we must kill one of our own."

"But he might have got away, sir."

"His papers would not be in order. He'd have been captured eventually."

"But what if he escaped altogether, sir?"

"Then, being in God's good hands, God would eventually punish him."

They shuffled on their feet. Looked wordlessly from man to man, questioning.

"So do you think, sir," Weisskopf said, "we're doing God's work here?"

Was it a challenge? Weisskopf always had something to add.

"We do army work, Weisskopf. We obey orders, we do our duty."

"So do you think, sir..." definitely it was a challenge... "that we sometimes go against God in our work?"

"I'm saying that we must use better judgment, Weisskopf. Enough men are dying in this war that we don't have to kill our own to add to it. Therefore, this is my order. From today, we do not fire on dodgers. We capture them, or we let them go." He looked from one earnest, weary face to the next. "We never again shoot down on our own. Clear?"

As a body they stiffened to attention and cracked their heels. "Yes *sir!*"

Really good men, every one of them. Much better than when he'd first taken command. Any man, he mused, could be made proud with fair discipline.

*

In March, when three weeks had passed without a letter from Britt, he put in another written request for leave.

The following day his memo returned to his desk, *Denied.*

For a while he just sat staring at it, his mind turning in slow circles. In the past week the numbers had not shifted. On the planning map nothing was pinned. North of Verdun the intense artillery war continued, but it did not reach the Salient.

Denied leave for what reason?

No use asking the colonel. He took the paper up the two flights of ornate stairs to the general's office and asked the general's secretary for an interview.

He had to wait only a few minutes.

General von Fuchs handed him a paper. "This clarifies your position. You're now officially attached to the Field Intendant Office, Detachment C. The Supply Services remains in the sector even when the army moves."

He couldn't absorb it. He didn't know where this came from. Without glancing down, he crumpled the paper in his fist and stayed at attention before the desk.

"Colonel Steiff remains your commander."

This was official, this was permanent. At last he blurted, "But I requested a transfer back to my regiment, sir."

"We go where we're ordered."

Ordnance, Supply, Transport... *Service* Corps.

"It comes with an advantage, Schellendorf." The general smiled dryly. "You would not refuse promotion."

"But not this way, sir."

"But this was how it comes. In direct relation to your responsibility." The general stood up and came around the desk, a small box in one hand. "You've been promoted, Schellendorf. To *captain*." The word he used was *Hauptmann*. Infantry. An insult.

Erich could not speak.

The general regarded him in deep thought. "Not quite what you dreamed when you joined."

This was not a stop-gap until they found the right man. They had found the right man.

"But," said the general, "if we keep you on the cavalry lists? And make it *Rittmeister*?"

"You can do that?"

"We can. You'll remain on the cavalry lists. A foot in each stirrup, as they say. You always have your regiment, they can't change that."

He could breathe a little better now. "Thank you sir."

The general placed the box in his hand. "Put on the extra pips now, and keep your regimental number on your epaulets. Then go grovel to the colonel."

He went down the ornate curving stairs, past the colonel's floor down to the front entrance. He stood in the open doorway and breathed in the late March air. Green things were suddenly growing. Grass spread a new velvet blanket in the chateau parkway. Trees that had survived the first shelling three years ago were coming into leaf, and birds flew everywhere. In the north at Verdun the guns growled. On the situation map over the past two weeks they had watched the shift, they called it the *Alberich* Movement. It was a withdrawal under the guns along the front, from Arras to Soisson. They were marching twenty kilometres back to prepared defences on a new line, the Siegfried Line they called it, to shorten and deepen the German defences. A strategic withdrawal, they said. Not a retreat.

But Erich knew the numbers. He knew the personnel and supplies that were requisitioned, and what the commanders were not receiving. He could see the obvious gaps not being filled, the casualties not replaced, inadequate rations, low stockpiles of ammunition, sick and killed horses not replaced, armaments and equipment destroyed and not replaced...

In combination with the numbers, the withdrawal to the Siegfried Line seemed to foretell a new and ominous direction of this war.

*

My dearest Erich ~ (Britt wrote in a careful hand) *We took your advice and sent one of our best managers to East Prussia to buy seed for all the crops, and shipped it back by railway. We sold one ingot to the bank, which brought in 8975 Marks. They say that the railways are now given over almost entirely to military needs and I believe it ~ 27 days from Königsberg to deliver two freight cars of seed, which cost in total 925 Marks! Never mind, today every one of the farms is busy planting. I have become almost a farmer myself handling the many problems. I work only four hours a day at the hospital and continue to attend Nadia until she comes to term*

Ah yes, he mused. Helping Nadia until...

Babies. Women's business. Men's responsibility. She lived in the doctor's house to help Nadia, so casual they could hold a lump of sugar on their tongue without melting it.

In two months he could apply for leave. They'd better have a replacement for him. Not that he could make any difference at home after all this time. So much already happened. Ménage à trios? Nobody there to stop them.

He stuffed the letter with the others in the fireplace grate. One of these days he would set a match to the pile.

He had a sudden yearning to write a letter home. Home to England. *England...*

He went out the chalet doorway and sat on the step in the evening air. The guns of Verdun added a distant drum-roll to the endless comedy. He'd released the troop for a free night. He could picture them now, carousing over there in the village estaminet, drinking themselves into a stupor, falling into a dirty little room for half an hour with an ugly French prostitute, and tomorrow brag it up to the boys. The measure of a man: how much to drink, how many whores to fuck...

One of the men sauntered across the railway track and came over to join him in the twilight.

"Ah Karl, have you nothing to do on a Saturday night?"

"Brought you a beer, *Herr Rittmeister*."

They sat side by side on the step, bottles of beer in hand.

Darkness fell and a full moon rose. One by one and two by two the men of the troop wandered across the railway tracks and came up the hill. They came casually, as if by coincidence, and sat down with him along the step that ran the full width of his little chalet, until twelve men crowded there elbow to elbow, quietly drinking beer in the moonlight.

Sometimes comradeship could make up for losing England.

Nothing made up for losing Britt. His heart, his soul, his reason for life...

In his mind he wrote a letter, *My darling Britt.* He stared out at the spring night... *I am promoted Rittmeister, four years ahead of peacetime advancement, is that not fine...?*

My Britt my Britt my Britt...

He could not bear this deep black hollow in his heart.

My darling Britt, what is happening with the doctor?

It all came down to that.

To the doctor.

Could it be the doctor?

* * *

CHAPTER 25

To April 1917

"The general wants you sir." The corporal ducked back out and marched away along the hall, no salute, though he wore his cap. Even headquarters staff suffered a loss of pride these days. Or perhaps *especially* headquarters staff had lost pride...?

He went up.

The general sat at his desk littered with papers and maps. He looked up, and then rose from his chair as Erich came through the door. He stirred papers on his desk. A handsome man, full beard and moustaches in the old style, a fine soldierly figure. An officer who, like Erich, had been shuffled aside to this inactive salient where his professional career had been long dying a slow death. Campaigns were in the north, Bapaume, Cambrai, Vimy, Lagnicourt... place names on the map that nobody had ever heard before this war, all raging in battle, while here an insignificant Salient straddled the French railway.

"Good morning Schellendorf."

"Sir." He snapped to attention before the desk.

"I don't know what to say." He found the papers in the pile. "Your leave pass and travel warrant. I give you eight days this time." He contemplated the papers, then passed them across the desk. "I understand that the colonel, your father-in-law, in recent days has not been in the best... ah... rational condition."

"He's just growing old, sir, nothing unusual."

"Last night he died. I received a telephone call this morning from the doctor."

Died?

Died? The baron...?

"He suffered a brainstorm, quite sudden. According to the doctor, your wife is taking it very hard."

According to the doctor...

The damned doctor...

"How *is* your wife, Schellendorf?"

"By her letters, sir, her health is restored."

"Ah good. Give her my condolences. We'll talk again when you're back, na?"

He stumbled away to the door.

"Oh, and Schellendorf! You must take leave more regularly. Attend to that lovely wife."

Erich went down the stairs in a fog of bewilderment that slowly, slowly turned to fury.

Take leave more regularly...?

*

Although he'd sent her a cable she did not meet his train. He wasn't surprised. She had other problems. Her father had died suddenly. A terrible shock. A huge vacuum left in her life.

And she had other distractions. *Doctors... Secrets...*

Was it Kirschner?

He walked up to the house with these ghosts in his mind, his brain tripping all over the little problems of the moment. Yet he must meet her, he must *look* at her. He must continue to pretend he knew nothing, thought nothing. He must pretend there had been no child, no abortion, no other man, no... no *affaire*.

Was it Kirschner?

The doors of the house were locked. He didn't have a key, he'd never before needed a key...

The baron was dead. This was Erich's house now.

The Benz now parked in the turnabout. The Benz was his Benz now. Oberon down in the garrison stable was his horse now...

No consolation. He'd never asked for any of that.

He walked down the hill, rucksack slung over his shoulder. He should have brought Kropp this time. He didn't know where the doctor lived, and so now he had to walk across the bridge all the way to the hospital to get the address. At the hospital they would not give him the address because they did not release personal information about the doctors. And no, the doctor would not be in his office today, this was Good Friday, a holiday even for a doctor...

Good Friday. Easter weekend.

He stopped on the embankment and stared into black water. Once again he verged on exhaustion because he'd been two and a half days on the stop-starting trains, buffeted by noise and too much thinking.

He went to the garrison mess, a familiar haven in a town that suddenly offered no other anchorage. In the bar he ordered a drink and swallowed it. Easter garlands decorated the bar and the windows and hung looped along the walls. Easter. Hadn't thought about it. Hadn't noticed. He picked up his rucksack and went around to the adjutant's office.

"I need a place to sleep, Captain," he said without preamble.

The adjutant rose from his chair, eyes popping at Erich's epaulets. "Well will you look at our young Rittmeister! Home a hero, I presume?"

"Home for the funeral."

He sobered at once. "Yes. Terrible. The old colonel gone. So sudden. He'll be missed. His stories."

"Perhaps you can find the home address of Dr Kirschner."

"Yes, of course." Suddenly all business and efficiency.

"First," Erich said, "I have to sleep, the house is closed, I need a bed."

"Yes. I can find you a bed. I have your kit, you know."

"What?"

"When you shipped to Königsberg? Just your ceremonial blues, you left them behind. Held in storage. If you like I can have them shaken out for the funeral."

"No." He glanced down at the greys he was wearing. "This will do. Somebody can press this up a bit, polish my boots. But above all I need sleep. Can you call me when the mess opens for dinner?"

They started along the corridor toward the visitors' quarters at the far end.

"Oh," the adjutant said as an afterthought, "did you hear? America declared war on Germany today. Aren't we in for a shitload of trouble now!"

*

The Kirschner house was an easy walk from the hospital. Erich stood for a while across the street to study the trees in new leaf growing in little gardens. The residential properties rose up the hillside, cut by the Philosophenweg where he and Britt used to ride. A happy balance, he mused, of middle-class modesty and comfort. Respectable, yet not too costly for a busy young doctor.

Respectable. Now there was an ironic word. *Ménage-a-trois* respectable.

He didn't know how he was going to handle this.

Eventually he crossed the street to the Kirschner door and pulled the bell. It shrilled inside. He did not ring again. After a time he heard the click, and the door opened.

A maid looked out at him. She smiled. "Herr Rittmeister von Schellendorf!" She stepped out of the way to allow him to step inside. "May I take your cap, sir?"

He gave it to her. She hung it on a hook. Stained-glass windows on each side of the doorway let in softened light, and the mahogany partitions gave privacy beyond. A small sign read *Office* over a door on the left. The floor was polished flagstone.

"Will you come in sir? Or shall I announce you?"

"Announce me please."

As she flitted away, his heart began to beat like the artillery at Verdun, *boomboom-boomboom...*

He heard footsteps. Then out of another door Britt came running so quickly he could not brace himself. She flew at him, driving him back against the wall, clutching him with rigid arms. "Oh Erich oh Erich oh Erich!" She was sobbing.

Her father had died. It had not seemed real to him until this moment.

He held her awkwardly. He folded his arms about her, and through the stays of her bodice felt how thin she'd become. She was dressed in black for the funeral two hours from now.

She held to him and gradually her weeping faltered. And still she held to him, her hair in his face. "Do you know," she said, muffled against his chest, "how good you smell to me?" She tilted her head to look straight at him, this beautiful woman of blasphemous purity, face glistening with tears. "Hold me," she whispered. "Kiss me."

He bent almost cautiously, and she gripped her hands behind his head and crushed her lips to his and opened her mouth to him... and he could not enter.

Even as he stood like an automaton, his mind was crashing with her artless rush into his arms, with her passion, her need that she signalled with this impulsive, intimate energy, as if... as if... as if this was not the woman of her careful letters...

"Oh my darling," she whispered, "oh my God, oh if only you could be here—"

"I'm here."

Now finally she sensed it. She stood back from him and looked into his eyes. "Oh." She touched his face, brushed his cheek with soft fingers. "Oh. You've changed." She smiled, her eyes still brimming over. "It's the war. Yes I understand. The war changes everyone. Are you all right?"

Her first concern? That he was all right?

"Can we go in?" he said.

"Yes. Yes..." She hooked her arm through his and led the way through.

"I went to the house," he said. "Nobody was there. The door was locked."

"Oh, it's all upside down." She was talking too fast now, almost hysterically. "All the servants left Tuesday for a week holiday, only Katja was there, and now she is here with me, and I had to lock it—"

"I don't care about the house." He stopped to face her, steadying her by the elbows. "Britt, it's all right about the house. It's all right."

She sighed and went silent.

In spite of his dreadful, unspeakable suspicions he drew her into his arms and held her. God, God, God... he could feel his heart bleeding.

She leaned into him like a child, her arms folded on his chest, her head on his shoulder.

"I'm here," he said vacantly.

*

It was a glorious spring day. The whole town of Heidelberg seemed to have gathered for the funeral of the resident baron, Colonel of the Regiment. More than half the crowd were infantry and cavalry in combat uniforms, wearing black armbands for the colonel. Most of the women wore black. Erich recognised many faces, and he nodded to them as he passed with Britt into the church, leaving most of the crowd outside in sunshine. The church was already full. Under a black veil Britt did not look up. She leaned on his arm and turned her head toward him as they walked down the aisle toward the high windows shining sunlight upon the coffin before the altar. When they came to the family pew she sat down woodenly and stared at the floor, and Erich sat nearest the altar. The doctor sat on Britt's other side.

The organ swelled softly. A choir sang so gently that the words were lost in the music.

It was a long funeral. The archbishop had much history to cover, many personal memories to relate, bringing the baron closer than he had ever seemed in life. A long queue of mourners added their personal eulogies.

Britt sat throughout, stiff and dry-eyed, never looking up. Erich too felt a dreadful distance. In that coffin lay the man who had freely, willingly, eagerly, given him hope for his future. This woman beside him, this child, this *stranger*... who had perhaps betrayed him with the other man beside her... this Germany, this uniform he wore so proudly... all were gifts from the man lying in the coffin. All of it a grotesque, monstrous mistake.

And all the doors of his other life were closed forever. There was no going back.

It made no difference. Three years ago he had sworn to the baroness his solemn oath to keep her daughter safe.

*

They returned to the doctor's drawing room after the burial. The coffin had been lowered into the open pit in the family plot beside the baroness. A new headstone waited to be placed into position, *Colonel the Baron Johann Gerhardt von Wittingen 1848 - 1917 Honour above All.*

There it was again, the endless call to honour.

The endless myth of honour.

They sat in dejected silence. Erich had set Britt down in a

chair beside the cold fireplace, and took the other matching chair opposite. Kirschner settled beside his wife on the sofa facing them. Kirschner's wife wore a free-flowing shapeless gown with a flower print, designed to conceal a huge mound of belly. She was a handsome young woman with a strong face and rich honey hair pinned high. She shifted on the sofa, perhaps uncomfortable, perhaps embarrassed by the mix of people in this room.

A maid brought a carafe of wine and placed it on the little table next to the doctor's elbow. Silently the doctor poured the glasses, and the maid passed them around.

Still silence.

Then the doctor cleared his throat and said, "An impressive funeral."

The tension in the room was palpable.

The maid retreated.

"When did you arrive?" the doctor asked Erich politely.

"Yesterday."

"I'm sorry, we should have met your train."

"I was not presentable. I went to the garrison to clean up."

"Ah." He nodded and sipped at the glass.

"The uh..." Erich ventured. "The baron. How did it happen?"

Frau Kirschner did not change; but both Britt and the doctor sat up higher, and darted glances at each other.

"It was sudden," the doctor said. "Middle of the evening, nobody with Brigitte except the maid. Thank God for the maid. A shocking..." He swallowed his wine and came to his feet. "May I speak with you in private? This has been extremely painful, I don't want to put the ladies through further suffering." Then he added, "Bring your glass."

Erich followed him back along the hallway into the front room labelled "Office".

* * *

CHAPTER 26

Easter 1917

The doctor closed the door and switched on an overhead light. The waiting room had one small window and sombre brown panelled walls and eight upholstered chairs along two walls. Kirschner sat down on one of the chairs. He waved a hand to Erich in silent invitation. "What did she tell you?"

"Who, Britt? Nothing." Erich hitched a chair a quarter turn where he could see the doctor's face in the light. "We didn't talk very much."

"She said that you seemed very... strange. Distant. She's been worried—"

"Well it's not important, what happened to the baron?"

The doctor leaned forward, studying him with steady eyes. "Yes, you are changed. I assume—"

"Please don't assume." He was choking with this man facing him so boldly, as if he'd never cheated with Britt. "The baron?" he snapped. *Had this man cheated with Britt?*

The doctor laced his hands on his lap. "I don't know how to tell you. This much I know for certain. Brigitte seems unaware of what actually happened. It was Tuesday night."

"Do you yourself know what happened?"

"Oh yes. Oh yes." He paused again to think. "Can I put this bluntly? Can I prepare you for this in any other way? I don't know what kind of man you are, how strong you are. Brigitte thinks the sun sets and rises on your command, so maybe—"

"*What?*"

The doctor peered across the space. "What?"

"What do you mean? '*The sun sets and...?*'" The pressure in the air between them made it hard to breathe. "What do you mean? What does she—?"

"Why, I mean the obvious. She adores you, she thinks you're the..." He broke off. He seemed to look inside himself. He sat up taller. "I'm sorry. We should have talked back then, right after the surgery."

"Never mind back then, the topic is now, the baron."

"Well..." Again he hunched inward to think. "Well..." He drew himself tall. "To be blunt, to cut all corners... Brigitte shot him. Killed him."

Erich snapped involuntarily to his feet, and stood staring down at the doctor.

"I could find no easier way to say it, I'm sorry."

"Tell me..." He sank down.

"Oh it was a long time coming to this." Suddenly the words flowed. "It was the reason I asked her to stay those months with us here, my wife's confinement being the obvious excuse, but she had her own house and the estates to care for, she couldn't stay with us forever. It was a long time coming, the old man lived in a fantasy, he kept mistaking Brigitte for his dead wife, he kept demanding his conjugal rights, it was a nightmare for her, she never knew when he might... I mean, that was why she worked at night, so that she could at least sleep undisturbed in the day and not be constantly on alert, she worked while he was at home, she slept while he was gone, she..." He stopped. He gazed past Erich, giving him time to absorb it.

Erich's head whirled in great confused loops, back over the months, all the way back to... "The surgery?" he managed to whisper.

"The foetus, yes. It was... Yes, her father's. She will never tell you this. The ramifications—"

"Oh my great God." His voice failed him. He'd thought... all that time... that she no longer loved him, that she had deceived him. He'd thought... this doctor, this good man... or some other man... Yet all that time she'd been in a desperate struggle for her own defence, for her safety, for her honour, and in all that time Erich had not been here for her. He'd done nothing to protect her. He'd turned his heart from her, he'd suspected her of unspeakable deception...

And now...

Driven to *murder*?

"How did it happen?" he managed to say. "The shooting."

"She was at home Tuesday evening. The servants had been released for the week. She thought she had a few hours before going to work at the hospital, but the baron returned that evening very early, it was his habit, you know, to stay late every night at the mess—"

"Yes, I know."

"Now unexpectedly he came home, he was raging, she said, she didn't know what it was about, he wanted this, he wanted that, he put a state of terror into the maid. Then apparently turned his attention to Brigitte with the intent of taking his wife to bed, and she was just as intent on escape, she said she went to the front for her coat but he intercepted her. She then ran to the gun room, she couldn't get to the front door or the kitchen and didn't want to go up the stairs, but he came after her laughing, she said, as if it were a game. And from the gun room of course there is no exit and..." He took a few deep breaths. "According to the maid she took the pistol out of the desk and fired one shot."

"According to the maid?"

"The maid had followed to try to intervene. So then, Brigitte fired the gun and the maid at once telephoned me. Brigitte has no memory of the gun."

"She doesn't remember she shot him?"

"No, no, we humans... you know... The human mind protects itself. One day when she's ready she'll remember. But not yet. I don't want you to speak of it to her. It may repeat the shock."

"But he's dead. How does she think he died?"

"I registered the death as by natural causes. As brainstorm. Nobody was surprised. She believes it herself."

"How could you get away with such a thing? Surely people would see the injury, people at the hospital, the undertaker?"

"I sent the body wrapped in shrouds straight from the house to the crematorium. It's not uncommon practice these days, with the war."

Erich stared at him. He could breathe now.

"It's a power we physicians enjoy. I send many bodies these days for burial. Just so many numbers."

"What was in the coffin?" he whispered.

"The baron's ashes, of course."

He noticed now the glass of wine forgotten in his hand. He drank it slowly down.

When they came back into the drawing room they found the women together on the sofa, Britt leaning sideways with her ear pressed flat upon Frau Kirschner's massive belly. "I can hear it gurgle," she laughed. "I can feel it kick against my cheek."

He stood watching them from the doorway, the doctor quiet behind him.

His heart would crack. She was so lovely, so sweet, so... so *brave*. She was his Britt again, his wife, his woman. But no, not again. She was the woman she had always been. The blunder had been his. He'd switched off his love and all feelings. He had condemned her without giving her any opportunity to explain. She had endured these terrible months without protest, without asking help, without his support, and still she could love him. And she could smile without envy over another woman's unborn child, even knowing that she could never bear a child of her own.

Then he realised his heart would not merely crack, it might explode from happiness. This was the woman who miraculously loved him.

He stepped into the room.

Britt looked up, and straightened. "Oh Erich, you should come and feel this baby inside! It's a miracle!"

Embarrassed, he laughed. The miracle was Britt. He held out his arms, and she leaped up from the sofa and came to him and put her arms about his neck and kissed him and clung to him. He cradled her, and swayed a moment with her. The nightmare was over.

*

There was just too much to do. He wrote notes to the accountant and to the lawyer, and Dr Kirschner sent a servant to deliver the notes to their offices. Tomorrow Germany would come to a standstill for Easter. Monday was almost as bad, and Monday afternoon he would jump on the train again to be back for Thursday morning.

He took the key from Britt and went up with Katja to the house, empty since Tuesday night. It was eerily quiet, as they walked through. Katja ran about opening windows.

He called after her. "Do you think she'll want to live in this house again?"

"Don't know, sir." From upstairs.

In the doorway to the gun room he stood looking about. This was where it had happened. Over in the corner the manikin stood stripped of its ceremonial blues. The baron had been cremated in that uniform.

Strange old man.

Damned old man.

And yet...

Amazing, demented old war-horse.

As Erich stepped forward, something caught the corner of his eye. He turned sharply. The wall beside the door was stained with a large splash of dried blood. He stood numbly staring at it. He went to touch the wall, ran his fingertips across the panel until he found the bullet embedded in the wood. He crossed to the desk and took the letter opener to pry the bullet out. A bit of twisted, bloody lead in the palm of his hand...

Monstrous.

On the parquet floor another dried splash where the head had struck.

And smeared lumps of brain matter, now dry.

"Oh sir!" Katja stood at his elbow. "I meant to clean it up, I must do it before the other servants get back, but Madame would never let me come alone!"

"Clean it up, Katja. You're a good girl, and I'm grateful."

In the kitchen she fired up the stove, ground some coffee beans, and put on a large pot to heat the water for coffee and for cleaning. He waited for the accountant and lawyer to call on the telephone.

"You saw it all," he said to Katja as the water heated.

By the stove she nodded.

"Come sit here."

Hesitantly she sat at the table opposite him.

"Tell me everything," he said.

"Oh, it was awful, sir, it happened before, but this time—"

"I know about Tuesday. Tell me about... about the night she had to go to the hospital for the surgery. Tell me that."

She burst into tears.

Astounded, he waited for the tears to pass.

Then, still sobbing, she said, "It was all my fault, sir! It was all my fault!"

The telephone rang in the hall.

Katja filled her bucket and escaped to clean the blood away.

*

The accountant arrived first, bringing with him the ledgers which they stacked on the kitchen table, while in the gun room Katja scrubbed. Dried blood was hard to clean. Too late Erich thought, *you don't use hot water to remove blood...*

"What can you tell me?" he asked the accountant.

"Just that your wife, sir, is not trained in business and she sometimes pays the bills as they come in and sometimes forgets to pay them and sometimes she forgets to advise me. So I am left until the cancelled cheques come back from the bank. That is easily fixed. But nobody makes the important decisions."

"How important?"

"Payment of last year's taxes, sir."

"Write the cheques for me to sign, and then post them out."

"Also, some of the estates have fallen below the profit line."

"Can you prepare a report and send it to me in France?"

"I can give it to you by hand on Monday."

He didn't know how he could fix all this. It briefly crossed his mind to sell the farms that were failing. Sell them at a loss if necessary, rather than keep them at a loss.

He didn't know how to do all this at a distance. Somebody ought to be here.

The lawyer, Herr Mundt, arrived. He brought the portfolios with him, and they spread papers out on the kitchen table while Katja poured coffee into cups.

The papers, transferring the baron's affairs and Britt's power of attorney, had been in place since December. No, there were no other immediate relatives or heirs to the estates. The lawyer would publish the death, as required by law, in case of legitimate claims, and wait the legal period of escrow before settling the estate.

"Can you recommend," Erich asked, "a reliable business manager? You yourself, perhaps?"

"Well, as I am your lawyer, it might be more functional to be your manager as well."

"Thank you. Work also with my wife. She has signatory power. I plan to sell some properties. Perhaps a land agent?"

"I will hire a good agent, and keep you daily informed." He smiled unexpectedly. "As I am just starting out, sir, I can use this experience. The entire firm stands behind me on your behalf."

They exchanged postal addresses, and the lawyer was gone.

He remained sitting with his cold coffee at the kitchen table. Somewhere upstairs he heard a thump as Katja moved something heavy. He waited a while longer until he heard her on the stairs, and he called her.

She poured fresh coffee from the hot pot for him.

"Sit," he said.

She sat at the table with a cup of her own.

"Now tell me."

She stared glumly at the table.

"We're being honest today," he prompted her. "There's no penalty for truth."

Tears again welled in her eyes. "She asked me how to do it. She..." She shrugged and began again. "When she took me into this house, sir, I was in terrible trouble. I was very ill. She took me in, called the doctor, paid my hospital expenses. Gave me work, gave me a safe place to live." She hesitated.

"Yes?"

"I was ill because... I wasn't married, see? I was with child. My mother'd kicked me out. I'd got nowhere to go. With a bastard child, sir, a woman is nothing. Worse than nothing. In the gutter, she is. So I got rid of it. You understand? I bin so ill with it, and she saved me."

He began to understand.

"So when *she* found her*self* with child, sir... And such a terrible thing, the husband away at the war, the father such a pig..." She looked at him with reddened eyes. "So when she asked me, I told her how I done it."

"How did you do it?"

She shook her head and looked away.

"No, tell me. It's all right, nobody will blame you, I need to know."

"A coat-hanger, sir. You unwind the ends, see, and you..." She winced, remembering.

"You what?"

"Push the wire deep inside. And turn it."

He put a hand over his mouth, but the groan squeezed out.

She wept again. "It worked on me, sir. But on her, it made her bleed. She's too delicate, I thought she'd die."

He reached over and touched her hand. "Katja. You're a good girl. You saved her life by calling the doctor. Both times, then and now. You understand?"

She nodded, her eyes wide and red and spilling tears.

"And you remain by her side. I thank God for that. My good and true Katja. I rely on you now."

"I'd never fail her, sir."

*

At last alone. After a brooding supper with the doctor and his wife they took a last small glass of wine to help them sleep, then went upstairs two by two to the bedrooms, Frau Kirschner heavy on the stairs, her husband's arm supporting her. Little gasps at the top, and she said, "Oh I'll be so glad to see the end of this." They parted right and left.

Britt's guest room backed on the hill, lights from the houses above shining through her window. She drew the blind, not quite darkening the room. The curtains fluttered. The blind bumped gently against the frame with spring mountain air soft through the open window.

He leaned back uneasily against the closed door. He watched her move across the room, watched her at the wardrobe bringing out her night dress, watched her shake it out and lay it across the generous bed. This beautiful creature now exhausted with too much death and horror. He was amazed at how profoundly he loved her truth and by her strength within that deceptive shell of 'delicate' woman.

A year and five months since last she had given herself to him. November 1915, the night of the baroness' funeral. The night when, over his reservations, she had been so hungry and eager and persistent and ready to make a child, and he had felt so guilty.

Now, today, another funeral marked the end of her family.

He watched as she slowly pulled her black silk gown apart at the little buttons and peeled it down over her shoulders, wearily, woodenly. He stood back against the door, unmoving.

He had no right to take this woman. He needed to apologise for the wrong he had done her by losing faith in her.

Yet he could not apologise for something she knew nothing about. And he could not speak until she spoke. And she would never speak.

"Are you coming?" she asked across the darkened room.

They lay awkwardly together in the strange bed, his awful guilt a new barrier between them. This was his guilt, not hers. He didn't know how to go past it. He didn't know how she felt about what had happened to her, didn't know how to ask. *After your father raped you, how do you feel about sex...?*

She stirred beside him. She turned to him. He held himself still... this had to come from her.

She put an arm across his chest. He'd brought no night clothes to this house, he was naked beside her. And now her fingers travelled his skin until his long months of drought suddenly let down the flood gates, and hot and urgent he turned over her and wordlessly took her.

It passed quickly. He lay holding her. She seemed to want to be held more than to be loved. "Just hold me," she whispered. "Just hold me..."

The ghost of the baron might always form a barrier between them. For both of them. For him knowing. For her not wanting him to know.

* * *

CHAPTER 27

Into Summer 1917

He came back to the same old duty. From his desk in the war room he could look over at the situation map where nothing ever changed. Day by day the lines in Flanders shifted a centimetre here, a millimetre there. From Ypres to Verdun the coloured arrows showed hard fighting over hills and farms and crossroads. The British/Belgians/French took a position, the Germans took it back, while thousands on both sides died in the exchange. Here in the Salient, fighting occurred in small senseless savage spasms when the French attacked a spot on the map. Then the Germans pulverised them, and for another day, another week, calm descended over the wasteland.

He came back on duty to his table in the war room. With a sense of unutterable irritation, aware that the other officers sent patronising smiles in his direction, he bent to untangle the chaos of paper. Just over a week on leave, and this. And this.

Toward ten the colonel came down, and stood for a time watching him sort the muddle of papers into stacks. Erich hadn't yet started his regular day's work.

"Glad you're back," Steiff said. "It's been impossible."

"Excuse me, sir," he retorted. "Am I the only man in the entire army who can do this? What do they do in other sectors?"

"The other sectors are not saddled with the dregs of humanity. Are my numbers ready yet?"

"Noon, sir." Curtly Erich dismissed him.

The colonel wandered away to look over the situation map.

Later when Erich was at lunch in the mess a letter arrived from Britt, as if she had written it the moment he'd got on the train. He finished his meal hastily, not participating in the table talk. The others had discovered a new lady of the night in the local estaminet, a *gamine* they called her, a prostitute child. They'd invited her into a chalet and plied her with drink and then lined up to take turns with her...

Erich escaped back to his chalet and ripped open the letter.

> *My darling Erich* ~ (she wrote in a hasty spiked hand)
>
> *My darling my darling, how I love you, how safe I felt when you held me in your arms with such tenderness, so sweet and gentle and patient with my foolishness, you made the sad times vanish when you held me. I hope you understand with Papi I was to the point of exhaustion...*

Papi? She called him *Papi*, after those many months...?

> *...Now on the orders of the doctor I am not permitted to work at night. He says I must rest. Therefore I work only when he himself is on duty so that he ensures I do not become overtired...*

The doctor again. Yes, yes, now he understood...

And, '*Papi*'? Not '*Father*'? He folded the letter. Perhaps she could be at peace about him. Perhaps she would never remember what had happened with the gun in the night. Damned old scoundrel. Let it be gone from her mind. He would not think of it again. He put the letter into his empty cigar box, and turned to the fireplace to salvage all those others that he'd stuffed into the grate...

The fireplace was clean as a wash basin. Cleaned. Scrubbed. Polished.

"Kropp!" he bellowed.

"Sir!" He bounced out of the tiny bedroom.

Erich waved at the empty fireplace. "What have you done!"

"I took the opportunity while you were away, sir, —"

"You burned my letters? You dolt! You burned my letters?"

The orderly stood petrified in the doorway. "I try to please you sir, I only try to please you..." Then, astoundingly, he melted to tears.

*

He rode on patrol. When he'd first taken command of this troop the men had been sullen and erratic, but now they laughed and joked as they rode. Time had blended them into a unit. It gave Erich pleasure to ride with them. As soon as he'd come back from leave the colonel had extended his rounds, stretching now from Avillers in the north to Vigneulles in the south, a long ride, in and out of the villages.

His days unfolded in the usual routine, but were longer now. He rarely got to bed before two in the morning, rising again at seven. He stopped changing uniforms at noon. Nobody corrected him for wearing cavalry greys all day.

From Verdun southeast across the St. Mihiel Salient the war stood forever in deadlock. The artillery on each side fired their token salvoes, the French shells struck into the unmanned First Line where only machine guns stood guard, and then the infantry rushed in afterward to repair the damage. The bulk of German infantry was held back on the Second Line, no harm done. In this sector the enemy had no British allies at their side to stiffen their spine. It was rumoured that the French were strung out thin, the troops exhausted and on the edge of mutiny.

On a lovely summer morning in the beginning of July Erich was called up to Steiff's office.

"Orders from the general," said the colonel.

"Yes?"

"He tells me that I must grant you leave."

"I didn't apply, sir."

"One week every three months. Just when you're most needed here. Choose your dates so I can plan."

He tried not to smile. "Thank you sir."

Back in the war room he found the officers clustered at the French window, peering out. He joined them. He was bursting with the news, *I can go on leave, I can go on leave,* like a child before Christmas holiday time. He choked it back. They would think him a fool if he spoke...

"See it there?" Immelmann pointed. The harsh fluttering sound of a motor came faintly through the open window.

They stepped outside to the lawn and stood in a group to look westward. Erich saw it now, the double wings and circular glint of the propeller in the sunlight. A biplane over there flew at treetop level above the roadway, coming straight on, coming, coming... the motor roaring now, coming straight at him. He stood rooted in fascination, then heard the chatter of the plane's machine gun, and he threw himself sideways to the ground and the window behind him shattered and in the same instant one of the officers flung a hand over his face and collapsed. The biplane sputtered over, sailing upward, rocking its wings. As it circled toward the village, he could see the British red-white-blue roundel on its fuselage.

They pulled themselves to their feet and gathered in a group around the body. Nobody called for a medic. Part of the head had been shot away, bone and blood and pinkish brain matter leaking out on the fresh-cut grass.

"My God, it's Georg," said one of the officers. "Who's going to write *that* letter to the next-of- kin?"

*

He rode with Britt on the Philosophenweg. Oberon pranced like a spring colt and had to be held down every step. Britt rode the adjutant's grey. Perhaps she was content at last to leave the colts and runaways to others.

"How do you like that one?" he asked her

"Very nice."

"Have you ridden Oberon yet?"

"Only in the riding ring."

The strain was there between them, vague and unspoken. Last night in bed, his first time home in three months, they had been careful with each other. Thoughtful. Reticent even, if making love could be reticent. His need for her was almost overwhelming, yet he'd held back until she'd made a move, and even then he'd felt that she was just performing a wifely duty. The joy seemed gone from her. *Damned demented scoundrel...*

On the upper paths they let the horses out to a hand gallop.

Erich watched her sideways, saw the flush of colour in her face, saw her smile. Then it seemed right again. They rode that way for a while, then slowed and stopped and looked out across the valley. All the cherry trees along the slopes were heavy with early fruit.

They got down and walked.

"How is the hospital?" he asked her, to make conversation.

"Busy. Terrible. I love helping the poor wounded boys, but I don't like to talk about it."

They walked, the horses' heads bobbing by their shoulders. He found her hand and folded it into his fingers. Few people walked on the paths today. The July heat pressed down. They came to their special tree and paused. He looked down at her and she looked up at him and smiled. He tied the horses to the special pine bough and sat with her at the base of their tree, backs braced to the trunk, half turned from each other to catch the magic.

"How is it with the war?" she asked in a muted voice.

"Our sector is almost inactive. Just the artillery to remind us. And aeroplanes flying over."

"Good, I'm glad."

"Where is everybody? Nobody's out walking today."

"Gone."

"Where?"

"To the war, I suppose. The accountant was called up last week. The lawyer is going next month. And anyway, nobody goes walking when they're hungry."

"Are things so bad?"

"There's no food, Erich. We're waiting for the first harvests. Babies are dying, don't you know? Mothers go to work in the munitions factories and—"

"But we have no factories in Heidelberg."

"They go on the train to Mannheim and Ludwigshafen, twelve-hour shifts, and every night home again, and the children just have to take care of themselves. The women do the same work as the men, but paid half the salary. Is that fair? Children are starving and neglected, just so the mothers can make more bullets?"

He reached for her hand.

"When the harvests come in," she said, "everything goes to

the army, in any case, so everyone will still be hungry—"
"But are you hungry, Britt?"
"We have the farms, Erich. We have the farms."
They sat a while longer, but the magic evaded him. No shimmering pocket of infinity, just distant sounds of traffic, and the hard rattle of chains as a barge moved on the river below.

*

His life settled into a pattern, three months at war, one week at home, and at least two days each way riding the stop-start trains, sometimes longer, never less.

In the Salient the artillery exchanged morning barrages, and sometimes at unexpected moments during the day to annoy those who took the shells on the other side. In the north the rumble of artillery rarely paused, day or night.

Soldiers on rest leave arrived from every part of the western front, stayed for a few days, then were shipped back. They spent their time sleeping and cleaning their gear, and being close-order drilled by their NCOs as if to remind them that they were still in the army. Then in the evenings they burst loose to carouse and sing outrageous barrack-room songs and share ladies of the estaminets and drink themselves blind..

'*Erschütterung*.' Every soldier in the trenches suffered some form of 'shell-shock', a word never heard before. Erich could tell by the look in the eyes, a vacant stare, deaf ears, body frozen in position while others frolicked around them. Weeping in a corner while others raised their glasses in a noisy toast. Crying out in sleep, to jerk awake in violent confusion. It came, they said, not only from the sight of monstrous death all around them, but from the screaming of shells and artillery thunder so overwhelming that the brain could not think through the din. It came from a solid rain of explosions which they had somehow survived while comrades had died beside them. Then, after a short rest in the Salient, sent back to the trenches in the North, to face it all again.

Erich often stopped these evenings to talk to the young veterans. Just a chat about families, wives, sweethearts at home. They didn't talk about the fighting, but it haunted their eyes. On his part, he somehow felt guilty that he was spared. He no longer wished to apply for a fighting command, and his guilt grey more deeply personal. In his guilt it was impossible to look a man in the eye when he arrested him for not having the correct papers. Nevertheless, Erich arrested him. Then sent him under escort, not to the guardroom, but back to his unit. That way he would not have to hear the rifle volley in the morning, or write letters to the next-of-kin.

They rode hard and long these nights, out and back almost thirty kilometres in each patrol. They'd been at it so long now that it had become routine. They happened upon fewer fugitives this way. When he followed a predictable schedule, the dodgers could avoid the patrol.

This October night they were trotting into Vigneulles, the southernmost limit of the patrol. It was an hour before midnight. A single streetlamp stood at the triple crossroad in the heart of the village, the place where they normally would turn back north toward Hottot. In the lighted intersection a fight erupted, seven or eight men pushing and shouting in the roadway. Erich pressed the troop forward at a trot. He thought they were drunk, and he only intended to ride into the mêlée and bump them apart and command them to go on about their business. Then one of the soldiers looked up and shouted a warning.

Everything stopped. The men stood shoulder to shoulder in unity, strongly shadowed by the lamp behind so that he couldn't see the features of their faces. One of them thrust another of them forward out of the group and said, "Here, take him! This here's tryin' to act like he's one of us, take the son of a bitch, could be a spy!"

Erich felt his stomach twist. Familiar figure, bedraggled uniform. The man turned away, hiding his face, but the men in the group buffeted him forward again. He would not face Erich, he kept turning his head away.

The troop, halted in formation, poised to move suddenly.

"Your papers, soldier," Erich commanded, sitting his horse above the man now.

The man shrank into himself.

It meant there were no papers.

"Name, regimental number, unit?"

Suddenly the man turned and reached for the horse's rein. His grip made the horse shy back a step. He stood holding the rein, looking up to Erich now, his face contorted with anxiety in the dull light of the streetlamp. "Schellendorf, for the love of God—"

"Ruperthal! My God..."

He wore a dishevelled, mud-smeared combat uniform a few sizes too large for him, insignia ripped off, jackboots cracked over the toes, one sole flapping loose... all plain to see in the light of the streetlamp.

Ruperthal the proud, the privileged. The sneak who had...

"All right you men." Erich waved the group off. "We have him, return to your units now. Behave yourselves."

They scattered away.

"Immelmann!" Erich called. "Bring the prisoner your horse, then go to the pool for another and find your way back. We'll take this one with us."

Little murmurs among the troop as Immelmann rode up. It had not been lost on them that these two knew each other. And to give him a horse...?

He stationed Ruperthal between two troopers all the twelve kilometres back to the chateau.

In his chalet Erich watched Ruperthal swallow the coffee Kropp had brewed for them. His filthy uniform smelled of blood and sweat. He had not shaved in days, his beard was crusted with dried mud. His trembling hands gripped the mug so tightly that he splashed coffee on the little table.

"Kropp," Erich said quietly, "fetch another bunk in here."

Kropp disappeared out the door.

It was almost three in the morning. Ruperthal had been close to exhaustion when they picked him up. The slow ride had been paced for him.

"What happened?" Erich drew his chair back from the table, farther from Ruperthal.

He shook his head. "I need sleep."

"Where's your unit?"

"My unit, oh hell my unit..." He began to cry. Tears flowed out of his eyes and his shoulders shook and he put his head down and sobbed into his arms folded on the table.

Erich had seen this often enough. The official opinion of shell shock was of cowards finding an excuse to avoid combat. Excuses didn't help. Either they went back, or they were shot.

He waited for the tears to pass. He felt nothing. This was Ruperthal. This was the nasty piece of work who once had tried to demerit Erich out of the academy. Slashed the sacred sword knot. For amusement had twisted a wire about Oberon's fetlock.

Ruperthal grew quiet, and then rested with his head on his arms folded on the table, breathing deeply, slowly. Regaining his dignity.

He moaned something into his arms.

"What was that?" Erich asked. "I didn't hear you."

"Don't let them send me back."

He smiled coldly. He had never dreamed this moment could arrive. And now that they had come to this, his contempt rolled up like a black thundercloud hanging high over their heads, waiting to let loose the lightning bolts.

He could have this man shot in the morning.

"What's this uniform you wear?" His cruelty was deliberate. "I don't recognise the regiment."

Ruperthal struggled to sit upright. He wiped a grimy sleeve across tear-wet eyes, smearing his face with a streak of mud. He looked twenty years older than last time. "You have no idea."

"Oh, I think I do, Paul. I see this every day."

"We were caught," he whispered hoarsely, "in no-man's-land. Artillery from both sides. Three days pinned in a shell hole full of water, I was the only one left, three days, three nights, dead men... *my* men... dead around me... all dead... I couldn't move for the machine guns, no food or drink except... that water... mud... blood... Constant bombardment... When I could finally get out, I was lost, I didn't know where... All that time without food or sleep..."

Erich drew his chair closer to the table. "What were you doing in no-man's-land?"

"We were on a raid."

"What's an officer doing on a raid? Where's your tag?" Deliberately he slipped the metal police gorget from around his neck and laid it on the table between them.

Ruperthal looked down at his hands. Then, as if it hurt to move, he felt inside his tunic collar and groped and stopped, his hand forgotten inside the collar. His eyes stared wearily at the floor. "I don't know."

"What uniform is this you're wearing?"
"Mine was in shreds. I was soaked and cold. This was dry."
"Where did you get it?"
Ruperthal stared at him wordlessly.
The silence stretched.
"Ah no..." Realisation, *dead, dead, left naked for the crows...* and a stir of sympathy.

Kropp came in, dragging with him the metal frame of a bunk. They watched as he clattered it over to the wall and set it on its legs and snapped the catches. "I'll get a mattress sir."

"That's for you," Erich said to Ruperthal.

"Really? You'd do this for me?"

He shrugged. "No, I leave it all up to you. I refuse to be responsible for the alternative."

"I'd sleep on the floor," he whispered. "I don't care."

Erich stood up now and stretched, weary to the bone. "Kropp will take care of you. I have to catch some sleep and be up early. What I think you should do, Paul—"

"Yes?" New hope in his eyes.

"Go to the orderly room in the morning and report for duty, Kropp can show you where. Otherwise it may go hard for you. I'll be there to identify you if you need me. Rely on Kropp."

"Thank you, Erich. Thank you thank you. I'm your servant forever."

"No, I don't think so, Paul..."

Kropp returned, wrestling a tick mattress through the door and around the table.

"No," said Erich with the tiniest thrill of triumph, "I value my servant more than that."

*

He didn't see Ruperthal again. He didn't ask. Didn't want to know. Life went on. The war went on. Winter would soon be upon them, the fourth winter of an impossible war, and he went about his duty in dogged weariness, and took his leave when his leave came up, and slept his leave away, and, still weary, came back to his eighteen-hour days.

So half another year dragged by.

* * *

CHAPTER 28

July – November 1918

In the spring of 1918, Hindenburg opened the last great German offensives at Lys and Givenchy and Passchendaele, and all along the Marne and the Aisne Rivers. By June the German advance had reached within 25 kilometres of Paris. From the east came news of the Brest-Litovsk triumph and the Russian collapse. Now everywhere they began to talk of a German victory

In his corner Erich attended to his numbers. As the western offensives surged back and forth, he watched on paper the enormous drain of personnel and equipment, sent north out of the Salient to fill the gaps of men and equipment lost in battle.

By July it seemed clear to him that, while they fought desperately in the north to hold the new positions, all advances had come to a halt. Paris had not been taken. The bleeding of men and equipment continued out of the Salient. Although General von Fuchs commanded eight divisions on paper, they were not divisions at all, but collections of disjointed army units thrown together without cohesion or spirit.

*

"Something's happening over there." General von Fuchs. had come down shortly after breakfast into the war room.

The senior officers gathered in a half moon around the situation map. At his desk Erich came to his feet to watch.

The general swept a hand along the whole salient front from

Verdun to Nancy. "Heavy American build-up over there east of the Meuse." He tapped the map. "Half a dozen divisions under General Pershing. A cavalry man."

The officers visibly relaxed. One of them laughed. Another said, "Americans! Puppies! Book soldiers! What do they know about real fighting?"

"That's hardly the question!" snapped the general. "They'll learn to fight soon enough! It's a question of numbers! Ask the *Rittmeister* here, he'll tell you about numbers!"

They all turned to stare at Erich.

"Tell them!" the general barked past them.

"We're stretched beyond our resources, sir."

"Louder, Captain! Louder! Make them listen!"

Erich raised his voice. "We have nothing left to fight with. We're not supporting our logistics in the line today."

"Exactly! If the French alone, weak as they are, attacked today, we would be hard-pressed to hold them off. With fresh Americans beside them..." He spread his hands and let the thought hang unfinished. He tapped the map. "General Gallwitz has just issued a directive to withdraw in good order to newly prepared installations along here..." He traced fortifications that had been built over the past winter on higher ground, "...which considerably shortens our line and will concentrate our defences more effectively, gentlemen, but it means we abandon the railway, it means the French in this sector then have more direct access to..."

Erich sat down and turned back to his papers while the general lectured his staff officers.

Withdraw.

Shorten the line.

Retreat.

The end was coming. The High Command had wanted to deal from a position of strength, but the spring offensives had petered out to a fizzle, with enormous losses both in casualties and prisoners-of-war. Erich knew the numbers...

Five hundred thousand in six months of fighting.

Half a million human beings. He couldn't visualise half a million faces, five hundred thousand, almost twenty times the population of Heidelberg...

General von Fuchs stood at his elbow.

He jumped to attention. "Sir!"

"My office."

He followed him up to the second floor.

The general sat at his desk to shuffle a personnel file. After a few moments he closed it and folded his hands on the desk. "You were instructed some time ago to apply for The General Staff. What happened?"

"But that was just the baron—"

"'*Just* the baron'?" He sounded surprised. "And von Moltke? *Just* von Moltke? Both your sponsors now dead, incidentally."

It made him somehow feel small.

"Schellendorf, do you know what separates you from those other officers downstairs?"

"They have more seniority?"

He snorted a dry laugh. "They follow orders. Anyone can follow orders. It takes a different kind of brain to formulate the orders."

"Well sir, I haven't ordered anything except my troop, and that's—"

"No. Wrong. You were born to command."

Self-consciously he stood digesting the words.

"You have the indefinable quality we call leadership. We're born with it, or we are not. You have it. I do not."

"But sir, you—"

"I'm a general because I beat my way up to it and because we need generals in wartime, and make no mistake, I command this sink hole salient because I'm not a very good fighting general and the only mark that I shall make in this god forsaken war will be by withdrawing my troops safely back to a stronger position! Understood?"

Was he supposed to agree? To disagree...?

"As for orders, Schellendorf, you have formulated them at a senior level quite competently for the past two years."

"But the colonel is the one who—"

"I only keep the colonel because..." He shrugged. "What else can I do with him?"

Erich stood in dumb silence, his head spinning with these confessions of a reticent man. Stupidly he said, "I thought it was just... the numbers."

The general laughed again cynically. "Colonel Steiff puts his signature to your numbers every day. Such is war, Schellendorf. Before you go on patrol today, pick up an application form in the orderly room. I want it on my desk tomorrow."

He cracked his heels and turned to leave.

"By the way, Schellendorf...?"

He turned.

"Just what was your relationship with von Moltke?"

He paused a moment to think about it.

"Na?" von Fuchs nudged.

"I didn't know the general, sir. I met him only once. At War School graduation."

"Ah. That's what I mean, you see. It's all in here." He tossed the file into his tray. "Before his death he inquired about you often. You caught his attention."

Erich did not point out the meddling of the baron.

Meddling? Or was it called sponsorship..?

*

The divisions of Detachment C prepared to withdraw to the new positions on high ground. The move would abandon the Meuse River on the western arm of the front, and the village of St. Mihiel with its vital railway link where Germans had entrenched in this salient for most of the war. Erich's numbers did not really change, but the logistics defined a different pattern. The pattern of retreat.

Erich went about his duties eighteen hours a day in dogged weariness. He took his leave late in July when his leave came up, and he slept it away. By the end of August, across no-man's-land the American build-up had solidified east of St. Mihiel as von Fuchs had predicted. The rumour was that the Americans were bringing up armoured tanks, a dreadful war machine, and aeroplanes by the hundreds. From the chateau they sometimes watched dogfights, half a dozen planes of both sides flying at each other in great loops high up there in the clean sky, with faint sounds of buzzing engines and chattering guns. Sometimes a stream of smoke burst out, or a wing ripped off, and a plane would tumble down and down and down. Around the chateau grounds and all along the front they had mounted defensive anti-aircraft seven-sevens. When they fired up at enemy planes, it sounded like a fast, iron heartbeat.

"What do you know," the general asked, "about a scorched earth policy?" He stood gazing at the Salient map that still had not changed, except for the growing numbers on the opposite side of no-man's-land.

They were alone in the war room. The others had gone to the mess for lunch, and Erich was late today with his reports. When the general spoke Erich left his desk and stood beside him at the frozen map. The little arrows had become a jumble of coloured pen scratches, like so many layers of barbed wire, until he could not tell what direction anything moved at any particular moment.

"When I served in East Prussia," Erich said, "I saw the Russians use scorched earth."

"Fairly devastating, was it?"

"Yes sir. Nothing left behind for the enemy to use."

"Ludendorff ordered scorched-earth when we withdraw."

He couldn't absorb the idea. Burn down barns and houses, poison wells, blow up roads and railway tracks, slaughter cattle. "We destroy all this?" he asked in shock.

"We're not Russian," mused the general. "I don't want to emulate barbarians. Lorraine is German land, we won this land in 'seventy, we can't burn it now." He sighed and turned away. "Schellendorf, take your leave early, we'll start withdrawing in about two weeks, you may not have another chance."

Erich finished his numbers and gave command of the horse patrol over to the sergeant. He was on the hospital train at two when it pulled out of Vigneulles.

*

Britt met him at the station. The train had been half empty, and he'd been able at least to sleep. "Your man Kropp telephoned all this way," she said. "He told me what time you left. I've met every train through here since yesterday evening."

"You're crazy," he said, delighted.

"The telephone is wonderful. If he can call me, you can call me from time to time."

"I never thought of it."

They walked arm-in-arm up the cobbled lane, his rucksack over one shoulder. At the great oak tree they stopped to look down at the town under a grey sky. The air smelled of rain.

The house had been built for a family of ten and a staff of sixteen. Now only two lived here, Britt sleeping in their lovely plush bedroom and Katja in the room opposite. The other rooms upstairs had been closed off. The attic was sealed off where the servants' quarters used to be, now empty. Downstairs the solarium, built so lovingly and used for only a few months, was locked. He looked through the glass door at weeds and shrivelled rosebushes littering the flagstone floor. The fountain had been shut down. He watch the little sparrows in their happy flocks.

He wandered through the house, poked into closed rooms, and felt the emptiness. "We should move out of here," he said to her. "We should sell this place, find something smaller, closer to the Kirschners over in Neuenheim—?"

"No!" she said too quickly. "This is my home."

The gun room had not changed. Over in the corner stood the headless mannequin dressed in walking-out blues, ready for the next roll-call. His mind stopped at that. He stared, puzzled by his own uncertainty, until he remembered that the ceremonial blues had been cremated with the baron, and now somebody had fitted a different tunic on the form.

"What is that?" he asked her. "Why don't you store that thing away somewhere?"

"It's how Papi wanted it."

"But..." He crossed over to the desk and found it exactly as it had been, with the same open appointment book and desktop blotter with the same jottings that had ended on the day of the baron's death, over a year ago. "What is this?" he asked again. "Why do you keep it like this?"

"I don't want to talk about it." She turned and walked back to the kitchen.

It was as if nothing could change, as if her life had been set in steel.

But that night in bed, confusing him yet again, she turned urgently to him, the old Britt filled with passion. He could respond now with his own passion, all pent up since the last time. Afterward they lay pressed together in the old glow, hot and sticky and smugly satisfied.

"You're back," he whispered to her.

"You're back," she echoed.
"I love you."
"I love you."

*

It was raining when he got off the train in Vigneulles. The village had changed. Gone were the casual crowds of off-duty soldiers wandering aimlessly, and the French civilians hunching through their daily rounds. Freight wagons were lined up along the eastern edge of the street, being loaded in the rain by soldiers passing bundles and crates from man to man out of the storehouses that they had made of almost every building. From clothing stores on the western edge of town more soldiers were loading trucks with folded grey bundles and crates of jackboots, stuff that Erich hadn't known were still on inventory. In the middle of the street, troops were lining up in formation. A command barked out through the clatter of truck motors, "Form to the right in column of two!" With the answering splashes of a hundred boots thudding down in mud, the company swivelled into marching order. The rain came down.

He stepped down from the railway platform into mud that covered his feet. Rain pattered across his shoulders and cap. *Welcome back to the war...* He collared a passing private. "Soldier, find me a horse."

"Yessir!" The fellow ran off toward the blacksmith shop.

Erich rode hard back to the Chateau. In the late afternoon he passed unit after unit of infantry and artillery marching in the mud away from the enemy, north-eastward toward Chambley.

Fuchs' headquarters was in commotion. As he presented his papers to the guard at the entrance he could hear shouted orders and slamming doors and the thunder of jackboots on wood.

So it was on.

Inside he threaded among soldiers who marched through the corridors carrying things. He found the war room empty. The situation map had been taken down. The tables and chairs had a blank look to them, like the lobby of a hotel, belonging to nobody. His own table was now covered with the residual disorder of the work of others. The filing cabinets remained. It wouldn't matter if they were captured, filled as they were with the records of past actions and wishful plans, useless to an enemy, *full of sound and fury, signifying nothing...*

He caught himself. He was still quoting Shakespeare? in English?

Did he still speak English in his sleep? Did Kropp have to listen to that, and wonder?

He stood immobilised in the middle of the room, hung up in thought. It was almost over. Perhaps he could go home again and, in his maturity and in his father's gentler age, bridge the great chasm and build peace between them. It would give Britt another family, another mother. Such comfort it could give to her. To all of them.

He turned and left for dinner. After two days on the trains, his stomach could wait no longer.

*

He woke to the guns. He sat upright on the creaking army bunk. Dark outside. A cold wind blustered through his open window, driving rain across the tiny room into his face. The guns seemed very close. A couple of bright flashes lit the window, and, fully awake now, he realised they were not guns but a string of artillery shells exploding. Then silence, and rain. Then another string, *blam blam bambam... bam...* and the chalet shuddered with each explosion.

He dressed in the dark. He had a weird fear... he knew it was weird... that if he lit a lamp it would give a target for the guns. They lay ten kilometres to the west, even farther to the south.

"Kropp!"

Kropp appeared in the doorway, pulling into his tunic.

"Am I packed?"

"No sir, you gave no orders."

He deserved that. "Get my kit packed and loaded on the baggage wagon. Stay with the wagon."

"Sir."

Keep him out of trouble...

Damn the rain.

The Americans were coming. This was it. Cavalry uniform, he wouldn't go into action in an infantry uniform. His heart was banging in his throat as he grabbed up his Luger and holster. He checked the action, checked the clip for cartridges, buckled on the belt. This was it, the great strategic withdrawal already begun but now under pressure of enemy guns. They hadn't planned for that. They'd thought they could just withdraw gently in the night. Now it would be a fight. The Americans might be green, but they had French veterans beside them to show the way.

He ran up to the chateau in the rain, his half tent flapping in wind gusts. A whistling cleaved the air overhead, and he threw himself to the ground. The earth heaved under him and a brilliant blast erupted and covered him with mud and grass, all too fast to realise until it was over. He lay for a moment in that wet cold place, then pushed himself to his feet and ran the last few metres to the rear entrance of the chateau. The guard didn't ask for papers, just opened the door for Erich to pass inside.

The corridors had gone strangely quiet. Of course they had loaded everything last night and had sent the wagons on their way. Now only staff remained to evacuate. As he ran to the front of the building he joined a growing crowd of officers moving out of rooms in the same direction. "Well this is a damned nuisance, na?" Some barked orders for no reason. Every man knew his part. Just that they hadn't planned on being driven out.

The headquarters would evacuate last. The telephone board in the foyer beneath the great stairway was still manned by intent operators, the very last of the last to go.

"Schellendorf!" Colonel Steiff intercepted him at the foot of the stairs. "The general wants you upstairs." He eyed him up and down. "God, you're a mess!"

"Sorry sir." He saluted, and ran up. He tried to brush off the mud from the shell explosion, but it only smeared. More shells were exploding out there. On the landing he paused to peer down through the open entrance. Blast after blast lit the darkness and shook the building. All misses so far, but coming. Coming. Trucks and motorcars lined up out there for the retreating staff.

The clock on the landing said quarter to three. He'd had three hours of sleep.

He ran onward.

The general was on the telephone. In an officious clatter several officers and NCOs were gathering cases of files. When Erich came in the general raised a hand to him and continued talking, then slammed the receiver into its box and turned. His face was black with fury. "You know..." He stopped and took a deep breath. "Schellendorf."

"Sir." He came to attention, his mud dripping to the floor.

The general seemed only now to look squarely at him. He broke into a sincere laugh. "God, you look terrible!"

"At least they missed me, sir."

"Yes, they're coming close, but it's still not..." He shrugged into his raincoat. He took up his briefcase, then laid it again on the desk, deep in thought. "Where's your troop?"

"At the guardhouse, I expect."

"Corporal!" he barked across at the men, "Call the guardhouse and order the police troop to report here and bring the captain's horse to the front door!"

"Sir!"

"Schellendorf..." He leaned on the desk, then sat on one corner of it and dangled a swinging boot. "Orders this morning from Gallwitz. Scorched earth. He issued the command to my divisions as well, overriding my authority. I have an assignment for you. Absolutely vital, you understand?"

"Sir."

"I want you to rescind those orders."

"I, sir? How—?"

"The telephone lines to the east are down. You will ride from one field HQ to the next, from Vigneulles to Nonsard, Pannes, Essey, Regniérville if you can get that far, locate each commander and pass the word that I have personally rescinded the scorched-earth policy. Can you do that? Then follow us to Chambley?"

"Yes sir."

"The French have started a major advance in the west from Troyon under a creeping barrage. I don't know what's happening east with the Americans. Take your troop. I'd give you a motorcar but you have to ride across country, avoid the traffic. I will not allow this land to be destroyed. If you can do this, Schellendorf, I personally will see you awarded your Iron Cross First Class, because I tell you, that's how important it is, and that's what it will take. You'll have to run close to the line."

*

Two hours yet to dawn. The last wagons and trucks were moving away northward out of the turnabout. The rain had let up, but the wind came in stiff gusts. Artillery roared all along the front in a wall of thunder that enveloped the air with vibration. From the high ground by the chateau he could look out three ways, east, south, west, and see fires lighting the night sky along a black horizon. Artillery? Scorched earth? Couldn't tell.

He gave the signal. The troop started forward south and east over their familiar beat toward the fires. They rode grimly, silently. They rode hard past his little chalet down across the railway tracks and through the splintered orchards, avoiding the village, avoiding the roads jammed with German troops and gun limbers and supply wagons, dodging French civilians with their bundles and their pigs and cattle and their babes-in-arms and whining children, all trudging in the dark through thick clay mud to escape a battle about to overrun this land.

On lower ground he could no longer see the flaming horizon. Artillery still wrapped his brain in a wall of thunder only a dozen kilometres away in any direction. They rode at a long trot. He was not sure precisely where he was going, he didn't know if any of the divisional headquarters were still on the map or if they too had moved out, leaving only a rear guard to face the enemy. The strategy had been laid for weeks. He knew the orders as well as anyone, but the enemy onslaught had tossed their schedules into the air and the commanders must now judge the situation minute to minute. Fuchs had also sent out the order not to throw troops into battle to delay the retreat. And so, riding toward the trenches, Erich didn't know what they were going into.

Wet and cold, they rode into Pannes. The wind gusted. The village appeared empty, and all the buildings had been torched. Fire fluttered inside the windows of the little church, and from a warehouse flames shot up through the roof thirty metres into the sky. A few French civilians stood in the road to watch, and when the troop rode up they shook fists at the troopers and scattered in the darkness.

A few kilometres from Pannes the rain came down again, blasting into their faces as they trotted into the wind. Soaked to the skin, God he was cold! No light fell from the heavy sky. The horses stumbled and shied at craters invisible to the rider in the darkness. One horse fell and the trooper cursed and somebody laughed. They rode on, and the fellow had to mount again and catch up the troop on his own. The only lights in this rain-driven night were reflected off the clouds from fires ahead. He didn't know if they were riding into artillery blasts or scorched earth.

They came on another burning barn. Around the raging fire an infantry company had fallen into formation to march on, rain slanting down.

Erich left the troop and galloped to the group, half a hundred black silhouettes, wet helmets gleaming in the dancing light. "You!" he shouted, "Who's in command?"

A man stepped out from the formation. "Erich, is that you?"

Startled, he drew his horse up. "Ruperthal? Paul?"

Ruperthal came to stand at the horse's shoulder. "My God look at you, the cat pulled out of the drainpipe." He put a hand on the horse's withers. He was smiling in the firelight.

"Well."

"Well."

"Well how are you, Paul? Better now?"

"God yes. Now look at me, we're burning barns. I wish I could ride with you. But you're going in the wrong direction."

"No, we have to put a stop to the scorched earth command. Everything is changed, the Americans are coming, don't stop to burn, just go."

"Is that an official order?"

"Direct from Fuchs. Where's your divisional commander?"

"I know where to find him, if you give me a horse."

"You'd leave your men?"

"My sergeant can retreat very well without me."

Erich turned to his troop. "Who volunteers his horse? He'll have to march to Chambley with this bunch."

They sat squinting at him, faces flickering in firelight. The horses stood with heads low in the rain. Nobody spoke.

"Weisskopf!" he shouted.

"Sir." Weisskopf nudged his horse one step forward.

"Give your animal to this officer and join the infantry. Keep them amused on the road with all your stories!"

The boys in the troop hooted with hilarity. "By foot, trooper, by foot...!"

It took a few minutes to make the transfer. Ruperthal spoke aside with his sergeant for a time, with nods of the head and waving of hands between them. *No need to explain yourself,* Erich thought impatiently. *Just give the order and be done.*

When they started onward, the light of dawn was paling over the eastern hills. Daylight would bring the first enemy infantry assaults. They had no time to continue this hare-brained mission. In every direction the fires of burning barns and buildings lit the sky, and companies of German infantry marched resolutely away over roads calf-deep in mud.

They forded the little river and turned toward Essey. Explosions here closed down on him from both directions, and he realised they were caught between two sides of artillery. "Where are they?" he yelled at Paul, and Paul waved his hand forward. They rode hard in the early light, and he thought, Good God, what are we doing here, we're already beyond scorched earth going straight at the enemy...

Out of formation now, they galloped over the rough terrain, dodging shell holes and piles of rubble in the fields They galloped past groups of soldiers trudging in the other direction in an impervious mass of movement, some of them without leaders. The first trenches, where Gerdt had died, lay only a kilometre ahead...

Ruperthal beckoned. The troop followed him into Essey. Flames rose up to the sky in roils of black smoke from every building, and the heat hit Erich even through the cold rain. The Cormier farm buildings had been flattened into scattered rubble. Fresh bodies lay shattered and bloody in the rain, soldiers, civilians, horses. Nothing in the village was left where a general might carry on his command. "Are you crazy?" he yelled at Ruperthal. "They were never here!"

"Erich, I was certain..."

A string of explosions erupted down where the blacksmith shop used to be, *boom boom boom*, running in this direction. The sun had risen now. He signalled the troop forward, away from the creeping barrage.

They rode at a long trot along the alley between opposing artillery lines, shells whistling overhead in both directions, across farmland pitted and pounded by a war that had gone back and forth enough to smash it into a wasteland. No cattle, no crops, no people. Few buildings, just holes in the ground and piles of stones and splintered bits of trees. Within a mile to the south lay the three levels of trenches sheltering a single brigade of soldiers stretched over a sixty-mile front, poised now to engage Americans. *Americans*, he thought, cold rain in his eyes, no longer feeling it on his body. How strange. Americans from beyond the ocean. He would like to meet an American one day...

Then beyond the familiar swamp the jagged stones of Regniérville rose ahead, they had just passed the last of the third position, and they were into fighting ground. They had not even seen any part of the advance, suddenly they were riding over ground littered with bodies and wounded men groaning. Men in German field-grey and men in American mud-brown. Bullets flew in the air from both directions. And over there he saw a wave of mud-brown uniforms bent low, running in a northern direction as if retreating from Erich's mounted squad, and the bullets flew in sheets. Erich realised that they had ridden somehow right into the battlefield on the heels of an enemy line that actually was on the attack...

On the heels of an enemy breakthrough.

Only now he saw it.

"We have to get out!" he shouted. He waved them north, and wheeled at the gallop. He glanced back and saw their faces, they all knew it was suicide, but they followed with perfect discipline, unsheathing their carbines. He drew his pistol and snapped off the safety. He saw an American soldier turn toward him, face shadowed under the helmet they were that close, and he fired at the face and saw it collapse backward. Other Americans turned and he fired, and his men behind him fired volleys at every turning face. At a hard gallop he led them at an angle up toward a ridge where he thought they would catch their own line, he hadn't seen the German line retreating, didn't know where it was, but galloped on, the horse stumbling now over shell-pitted rubble and fighting the bit and snorting at the stench of blood and shattered human carcasses. Roar after roar of artillery battered his head, shells screamed, bullets whizzed and pinged in all directions, and they raced up to the crest of the ridge, turned over the top, from the corner of his eye he saw two riders down, a horse screamed somewhere, and...

BOOM! the earth opened in a gigantic blast, debris in the air, his horse suddenly gone from under him in an explosion of blood and flying shards of bone and flesh and metal...

* * *

CHAPTER 29

To 11 Nov 1918

"Don't move *Hauptmann.*"

The voice reached him from a great distance. He floated deep in a blackness, and then pain struck a steel hammer into his chest that jerked him sideways.

"*Rittmeister,*" he tried to say.

Somebody was holding him by the shoulders. The world jolted, like a wagon without springs on a rough road. He opened his eyes and saw the overcast sky above, and then dreamed that an upside-down face stared at him.

Then he thought smiling, he was in a wagon without springs on a rough road, and that face really was a face leaning upside down over him, holding him steady by the shoulders.

And he thought, *The rain stopped.*

"Don't move, Captain, or you could bleed to death."

Then the wagon jolted and white heat engulfed him through the chest...

There followed a millennium of insensible suffocating darkness, in and out of consciousness, wave after wave of pain that radiated from a spot of unbearable burning along his spine, and always somebody at his side, "Don't move, Captain..." Then one day he opened his eyes to a woman bending above him, tugging at his tunic.

"Don't..." he said in English, and died again.

Next time he woke to a man screaming. He'd heard that noise before somewhere, the echo of another familiar moment. He lay staring up at wondrous geometric flower designs stamped on a grey ceiling, and the man screamed, and it took a direction over to his left. He turned his head and the move caused him agony and he saw lines of beds along the dim wall and across the way more beds lined the opposite wall and he knew he was in a hospital, and he thought, "God be thanked, I'm alive, I'm safe..." The pain was an overwhelming pressure in his chest. He slept.

*

"Wake up now."

Erich opened his eyes. Sunlight battered him from a window across the room. Dr Kirschner stood above him floating in a golden haze, smiling down.

"Hello," Erich said, surprised. Pain stabbed through his left chest and made him gasp, driving a harder pain up through his spine into his head. He closed his eyes.

"You're a tough nut. You should be dead."

"Thought I was." His voice came out in a careful whisper. "Where am I now?"

"Home."

"Britt—?"

"I haven't told her yet."

"What happened?"

"Best I can tell, your horse was hit by a mortar and you took shrapnel in the chest."

"Ah..." He felt over his chest, found the bind of bandage. The ribs below his heart shot out pain with every breath.

"I won't tell her until you understand the danger. That bit of shrapnel is still in there, it damaged a small artery inside your chest, down on the left against the spine, and you've lost a lot of blood, a miracle you didn't drown in it. If you move, it may tear the vessel again. We can't open you up, chest surgery is more dangerous than the shrapnel. You understand? If you'll be quiet so it can heal, I'll allow her to visit, na?"

He nodded. He couldn't move in any case without the pain crushing his consciousness.

He slept and woke and slept again.

Nurses rushed from bed to bed in the stench of blood and

pus and gangrene. The moans and groans and whimpers in the night never stopped. Never a moment of silence. Erich woke in pain out of a feverish doze and Britt smiled down at him from dark amethyst eyes, "Hello my darling. Try not to move, I'm here, I'm here." She kissed his eyes, his mouth, she turned away from the horrors of men dying around them and laid her head beside him on the folded blanket that was his pillow, "I'm here, my darling, I'll take care of you." Then more days of pain, of sleeping and waking, and agonizing changes of bandage, and a cool hand on his brow and the screams of men dying all around. Britt popped by in her busy day to stick a thermometer in his mouth and take his pulse and finally, when he felt up to it, to give him his first shave.

"Kropp told me." She lathered him up, warm soapy foam in his nostrils and ears. "About how it happened."

"Kropp wasn't there."

"No, but he spoke to the men who were. He told me how your men adore you. So, you know, when you fell, they couldn't leave you in the battlefield, especially the other officer."

"Other officer?" He knew... *Ruperthal...*

"The one who was shot getting you out, I don't know his name."

Ah no, ah no... He had never wished that on Ruperthal...

*

She came often during the day. She sat with him now to see him eat the horrifying sludge they dealt out at mealtime. She offered nothing better even though they had the farms. "Bring me a fresh egg," he said to her one day at noon over a bowl of cabbage soup with tiny specks of ham floating in it. To chew the woody black bread he had to soak it in the watery cabbage soup.

"Not in front of the other patients."

In the third week they finally allowed him to sit up. Every move still shot lightning pains from his ribs and a deeper grind along the spine. That afternoon the garrison adjutant came to his bedside. "Mail for you." He gave him a bundle of letters from men of Detachment C. And one, a surprise, from General von Fuchs, scribbled by hand...

"*...been informed of your efforts in obeying an impossible order, and although you could not carry it through, a promise is* *sacred to the honour of every...*" He wasn't sure what it meant.

The next afternoon a group of five garrison officers gathered in a tight knot at the foot of his bed, chuckling at some joke. He smiled, not knowing the joke, and they parted ranks.

Ruperthal stepped forward.

"Paul! They said you were killed."

"Yes, I heard that rumour too." He held up a bandaged hand. "Shot off my little finger, so I'm on recuperation leave. Came all this way to visit. How goes it now with you?"

The next afternoon they returned carrying bottles of beer from the mess. They sat around his bed like a barrier of laughter against the misery around them, drinking, making silly toasts and telling war stories as if they were in the mess and not surrounded by men dying. Then Britt descended upon them in a fury and beat them out of the ward. "For shame," she said to Erich. "Tell your friends to take their nonsense somewhere else."

"That was Paul." He grinned. "The one who got me out? The one who Kropp said was killed?"

"Oh darling darling, I'm sorry, tell him I'm sorry!"

"Don't keep them from me, Britt. God, it's terrible here..."

After that it was quick progress to standing up, and then to short walks around the ward from bed to bed where he stopped to talk to other wounded, some of them missing arms or legs, some with raw wounds leaking pus that might never heal. Forty men in this ward, officers and non-coms mixed in together. Civilian hospitals made no distinction. A patient would die, his body lugged away like an empty lunch tray, and ten minutes later a new agonised figure would be set gently on the freshened bed to begin the next cycle of pain.

"They got these in today," said Britt. "All the way from Spain." She had smuggled in an orange, peeled and broken in sections and hidden in a handkerchief. "I stole this from the kitchen for you."

It filled his mouth with delicious acid nectar, flowing new life into him. "Can you bring me an egg," he begged. "Smuggle it in. An egg is smaller than an orange. I'll eat it raw."

"Oh darling, just wait until you come home."

"Tell Kirschner to release me."

"He will when you're ready. Then, all the eggs you want...

and anything else..." She leaned closer to whisper, "I can hardly wait to have you home..."

When Paul and the boys came in the afternoons, she went back to her work. They brought news of the war and smuggled beer to him and titbits from their dinner in the mess. He felt his strength coming back. The pain receded to a dull ache, and the evening nurse no longer pricked his arm to put him to sleep.

Then one afternoon the boys were still visiting when a hospital orderly brought his clothes and boots and set them on a chair. "You're released, sir. We need the bed." He handed Erich written instructions for his recovery, signed by Kirschner.

The boys helped Erich dress. His uniform had been cleaned, but still showed the battering of the day they had dragged him out. "God, you should have been there," said Paul, holding up the tunic.

"Well I *was* there, you idiot—"

"Ah, you were out of it, thank God. Look here at this." He turned the tunic so that Erich could see the rip in the grey worsted under the left breast pocket, mended with tiny black stitches. "It missed your heart by a hair. I don't know how you're still alive."

The boys paused to finger the damaged tunic.

Erich met Paul's eyes, held his gaze. "Remember? The jump-off?"

"Remember...? Yes. I was wrong."

"And now you've saved my—"

"September you saved my life. I was exhausted, I didn't know what to do, I thought without papers they'd shoot me as a deserter and I thought you'd caught me cold, but you said, 'Go report for duty', I hadn't thought of anything so simple as that, and I reported for duty and that was the end of it."

"You risked yourself to pull me out."

"The code of the Corps." Paul grinned. "And so it goes, Engländer."

Erich punched Paul in the arm, shooting a scream of pain through his own ribs and spine.

He signed out from the hospital, and they went with him in a riotous group to report to the garrison adjutant. As they rode in the motor taxi, all seven crammed in front and back, he carried forever with him a vision of the hospital corridors, lined with men on pallets groaning for a bed. Somewhere in all that misery Britt would work until after six.

*

"*Eins-zwo-drei oopah!*"

They raised their glasses. The objective was to empty the glass in a single swallow. Erich choked and the cognac burned the lining of his nose and he sprayed it out into the air. Roar of hilarity, ribs grinding, spine aching. He couldn't see through the tears in his eyes from cognac in his nose and from the alcoholic haze of the last few hours. *Early to bed* the doctor's instructions read. Perhaps tomorrow.

Unbidden, the bartender splashed cognac into glasses lined along the bar.

After supper in the mess their little party had grown to a dozen, the entire complement of officers left in the garrison. These were the rear guard of Heidelberg. Even the adjutant, a dedicated family man, drank with them through the evening.

"Gentlemen!" He raised his glass. "I give you peace!"

The noise softened. The laughter stuttered to silence.

"Peace," said somebody.

They raised their glasses. "Peace." With drunken solemnity they drank.

Erich mused in his haze that the news from Compiegne was of armistice, though nobody could yet be sure. The rumour was that armistice depended only upon the abdication of the Kaiser. "Paul," he turned to Ruperthal, "if the Kaiser abdicates, where will we be then?"

"What?"

"I took my oath to the Kaiser. What happens if he's forced to abdicate?"

"Oh my God, will you give this man a drink? He worries too much!"

At the end of the bar Heinz, Erich did not know his last name, raised his glass, "Gentlemen, I give a toast to abdication! Long may the Kaiser live! But may he live somewhere else!"

Silence fell again. Each man turned every way to see who would raise his glass.

"Come on, come on, be serious, a serious toast here."

"Peace!" shouted somebody.
"We already drank to that! What else?"
"Victory! I drink to victory!"
They laughed uproariously, and raised their glasses.

*

The cognac had run out. They were into the schnapps now, tall glasses, every toast a delicate sip. He didn't know what time it was. Somewhere along the bar somebody murmured, "I drink to my lovely wife, wherever she is tonight."

They chuckled and raised glasses.

Lovely wife.

"Speaking of lovely wives," Paul said, butting his shoulder against Erich's shoulder, "was that not your lovely wife who kicked us out that day? I remember she visited the War School?"

"That was indeed my lovely wife." His tongue felt too large in his mouth.

"My God I never saw so beautiful a woman in my lifetime, where is she tonight?"

Erich was about to say 'Home', but Paul turned to the adjutant. "Did you ever meet his wife? Did you ever see such a vision of such glorious pulchritudinous beauty?"

"I did indeed meet her," the adjutant said in sodden dignity. "Many times. Many many times. She is the daughter of the late colonel of this very regiment." He stepped around Paul to stand close to Erich, nose to nose. "What in hell are you doing here, Schellendorf?"

"I'm... I'm here." He couldn't think through the fog. "I'm just here because... I'm here."

"You want to go home to your wife."

A slow nod of agreement made his head swim. "Yes, I most certainly do want to go home to my pulchritudinous wife."

"Look at you. Drunk! Look at your uniform. A mess!"

He looked down through the haze. Wrinkled, torn, scuffed, patched. The others were neat enough for parade.

"I'll fix you up," said the adjutant. "Your ceremonial blues are here in storage, you know."

"What?"

"Come on boys."

In a phalanx they marched him out of the mess to the

barracks end of the building, five fellows including Paul and the adjutant. In a visitor's bedroom they ripped the wrecked, battle-torn uniform from his poor body throbbing in the ribs, and then dragged him naked into the shower room and turned on the spray, "My God, would you look at that scar!" and while two of them scrubbed him down, the adjutant disappeared. They were rubbing him dry when the adjutant returned and thrust a razor into Erich's hand. "Now shave." They stood him before a mirror. He looked terrible through the haze. "Let me," said Paul, and lathered him up and began to scrape the razor across his jaw. "Should we trim his hair?" "No, no, get him dressed." They made him stand there naked until Paul finished the shave.

In the bedroom they sat him on the bunk and dressed him as if he were a child. Underwear, socks, breeches, boots newly polished by a barrack orderly, spurs attached, he didn't know where they found spurs for him. Then, more carefully, the ceremonial tunic with its dozen gold buttons and the gold braid and the high stiff collar. He stared at it through the wavering haze of alcohol and remembered his first sight of this uniform six and a half years ago.

"This has lieutenant's insignia."

"Doesn't matter, his wife won't know the difference."

"She knows the difference, she's the colonel's daughter—"

"Here." The adjutant tugged at Erich's belt, attaching the scabbard, "wear your sabre proudly, my son, and charge up that hill and sweep your pulchritudinous wife straight into heaven! Na? You're elegant!"

Outside they gathered about in the cold November night, other officers coming out from the bar to join in the festivity. Somebody brought up a horse. In the light of an autumn moon he recognised the adjutant's grey gelding. *First the horse, always the horse...* "Who'll come with me to bring him back?" he asked in his thick fog.

"Listen, he's a bird-dog. Just turn him loose, he'll come home by himself."

Somebody said, "The horse is sober."

They laughed uproariously and hoisted him up and set his stirrups for him. Then a slap on the rump and the horse cantered along the grassy verge of the road, so softly gaited it did not even jolt his grinding ribs.

Across the Karl's Bridge he saw no sign of traffic, not even a pedestrian. Street lamps glowed dimly at major intersections. The river below shone silver under the moon. The horse's rhythmic hoof-beats rang sharp iron on stone cobbles, as loud as rifle shots, and echoed from the sleeping stone buildings. Cold air revived his stifled lungs.

Up the slope past the old oak, he stopped the horse in the turnabout by the garden gate and listened in the moonlight. Quiet as a cathedral. He was chilled now. He slid from the saddle and tied the reins to a saddle ring so the horse wouldn't drag them over the ground, and gave him a slap; and the horse turned and trotted away in a straight line down the cobbled lane, good old bird-dog.

He staggered through the gate, unfocussed with drink, cold inside his chest with this awful wound still raw. Stepped up to the door, reached to turn the bell, but stopped, because this was his house, this was *his* house, and he opened the door gently and stepped into the dark and silent house and weaved bumping along the silent hall, *shhh*, softly he trod his boot-heels *shhh* on the parquet stairs, and at the top where the electric nightlight glowed on the wall he reached for the handle of the bedroom door...

No, he should knock. He knocked.

He heard her drowsy voice beyond, "What is it Katja?"

He opened the door and gripped his scabbard, and stumbled drunk and cold and hurting across the threshold into the dark bedroom, one boot-heel thudding on hardwood, the nightlight behind him casting his long shadow into the room...

She reared upright in her bed and screamed...
    and screamed...
        and screamed...

*

Katja called on the telephone for the doctor. Britt sat like a stone at the kitchen table staring straight ahead. When Erich touched her she felt as hard as a piece of wood and when he spoke to her she did not move. She didn't seem to know he was there. The doctor came within the hour and gave her a bromide and put her to bed, while Erich tried to shake the alcohol from his head.

"It's hysteria," the doctor told him. "It should pass."

Through the haze of cognac he shook his head, no, no, no, Britt had never been the hysterical sort...

Late the next morning he woke with a blinding hangover, and heard news of the imminent cease-fire. Another of those incredible compound words devised out of three other unrelated words, *Waffen-still-stand*. Weapons-at-a-halt.

Armistice they called it in English.

The English had a word for everything.

* * *

CHAPTER 30

May 1919

Whole strings of silent artillery blasts exploded in white brilliance inside his head, buffeting him with painless cushions of light, nothing solid. Then again the black void. Somewhere there was a horse, but he could not find it in this darkness, a horse to carry him out of the barrage, he knew there must be a horse, it was white, you didn't want a white horse in battle, white was a target, and while he groped on hands and knees over rough black ground searching for the horse in the flashing darkness he knew the artillery had found the horse and with glittering yellow devil eyes was creeping reaching leaping now for him...

He reared awake in a cold sweat, bolt upright in darkness. The explosions fluttered and were gone. He felt over his body for injury, he flexed each joint...

She slept undisturbed. Usually she woke, but perhaps this time he had not cried out.

The dreams came almost every night. Silent explosions. Dead Cossacks piled in snow, eyes fixed on eternity. A Russian officer slashed down through the shoulder into the chest who sometimes in the dream stood up and waved a sabre in the air. And Gerdt smiling in mud. The ghosts came during sleep, or drifted in the back of his head even when he was awake, while he was at mess, or drilling the men. Or riding the train home.

And now, as he sat upright in the darkness, Gerdt's voice whispered from a long way off, *"Tell Annette..."*

Tell Annette *what?* He'd never known...

He sank back down beside Britt and stared at the dark ceiling. Did everyone have war dreams? Did *anyone* have these dreams? These voices whispering from the dead?

Weary, he slept.

*

It was all coming apart. At Versailles, instead of armistice, they were talking surrender. Unconditional surrender. They were talking about *Reparations*, they were talking *billions of Marks* in reparations. *Billions.* A billion was a thousand million. Write down a list of numbers on a piece of paper, starting at 1, one number per line, how many years would it take to write to a billion ones? How many sheets of paper?

And they were talking of Germany, Germany, Germany. Not Serbia who had assassinated Franz Ferdinand, not Austria who had retaliated, not France who had first grabbed for Lorraine and Alsace, or Russia who had invaded East Prussia almost before hostilities were declared...

Germany. Sole responsibility for the war to end all wars.

So. The world gathered at Versailles to beat out the terms of truce and then turned it into unconditional surrender. Wilson had arrived with his Fourteen Points, and had not spoken. Germany sent delegates who were not permitted to speak. The headlines of every newspaper in the western world today shouted, *Unconditional surrender*. Not the negotiations they'd discussed at the cease-fire last November. Not armistice.

Surrender.

Unconditional.

He folded the newspaper and set it aside for Britt. His coffee was cold. He could hear Katja banging at something on the stairs. The girl moved like a ghost, but she dropped things, and banged things, as if her hands were not attached to her brain.

Twice she had saved Britt. The first time, the coat hanger, the second time, the gun. Precious Katja. He must hold tight to Katja with her animal cunning.

She rustled into the kitchen. As she passed she picked up his cold coffee cup to refill it at the stove. "Breakfast, sir?"

"What do we have?"

"Porridge with a bit of butter. And bread I baked yesterday."

"Yes, fine. Where is Madam this morning?"

"At the hospital, sir."

Twinge of irritation. The war was over. The hospital still managed the chronic cases, the blind, the crippled, the legless, the tubercular, and those made mad by war. Hospitals no longer needed their hordes of volunteers.

"What time did she go out?"

"Quite early, sir. About six."

"She didn't want to wake me?"

"No sir."

No. Don't wake the captain. Don't disturb the captain. Almost every Friday evening he came from Schwetzingen home for the weekend, but found himself a mere visitor in an empty house filled with ghosts. Katja, the ghost who pattered endlessly about doing housework. The baroness, sun spirit of the desolate solarium. The baron in the blood-spattered gun room with his appointment book open on the desk. Of all the family only Gerdt did not haunt this house. Gerdt, who died smiling in the mud of Lorraine.

"So," he said to Katja at the stove, "there's been no mail from England this week?"

"No sir."

Six letters he'd sent home since the armistice was signed in November. Three in December, two in January, one in March, *Dearest Mutti, of all the things I missed the most, it was you at Christmas. How have you come out of the war? Here we find it difficult with many shortages, but we manage well enough...*

Six letters. He would not write again.

They would lose it all, he knew it now. He'd sat down yesterday with Herr Mundt and the accountant, both newly back from the war. He'd sold the Benz to pay their professional fees. He hadn't imagined it could be this bad, but there it was, two years of delinquent property taxes for thirteen farms and seven villages on seven estates. Property taxes never collected, never paid. Thousands and thousands of Marks owing, nothing coming in except token farm produce. No cash coming in except his captain's pay. When the baron died, his feudal system had collapsed. The farmers had joined a raging proletariat movement and claimed their rights, and all Erich could do now was sell the land from under them to pay the delinquent taxes.

But it was Britt who worried him the most. Hospital work exhausted her, yet she refused to stop. He'd thought the end of the war should make her joyful, yet she walked in a trance. He'd thought by loving her he could open her heart again, but lately she could not tolerate him touching her. When the baron died she seemed to have died with him.

He thought he understood. But her melancholia had intensified since he'd come home, as if he himself had caused it; and it continued on and on and on.

*

He went down to the hospital in the warm morning. Walking in town, he no longer wore the uniform for fear of attracting Spartakists and other revolutionaries who often roamed the streets to spread their leftist gibberish and to beat up right-wing conservatives. Soldiers were a favourite target. Soldiers had lost the war, after all. So they said.

On the Hauptstrasse outside the newspaper office he passed a knot of angry people reading the latest headlines about Versailles. Fists in the air. A crack in the plate glass window where a fist had struck. Strange, half-savage times. The rule of law seemed vague these days. Even at Regiment they were hard pressed to keep discipline. War-weary soldiers just wanted to go home.

He no longer knew what he felt. He was not himself. Walking in shoes instead of boots, wearing civilian slacks and jacket, wearing a tie after six years without, a grey fedora hat instead of his service cap. He felt like a leaf on a large tree fluttering in the wind, a part of the faceless mass. A nothing. Consciously he squared his shoulders, lifted his head high, set his eyes front and met the gaze of others walking past him on the pavement. He was a soldier, God damn it...

He was a soldier in a land where they said the finest soldiers in the world had failed. He would never believe that. The soldiers had not failed. They had fought and fought and had never stopped until they'd run out of guns and ammunition and equipment and food, and finally the support of their own government. The rumour was growing at Regiment that the whole thing had been misbegotten from the start.

*

He didn't wait long in the office. In a rush as always, Kirschner burst through the door. "Take off your shirt, let me have a look."

Erich laughed. "It's not an appointment."

"Ah!" He uncurled his stethoscope from around his neck and tossed it on the desk.

"It's a... shall we say, a social call?"

"How are you, then?" He sat down.

"I'm well, back on duty, policing the police at Regiment."

Kirschner laughed. "I'm sure that means something."

"I came, in fact, to ask about Britt."

"Ah! I believe she's at work today."

"Yes indeed she is. I came to ask why. The war is over. It's the weekend. I only come home on the weekend."

Head lowered between his shoulders in thought, the doctor gazed at him across the desk. "Well, I should tell you the truth. She needs a little cash from time to time. The hospital pays her a small hourly wage. Higher rates on the weekends."

Slap in the face. Erich blinked, confused. Anger curled in his gut. "I send her my pay every month! Two hundred marks every month!"

"A loaf of bread costs twenty marks right now, and rising every day."

"We bake our own bread, for God's sake!" *Stupid thing to say.*

The doctor smiled.

They sat that way in reflection, staring across at each other, not seeing.

"My God," Erich said.

There was money in the bank. He'd checked it yesterday with the accountant, twenty-seven thousand and change. Tied up until the back taxes were paid. He would not touch the gold bars in the upstairs safe. Britt's dowry remained in a separate account under her name: he would never touch it. But even that was losing all value to inflation.

"God," he said again. He squared his shoulders. "I came to ask you, what is wrong with her these days, she doesn't act herself."

"How does she act?"

"She's in a trance. Nothing touches her."

"Example?"

"She never smiles. She used to laugh at everything. Now she decides to work on weekends, the only time I can be home. She doesn't ride, she's always tired. She... she doesn't want my affection—"

"The war has been hard on all of us."

"But... I wonder about the father. The gun. She's never spoken of it."

"Yes, that too. She adored her father, of course. Terrible shock. Also, of course, his physical attacks, I don't know how often. Not often," he added hastily. "We tried to protect her—"

"I know, I know." A blackness filled the pit of his stomach. "How long will this... do you think... will this continue?"

"I don't know."

"And I mustn't mention anything to her? About the gun?"

"A psychiatrist colleague insists it would drive her deeper."

"It's just... I miss my wife. You know?"

"Patience. Restraint. Such incidents which shock the mind may be lost to the patient's memory for a short period. It's not uncommon—"

"But it's been months and months."

"Eventually she'll see the truth as it was. Just wait. It will come right in the end."

*

On Wednesday in the Schwetzingen mess when he was at lunch with the boys, Kropp brought two letters to him. He stuffed them into his pocket for later, the conversation around the table was more compelling. They all talked over each other, raging about the Treaty just published in the morning newspapers...

"We were supposed to negotiate as equals—"

"The world's ganged up against us, that's the—"

"Ah no, this is Clemenceau all the way, the French are getting back for Sedan, they're taking everything back and then punishing—"

"The whole world envies us you know—"

"They had to gang up together to defeat us—"

"They never defeated us! We only agreed to a truce because *they* agreed to negotiate!"

"So now they change their mind."

"The victor rules, that's war."

"But this, but this! Only four thousand officers! A hundred thousand men! Five divisions? From a hundred divisions in the field? We can't even defend East Prussia with that!"

"Ja, well Karl, you have to ask, who stays in the army? Who goes?"

"The Engländer, he can always go home to the victors."

They turned, surrounding Erich with a ring of eyes.

"I'm going nowhere," he said. *False courage. The door was indeed open...*

Karl raised his glass. "Here's to going nowhere."

"Ooopah!"

"Prosit!"

Morosely they drank.

*

Alone in his small barrack room he pulled the letters from his pocket. One from England...!

> *My dearest Son!* (she wrote in German)
> *Greetings from your grateful Mother at this strange historic hour! I thank you endlessly for writing to us. I thank God you survived the awful war. We have heard stories of mobs in Berlin, and about that awful woman Rosa Luxemberg in January shot by crowds of soldiers running wild. I am glad to know that you are safely returned to your Regiment.*
>
> *I have worked hard upon your Father over time. It is impossible for him to write to you, out of pride, you understand. At the same time he is pleased to repeat to me endlessly, 'I told him so.' He now expects that you will come home when you have arranged your wife's affairs and are released from the army. A place awaits you always in The Partnership where you might study anew toward...*

He sighed. *Always the Partnership. The Law.*

The second letter came from Kassel, where the Army High Command had withdrawn to temporary headquarters. Perhaps his release papers. Everyone was getting their papers. He was the *Engländer*. They would throw him out to leave room for a true German.

He sat on his bunk to rip it open.

Envelope within an envelope. *Geheime.* Secret. It came from the office of Lieutenant-General Wilhelm Gröner, Deputy Army Chief of Staff, dated 14 May 1919, "...*You are ordered to report to the War Academy on 1 Sept 1919, to commence officer's training to The General Staff...*"

He crushed it in his fist. This letter was obviously written before the treaty terms were published. According to Versailles there would be no War Academy. No General Staff. Hardly an Army.

The end.

One door closed, another opened. As soon as he could sell the properties and settle Britt's 'affairs', as his Mutti called it, he would be almost obliged to crawl back to England, nothing left in Germany to sustain them as a family. Britt would be happy to escape from the memories. The hidden, the buried memories. That damned house.

This was probably best. Complete break. New horizons.

To think that he'd gone through a bitter war on the wrong side, only to end up where he'd started.

I told you so... He would have to live with that. Probably for the rest of his life.

He could finish at Cambridge. His father would gladly pay the fees, triumphant in his own righteousness, delighted to forge the prodigal son into an English barrister and elevate him into his Old Chambers.

God.

Grotesque.

Perhaps for Britt he could do it...

Kropp stood in the doorway. "The commandant wants to see you sir."

*

"Parade tomorrow," said the colonel. "You and three others to receive the Iron Cross, yours is First Class for your charge in

November, wounded on the battlefield under heavy enemy fire, bravery leading to the disruption of a full enemy assault, etcetera." He smiled grimly. "Even if it didn't exactly stop the Americans."

Erich laughed at the irony. Fuchs had made him a promise that must be honoured.

The colonel held up a copy of the same letter Erich had received from the Chief of Staff. "Now this matter."

Erich shrugged. "So it's been cancelled?"

"Why?"

"The Treaty? Versailles? Dissolving the General Staff?"

"Of course it's not cancelled. But it *is* classified most secret. Training will proceed as ordered, only that you will not discuss it, not even with your immediate family, you understand?"

"But if the army is cut back by ninety percent—?"

"You'll undertake training in the guise of post-graduate university education. The General Staff is officially dissolved. '*Officially*', I say. *Un*officially it is now called the 'Troop Bureau'. On orders from the Deputy Chief of Staff, you are among the four thousand officers to continue serving in uniform. Other personnel will go into mufti and train on weekends and holidays."

In a silent clap of thunder, like the silent artillery of his nightmares, he had just been handed membership in a colossal conspiratorial thumb of the nose at the enemy...

At *England*.

The colonel's smile widened. "You were acquainted with von Moltke? And now with von Fuchs?"

"Ah no, not again—"

"Tradition, Schellendorf. Patronage. Understood? Use it."

Ah yes, he understood now. The Army flourished, Prussian patronage flourished. He smiled. Everything had merely gone underground in the guise of different names.

Just that he would not be part of it...

*

After parade and for the rest of the week he waited for Friday. Again and again he pulled his mother's letter from his pocket and read it, and smiled. His father would be no bother now. *Yes Father, you probably told me so, but look at my gorgeous adorable Britt and tell me I was wrong...*

Homesickness fell over him like a hunger. He couldn't concentrate on duty, he left it to the non-coms. He wanted to shout, "I'm going home to England!" but spoke to nobody about it. What did the English say? *...many a slip 'twixt the cup and the lip.* Nothing must happen before he turned in his resignation.

He hadn't realised the great gap of England from his life. The green settled fields, the terrible island weather, the filthy city. English accents in his ears. The subtlety of English humour. Polite smiles and understated clothing and quiet manners. The moderation of all things English, so far away and so long ago he could hardly remember.

Goodbye to *eins zwei oofah!* Hello *cheers...*

He had to prepare. He needed clothing. One jacket, one shirt, one tie, one pair of trousers. His old clothes from student days no longer fit the hard muscle he'd developed on arms and chest and waist and thighs from five years of handling horses day in, day out. Mutti would be impressed with her soldier son.

Now that he had really decided, he couldn't wait to tell Britt on Friday. "We're leaving this place," he would say to her. "No more hospitals, no more hunger, no more nightmares for either of us..."

He hadn't seen her smile since the day before armistice, that November night when he'd jolted her out of a bad dream. Finding distance from the memories would give her freedom to smile again.

*

On Friday she surprised him meeting his train. How long since she'd last done that? He couldn't remember. But there she was, waiting beyond the barrier wearing a bright pre-war summer frock, a stand-out in the drab post-war crowd. Warm sun, not a cloud in the sky, a wonderful day for planning. He met her beyond the barrier. She turned her cheek for him to kiss. They walked together up the cobbled lane, pausing at the great oak tree to look down at the river and the old stone bridges, and he thought, We'll come back on holiday from time to time.

Aloud he said to her, "I must buy new clothes tomorrow. I need your advice on that."

"I go to work tomorrow."

"Britt..." He bit back his irritation. "Tell them you want the weekends free."

"I'm needed most on the weekends."

"Then tell them your husband wants this weekend."

"I need the money, Erich." Her voice was flat.

It made him cringe inside. She'd never before complained, that was the thing. Never complained.

This was not the right moment to speak of England.

They walked on, side by side. Separate.

The heaviness between them bewildered him. If anything, it was getting worse. The shimmering invisible barrier that had once enfolded them together against the outer world now seemed to rise like a wall to separate them. Invisible. Impenetrable.

A stork stood on the roof over its pile of sticks by the front chimney, wings spread wide to give shade to the nestlings against the afternoon sun. Gerdt had called the storks their cosmic good fortune. A good sign. Yes.

The garden was going to weeds. This, Erich thought as they stepped up to the door, was his weekend duty while she worked at the hospital. Cut the grass, trim the borders, weed the flower beds where new shoots grew wildly out of last year's neglect. Britt was a horsewoman, not a gardener.

Tidy it up. Then put it up for sale.

*

She undressed out of sight in the bathroom. When she came out she wore a flannel gown that effectively concealed her lovely shape. He wore nothing at all, waiting under the covers like a bride. Had they reversed roles? He smiled.

"It's that time of the month," she said, sitting on the edge.

"How can it be...?" *She'd had that surgery...* "I thought—"

"It's the wrong time, I say."

Gently, gently...

Suddenly he realised. This had become her code, *please don't touch me...*

"It's all right, Britt."

Now they were both lying about it.

She came in beside him. He put an arm about her and drew her close, and felt her go rigid. There was a word for this, it was called... it was called... frigid...? Frigidity?

God, if she hadn't shot the old man he would have shot him for her...

He held her quietly. Gradually she relaxed beside him.

"I made a big decision this week," he said. This was the right time. They'd had a nice supper, the inevitable ham, with cabbage and potatoes from the cellar, and white Rhine wine. And pleasant conversation about her work in the hospital. She would never be more relaxed than this, never more safe and warm beside him.

"Mutti finally answered my letters," he said.

She said nothing.

"They want us to come home."

"Us?" Dry flat voice. "They refused to meet me last time."

"You'll love my mother. You'll feel at ease with her. She'll most definitely love you."

"And your father?"

"He apologises." *He was becoming such a liar.* "He wants to see us home."

She sighed. "When? I have to arrange it with the hospital."

"Darling, you don't have to ask the hospital's permission to move away to England. Just tell them we aren't coming back."

"What?" She sat upright, twisting out of his arms. "*Move*, you say? Not coming *back?*"

"We don't need to go immediately, Britt. There's so much to do, prepare the property for sale, put it on the market, resign my commission, it all depends on the army."

She sank back beside him. "No, I don't think so. We don't 'prepare' this property for sale. We don't sell this property. I've lived here all my life, Erich, this is my home. I will never leave this house."

"Britt, we have no future here. We can't survive on my captain's pay scale, we—"

"I don't want to talk about it."

"No, fine..."

He held her. Gradually she relaxed again, gradually she sank into sleep.

He stared at the ceiling, his body rigid in a silent scream for her, his brain whirling with her absolute, *I will never leave this house I will never leave I will never...*

*

"No." She stood before the hallway mirror and adjusted her hat. It had a wide, down-turned brim to protect her face from the sun.

He couldn't see her eyes. "We should talk about this."

"You may do as you wish, Erich. Go to England, that's fine. You can go. Why do you ask?"

"I'm not asking, Britt. My decision is to go to England. As my wife, you come with me. You don't decide. You go with your husband."

She tucked the back of her hair under the hat. He used to see his own Mutti perform that exact move in a similar mirror. It was as if Britt had finally accepted the corsets of female convention. And in the same move, with that one implacable word, *No,* had returned to her childhood rebellion.

Wifely obedience would never be part of Britt. He saw it perhaps too late.

"I finish at five today," she said, walking out the door. On the step outside she paused and turned again to him where he had followed to the doorway. "This is my home, Erich. Go where you wish, I will never leave this house."

*

He stared from the train window. He could hardly remember first coming to this country. Easter 1912. Seven years ago, almost to the day. Before the war to end all wars. When peace had been a reality, not a desire. He could hardly remember himself in 1912, a schoolboy desperate to succeed, but too young and fresh and inexperienced to know how to handle an implacable father.

Did he really dream of returning to that?

She would not go with him. There was no point in asking, and stupid to insist. Cause-and-effect, she would not go. He could not force her to go. He could not go without her.

It bewildered him. His love for her had settled into this deep stillness, an unbreakable bond, a profound need to protect her, to touch her, be with her, laugh with her, ride with her...

When had she cast that aside? How did it happen? He stared out at the land passing, at the groves of cherry trees in early fruit and the tidy rows of green crops sprouting on brown slopes and the spotted cattle grazing along the hillsides and the evergreens thickening now toward the higher foothills in the south. So different from England, yet the same timeless pastoral power, foundation of the land.

No decisions were left to him. Tomorrow he would sign the application for General Staff training. For the *Truppenamt,* the 'Troop Office'. For the vast conspiracy against the victors into which he had already been inducted.

Of course he could not run away to England. He was responsible. The ring was heavy on his finger, *"Dienst ~ Mut ~ Treue".* He could not take it off.

The terms of the Versailles Treaty were intolerable. Without conscience, without honour. He would observe his oath of allegiance to the new government at Weimar. He would stay and fight. *Duty. Courage. Fidelity.* He would stay and fight the dreadful injustice of that treaty. From this day, the unpardonable treaty.

And Britt.

Dienst. Mut. Treue. He'd *married* her. He'd made promises to Britt and to God.

In the distance of time he could hear again the voice of the baroness, *"...no matter what happens in this war, or in life itself, you will keep my daughter safe..."*

Yes.

He must help Britt break loose from the past. He must be patient. He must prove again to her that his love was real and caring, that he would not leave her, that he was her shield against a ruthless world, and nothing would ever hurt her again.

She had loved him. Hadn't she? Before it all went wrong?

Somehow he must prove all of it her way, and then she would love him again. It would happen. She would go past this horror and come back to him one day and love him again.

Then... One day...

Perhaps England.

* E * N * D *

Lyn Alexander

Historical Afternote

The treaty of Versailles, mentioned in the final chapter, was hammered out at Versailles in 1919. Its provisions were designed to render Germany incapable of offensive military action, and to accomplish international disarmament.

As the Germans saw it... revenge.

The treaty forced Germany to pay reparations to the Entente powers. The total cost of these reparations was assessed at 132 billion Marks (at that time, 31.4 billion dollars, or 6.6 billion pounds sterling, roughly equivalent in 2014 to US $442 billion or UK £284 billion).

Germany was to demobilize, leaving an army stripped down to 100,000 men in a maximum of seven infantry and three cavalry divisions. The General Staff was dissolved, and conscription abolished. Military schools for officer training were limited to three, one school each for army, navy, and air force. To prevent Germany from building up a large cadre of trained men, soldiers in the ranks were to be retained for a twelve-year term, and officers would serve a minimum of 25 years.

Because Germany was not allowed to participate in the negotiations, the German government issued a protest against what it considered to be unfair demands, and a "violation of honour", soon afterwards withdrawing from the proceedings of the peace conference.

The German economy was greatly weakened by the war, and only a small percentage of reparations was paid in hard currency. Nonetheless, reparations placed a significant additional burden on the German economy. Germans blamed the near-collapse of their economy on the Treaty of Versailles, and some economists estimated that reparations accounted for much of the German hyper-inflation of 1923.

FINALLY

Had the Treaty of Versailles been negotiated democratically, Adolf Hitler could never have risen to the forefront of world politics, and World War Two would not have happened.

* * *

Printed in Great Britain
by Amazon.co.uk, Ltd.,
Marston Gate.